TO HELL

LOOK FOR THESE EXCITING WESTERN SERIES
FROM BESTSELLING AUTHORS
WILLIAM W. JOHNSTONE AND J.A. JOHNSTONE

Published by Kensington Publishing Corp.

HALFWAY TO HELL

WILLIAM W. JOHNSTONE

AND J. A. JOHNSTONE

P

PINNACLE BOOKS
Kensington Publishing Corp.
kensingtonbooks.com

PINNACLE BOOKS are published by

Kensington Publishing Corp.
900 Third Avenue
New York, NY 10022

All Kensington titles, imprints, and distributed lines are available at special quantity discounts for bulk purchases for sales promotion, premiums, fund-raising, and educational or institutional use.

Special book excerpts or customized printings can also be created to fit specific needs. For details, write or phone the office of the Kensington Sales Manager: Kensington Publishing Corp., 900 Third Avenue, New York, NY 10022. Attn. Sales Department. Phone: 1-800-221-2647.

First Printing: March 2025
ISBN-13: 978-0-7860-5142-7
ISBN-13: 978-0-7860-5143-4 (eBook)

10 9 8 7 6 5 4 3 2 1

Printed in the United States of America

Prologue

Gerald Filmore knew the scrip was a bad idea.

The great railroad strike of 1877, which had started back east with the B&O, had exploded big, spread like fire, and then eventually petered out by the end of July for lack of leadership. Simple anger hadn't been enough to fuel such a fire. Now it was September.

And the crews were still muttering. He had all kinds working for him, Poles, Czechs, Negros, Chinamen, and whites, of course—some local and some just Irishmen.

Discontent sounded the same in every language.

Filmore didn't like it.

According to the foremen, the mutterings from men who'd had enough being treated like dirt were getting louder with talk of strikes and just plain violence.

Thing was, they weren't being treated *so* bad, not really. They just couldn't put up with the scrip Gladstone Railways used to pay them. Filmore supposed he couldn't blame them. The stores in town didn't take it, and the towns were all too far to go anyway. That left the company store, which was woefully understocked and overpriced, and clearly a scheme to take back some of the money Gladstone was laying out for labor.

It started with a slowdown. Suddenly the crews were laying a mile and a half of track a day instead of two. Daily track laid could vary, of course—terrain or weather—but all four crews? Nobody doubted it was intentional. And then Filmore had found out that nobody had bought anything from the company stores for a solid month.

Grumbling got worse. Work slowed further. The company stores were ghost towns.

Finally, a laborer from each crew—some hearty fellow voted into authority by his brethren—approached each foreman to deliver the exact same message. Work would stop unless they were paid properly. The scrip had to go. The men each wanted pay for three months' work, from the time Gladstone had started using the scrip. And they wanted it in gold. If they weren't paid properly, work would stop. Tools would go missing. Unfortunate things might happen to the track already laid. If they were fired, then any new laborers Gladstone hired would meet with . . . trouble.

Filmore realized with cold, leaden certainty that these men had something the strikers back east didn't have enough of. Leadership. Who was organizing these men? Filmore didn't know, but the man's presence loomed over all like a dire specter. These men clearly intended to carry out the threats they were making if not treated fairly. The new rail lines would be severely delayed or perhaps not completed at all.

And that simply wouldn't do.

Gerald Filmore was the man Gladstone had put in charge for the development and construction of all branch lines in the region. He had the authority to handle the situation any way he thought best. The only thing Gladstone really cared about was completing those lines. To this end, Filmore considered a drastic and revolutionary solution to the problem.

Why not just give them what they want?

After all, the men weren't asking for *more* pay. They simply would no longer tolerate being paid in scrip.

And, yes, the Gladstone executives might argue—in private—that paying them in anything other than scrip would, in a way, constitute a raise, since the company store would be effectively out of business, and Gladstone could no longer use it to bilk the men out of their wages. Filmore didn't care. Fair pay for fair work. What was wrong with that?

The penny-pinchers in the home office would scream like stuck pigs, but in the long run, it would be worth it. They'd have to see that, wouldn't they? The setback from a complete shutdown would— Well, Filmore hated to think what that would do to stock prices. So, with the recent strike fresh in everyone's memories, they'd have to agree with him.

So: four crews, three months' pay. Nearly five hundred and fifty men.

That came to fifty thousand.

In gold.

Filmore felt his heartbeat kick up a notch. Yeah, that was a lot of money. Maybe this wasn't such a good idea after all. Maybe—

No. He was the regional boss. Time to step up and make a decision.

Filmore quickly sent the telegram to the bank in St. Louis before he changed his mind. The fifty thousand would come as far as Cheyenne; then it would be divided up and sent to the paymasters for each crew. A handful of Pinkertons would escort the money as a matter of course, but secrecy was their greatest security measure. The gold would arrive with little fanfare.

He'd have to say something to the laborers to fend off a strike. The money was coming. When? Soon. Yes, in gold.

Then the men would be paid.

Work would continue.

Okay, then, the decision had been made, the plan put into motion. Solutions to problems, that was Gerald Filmore's specialty. And he himself would be in charge of all the arrangements to bring the gold west.

And then Gerald Filmore had an idea.

Grady Jenks boarded the train in Grand Island and took his seat. He didn't look for the others. The whole point was not to appear suspicious or threatening, and few things were more threatening than an outlaw gang, which was surely what they'd all look like if they bunched up together.

So Bill Farkas and Little Joe Tillis had boarded at Fremont. At least, Jenks *hoped* they had. He twisted in his seat looking all around but didn't see them. Probably, they were in the next car or the one after. It was a long train, going all the way to the West Coast. The Morris brothers—Lester and Eugene—would get on at the Platte River Station.

And then once they'd cleared Nebraska, they'd make their move before hitting Cheyenne.

He wished Frenchy LaSalle was with him. Jenks always thought six was a good number for a gang. Any fewer, and you were shorthanded and maybe outgunned. Seven started getting to be too many mouths to feed, so to speak.

No, six was best. Except he didn't have six, because Frenchy LaSalle was waiting at the river with his own job to do.

Well, there was no help for it. The plan was the plan.

The train lurched forward, and soon they were rolling along. Nebraska passing by outside the window no more interesting than it ever was. The train rocked . . . and swayed . . . and jostled . . .

Jenks snorted himself awake, sat up, and rubbed his eyes. He'd been lulled into a snooze, and the train whistle announced they were coming into the station. Platte River already? No, he hadn't come that far, but he was close.

An hour later the train slowed into the Platte River Station, hissing steam, the steel wheels moaning and groaning. Jenks glanced out the window and saw the Morris brothers coming along the platform. They were an odd-looking couple, who Jenks wouldn't have figured for brothers. There was some family resemblance but nothing anyone would notice right off—probably because Lester was the oldest of five brothers and

Eugene the youngest, the brothers in between not worth a tinker's damn, according to Lester.

Jenks watched them board and take a seat three rows behind him. Lester leaned back, pulled his hat down over his face, and crossed his arms and stayed that way. He had gray at the ears and in his mustache, and was just flirting with middle age, lean and hangdog, and with a look in his eyes that said he had already heard anything you might have to say.

Eugene, sixteen years younger, still had a youthful softness around the face. He went clean-shaven because a proper beard was something he hadn't been able to manage and only seemed to draw more attention to his youth. He kept looking every which way except at Jenks, as if to prove beyond a shadow of a doubt to any onlookers that he didn't know the man.

Jenks turned back around, shaking his head. He had little use for Eugene on his own, but the brothers worked well together, so Jenks was obliged to take them as a set. Anyway, they'd be over the line into Wyoming soon, and then it would be time to get to work. Everyone knew what to do. Even Eugene.

The locomotive hissed steam, the clank and jangle of the entire train summoning the gumption to move, and in no time, they were bouncing along again.

Going over the plan in his head one more time, Jenks pictured the train. The locomotive and the tender. Then four passenger cars. Then five freight cars. Then the caboose. If the railroad man's information was correct, the gold would be in the freight car right before the caboose. The four Pinkertons were in disguise, dressed like freight men, in work clothes, but Jenks knew they'd be armed like Pinkertons, not freight men.

Jenks supposed security for so much gold was a conundrum. Keeping the gold secret was obviously the best thing to do, but wouldn't more guards be better? On the other hand, more guards meant attracting more attention. Maybe it was the best they could arrange on short notice. The railroad man had said Gladstone was in a hurry.

Well, Jenks didn't create the situation. His job was to take advantage of it.

They crossed the state line, and Jenks stood. Time to get this show on the road.

And finished before reaching Cheyenne.

He headed back toward the caboose, giving the Morris brothers a barely perceptible nod as he passed.

Eugene nudged Lester, and the older Morris sat up and straightened his hat. They gave Jenks a ten-second head start before following.

They passed through the next passenger car, where Jenks spotted Bill Farkas and Little Joe Tillis.

Predictably, Little Joe was one of the biggest men Jenks had ever seen, barrel-chested, shoulders big enough to park a wagon on, legs like tree trunks, and a head taller than the rest of the boys in the gang. A round, friendly face with a well-trimmed red-brown beard. He had a Peacemaker slung low on his hip.

As did Bill Farkas. Carrying a similar revolver was where the similarities ended. Bill was barely five and a half feet tall, a compact, mean little package: little black glittering eyes, a hawkish nose set in a lean face, a tall hat in an attempt to give him some height, which fooled nobody.

The two men fell in behind Jenks and the others, and the five of them exited the passenger car into the first freight car. It was full of barrels and crates, a narrow path between the freight running the length of the car.

"Who's going up top?" Jenks asked.

"Me," Farkas said. "And Little Joe."

"Okay." Jenks reached inside his vest and came out with two fat cigars. He handed one to Farkas. "You got matches?"

"Yeah."

"Get up there then."

"Here?" Farkas asked. "That's a long walk."

"We don't know for sure what's in the next cars," Jenks said. "You won't run into nobody up there."

Farkas frowned but nodded. "Right."

They went to the end of the car, opened the door, and went out, the sound of the chugging wheels hitting them—and the wind. Instead of crossing to the next car, Farkas swung out, grabbed the iron ladder on the side and climbed up to the roof. Little Joe followed.

Jenks watched until they were out of sight then turned back to the Morris brothers. "Come on, then."

They entered the next freight car and found more of the same. They kept going until the end, and Jenks found his Smith & Wesson Schofield in his hand with no memory of drawing it. He supposed he was bracing for what was to come. They reached the final freight car but didn't go in.

"Let's give the boys a minute to get into position."

Jenks holstered the Schofield and stuck the other cigar in his mouth. He struck a match, puffed it to life, then shook the match out and tossed it over his shoulder. "Wait here. On either side of the door might be safest."

Eugene stood on the right side of the door, Lester on the left. They ducked down into a squatting position.

"Wait for the second one," Jenks reminded them. "Or we'll be putting you into a hole in the ground."

Jenks opened the door and stepped across to the final freight car, but didn't enter. He put his ear to the door, though he couldn't hear anything over the rattle and chug of the train. But they were in there. If the railroad man's information was right, the four Pinkertons would be inside—hopefully, not expecting what was about to happen.

Jenks reached into the vest again and pulled out a thin stick of dynamite, turning his head slightly to make sure he didn't have a disastrous accident with the cigar. The dynamite made him nervous, and he wished there was some other way, but they needed to get through quick and preserve their surprise. He lodged the dynamite into the door handle, angling it to be good and tight, so a sudden bump wouldn't knock the thing loose. The fuse would give him maybe eight to ten seconds.

He stood back and waited.

A minute later, an explosion came from the far side of the car. Jenks lit the fuse as a rapid-fire smattering of pistol shots came from within: Farkas and Little Joe trading lead with the Pinkertons.

Jenks grabbed the safety bar on the side of the car

and swung himself out, clinging to the side of the freight car and counting in his head. The dynamite went off a few seconds early—you could never completely trust a fuse—with a sharp, thunderous crack. He swung back to find the door blown clean off, lots of smoke, Lester and Eugene coming out of the other car.

"After 'em!" shouted Eugene as he dove into the smoke, Lester and Jenks right behind.

A twelve-gauge boom shook the interior of the freight car. Eugene flew back, hit the corner, and melted into a pile, his chest a raw mess of blood.

Jenks's Schofield flashed into his hand, and he fanned the hammer twice, blasting the figure in the smoke ahead. Farkas and Little Joe had been told to stay out so they wouldn't all gun each other in the crossfire.

There was another man dead on the floor, but two more rose up, shots fired, lead zipping past Jenks's head.

Lester had his six-shooter out now, and both men blazed away until their revolvers clicked empty.

It was suddenly quiet in the freight car except for the normal rattle and chug of the train. The bodies of the four Pinkertons lay in the center, draped over one another. Farkas and Little Joe stuck their heads in the other blasted doorway.

"That got 'em?" Farkas asked.

"Yeah. Get up top and yell when you see the bridge."

"Right." Farkas disappeared.

Jenks broke the Schofield in half and let the spent brass fall and *ting-ding* on the floor. He looked over at

Lester as he thumbed in new shells. The man knelt over the body of his brother who was clearly dead.

"Lester, I'm sorry about Eugene," Jenks said.

Lester didn't move, didn't say anything.

"I'm sorry, but there's still work to do." Jenks tried to sound firm but not harsh.

"Is that what I'm supposed to tell his ma?" Lester said bitterly. "Work to do?"

"Lester."

"I know, I know." Lester stood with a grunt.

"Head back up to the first passenger car and see if anyone's coming this way," Jenks told him.

The sticks of dynamite had been small, but they'd each produced a good bang. All the way up in the locomotive, maybe they'd heard something or maybe not. Maybe heard something and ignored it, after the train kept going with no problem. Or maybe the noise had made a passenger curious. Or maybe a conductor had heard and felt dutybound to investigate.

Or maybe any of a hundred different things.

Lester looked down at Eugene one more time, shaking his head and muttering curses under his breath. He looked back at Jenks. "Yeah, I'm going." He left, heading back toward the passenger cars.

Jenks motioned with his revolver toward a crowbar hanging on a nail. "Get it. You know what we're looking for," he said to Little Joe.

"Right." Little Joe took the crowbar and went to work. There were a dozen large crates in the freight car.

Jenks exited through the car's blasted back door and

crossed to the caboose, went up the iron ladder, and found Farkas on the roof. "Any sign of the bridge."

Farkas shook his head. "Not yet."

"Give us plenty of warning," Jenks said. "We're only on the bridge a few seconds."

Farkas frowned. "I know it."

Jenks went back down the ladder and into the freight car. "Anything?"

Little Joe had cracked open about half the crates. "Working on it."

Jenks started to feel nervous. "Well, hurry up."

Little Joe was about to snap back at him when Lester returned.

"Nobody's coming," he said. "We're in the clear."

"Good, but watch the door anyway, just in case." Jenks turned back to Little Joe. "Keep going. The bridge is coming soon."

Little Joe redoubled his efforts prying open the crates. When he got to the last one, Jenks felt sick, a feeling that soon turned to fury. Duped. All the planning and effort. Eugene dead. What in blue blazes were those Pinkertons guarding if there was nothing—

"It's here," Little Joe said.

Jenks blew out breath he hadn't known he'd been holding. "Get it out of that crate."

"Pretty heavy."

Jenks could imagine. An iron chest plus the contents. Heavy indeed.

Farkas stuck his head through the doorway. "Bridge coming!"

Jenks cursed. "Farkas, get over to the side door. The rest of you lift this thing."

Lester and Jenks got on one side of the chest, Little Joe on the other. They heaved, muscles straining, sweat breaking out under their arms and across their foreheads. They removed it from the crate then let it drop back to the floor with a heavy metallic *clunk*.

Farkas slid open the car's big freight door, and wind whipped through, tugging at their clothes.

"Drag it over!" Jenks shouted.

They shoved it right to the edge.

Jenks stuck his head out and looked forward just in time. The locomotive was just crossing onto the bridge over Crow Creek. They only had a few seconds to get this right.

"On three," Jenks shouted over the wind. "One . . . two . . ."

The freight cars rattled along the tracks and onto the bridge, and then they were coming to the creek . . .

"Three!"

They all shoved the iron chest out the door.

Frenchy LaSalle sat on the bench seat of the buckboard, just inside the tree line along the edge of Crow Creek. It was a good spot for staying out of sight while still affording him a clear view of the bridge.

Frenchy bit into a strip of jerky and chewed without relish. He was a long way from Paris and the cuisine there. That's what happens when you kill a man and then run, he supposed. You end up in America, fallen in with other cutthroats and blackguards, which was fine—except he wished the food was better.

The train whistle in the distance brought Frenchy back to the here and now. He watched and waited.

Two minutes later, he saw the smoke. The train appeared, rumbling across the bridge, and then Frenchy saw it, the open door in the last freight car right before the caboose. Then the chest came tumbling out and fell and fell and—

It hit the dead center of Crow Creek with a loud, wet *whap*, bobbed a moment, then rapidly sank. Frenchy clicked his tongue and flicked the reins, and the buckboard moved forward, stopping right on the edge of the creek with the horse's forehooves in the water.

Frenchy climbed down from the buckboard with a coil of rope. He tied one end to the buckboard. "Wait here, my friend," he told the horse.

He let the rope uncoil as he waded into the water toward the spot where he'd seen the chest go in. In mid-September, it was still plenty warm, but the water was biting cold. He didn't complain. He'd been picked for the easy duty, well away from any gunplay. If a little cold water was the worst of it, then Frenchy LaSalle had come out on the good end of it.

He found the chest in waist-deep water and tied the rope to one of the handles with a good knot. He trudged back, dripping wet, climbed onto the buckboard again, then gave the reins a good flick. It took a bit of work, but the horse pulled the chest onto dry land, and Frenchy parked the buckboard next to it.

He tried to lift the chest into the back of the buckboard and burst into laughter. No way on God's green earth was he going to be able to lift that all by himself.

I guess nobody had thought of that. He fingered the big padlock keeping the chest secure. He stood back, looked around, then drew his revolver. It took three shots to get the lock off.

Frenchy knelt in front of the chest and threw it open. Canvas bags. Lots of them. He picked one up. Heavy. He was sorely tempted to cut one open and see the gold glint in the sunlight, but he'd tarried too long already, and the gunshots might bring somebody.

He took the bags out one at a time, heaved the chest into the buckboard, then refilled the chest, closed it, and threw a horse blanket over it. First, the hiding place for the gold. Then the rendezvous with the rest of the boys.

And then he would be rich.

Frenchy LaSalle felt himself grinning as he pointed the buckboard north. He was home free now.

CHAPTER 1

Parker Jones was just about to lock up when the man with the two-gun rig walked in.

He was tall and lanky, black hair coming down from under his hat to fall over his neck and a mustache that curled down over his upper lip. Except for a starched white shirt, the man was dressed entirely in black.

Silver spurs gleamed as did the twin nickel-plated Remingtons on his hips with the ivory handles. He stood erect , entered the office with a purposeful stride and fixed Parker with piercing blue eyes.

"Name's Best," he said. "Tanner Best. I want to see the sheriff. That you?"

Parker stopped himself from sighing. Two more minutes and he'd have had the place locked up and been on his way to Clancy's Saloon for a much anticipated beer. Still, the man had a no-nonsense way about him, and if he was looking for the sheriff then maybe it was something important. To Parker's way of thinking, there were only two sorts of man who'd sport pistols like that. One sort was a fella too fancy for his own good, not somebody to take seriously. The other sort was a man who could back them up with action, a man who'd maybe earned the right to carry any kind of six-guns he wanted, and woe unto anyone who elected to criticize.

Parker decided he wasn't about to criticize.

"Sherrif's due back from Joplin tomorrow," Parker said.

"You one of the deputies?" Best asked.

"The only deputy," Parker told him. "Rory's Junction tends to be fairly law-abiding."

"I'll direct my questions at you, then," Best told him.

Why me?

Maybe if Parker answered the man's questions quickly, he could be on his way to that beer. "I guess I got a minute."

"Son, you got as many minutes as I need. Now, listen up."

Parker frowned. *Son?* The man was only ten or twelve years older than he was. "If it's some simple question, I can try to answer it. Otherwise, the sheriff's back tomorrow, and you can ask him. I was actually just about to close up."

Best smirked. "Close up? You might lock these doors and go home, but the law never sleeps, boy."

Parker wanted to roll his eyes but didn't dare. "I see. You know something about the law, do you, Mr. Best?"

Best looked down at his jacket and laughed. "Oh, yeah. Forgot. I don't like to call attention to myself when I'm traveling." He dipped two fingers into his vest pocket, came out with something. Parker caught a glint of metal. Tanner Best pinned the badge on his lapel.

U.S. marshal. Well, damn.

"Beggin' your pardon, marshal," Parker said. "What can I do for you?"

"I heard tell Grady Jenks was seen in the area," Best explained. "I was wondering if you or anyone around here has heard or seen anything. Maybe saw some strangers wandering through."

Parker paused to show he was thinking about it and then slowly shook his head. "No, can't say I've ever heard of this Grady Jenks character."

"Never heard of him, huh?"

"Should I have?"

Best made a sort of low growl in his throat like he was reminding himself to be patient with a small child. He turned and took three lazy steps to the wall on Parker's right, spurs jingling as he went. The jailhouse wasn't big. Rory's Junction didn't need much. One room with a desk. A jail cell behind him. A rack on the other wall with rifles and shotguns.

But Best had gone to the opposite wall, the one with the big corkboard. Three layers of calendars and announcements and handbills pinned there. Sometimes the sheriff would hang up something he'd cut from the newspaper.

Best rapped a knuckle on a wanted poster. It depicted a rough line drawing of a shady-looking character, the words **GRADY JENKS** underneath his face.

WANTED FOR HIGHWAY ROBBERY.
$500 REWARD.

"He's been staring you in the face all day," Best said.

Parker felt himself go pink in the cheeks. "I guess there's so much hanging on that board, we don't even see it no more."

"Maybe sort through it," Best suggested. "Cull the old news."

Parker nodded. "Right."

"But you ain't seen anyone who looks like that?"

Parker shook his head. "No, sir."

"Well, the likenesses ain't always too good on them posters." Best reached into his jacket and came out with some folded papers. He unfolded one and set it on the desk in front of Parker. "The younger one's dead. Seen the older one?"

Parker squinted at the wanted poster.

THE MORRIS BROS. LESTER AND EUGENE. $250 REWARD EACH.

"Not familiar, sir," Parker said. "Sorry."

Best refolded the wanted poster and stuffed it back into his jacket. Then he unfolded the other one and slid it across the desk. It was another line drawing of a face, reasonably detailed. Middle-aged. A round, affable face. Thick cheeks and bushy eyebrows. A big nose. But there was no name. No dollar amount for a reward.

Best must have read Parker's mind.

"This isn't a wanted poster," the marshal said. "This is just someone I'm looking for. I'd like to ask him a few questions. Gerald Filmore. He's a railroad man. That face look at all familiar?"

Parker would have remembered anyone who'd looked like that, but again, he made as if to study the drawing an extra few moments to assure Best he was taking it seriously. Finally, he said, "No, sir. Never seen him."

Best sighed as he folded the drawing and stashed it back inside his jacket. "Is there a hotel in this town?"

"Lana Ross, at the end of the street, runs a boarding-house," Parker said. "She might have a room."

"Okay, then," Best said. "Maybe I'll catch the sheriff in the morning before I leave. If he's back in time. You have a good day, deputy."

Parker watched him go, the jangle of the marshal's spurs playing him out the door. He finished locking up and headed straight for Clancy's. People were just starting to wander in, and there was still plenty of room at the bar. Parker bellied up and waved at Clancy. The old man brought a beer for Parker without having to be told.

"Another peaceful day in Rory's Junction, deputy?" Clancy asked.

"Told some loud kids to be quiet," Parker said. "They were disturbing the fellows over at the barber shop."

Clancy grinned. "What would the townsfolk do without you to protect us from such villainy?" He kept grinning as he wiped a cloth back down the bar.

Parker shook his head, laughed, then drank half his beer in one go.

More men drifted in, some taking a moment to exchange bland pleasantries with Parker. *Yes, it has been warm. Did you hear Martha Quinn's shepherd had a litter of puppies? Old man Perkins still has the fever and might not make it. A damn shame.*

And so on.

Parker saw Marshal Best enter the saloon and turned away, hunching over his beer, trying to look inconspicuous. It didn't do any good.

Best bellied up next to him at the bar. "Deputy."

Parker didn't look up. "Marshal."

"Thanks for the tip on the boardinghouse," Best said. "She had a room for me."

"That's good."

Best waved for the bartender to bring him a whiskey. "Leave the bottle."

Clancy left the bottle.

Best filled his glass, shot the first one back, smacked his lips, and refilled his glass. He held the bottle up to Parker. "Drink?"

Parker didn't really want to prolong his conversation with Tanner Best. On the other hand, a free drink was a free drink.

Parker reached behind the bar and helped himself to a shot glass, set it on the bar, and Best filled it for him.

Parker held up the glass. "Appreciated." He threw it back, felt the pleasant burn down his throat.

Best filled his glass again without asking.

Parker felt obliged to offer some conversation. The marshal was pouring whiskey after all.

"So, those men you're looking for," Parker said. "They rob a bank around here or something?"

"Those men done a lot of bad things, but nothing

around here," Best told him. "As for me, I'm after them because of the big train robbery."

Something tickled Parker's memory. "That thing out in Wyoming?"

"That's right," Best said. "There's a lot of gold still missing, and none of the men have been caught except for one of the Morris brothers—although, I wouldn't quite say he was *caught*. Found his body in a freight car."

Parker remembered the newspaper article a little better now. The conductor and engineer thought they'd heard some kind of commotion, but then thought nothing of it when the train continued to run smoothly. It was only after they'd pulled into the Cheyenne station that they discovered both doors had been blown off the final freight car, which was littered with the corpses of incognito Pinkertons. By the time the law was called in, the train passengers had all gone on their merry way. A spokesman for the railroad claimed not to even know there had been such a substantial amount of gold aboard the train. From the article, Parker got the impression the whole thing was a big, confusing mess.

"If the train was robbed in Wyoming, I guess I'm wondering what you're doing in Missouri, marshal," Parker said.

Best sipped his whiskey. "The only clue they had was Eugene Morris's corpse. Him and his brother were known members of the Grady Jenks gang, so that's who we have pegged for the crime." A shrug from the marshal. "Although that other man, Gerald Filmore? Well, he has my interest."

"Oh? How so?" Parker nudged his empty shot glass toward the marshal, hoping he'd take the hint.

Best refilled the glass. "That sketch I showed you. The one that's not a wanted poster. He's a railroad employee that's gone missing. I wouldn't mind asking him a few questions. I don't believe in coincidences, him going missing right around the time of the robbery? No, sir. I have questions."

"What makes you think he's in Rory's Junction?" Parker asked.

"I doubt he is," the marshal replied. "But the man's mother lives twenty miles from here in Neosho. I'm showing his sketch in every little town I pass through. Worth a shot."

Parker pushed away from the bar. He was generally a beer man and was starting to feel the whiskey in his legs. "Well, I wish you luck, Marshal Best. Rory's Junction is the sleepiest place this side of the Mississippi, so I doubt it's the sort of place that would attract a hardened criminal with a pocket full of gold. But I'll keep my eye out."

A brief smile flickered across the marshal's face. "You do that, son."

It was dark when Parker left the saloon and began walking the road home by moonlight. He knew the way and could do it with his eyes closed. Just out of town, the road took a lazy turn to the right to parallel Harold's Creek. Ten minutes later he arrived at the little flour mill. The creek turned the wheel, and Parker's brother-in-law, Caleb Burnside, made a decent living with it.

Caleb was just coming out of the stables as Parker

walked up out of the darkness. He frowned at Parker. "You missed dinner." He was short but broad, mouse-brown hair thinning on top, a good twenty years older than Parker, ruddy red cheeks, and white stubble on his jaw. "Get home sooner and you can eat."

Parker shrugged. "It's okay."

Caleb grunted like it made no never mind to him either way, then turned and went inside the small house.

Parker turned the other way and entered the mill through the little side door. There was a room in back that had been for tools and spare parts for the mill, but they'd cleaned it out when the twins had been born to make a place for Parker. The miller's house was small, and Parker had begrudged it when his sister and brother-in-law said they needed the room for their children. When Parker's parents had died, his older sister had been of marrying age, and Caleb had always been fond of her. Parker had still been in school. It had been kind of Caleb to put a roof over his head, and Parker maybe didn't blame the man for wondering when he would finally move on.

But Parker hadn't moved on. And now he lived in the mill's old tool room, slept on a narrow cot. He liked working as a deputy, but the pay was a laugh. He kept waiting for some opportunity to present itself.

It never did.

He lit a lantern and sat on a stool and pulled off his boots. He was hungry, and that was for sure, but he'd just have a big breakfast. Anyway, a man didn't notice his hunger so much while he was asleep, so he supposed he'd just collapse into the cot and close his eyes.

A knock at the door.

"Come in."

His sister entered, holding a tin plate with a red-and-white-checkered napkin thrown over it. The smell of the food hit him, and Parker's mouth watered.

"Your husband said I missed dinner," Parker said.

She rolled her eyes. "Oh, don't listen to him."

She handed him the plate, and Paker snatched the napkin off the top. A biscuit and a chicken leg. Turnip greens. White beans. Parker immediately bit into the biscuit.

"You're the best," Parker said, as he chewed.

She grinned down at him, leaning back against the wall and watching him eat. "Can't let my little brother starve."

Sarah Jones—now Sarah Burnside—was still a handsome woman. She was nine years older than Parker, with the same auburn hair and fair complexion. She'd been a catch back in the day, and Parker always thought she could have done better than Caleb, although maybe thinking that wasn't so generous. Now she looked a bit haggard, especially around the eyes—not bad, but tired, keeping house, running after the twins, helping Caleb at the mill.

Not for the first time, Parker felt a pang of guilt. He should have been off on his own before now. He was young, sure, but a grown man.

Maybe Sarah was thinking the same thing, because she said, "How long you think you're going to live in this flour mill, Parker?"

He shrugged. "Has Caleb said something?"

"He's concerned you're not—well . . . living up to your potential."

Parker spooned in a mouthful of beans, wondering just exactly how much potential he actually had and how a fella went about getting it up and running. "I just— I need to figure things out."

"No, I know." She nodded, reluctant to press him. "I know."

He ate faster, biting a chunk out of the drumstick.

"You thought any more about the army?" Sarah asked.

Parker shrugged, spooning more beans into his mouth. His father had gone into the army and come out a sergeant. He'd told Parker it was a good way for a man to get a start. Yeah, Parker had thought about it. And then he'd stopped thinking about it.

He finished eating, wiped his face with the napkin, put it back on the empty plate, and handed everything back to her. "Thanks."

"You're welcome."

"Well, I guess I'd best get some shut-eye."

She nodded and smiled weakly. "Sure, Parker. Sleep well." And she left.

Parker stretched out on the cot. He closed his eyes and was asleep in no time, dreaming of nothing at all.

CHAPTER 2

Six rapid shots—three exploding bottles, and two metallic *tinks* as the tin cans were knocked off the fallen log.

Parker emptied the six-shooter and thumbed in fresh shells. He liked the feel of the revolver. Liked its weight.

His pay for being deputy sheriff in Rory's Junction was pretty pitiful, but since he didn't pay anything for food or a roof over his head, he could save for things he really wanted. A decent horse, for example. The saddle was a little beat up, but the price had been good. He'd purchased the Colt Peacemaker secondhand, but the previous owner had kept it clean. There was some room in the sheriff's budget for ammo each month, and Sheriff Crabtree let him have a box now and then to practice.

It was the only thing he was really good at. Shooting. Maybe it was because it was the only thing he really practiced. From twenty feet—or even thirty—he simply didn't miss. And that was from the hip. He was fast, too. Another thing he'd practiced a lot. Quick draw.

Parker set up four new cans on the log. He was

shooting toward the creek, with the woods beyond, so he didn't have to worry about stray shots. He walked back to his spot, turned, letting his right hand dangle down near the Peacemaker, ready to see how fast he could draw and still hit the cans.

He heard voices.

Mary Lou Shaw and Bonnie Morgan were walking together down the road and would pass right by Parker on the way into town. He decided not to shoot until they got closer so that he could show off a bit.

He watched them come in the corner of his eye, saw them turn their heads to look at him.

Parker whipped the six-gun from his holster and fanned the hammer four times.

Boom-tink. Boom-tink. Boom-tink. Boom-tink. Four dead tin cans.

Parker spun the revolver on his finger with a flourish as he returned it to its holster.

The girls put their heads together and giggled.

Then Mary Lou shouted. "I'm sure glad you're around to protect us, Deputy Jones, in case Rory's Junction is overrun by all them villains from Dodge City and Tombstone."

Parker knew when he was being made fun of.

"The law is a serious matter, ladies," Parker said sternly.

The girls giggled, rolled their eyes, and kept walking.

"Hold on, now." Parker walked after them. "You two don't have time to pause and chat?"

The two girls looked at him, then put their heads

together again. Then Bonnie kept walking. Mary Lou came toward him.

Parker would have preferred it the other way around. There wasn't one single thing wrong with Mary Lou. Hair like copper, freckles across her nose and cheeks. Bright green eyes and a nice slender figure. But Bonnie was the one who'd always had Parker's attention. Bonnie had corn-yeller hair and perfect teeth, and eyes as blue as the sky, and an hourglass figure.

"Where's she going?" Parker asked when Mary Lou was close enough.

"She wants to make sure she gets a seat close to Lawrence Foley in church," Mary Lou told him.

"Lawrence Foley? What for?"

Mary Lou shook her head and rolled her eyes, amused. "Parker Jones, don't you keep up with current events?"

"I was thinking I might call on Bonnie myself." Parker hadn't been thinking that, but he began to suspect maybe he should have been.

Mary Lou shook her head again, but the amusement faded. "Parker."

"I'm better looking than Lawrence Foley," Parker said. "And taller."

"Parker, we're not kids in school no more," Mary Lou said. "There's more to a man and woman being together than just looks."

"Lawrence's family is farmers," Parker said. "What's so special about that?"

"The Foley farm is over a hundred acres," Mary Lou told him. "They're building another house on the other side of the property for Lawrence, with a porch and everything. A woman wants to know she's marrying into something besides a nice smile and good hair."

Back in school, Bonnie had eyes for Parker, and he'd known it. But she was younger. He always thought she'd keep, that she'd be waiting for him when he was ready. That was foolish. He realized that now.

"Well, I didn't really fancy her all that much anyway," Parker said.

Mary Lou put her hand on his arm and gave it a friendly squeeze. "Sure, Parker. I've got to get going, okay?"

"See ya."

Parker picked up the cans and saved them to shoot again later. Then he walked into town and opened up the sheriff's office. He took the broom from the corner and gave the place a good sweep. He sat behind the desk awhile, in case anyone needed him for something.

Nobody did.

Just before noon, the sheriff walked through the door.

"Howdy, Parker. Get along okay without me?"

"Nothing but peace and quiet."

Sheriff Mason Crabtree retired from the army as a major. He had no wife and no kids, and had taken the job of sheriff as a courtesy and simply to keep busy. He was in his late fifties, salt and pepper hair in a sharp widow's peak, bland brown eyes, clean-shaven except for a thin mustache. He had an easy, unexcitable way about him: even-tempered and thoughtful, but with a kind of quiet strength that made him a good choice for a lawman, at least in a sleepy place like Rory's Junction.

"Oh." Parker just remembered. "There was a federal marshal here, asking for you."

Crabtree raised an eyebrow. "For me?"

"Well, for the sheriff."

Parker related the details of Tanner Best's visit, looking at the wanted posters, and Best's theories concerning the train robbery.

"He wanted a room, and I sent him down to Miss Ross's place," Parker said.

"Huh." Crabtree gave that a few seconds thought. "I reckon I'll mosey around to the boardinghouse and see if he's still there. I need to make the rounds anyway. Half a sheriff's job is being seen. Folks like to know the law's around—just in case."

"Okay then," Parker said. "I'll hold the fort, here."

The sheriff left, and Parker looked for something to do. He took all the rifles and shotguns down from the rack and cleaned them, even though he couldn't remember the last time they'd been fired.

The sky had grown dark by the time Crabtree returned, even though it was only early afternoon.

"Storm coming," Crabtree said. "I got things handled here, if you want to head home before it starts coming down."

If Parker went home now, his brother-in-law would find some chore for him to do.

"I can keep you company."

The sheriff eased himself into the chair behind the desk. "Suit yourself." He opened a newspaper and began reading.

Parker plopped into the chair on the other side of the desk and twiddled his thumbs.

Crabtree slowly lowered the newspaper and looked at Parker. "Son, how long you plan to do this?"

"Well, until Clancy's opens maybe," Parker said. "Not sure."

"I don't mean today," Crabtree told him. "I mean the rest of your life."

Parker wasn't sure what the sheriff was asking him. The confusion must have been plain on his face.

"I knew your father from the army," Crabtree began. "Good man. And I wanted to look out for you and Sarah when your folks passed. But of course, Sarah was already engaged to Caleb. I brought you on as deputy to—oh, I dunno—have you where I could keep an eye on you. Give you something to do. Fact is, Rory's Junction barely needs a sheriff, let alone a deputy. I had to mess the budget around a bit to give you your paltry paycheck. Anyway, I thought it would only be for a little while."

"I got no complaints about the pay, sheriff."

"Okay, but that's not the point," Crabtree said. "You're still young, but you're not going to stay that way. You might want to think about—well . . . a path."

"A path?"

"An idea what you're going to do with your life," Crabtree said. "A goal you're working toward. A life you want to make for yourself."

Parker wondered if Lawrence Foley had chosen his path. To Parker, it seemed more like Lawrence had rolled out of bed and already found his path under his feet, just doing what his folks had done before him. How was waking up at dawn every morning to work the dirt and feed chickens and slop hogs better than what Parker did every day?

Except that Bonnie thought it was. Score one for Lawrence.

"I guess I'm just slower than some about figuring that out." Parker rose slowly from his chair. "I might take the long way round to Clancy's. Good for the law to be seen. Like you said." He tapped the tin star on his vest as he headed for the door.

"Parker."

Parker paused in the doorway, looked back at the sheriff.

"You're a good young man," Crabtree said. "Affable. Thoughtful. I'm not picking on you. I'd just like to see you be something is all."

Parker nodded. "I understand. I'll think on it."

When Parker stepped outside, the wind almost took his hat away. The sheriff had been right. A good blow was coming, the sky getting darker by the minute. He took the long way round to the saloon, just as he'd told Crabtree, but there weren't a lot of folks on the street. Everyone was locking up tight in anticipation of the coming storm. Parker started walking faster.

The rain started coming down just as he stepped through the front door into Clancy's. Parker took off his tin star and stashed it in his shirt pocket. He was off duty.

"A little early today," Clancy said.

"A good day to be indoors." Parker bellied up to the bar, and Clancy brought him a beer.

Thunder cracked so loudly overhead, it made both men flinch. Lightning lit up the windows. Rain lashed the world.

Clancy shook his head. "Gonna be a slow night. Folks don't venture out when it's like this, not if they can help it."

Parker nursed his beer. Time crept past.

A few others stumbled in, holding their coats closed in front of them, water dripping from hats, leaving wet footprints across the rough wooden floor. It wasn't a night for talk or jokes or fellowship. Men hunched over their mugs of beer or glasses of whiskey, each alone with his own thoughts, simply glad to be out of the rain. Thunder rumbled. After a while, the rain eased, but not much.

The saloon doors flapped open and another man stumbled in, posture and bearing indicating deep fatigue. He was soaked through. He went to the nearest table and half sat, half fell into a chair and didn't so much as look up. Usually, if a man wanted a drink, he'd go to Clancy for it, but since it was a slow night, Clancy came out from his place behind the bar and crossed the saloon to lean in and talk to the newcomer.

Parker watched the exchange but couldn't hear their words over the storm.

Clancy came back to the bar and filled a glass with whiskey. He shook his head and *tsk*ed.

"What?" Parker asked.

"Fella looks like ten miles of bad road," Clancy said. "Face white as a ghost. I guess he's been traveling all day, which I don't envy in this weather." He took the glass and bottle back to the stranger.

Parker tried to see what the man looked like, but he was facing the other way. Somebody passing through town hardly qualified as an interesting event in Rory's Junction. Then again, in light of Tanner Best's recent visit, Parker found himself curious. He didn't really think notorious outlaw Grady Jenks was within five hundred miles of Clancy's, but the villain's image was still fresh in Parker's mind from Best's wanted poster.

Parker eased away from the bar, bringing his beer mug with him, sipping causally as he took a slow stroll along the bar, trying to get a look at the man's face while doing his best not to be obvious about it. He went to the front window on the pretense of checking the weather, tilting his head and squinting up into the dark sky. He *tsk*ed and shook his head as if to say, *Looks like I'll be here awhile. Better order another beer and get comfortable.*

He made a slow turn back to the bar and was afforded a clear view of the stranger's face. He was simultaneously shocked and disappointed.

Disappointed because the man was clearly not notorious villain Grady Jenks. The likenesses on the wanted posters were often short on accuracy, as Tanner Best had said, but this man's face wasn't even close to a match. It probably wasn't too intelligent, hoping for a dangerous outlaw to pass through town and pause for a whiskey at Clancy's Saloon. But Rory's Junction was such a sleepy place—who could blame Parker for wanting a little excitement?

Even though he wasn't an outlaw, the stranger's appearance was shocking nonetheless. His face was white as a ghost, lips nearly blue. He was dripping wet and held his coat closed in front of him as if he couldn't get warm. His eyes looked glassy and dazed, as if maybe he was about to drift off.

Parker stepped up to the man's table. "Mister, I hesitate to pry into another fella's business, but are you okay?"

The man hesitated a moment, eyes blinking. He looked up slowly, expression blank, eyes slow to focus. He looked around as if trying to remember where he was, then looked back at Parker. "Come again."

"You don't look so well," Parker said. "Do you need any help?"

The man smiled, but it looked forced. It looked like pain. "As a matter of fact . . . any chance . . . maybe . . . this town has . . . a doctor?"

"You hurt?" Parker asked, a little more earnest now. "I can fetch him."

A flash and a crack of thunder shook the whole saloon and made Parker jump.

Sheriff Crabtree burst into the saloon, water streaming from his glistening raincoat, his tin star catching a bit of lantern light. He took his hat off and shook the rain from it.

"It's a gully washer out there, and that's for sure." Crabtree stalked toward the bar. "A shot of whiskey, Clancy, but just one. It's early to bed for me tonight."

Clancy poured his whiskey. "There ya go, sheriff."

Parker looked back at the stranger. "Sorry, mister, you were saying? About the doctor?"

The stranger's eyes went to the sheriff for a moment, then came back to Parker. "Never mind. Just—my stomach. Something I ate maybe. It can wait until morning."

Crabtree tossed back his whiskey, then set the empty glass on the bar. "Thanks, Clancy. Put it on my tab." He paused on the way out and gave Parker's shoulder a friendly squeeze. "You know I wasn't getting on you. Earlier, I mean. I'm just thinking about what's best for you."

A wan smile from Parker and a nod. "I know."

"Okay, then. Stay dry, if you can." Crabtree left without noticing anyone else in the saloon, probably intent on getting home to his warm, dry bed.

Parker stood a moment. Maybe his pa had been right. Maybe Parker should have joined the army. If he'd joined first thing, he'd probably be an officer by now. He could retire a general, maybe. Then what would Bonnie think of that, him riding back to Rory's Junction with shiny buttons on his uniform and a lot of gold piping, and a sword hanging from his belt?

He grinned and shook his head. Naw. He was kidding himself.

More thunder, but not a sharp crack this time, more like a rolling rumble spread out over the width and breadth of the land, like the sky itself was tumbling down and piling onto God's earth. The rain kept steady, and Parker was starting to think he'd have to walk home in it. He'd surely missed dinner, and if he continued to linger at Clancy's, Sarah would go to bed. No counting on her sneaking him out a plate.

The thought of him slinking home wet and hungry was suddenly as depressing as hearing Bonnie was going to marry dumb old dirt farmer Lawrence Foley.

He sighed. It had been that kind of day.

Parker turned to the stranger again. "Well, mister, if you're not in a hurry for the doc tonight, then I guess I'll be getting along."

The stranger sat with his eyes closed, chin on his chest. He was still dripping wet all over, a puddle under his chair from his wet trousers. Parker looked closer. Red dripped wetly, along with the rest, down into the puddle, making it go sort of rosy.

Parker took a half step closer. "Mister?"

For a moment, Parker thought the man was dead, but when he got closer, he could see the stranger was breathing. Parker tentatively put a hand on the man's shoulder.

The stranger's head came up slow as molasses, eyes creaking open, voice barely above a whisper. "Maybe . . . that doctor . . . after all . . ."

He fell out of his chair and rattled the floorboards with a thud, his hat rolling away.

The few patrons in the saloon turned and gasped. Clancy came out from behind the bar with an alarmed look on his face.

Parker looked down at the sprawled stranger. His coat had come open, revealing a big, wet red blotch on his shirt right on the belly, just a little off to the left.

"I'll run after the sheriff," Clancy said, heading for the door.

"Get the doctor first," Parker called after him. "This fella looks pretty bad."

The other saloon patrons edged closer, looking from the wounded man to Parker and back. Parker figured he should say something. He was a deputy after all.

"Let's not crowd him. Give him air," Parker said. "Clancy's gone for the doc."

The patrons shrugged and went back to their drinks.

Parker heard something and realized the stranger was trying to speak to him. He shifted his eyes from the man's belly wound to his face. With his hat off, the man looked familiar. A round, affable face. Bushy eyebrows. He gestured for Parker to come closer.

Parker knelt next to the man. "We've sent for the doc. Just take it easy."

The man was still trying to say something, a sort of urgency in his eyes.

Parker leaned in and turned his head, bringing his ear near the man's mouth.

The whisper leaked out of him, a sigh of wind over dry leaves, barely audible but plain. "The gold."

CHAPTER 3

Grady Jenks had to hand it to that Kansas marshal. The man had raised a posse a lot quicker than Jenks thought he could and had offered dogged pursuit as Jenks and the boys made for the Missouri line.

The train robbery had gone perfectly with the exception of Eugene's death, but that was the risk in their line of work. When the lead starts flying, anything can happen. All in all, the plan had worked well.

The luck had been all bad ever since. They'd gone to meet Frenchy LaSalle at the rendezvous point, an abandoned mine. That's where they'd intended to split the gold and all go their separate ways. For Jenks, it was his final score, as far as he was concerned. With so much money, he could set himself up somewhere. Take a new name. Do whatever he wanted.

They'd found Frenchy at the rendezvous all right. Dead. No gold.

It didn't take a genius to figure what had happened. The railroad man had double-crossed them.

Grady Jenks muttered a curse.

They reined in their horses on a low hill and looked back at the pinpricks of light following them in the dark, lanterns in the distance.

Grady *tsk*ed. He'd hoped following the stream a few miles would throw them off, but they must have had some good trackers with them.

Lester sat astride the horse next to him. He leaned over, spit a wad of tobacco juice, then said. "They don't quit, do they?"

Grady scowled at him, a wasted effort in the darkness. "It's your fault they're back there. Why'd you shoot him?"

"He was trying to get away," Lester said.

"If you kill him, how do we make him tell us where the gold is?" Jenks asked heatedly.

"You've made that point several times. I told you it won't happen again," Lester said in that calm way that indicated he was really getting angry. "Lay off."

"None of this bickering is solving our problem," pitched in Little Joe.

"You got any bright ideas?" There was a hint of sarcasm in Jenks's voice, but he wouldn't turn away a good idea if anybody had one.

"Who's got the fastest horse?" Bill Farkas asked.

"Me," Jenks replied.

"And I'm the best rifle shot," Farkas said. "We agree?"

"Let's say nobody disagrees," Jenks told him. "You got something?"

Farkas twisted in the saddle, looking toward Missouri

but, of course, only seeing the dark of night. "We should make Shoal Creek soon."

"And?"

"They'll have to come across slow after that rain," Farkas said. "We can lay into them from the opposite bank."

"There's at least twenty," Jenks reminded him.

"We open up on the first ones across, really let them have it," Farkas said. "The ones who haven't started across will jump off their horses and take cover, maybe even panic and scatter. Then you fellas take off and ride for all your worth. I'll stay a bit and keep shooting. They might even wait to cross in daylight. Give me your horse, and I'll catch up."

"How come you're a hero all of a sudden?" Little Joe asked.

Farkas shrugged. "Gotta try something."

Jenks thought about it, but the only thing that happened was the posse got a little closer.

"Okay, we'll try it," Jenks said. "Let's go."

They reached Shoal Creek an hour later. They had found the best spot for crossing and hoped the posse would agree and come right to them. The recent downpour had indeed swollen the creek, and the current was strong. The going was difficult. Twice as difficult while being shot at, Jenks hoped.

They found good cover on the other side and checked their rifles.

"Lead the horses away quietly when it's time to go," Farkas said. "I want them to think I got company over here for as long as possible."

Jenks nodded. "Right."

"Where we gonna meet up?" Farkas asked.

"I been thinking about that," Jenks said. "I don't know Missouri."

"Eiger's," Little Joe said. "It's a trading post just over the line. Everyone knows it, so you can ask around if you get lost."

"Eiger's, then," Jenks said.

Everyone grunted agreement.

They waited.

As feared, the posse had caught up to them a little, as they arrived at the creek ten minutes later. They hesitated a moment, maybe talking it over. The couple out front swung their lanterns low as they nudged their horses back and forth along the bank, maybe seeing where Jenks and his boys had entered the creek. He could hear them talking it over—not the actual words, but voices, muffled by the babbling water.

Jenks's palms were sweaty on his rifle. Maybe this was a bad idea. Probably they could have kept riding and shaken off the posse, then crossed into Missouri.

Too late now.

The first five eased their horses down the bank and into the creek, two in front and three behind, the rest of the posse watching from dry land. Jenks and his gang waited until they reached the deepest part in the middle.

Then he lifted his rifle and fired, the crack of the rifle shot echoing in the night, drowned out in the next second by the barrage of gunfire from all four of them. They methodically shot, levered in a new shell, then fired again, taking careful aim each time. The men in the posse were practically asking for it, targets lit up by the lanterns some carried.

Four of the five men in the creek were shot out of their saddles, bodies tumbling into the water, the current taking them away. The fifth managed to turn his horse in an attempt to ride back before taking one right between the shoulder blades. His foot caught in a stirrup, and he was dragged downstream by the panicked horse.

The ones left along the opposite bank were all doing different things. Some immediately returned fire, shots going wide. Others dismounted to find cover first. A few turned their horses to ride away. Farkas had been right. It would take them a while to get organized again after this.

"Once more before you go," Farkas said.

The four of them reloaded their rifles and then emptied them again at the men across the creek, the air filled with the rapid crackle of gunfire. Some of those damn fools in the posse still had their lanterns lit, and that's where Jenks concentrated his fire.

A smattering of return fire, then a brief, confused silence.

"Go on," Farkas whispered. "Leave that fast horse of yours."

"Good luck," Jenks whispered back. "See you at Eiger's."

Jenks led Farkas's horse away, keeping low and quiet, Little Joe and Lester close behind. They went for about a mile like that before mounting up and riding away fast, the sound of scattered rifle fire echoing behind them.

Jenks shook his head and muttered a curse. The train robbery was supposed to be so well planned that there'd be no trouble afterward, and now they had a posse after them, just what Jenks wanted to avoid. That double-crossing railroad man, Filmore, had caused them too much trouble, and Jenks planned to throttle him when they finally caught up.

After he told where the gold was, of course.

A federal marshal's badge could do a lot of things. It could open doors. It could make tough men step aside. It could even catch a woman's eye, if she was the right sort of woman. A marshal's badge meant power, because anyone with half a brain knew they didn't hand those badges out to just anybody. The man who wore the badge was hard as a coffin nail, spoke hard words, and gave hard lessons.

And the hardest of these hard men was Tanner Best.

But one of the things a marshal's badge couldn't do was keep the rain off.

Best slouched in the saddle as his horse clopped through the mud into Garyville, water running off his raincoat and the brim of the hat pulled low. He was cold and wet and hungry, and in no mood for nonsense.

He'd been through a lot of little towns up and down the border Missouri shared with Kansas and Oklahoma, showing his wanted posters and the sketch of the railroad man with no luck. His mission in Garyville was something different. He was looking for a one-legged man named Nolan Conroy, with the intent to make the man talk.

He dismounted in front of a hotel called The Scotsman and looped the reins of his horse around the hitching post. The rain had let up some and wouldn't bother the animal. Best hoped he wouldn't be here for long.

He climbed two steps, paused under the protection of the covered porch, and turned to look up and down the street. Nobody around, not a surprise, with the poor weather. It was late, but not too late. Nolan Conroy didn't strike Best as an early-to-bed sort of man.

Best entered the hotel. The lobby was empty. He went to the front desk and rang the bell.

A moment later, a little man with thinning gray hair and a napkin tucked into his collar emerged from the back room, a vacant look on his face. He held a half-eaten spare rib in one hand.

"Sorry to interrupt your dinner," Best said. "I need to confirm that a man named Nolan Conroy is a guest here."

The little man offered an apologetic shrug. "Sorry, mister. Can't give out information like that."

Best pulled aside his raincoat to let the badge show.

The hotel man squinted at it. "Oh."

Best took off his raincoat and hat and hung them on the nearby wall pegs. "Room number?"

The hotel man consulted his book. "205."

"Thanks."

"Uh, you want me to fetch him down."

Best shook his head. "I'll go up."

"Uh, is there going to be trouble."

Best grinned. "Only if he starts some."

"Should I—"

"You should go back to your dinner."

The hotel man stuck the rib into his mouth and rapidly retreated to the back room.

Best crossed the lobby and headed up the stairs, pausing halfway to cock his head and listen. He didn't hear anything worrisome. He began climbing again. Each step creaked a little. On the second floor, he found room 205, leaned an ear toward it but heard nothing. Light from under the door. Probably not sleeping, then.

He listened again, thought he heard some movement, but nothing significant. Best drew one of the Remingtons and eased back the hammer with a thumb. He took a step back then kicked the door hard.

The door swung inward with a crack, pieces of the doorframe flying. Best swung the pistol from right to left, taking in the room's interior in an instant. Bed, table, chair. All the way on the left side of the room, near the window, was a tub, and in the tub sat Nolan Conroy, covered with suds. He saw Best, his eyes popping wide.

A ladderback chair sat next to the tub, a gun belt hanging from one side, and Conroy's wooden leg hanging from the other. Conroy came halfway out of the tub, reaching for his six-gun.

Best leveled the Remington at him. "Don't."

Conroy froze, hand a few inches from his revolver, water running off his rubbery white flesh, the expression on his face showing how deeply concerned he was about his predicament.

Best walked into the room, his gun still pointed at Conroy's face. He shut the door behind him as well as he could, considering the busted frame. "You stay just like that, Nolan. Don't twitch a muscle."

"I ain't done nothin'," Conroy said, making sure not to move. "I served my three years. I'm clean."

"You haven't done anything that anyone *knows* about," Best said. "But I know better than to think you're clean, bath or not. I'm sure you've been up to no good. Maybe I'll look into that and maybe I won't. Depends."

"On what?"

"On you answering my questions," Best said. "And if I like your answers or not."

Conroy frowned. "That tin star don't make you God Almighty."

Best crossed the room in two long strides and grabbed Conroy by the back of the neck. The marshal dragged Conroy over the side of the tub with a splash of water. Conroy landed in his own puddle, fish-belly white skin glistening with bathwater and fluffy white soap suds. His left leg had been cut off just below the knee, the flesh at the end a mass of twisted, puckered scars.

"I'm looking for Grady Jenks," Best said.

"I never ran with him," Conroy said. "Never even met the man."

"But you ran with the Morris brothers."

"So what?"

Best took the wooden leg from the chair and held it

by the ankle. He raised it high then brought it down hard across Conroy's back with a wet smack.

Conroy howled.

"So what?" Best mocked. "So I'm looking for Grady Jenks, fool. And the Morris brothers are part of his gang. Or Lester still is. Eugene is dead."

"Dead?" Conroy said. "I didn't know."

"Well, what *do* you know?" Best demanded. "If I know where to find Lester Morris, then Jenks will be right there with him."

"How am I supposed to know where Lester Morris hangs his hat?" Conroy said bitterly. "It ain't like we correspond."

Best slammed the wooden leg across his back again. Conroy shrieked.

"You can't beat a man with his own leg," Conroy said, a note of hysteria in his voice. "That ain't right."

"I'll use it to crack your thick skull next," Best told him. "Unless you think of something useful."

"I don't know a thing, I'm telling you."

Best raised the leg to crack him again.

"Wait! Little Joe," Conroy said quickly. "Little Joe!"

Best lowered the leg. "Joe Tillis?"

"That's him," Conroy said. "He still running around with Lester?"

"Yeah, he's with Jenks's gang."

"Eiger's then," Conroy said. "Little Joe always liked to use it as a stop-off place between jobs."

Marshal Best had heard of it, a little place right before crossing the line into Kansas.

"And you're positive he'll be there?"

"No, not positive," Conroy said. "But you said to think of something, so I thought of something."

"Okay, then." Best tossed the leg, and it rattled away across the floor. "I guess that's the best you can do."

"You gonna leave me alone, then?"

"I reckon." Best crossed the room to the little table and grabbed the other chair and slumped into it. He took off his hat and wiped sweat from his forehead. "What are you doing in this little nothing town anyway?"

"Passing through," Conroy said. "Heading west."

"To do what?"

"Look for work."

"Uh-huh." Best put his hat back on. "You seen Ned Gorman when you were in stir?"

Conroy rolled over and backed up against the tub in a sitting position. "Some."

"He still want to kill me?"

"He does," Conroy confirmed. "But there's plenty men in there who do. Men you put there, marshal."

"Most are talk," Best said. "But Gorman always struck me as the type who could hold a grudge a good long time."

"Maybe."

Best sighed. "You know, I'm thinking this isn't going to work, Nolan."

"What isn't going to work?"

"Just leaving you alone."

Conroy's face turned worried. "I told you all I could," he said, voice small.

"Yeah."

"Okay, then."

"But what happens if you see Jenks or Little Joe before I catch up with them?"

"I won't see them," Conroy said.

"But what if you do?" Best insisted. "You'd tip them off I was after them. I can't have that."

"I wouldn't say anything."

Best shook his head. "Can't take that chance."

Conroy's face went blank.

Best tossed his Remington on the bed and let his left hand dangle over the other six-shooter. "I'm not as fast with my left. I believe in giving a man a chance."

Conroy's eyes flicked between Best and his gun belt still hanging from the chair. "This ain't necessary. I won't say anything."

"This is happening, Nolan."

"Please."

Best let his face go hard. "You want me to count it down?"

Conroy leaped for the chair, falling across it as he got a hand on the butt of his pistol. Best let him get the revolver halfway out of the holster before drawing the Remington and firing, the pistol's thunder filling the little hotel room.

Conroy took the shot between the eyes, head snapping back, blood flying in an arc. He fell back against the tub, water splashing over him, and slumped into a slick pile of white flesh.

The little hotel man was up from the front desk the next moment, pushing open the busted door, eyes wide.

"He drew on me," Best said matter-of-factly. "Guess you better fetch the sheriff and get this mess cleaned up."

CHAPTER 4

Parker looked up quickly, eyes darting around the interior of the saloon. If any of the others heard the word *gold*, they weren't letting on, all seeming more interested in their whiskey.

Parker leaned in closer to the wounded man and whispered, "What was that? Gold?"

"I'll . . . tell you. Tell you . . . where." The stranger's voice was weak. "Just get me . . . a doctor. I don't . . . want to die. Get me a doctor, and . . . I'll tell you."

"Tell me what?" Parker asked.

"Where . . . to find the gold."

Parker let that sink in. He knew the man's face now, realized it was one of the sketches Tanner Best had showed him, not one of the outlaws on the wanted posters but the one of the railroad man.

Gerald Filmore.

Parker's head swam with the possibilities. Here was the man who'd—what? Orchestrated the train robbery? Marshal Best said he was a man he wanted to question, but what did that mean? What did Gerald Filmore know? What had he done?

He noticed Filmore was gesturing to him with a trembling hand. Parker lowered his head. "M-mother's . . . the . . . general."

Parker blinked. "General?"

Filmore's eyes rolled back, a long, ragged sigh leaking out of him.

Clancy burst into the saloon, face red and puffing, Doc Abernathy right on his heels.

Doctor Silas Abernathy had graduated medical school in Philadelphia, packed his bag, and headed west to make his fortune in California. He got as far as Missouri, met a girl, and had stayed thirty-five years. Parker guessed Rory's Junction had probably grown up around him. He was a compact little man with a no-nonsense face, round spectacles, and a shock of mussed white hair. His striped nightshirt had been poorly tucked into his trousers, the tail of it flapping in the back. He gripped his black doctor's bag in one hand.

"One side, boy."

Parker moved out of the way, and Abernathy knelt next to Filmore. He pried up the man's eyelids. Then he ripped open his bloody shirt and looked at the wound, poking and prodding. The doc touched his wrist then a spot on his throat, shaking his head and *tsk*ing. "He's gone."

Clancy leaned in to look over the doc's shoulder. "That's a shame."

Abernathy stood and sighed. "Well, I'm awake now. Clancy, you got a blanket or something to throw over him? And bring me a whiskey."

By the time Clancy returned with the blanket and the

doc's drink, Sheriff Crabtree had arrived. "What's the word, doc?"

Abernathy sipped whiskey. "Too late for me to do anything."

Crabtree knelt next to the corpse and began going through his pockets. "Let see what he's got."

Parker stood dumbly, watching.

"You okay, boy?"

Parker blinked, looked up at the doc. "Sir?"

"Your first time seeing a dead body?" Abernathy asked.

Parker shook his head. "My folks."

"Oh, yes. Of course," Abernathy said. "Still, not the same as seeing a man dead from a gunshot."

The sheriff looked up. "That's what did it? You're sure?"

The doc nodded. "I'm sure."

"Huh." The sheriff kept searching the corpse.

"Quite a thing, killing a man," Abernathy said. "Not that I've ever killed anyone, but I've seen plenty of men die. Everything they ever had or were going to be, all of their plans for their own lives, all gone up in smoke." A shrug and a sip of whiskey. "Although I guess life can do that as well as death. Life gets in the way."

Parker had only been half listening. "How's that?"

"Life gets in the way," Abernathy repeated. "Take me for example. I was going to California. But then I met the little woman. Don't misunderstand, I'm not sorry. But I wonder sometimes what my life would be if I'd kept going to California. What about you, boy? You ever wonder?"

Parker didn't answer him.

"Well, he's got a pocket watch, forty-three dollars, and an unsmoked cigar," Crabtree said. "But nothing to say who he might be—or might've been. Parker, he say anything to you about what he was doing in town? Maybe he said his name."

His name was Gerald Filmore, thought Parker. He could have told the sheriff that, could have explained recognizing the face from Marshal Best's sketch, told the sheriff Filmore's final words. But the deputy didn't mention any of that to Sheriff Crabtree.

Parker shook his head. "He didn't say."

And that's when Parker realized he'd made up his mind. He was going after the gold.

Parker checked his saddlebags. They contained everything he owned in the world.

"Are you sure about this?" his sister asked.

"Got to start making my own way somehow," Parker said.

"You heard the man." Caleb gave Parker a manly slap on the back. "He knows what he's doing."

Caleb was practically beaming. Parker knew that deep down his brother-in-law was a good man and wished him well, but he also knew the primary reason for Caleb's lighthearted mood was that he was getting rid of what Caleb considered so much dead weight in the shape of his wife's lazy little brother.

Parker didn't take offense. Caleb wasn't entirely wrong. Yes, Parker needed to make his own way. He'd only been waiting for the right opportunity to nudge him out the door.

That opportunity had finally arrived.

He gave his sister a peck on the cheek, shook Caleb's hand, and then climbed into the saddle.

"Just be careful," Sarah told him for the hundredth time. "A lot can happen between here and California."

Parker had told them he was heading west to be part of the Rio Dell gold rush. He figured it was good cover for what he was really doing and would provide an easy explanation if he suddenly struck it rich. "I'll be careful. And I'll write."

He gave them a final wave as he rode off toward Rory's Junction.

He stopped at the sheriff's office, dismounted, and went inside.

"So you're really going through with it," Crabtree said.

"It was your idea," Parker reminded the sheriff.

Crabtree looked sheepish. "Well, I wouldn't quite say that. I just wanted to give you some things to think about. I didn't think you'd be pulling up stakes and leaving town so sudden."

"I'm not laying this on you, sheriff," Parker assured the man. "It's time, that's all. You just helped me see it. One more thing. I didn't want to leave town without giving this back to you." Parker set his tin star on the desk.

Crabtree picked it up and looked at it a moment with a wry smile before handing it back to Parker. "Let's not say you're quit. Let's just say you're on leave for the time being. Anyway, you never can tell when one of those stars might come in handy. It might open a door for you—although keep in mind, it can also make you a target. The trick is guessing right."

"Thanks, sheriff." Parker tucked the star into his shirt pocket. "I guess this is it, then."

Crabtree held out his hand. "Good luck, son."

They shook.

Two minutes later, Parker was back on his horse, heading out of town toward Neosho.

The trip to Neosho was easy riding on good roads, and Parker got there about an hour after lunchtime. He rode into town with his head up and a good feeling in his chest. Some dang fool might even have mistaken the feeling for—what? Pride? Enthusiasm?

Parker had embarked on a grand adventure. He might be a rich man by the end.

He just had to figure out how to begin. He knew the man's name, knew his mother lived in town. Surely that was enough to get started.

Parker eased his horse down Main Street and stopped at the first businesses he saw, a place called Bently's Mercantile. He dismounted, secured his horse to the hitching post, and walked inside. The place was empty of shoppers, and a man in an apron, behind the counter, was replacing bags of coffee beans on a high shelf with the aid of a short stepladder. He was bald and chubby, handlebar mustache oiled into an elaborate curl.

"Sir, can I ask you a question?" Parker said. "I apologize for bothering you. I can see you're busy."

The man came down from the ladder. "No trouble. I just try to keep busy during the slow hours. You know how it is. What's your question?"

"I'm looking for the Filmore house," Parker said.

The man chuckled. "That's about ten different houses in these parts. A prominent family."

"Gerald Filmore ring a bell?" Parker asked. "I'm looking for his mother."

The man's eyes narrowed. "What would you want with her?"

Parker thought a moment before speaking. If in doubt, a man could always fall back on the truth. "I need to deliver some news of a personal nature. Sort of delicate-like." He hastily went into his shirt pocket and came out with the star and pinned it on his vest. "Not my jurisdiction, so I wasn't wearing it. Just sort of here as a courtesy, so to speak."

The mercantile man squinted at the star. "Oh. Well, that's okay then, I reckon. The Filmores are an old family around here, going back to the founding of the town, and the dowager is the oldest of all—*dowager* being a sort of term of affection. Esmeralda is her name. The family used to be much more well-to-do before the bust of '73, but they're still respected around these parts. I don't personally know the family well, but that's all common knowledge."

"Any chance you could point me in the right direction?"

"Keep going down Main Street," he told Parker. "The

first house right as you leave town, big two-story thing, white with blue shutters."

Parker thanked him and left.

The house was right where the mercantile man said it would be, large and clearly the home of a person of means, although at a second glance, he realized the dwelling would soon be due for a new coat of paint. The yard wasn't overgrown, but neither was it tended as well as it could be. Parker wondered what the place would look like if he came back in another five years, or ten.

He tied his horse to the low limb of a young maple at the edge of the property, then took the walkway toward the house, looking for signs of life in the windows but seeing nothing. He climbed the step to the wide front porch. There was a brass knocker on the front door. Parker knocked and waited, belatedly snatching his hat from his head as the door slowly creaked open.

An old negro stood there in a butler's uniform, stooped, face lined, hair thinning and white, watery eyes bored. "May I help you, sir?"

"I'm Parker Jones, just up from Rory's Junction. I apologize for coming unannounced, but I was hoping to speak to Mizz Filmore."

The butler's eyes slid momentarily to the tin star on Parker's vest, which he'd left pinned there for just this purpose. Sheriff Crabtree said it might open doors on occasion, and Parker was betting this was one of those times.

The butler stood aside and gestured for Parker to

enter. "If you can wait here in the foyer, I'll see if Missus Filmore is available."

"Much obliged."

The butler left.

Parker waited.

The foyer was big, much bigger than the little room he'd called home in the flour mill, arched doorways to the right, left, and ahead of him. He glanced upward. A crystal chandelier hung from the twelve-foot ceiling. He looked closer and saw it was covered with cobwebs. Indeed, the foyer told the tale of a wealthy family now diminished: scuffed floors, threadbare rugs, peeling paint.

The butler returned and gestured to his left. "Missus Filmore will join you in the parlor."

Parker followed him in, and then the butler withdrew, and Parker just stood there holding his hat and wondering if he should sit. He took in his surroundings. A sitting area, furniture matching but the fabric faded—divan, sofa, love seat. Painted lamps with a very light layer of dust. An oil painting over the mantel, some military fellow in an odd-looking uniform.

"Thank you for waiting."

Parker turned to watch the old woman shuffle into the parlor. "No problem at all."

Esmerelda Filmore was very old and very stooped, and to Parker it looked like a good sneeze would knock her right over. She wore a muted pink dress with a tight floral pattern, a brooch at her throat with a large red gem. Parker didn't know much about jewelry. A ruby maybe.

Or glass—he wouldn't know the difference.

Her skin looked like wet tissue clinging to her bony head. Her hair was piled up in a wiry, gray bun. One eye milky, the other a bright, alert blue.

Esmerelda stepped closer, her good eye examining his face carefully before going to the star on his vest. "You're not one of Dalton's."

"Dalton, ma'am?"

"Our sheriff."

"Oh, no, ma'am," Parker said. "I apologize if I gave your man that impression."

"You did not," she said. "Who are you?"

"Parker Jones, ma'am, up from Rory's Junction," he told her. "I'm a deputy there."

"Have a seat, Deputy Jones. Damon is preparing tea for us."

"That's generous, ma'am, but I wouldn't want to put you out. I just wanted to ask a few—"

"I'll be the first to let you know when you're putting me out, deputy," she said politely, but with just enough authority. "I am eighty-one years old and receive precious few visitors. You'll indulge me to make the most of it when afforded the opportunity. Please have a seat." She gestured to the love seat.

Parker sat on the edge, hat in his lap. The old woman perched on the sofa across from him. It struck him suddenly that he was about to tell her that her son had been shot and killed, and he doubted she'd want to sit and have a pleasant chat over tea afterward. Somewhere in this house—Parker had assumed—was a clue to the whereabouts of the missing gold. His plan was—what exactly? He couldn't simply rummage through the woman's home with her standing there watching.

"I understand you have questions for me," Esmerelda said.

"Yes, ma'am, but first, I have some unfortunate news to deliver," Parker told her. "About your son." It seemed cruel to withhold the information for his own greed. His only choice was to give her the bad news as delicately as possible and then try to find out something useful about the gold afterward.

"There was another lawman here a few days ago, looking for Gerald," she said.

"I imagine that would be Marshal Best, I reckon."

"Indeed. Gerald had already gone by the time Marshal Best paid his visit, so I wasn't able to help him. I hope you're not here to tell me Gerald is in some sort of trouble," the old woman said. "He's always been hard-working and law-abiding."

Before Parker could reply, the butler returned, wheeling in a tea service on a rickety trolly. He filled a bone china teacup from a matching pot, set it on a saucer, and handed it to Esmerelda. He repeated the process, handing Parker his cup.

The old woman sipped.

Parker sipped.

"Anything else, ma'am?" the butler asked.

"Thank you, no, Joshua."

Damon bowed and left.

Parker was feeling more awkward than ever. He couldn't remember the last time he drank tea. He should have come to the point sooner, before she went to the trouble.

"Gerald," Esmerelda prompted. "I was asking if he's landed himself in some sort of trouble."

"No, ma'am, leastways not in the way you're thinking," Parker said. "I feel like I don't know how to tell you this any other way than just coming out and saying it. Someone shot and killed your son, ma'am. Gerald Filmore is dead. It happened in Rory's Junction. I'm as sad as I can be to be the one to bring you the news."

Esmerelda went rigid, the teacup halfway to her lips. A frozen moment passed that way, and Parker could see it in her eyes, turning over the information, swallowing the bitter pill and digesting it, and suddenly Parker wished he were anywhere else, gold or no gold, and that it had been somebody else to bring this poor old woman such awful news.

"I can come back later, ma'am, if that's better," Parker said. "In case you need to . . ." He trailed off, not really knowing what it was she might need to do.

"Need to do what, deputy?" she asked. "Cry? Rend my clothing and throw myself on the floor in a fit of grief?" A long, tired sigh leaked out of her, and she set her cup and saucer back on the trolly. "My husband died twenty years ago. I lost three sons before Gerald. One at Bull Run and another at Vicksburg. The third was killed by Jayhawkers. A woman's heart hardens to such things, although I thought it would be different with Gerald. A safe, responsible job with the railroad. It's just me now alone in a big house. I will cry about that when the time comes."

Parker swallowed hard and remained silent. Should he go—make his excuses and leave? It felt like he was waiting for the old woman's permission.

"I'm just glad you're here," she said. "Glad you're on the trail of the murderer who killed my boy."

Oh?

But of course. He was a man with a tin star on his vest. She had assumed he was hot on the killer's trail, the law come to see justice done.

"If there's anything I can do, any questions I can answer to help you solve this terrible crime, please don't hesitate to ask," she said.

Parker hesitated, but only for a moment. He recognized the opportunity she was offering. "Ma'am, does he have a room or someplace he keeps his personal effects? There might be a letter or something to tell us if he was having a dispute with somebody."

Parker Jones had no idea who might have killed Gerald Filmore. Probably a random highwayman looking to make a fast buck. A quarrel over a hand of cards. Maybe Filmore had taken an improper fancy to another man's wife.

Parker didn't have one clue, and deputy or not, it had only just occurred to him that it should be his concern. He'd had gold on his mind and little else. He wasn't especially proud of his greed, and he felt bad for the old woman, but if he was being honest with himself, it wasn't troubling him all that much. For the first time in Parker's life, there was ambition driving him further than his next meal or mug of beer, a self-centered sort of ambition, yes, but a direction, an endeavor he could pour all his energies into.

A pile of gold could sweep away nagging feelings of guilt easy enough.

Esmerelda Filmore twisted in her seat and called over her shoulder, "Joshua!" She faced Parker again and said, "He is a grown man and of course maintains his own home near his work with the railroad, but he still has his room here for when he visits. Many of his things are still up there. I'm not so very fond of stairs these days, so I'll have Joshua show you the way."

The servant appeared and bowed slightly. "Ma'am?"

"Joshua, take Deputy Jones upstairs," Esmerelda said. "He has my permission to search Gerald's things."

"Yes, ma'am."

The butler led Parker upstairs and down a wide hallway to a door at the end, opened it, and gestured that Parker should enter. Parker went into the room, eyes going from one corner to the other, wondering what he should be looking for. There was a large double bed with a checkered quilt and an ornate, polished wooden headboard. A table with a water pitcher and basin. A mirror behind it. A rug. A dresser with five drawers and a little wooden box on top. There were a couple of fly-fishing poles in one corner, a wicker creel basket on the floor, presumably with flies and other tackle inside.

Parker didn't know where to start.

Joshua stood in the doorway, wringing his hands as if uncomfortable with letting a stranger rummage through the dowager's household.

"I'm not sure exactly what I'm trying to find,"

Parker admitted to the butler. "Something to tell me if Mr. Filmore had any enemies maybe. I have to be methodical. Might be a few minutes."

"Then if you don't need me, sir, I'll get to the kitchen," Joshua said. "Missus Esmerelda eats early these days."

"Thanks. I'll get along fine."

Joshua bowed and left.

Parker sighed and looked around the room again. He started with the dresser, opening one drawer at a time. Clothes, some fancy enough for church, others for working in a field or garden. He felt around under the clothes in case there was something hidden. There wasn't. He checked the box on top of the dresser. Cuff links. A silver watch chain but no watch. A tie pin with a pearl. A comb. A paisley bowtie.

He checked the wash basin, looked inside the pitcher. Nothing.

He looked at the fly-fishing rods. They seemed of good quality—although, really, Parker knew little of such things—but looked worn, as if they'd seen a lot of use. He knelt next to the creel basket and opened it. He thought he detected the very faint smell of old fish, but maybe that was his imagination.

The basket contained spools of fishing line, hooks and weights, and various flies. It occurred to Parker that as he trekked west, crossing the wilderness and sleeping outdoors every night, some fishing gear might come in handy. He looked over his shoulder, confirmed he was unobserved, then slipped a spool of line, a handful of hooks and weights, and the flies into his inside vest pocket. The man was dead after all and wouldn't miss these things, and it wasn't like old Dowager Esmeralda was going to take up fly-fishing anytime soon.

Parker checked under the bed next. A few lumps of something he couldn't identify in the darkness.

He went to the windows and spread the curtains. The angle was perfect to let the late afternoon light pour through the dirty glass. He pushed the bed aside. It slid quietly across the smooth floor.

Parker could see now the lumps were just a pair of old work boots, caked with old, dried mud. His shoulders slumped. There was nothing here, nothing to lead him to gold or even offer a hint.

Parker stood, turning slowly to take one last gander. There was nothing left to see, no more clues to find.

He went back downstairs.

There was no sign of Joshua. Esmerelda had fallen asleep on the couch where she'd been sitting, head down and tilted slightly to one side, mouth hanging slightly open. For the briefest moment, Parker worried the old woman had died, but the slow rise and fall of her chest was proof of life.

The house was strangely quiet now, the old man in the odd uniform looking down at Parker and the sleeping dowager like some grim, ghostly guardian. Who was the man? Some ancestor maybe, a cavalry officer in some Napoleonic conflict or perhaps . . .

Perhaps a *general*.

As Gerald Filmore lay dying, he'd said something about a general. Who else could it be but the man in the portrait?

Parker glanced at the sleeping woman again, then

approached the painting which hung above the mantel.
He took a lesson learned from searching the bedroom
earlier and examined the dust around the painting and
on the mantel below. As Parker had guessed, the dust had
been disturbed. He looked once more back at Esmerelda
before carefully and quietly lifting the paint from the
nail on which the portrait hung. And behind the painting was—

Nothing. A blank wall. Parker wasn't sure what he'd
expected. A secret safe set into the wall, full of all the
gold. It was nonsense, of course. Gerald Filmore had
said something about a general, but the man had been
dying, probably out of his head from pain and loss of
blood. He probably had no idea what he was saying
or why, and Parker was chasing after ghosts, based on
a dying man's final delusions.

He made to return the portrait to its place on the wall
before he was discovered and forced to come up with
some kind of explanation.

He paused.

Something was stuck into the back side of the frame:
a folded piece of brown paper, tucked between the
frame's rough edge and the back of the canvas. Parker
snatched the paper, his heart quickening as if he expected to be caught any second. He shoved the paper
deep into his trouser pocket and hastily replaced the
painting.

Esmerelda hadn't so much as twitched.

Parker touched her gently on the shoulder, and the
old woman's eyes creaked open.

"Sorry to disturb you, ma'am," Parker said. "I'd best

get along. Thank you for your time. You can contact Sheriff Crabtree in Rory's Junction about your son's body. I'm sorry for your loss."

Slowly, her eyes focused on him, and there was a long moment as if maybe she was trying to remember who Parker was and what he was doing in her house. "Good luck, Deputy Jones."

As slow as a sunset, her eyes closed again, and she was back to sleep.

Parker let himself out, walked back down the walkway trying not to look like he was in a hurry. He mounted his horse and headed out of town, looking over his shoulder occasionally, although, obviously, nobody was coming after him.

He reined in his horse a mile down the road, took the paper from his pocket, and unfolded it.

It was immediately clear to Parker he was looking at a map, drawn with care, in black ink. In the middle of the map was a large—something. It looked like a huge tree stump, thrusting up from the ground. Lower and to the left a bit was a long, curving line. A road. Arrows with numbers to indicate—yards? Feet?

Parker examined the map a good five minutes, poring over every detail.

He sighed and shook his head.

It meant nothing to him.

CHAPTER 5

Parker passed the night under the low branches of a willow tree, the cold ground making his cot and small room back in his brother-in-law's mill seem luxurious by comparison. His blanket was too thin even for this time of year, and his saddle made for a poor pillow. He stood and stretched, every part of him sore and out of sorts.

Last night's modest fire had gone completely cold. He built another and made coffee. He put the feedbag on the horse while the coffee brewed and ate a cold biscuit. He and the horse, both, would run out of food in another two or three nights, and he reminded himself he needed to purchase supplies before heading west in earnest.

But . . . should he?

The west was vast. He's spent one night on the ground and was already miserable, and his visit to Esmerelda Filmore's house had not produced the clues he'd hoped would help him find the gold, at least not without a lot of hard thinking. He could slink back to Rory's Junction with his tail between his legs. His sister would be happy to see him back, and of course, Crabtree would let him continue as deputy.

But the look of sour disappointment on his brother-in-law's face would be too much to bear, partly because it would remind Parker that he was not completely welcome.

Mostly, it would be a reminder that his brother-in-law was right, that Parker had not only failed as a man, failed to go out and make his own way, but that he'd done it in record time, crawling back before the sheets on his narrow cot had even cooled.

No, Parker would go on, somewhere and somehow. The idea of finding the gold had been foolish. He could see that now. So then, what? Parker Jones still needed to find his own path, be his own man. West was as good a direction as any.

He finished the coffee, saddled the horse, and kicked dirt on the fire. Time to mount up and go. He headed north up the road.

Parker soon enough found himself in farm country and just after midday stopped next to an old farmer mending a fence.

"Howdy, mister."

The old man looked up, pushed his hat back. "Howdy yourself, young fella."

"Hope you can point me in the right direction," Parker said. "Heading out on a long trip, and I need to get supplies someplace."

"Which way you headed?" the farmer asked.

"West."

"Eiger's, then."

"Which way?"

The farmer waved up the road. "Just like you're going. Another ten miles maybe. Then the road forks. Go left. You'll hit Eiger's right before the Kansas line."

Parker touched the brim of his hat. "Obliged."

The sun beat down, and the day stretched on as Parker headed for the fork. He took the map out and looked at it again. The big tree stump—to Parker, it didn't look like anything else—was clearly meant to be the starting point of the map. It had been drawn carefully, lines down the side to give it texture. The numbers and other directions were useless without knowing the starting point. How many tree stumps in the world could there be? A million? He shook his head and put the map away.

Eiger's Trading Post sat in a bend in the road where two other roads branched off, one—more of a trail really—meandering vaguely north, the other shooting due west straight as an arrow. The trading post was a long log building, low, with a turf roof, corrals and stables around the side and back, and a little blacksmith's setup next to a barn that badly needed a new coat of paint. There was a single horse out front, its reins looped over the hitching post.

The weather had turned. The sky was an even slate gray, the sun dulled to a faint glow, a cool misting rain insistent and unceasing. Parker wiped water from his face and sighed, and approached Eiger's at a walk. He dismounted and tethered his horse next to the other, paused, and cast an eye over the establishment.

It was a rough, uninviting looking sort of place, but

Parker wasn't here for a vacation. He planned to supply himself and be on his way.

He entered and let his eyes adjust to the dim lighting. The interior of Eiger's was dank and smoky, probably from lanterns burning cheap oil. There were shelves of dry goods, feed sacks in a pile along one wall. There were two men inside.

The first stood behind a counter made of two wide planks laid across a pair of barrels. He had the loose skin of a man who'd slimmed down too fast, a sparse and ugly brown beard, a head full of greasy curly hair. He wore a dirty apron and leaned on the planks like they were the only thing holding him up. He regarded Parker with vacant, watery eyes.

The other man in the room sat at a rickety table in the far corner, slouched in an old chair, nearly unnoticeable in the murk of the trading post's interior. A short fella with a hawkish nose. He had a haggard, worn-out look about him, a deep weariness in his eyes. He filled a wooden cup with clear liquid from an earthen jug, and even from across the room the acrid moonshine stink scorched Parker's nostrils.

"Do you for something?" the man behind the planks asked.

Parker stepped closer to the makeshift counter. "You Eiger?"

"Eiger died in sixty-eight. I bought the place from his widow. I'm Chester."

"I'm heading west," Parker told him. "Need to feed myself a while and not spend too much."

"Huh." Chester reached behind him, then dropped

a sack of dried beans on the counter. "There's jerky. Not too old."

"Beef?"

"Horse."

"Cheap?"

Chester nodded. "Trying to get rid of it."

"Okay."

"Coffee?" Chester asked.

"How much?"

"Twelve cents a pound."

"What about two pounds for twenty cents?"

Chester shook his head. "Twelve cents a pound."

Parker frowned. "Just a pound then."

Chester put the coffee next to the beans and the jerky, then added a small sack of flour. Some lard. A bag of red apples which were too expensive, but Parker loved a good apple. All told he spent a dollar. He'd probably get sick of beans, but he wouldn't starve.

He moved his eyes across the interior of the trading post, the shelves and stacks and bags. He had no idea the extent of the supplies he'd need, not really. His sister had brought him his meals. He'd lived a simple, uncomplicated life—spoiled, some might say—although he thought the word applied more to the idle rich, and whatever Parker might have been, it dang sure wasn't rich.

"Okay if I look around and see what else I might need?"

A vague wave of the hand from Chester. "Help yourself."

Parker circled around behind one of the shelves,

wondering what he could use and what he could afford. He spotted sacks of oats and remembered he'd need to feed his horse, too. There was probably a lot he wasn't thinking of.

He heard the trading post's front door creak open, and somebody entered. Parker bent and looked through the shelves' open spaces to see the newcomer but caught only a dark figure, dripping wet.

"Name's Grady," the newcomer said. "I'm meeting somebody here."

"You look soaked," Chester said. "I was told you'd be along. Bill's in the corner."

Parker's ears twitched at the name *Grady*, some recent memory trying to make its way back to the surface. He eased around the side of the shelves for a better look as Chester and the newcomer Grady conversed in low tones. Parker got a better look at the man's face, and the memory solidified instantly.

The outlaw Grady Jenks. Parker remembered the face from the wanted poster Marshal Best had shown him. Best had complained that often the illustrations weren't quality, but in this case, the image was right on the money. There was no mistake that the man talking to Chester was the villain wanted for the train robbery in Wyoming.

And there was a reward for the man.

Parker took the tin star from his shirt pocket and pinned it to his vest. He eased the Peacemaker from his holster but didn't thumb the hammer back. He didn't want to get nervous, twitch, and accidently shoot the fellow. Grady Jenks would be Parker's first prisoner, and he intended to take him alive.

Parker came from around the shelves and leveled the revolver. "Grady Jenks, you're under arrest. Drop that gun belt right now, and nobody has to get hurt."

A long silence stretched.

Then Jenks scoffed. "Boy, leave us alone. Men are talking."

Parker frowned. "I'm not joking, mister."

"I ain't laughing," Jenks said.

Parker heard a chair scrape across the floor. In the corner of his eye, he saw the short man in the corner stand, hand resting on the grip of his six-shooter.

A wicked grin quirked across Jenks's face. "Friend of mine."

Parker swung his Peacemaker between the man in the corner and Jenks. "Just hold still, both of you."

Thunder rumbled outside, and the rain came harder. Lightning flashed in the window.

The front door slammed opened again, and two more men rushed inside, grumbling and wiping water from their faces, hats dripping. They froze, the grumbling drying up as soon as they saw Parker with his gun drawn.

"You men stay clear of this," Parker said. "Official deputy sheriff's business."

The men straightened and eased into the room, taking up positions on either side of Grady, their faces going hard, hands hovering over their guns. Parker's eyes kept darting to the man in the corner. Nobody moved. They hadn't shut the door, and wind and rain continued to howl outside, punctuated by an occasional clap of thunder and flash of lightning. Chester stood stone still behind his makeshift counter, but to Parker, he seemed coiled to strike. Chester looked at the deputy with cold hatred. There was no doubt he was on the side of the outlaws, or at the very least wasn't planning to lend Parker a helping hand.

"I think you bit off more than you can chew, boy," Jenks said. "Stupid got you into this situation. I doubt stupid will get you out. So maybe don't be stupid."

Parker swallowed hard. Stupid was, in fact, exactly how he felt.

"Put that gun down, and you live," Grady said. "You can walk out of here and think about how to be smart from now on."

Parker licked his lips. "You said not to be stupid. I guess that's good advice. I sort of doubt you'll let me stroll out of here like nothing happened."

"See, now you're thinking realistically," Jenks said. "We'll let you walk. But first we collect an inconvenience fee. That's the cost of stupid. We'll take your gun and your horse and everything you have. We'll even take your clothes. You can walk naked to the nearest town. Someone will have pity on you and give you some old clothes. There's still good-hearted people out there. They'll laugh at you, but that'll drive the lesson home, and you'll know better for next time. That's how hard lessons work. They sting, but you can come back from a hard lesson. You can't come back from a bullet between the eyes."

Parker wondered how many he could get if he just started shooting and decided not enough. He didn't want to die, but he didn't like the idea of walking out of here naked in the cold rain, either—but mostly he just didn't believe Grady Jenks. If Parker put his gun down, the man would shoot him dead. It was just that simple. Parker didn't know what to do.

So he just stood there.

Jenks shook his head and sighed. "Okay, then. I'm going to count to three. If that gun ain't on the floor by then, you know what happens next."

Parker felt his heartbeat kick up a notch.

Jenks's face went hard. "One."

Shoot or drop the Peacemaker? Parker felt his head go light, palms sweaty.

"Two."

This was it. This was happening.

Jenks opened his mouth to say *three*, but never got the word out.

A clap of thunder cracked directly over the trading post like the sound of the world ending, and everyone flinched, the lightning flash momentarily flooding the interior of Eiger's with blinding light.

When they'd all blinked their eyes clear, someone stood in the doorway, a dark figure, his rain slicker billowing around him and shoved back to reveal a pair of gleaming six-shooters.

"Let's all just calm the hell down," he said.

Parker immediately recognized the voice of Marshal Tanner Best.

All eyes in the trading post went to the man standing in the doorway.

"Mister, you're pushing your face in where's it's not wanted," Jenks said. "This ain't your business."

"I'm Tanner Best, a U.S. marshal. That makes it my business, Jenks," Best told the outlaw.

Jenks frowned, obviously not liking his name and the words *U.S. marshal* in the same sentence. Jenks's eyes narrowed, suspicious. "Have we met? I don't recall."

"No, but I know you all the same, by reputation," Best told him. "Looks like you've got Joe Tillis and Lester Morris with you. My condolences for Eugene, Lester."

Lester scowled at that.

"And I guess that's Bill Farkas back in the corner," Best said. "Bill, there's no paper on you that I've seen. Holster that hog leg and have a seat, and we can quarrel some other time."

Farkas's eyes went nervously to Jenks, but he didn't sit.

Parker stood and said nothing, the Peacemaker growing heavy in his hand.

Jenks looked at Parker, then back at Best. "You with him?"

Best chuckled. "I reckon I am now."

Jenks suddenly grinned like a maniac. "Then I guess you can die with him."

And everyone went for their guns.

Little Joe Tillis dove over the counter and squeezed his bulk behind some packing crates, ducking his head low.

Chester moved with surprising speed, producing a double-barreled shotgun from nowhere. The blast shook the interior of the trading post and obliterated a row of crockery just above Best's head. The marshal had ducked low, the twin Remingtons filling his hands.

Everyone ducked every which way, pulling pistols. Parker threw himself on the floor. Lead filled the air.

Best raised his Remingtons and fired each. Chester twitched as fresh blooms splashed red across his chest. He dropped dead behind the counter as Best brought his revolvers to bear on the others. Jenks dove for the floor and rolled.

Lester's gun was in his hand but not fast enough.

Best fired, and Lester's left knee exploded with blood.

He screamed and hit the floor hard, writhing and squirming and screaming some more. He slapped one hand over the ruined knee, thick blood oozing red between his fingers. With the other hand he waved his six-shooter around on the chance a target wandered into his line of sight.

Jenks scrambled around to the other side of one of the barrels used for the makeshift counter, and Best chased after him with lead, firing three holes into the barrel, wood chips flying. The holes in the barrel squirted liquid, and Parker smelled brine.

He's killing the pickles.

Best squeezed off two shots into the corner to remind Bill Farkas he hadn't been forgotten. Farkas upended his table and dove behind it.

Jenks popped up just long enough to fire twice, and Best scurried behind the other end of the same shelf under which Parker was hiding.

Parker wasn't keen on being in close proximity to a man making a target of himself. He belly-crawled across the open space to the next shelf just as Jenks popped up again and took a couple of wild shots at him.

Earthenware jugs exploded on the shelf above his head. A moment later, Parker felt something thick roll down the side of his face, and he was sure he'd been shot.

Some of it got into his mouth. Sweet. The jugs directly above Parker's head were full of maple syrup.

"My knee!" screeched Lester. "It hurts like fire!"

"Will you quit that yammering?" Best shouted at him.

Jenks stood and fired again, mostly just to make Best duck his head. The outlaw turned and ran toward Farkas. "Out the back!"

Tillis sprang from his hiding place and followed.

The three men vanished around the corner and into the murky depths of the trading post.

Tanner Best leaped to his feet to give chase.

Lester cocked the hammer on his revolver, gritting his teeth against the pain in his knee as he aimed and fired.

Best's hat flew off his head and spun away.

The marshal spat a string of inventive curses as he dove to the floor. Lester fired again, but the shot flew high.

Best got to his hands and knees, and put his shoulder against the shelves. He grunted and pushed. At first, nothing happened, but then slowly . . . slowly . . .

The shelf toppled and landed hard with a calamitous racket right on top of Lester Morris, jars, pots, cans, and bottles clattering in every direction.

Best stood panting from his exertion and moved toward Lester.

The outlaw groaned, but then slowly tried to lift his pistol. Parker had to hand it to him. He was still game.

But that didn't do him any good.

Best cocked one of the Remingtons, then shot Lester square in the face. The violent action made Parker flinch.

Lester's leg twitched once, and that was the end of him.

Best picked his way past Lester and the ruined shelf, chasing after Grady Jenks, Bill Farkas, and Joe Tillis. He came back a moment later, then went to the front door and looked out, shaking his head and muttering additional curses. "They took their horses. I'll never pick up the trail in this rain."

The marshal sighed and holstered his six-guns.

He turned back to Parker still cowering on the floor. "Might as will get up, boy. It's all over now."

CHAPTER 6

"I know you, don't I?" Tanner Best thumbed a fresh wad of tobacco into the bowl of his pipe, struck a match and lit it, puffing vigorously. "The deputy from Rory's Junction."

"Yes, sir. Parker Jones."

"A bit out of your jurisdiction."

Parker knew he had to tell the marshal something and decided to rub up against the truth as much as possible. "Somebody killed Gerald Filmore. He stumbled into town all bloody. I made the trip to tell his mother."

Best nodded as he puffed the pipe. "Eiger's a bit out of the way for that."

"I'm heading west," Parker said. "Notifying his mother was my last act before striking out on my own, but then I recognized Grady Jenks from the wanted poster you showed me."

"And you thought you'd collect the reward."

Parker shrugged, sheepish. "Something like that."

Best looked down at the Peacemaker still in Parker's hand. "You do anything with that?"

Parker shook his head. "Never even got a shot off."

"It can be tough to know," Best told him, "when to draw and when to shoot. Once the lead was flying might have been a hint."

"Sorry. I never arrested nobody before."

"Could have been worse, I reckon," Best said. "Somebody might have been paying a visit to your mother to give her the bad news."

Parker didn't bother telling the marshal he had no mother. The point was made.

"Still, keeping your lack of participation in mind, I suppose I'll be collecting the reward on Lester Morris all on my own."

"I suppose that's about right," Parker admitted.

"Be right back." Best stuck the pipe between his teeth and moved toward Lester, stepping in blood and syrup and pickle brine. He bent to grab the corpse, heaving the dead man over his shoulder. He left the trading post, then returned a few minutes later.

"I tied Lester to his horse," Best said. "I'll take him to the local authorities. I'll report what happened here. Did Filmore's mother have anything to say?"

Parker knew what the marshal was asking. Had she said anything about outlaws or gold or train robberies. "Just that she was sad about her son."

"Huh." Best tapped the pipe stem against his teeth, pausing for thought. "Well, I'd better get going." He waved vaguely at the interior of the trading post. "I'd help myself if I were you."

It took Parker a moment to realize what the marshal meant. "That's all private property, ain't it?"

"There's the law, and then there's the law," Best told

him. "One law is written down by politicians, safe behind some desk somewhere. Then there's the law of reality and survival. You'll find *that* law becomes a little more important the farther west you go. The man running this place fired a scattergun at a U.S. marshal. He forfeited any consideration that was coming to him. But you do as you like, and good luck to you."

Tanner Best stuck his pipe in his mouth and left.

Parker stood there a moment, pickle stink filling the air, head sticky with syrup.

He poked around the place, trying not to step in the mess, and found a rag, more or less clean. He wiped off the syrup the best he could, then tossed the rag back into the mess. He stood another moment, thinking about what the marshal had told him.

He didn't think too long.

He found a sack and filled it: more apples, butter, bacon, lard, corn meal, eggs, more shells for his Peacemaker, another bag of oats to feed the horse, sugar, more coffee, a couple of good blankets, rope, a lantern, a slab of salted pork, a shovel, and a few other random items.

Two bottles of whiskey found their way into his bag also.

Two shirts and another pair of trousers, not fancy but clean and new.

More saddlebags to transport it all.

Finally, he found the double-barreled twelve-gauge behind the counter near Chester's corpse. He had to wipe pickle juice off the butt but figured the thing might come in handy. A box of double-aught shells.

Parker felt a little like a burglar but reminded himself he had Mashal Best's permission.

He walked out of the trading post. The sky was still gray, but the rain had stopped. He secured all of his new provisions to the horse, packing as much into the saddlebags as possible. He was about to mount but paused, another idea nagging at him.

Parker went back into Eiger's and searched behind the counter. It didn't take him long to find the little tin box. He figured if it was a place of business, Chester would need to make change somehow. He opened the little box and counted the money.

Just over twenty-two dollars in coins and paper money. Was this going too far?

He stuffed the money into his pocket. Somebody else would take it if he didn't.

Parker went back outside, mounted his horse, and took the road west. He rode until sundown, then made camp in the shelter of a shallow dell. He was reasonably certain he'd crossed into Kanas, but he'd never been there before, so he couldn't be sure. There'd been no sign, no fanfare of trumpets. The landscape didn't look any different. He didn't quite know what he'd been expecting. It was ridiculous in a way. He'd lived within a stone's throw of the Kansas line his entire life and had never thought to go, had never seen the need.

And of course, Kansas wasn't the point really, not all on its own. It was merely the first place he'd never been before of an entire world. So he rustled himself up a big meal to celebrate Kansas, to celebrate his first step into a bigger life, a life he'd have lost at the hands of outlaws if Tanner Best hadn't come along.

A lesson learned. The first of many to come, he reckoned.

He cracked three eggs into a pan and sliced some of the pork.

Afterward, he reclined on his saddle with a full belly, sipping from one of the whiskey bottles, looking up at the stars. Not bothering to count them. That was something children did.

Parker drifted off, dreaming of big tree stumps and mysterious maps, smelling the cloying odor of maple syrup.

Parker awoke the next morning with a headache. Too much whiskey.

His body ached, too, but not quite as much as the previous morning. He'd slept with the extra blanket folded up beneath him. Coffee, a bite of jerky for breakfast. He fed and watered the horse.

Saddle up and go.

A week later, and the ground was more comfortable, but his grand adventure had grown tedious. The stars looked the same. He'd learned he'd rather drink beer than whiskey. He wasn't sure where he was going, but he knew it was a long way there.

Parker slumped in the saddle in the middle of a seemingly endless ride, the horse clopping along, and not for the first time, he'd wondered if it were all a mistake. The previous evening, he'd discovered he was lousy at making biscuits. His room in the mill hadn't been much, but he'd never been troubled by insects and critters in the night. And mostly—

Mostly, he was lonely. Parker hadn't spoken to anyone but his horse in days. His sister cared for him. Sheriff Crabtree was the wise, older man he could go to for advice. The fellas down at Clancy's Saloon were always good for a laugh.

Parker even missed his brother-in-law. It had been sort of fun annoying the man.

Kansas went on and on like it was trying to prove something.

He angled north a bit, with the vague idea he'd eventually end up in Wyoming. That's where the train robbery had occurred after all. Maybe that's where the gold was hidden. Maybe he could ask around, pick up a clue.

Maybe a lot of things.

Parker stuck to the road when it went in the right direction and cut across open country when it suited him. He camped near streams, when possible, for fresh water. Occasionally, he'd spot some small town in the distance and consider diverting toward it. Maybe they had a saloon. Maybe a hotel. Parker had never slept in a hotel before. Were they expensive? Would he burn through all of his carefully hoarded money if he yielded to the temptation of creature comforts.

He didn't know, so he rode on.

Low hills, green and treeless, rolled out before him. The sky grew so wide, it was almost dizzying. He felt small but not bad for it. It was an odd but not unpleasant sensation to be a speck in the middle of the vast wilderness. The days melted one into the next, and Parker felt a natural part of it all. He realized he felt alive and realized also that the feeling was not what he'd expected. Sometimes, he'd hear people get all poetic about being alive, and Parker had always associated the sensation with a wild surge of energy.

But that wasn't what Parker felt at all. He felt calm, swaying in the saddle, the day warm but not oppressively so.

The sky opened up the next day and ruined everything. There wasn't any shelter for miles. All Parker could do was slump in the saddle and let the rain beat down on him. He no longer felt alive. He felt cold and wet and tired.

The next morning, he changed into one of the shirts and the other pair of pants he'd taken from Eiger's. He climbed into the saddle and rode on with little relish. He had no enthusiasm for going forward, but he'd come too far to turn back.

He spied a town a few days later and succumbed to the temptation to enter it and spend some of his money. He found a sleepy saloon and ordered a beer. He tried to start a conversation with a couple of surly farmers who clearly had no interest in talking with a random stranger. The experience wasn't worth what he paid for the beer. He caught sight of himself in the mirror on the way out of the saloon. Disheveled from long days on the trail, unshaven and unbathed.

Parker supposed he didn't blame folks for not wanting to speak with a dirty vagabond. He left town and kept riding.

A little over two weeks had slipped away since Parker had left Missouri, and he now strongly suspected he'd crossed into Nebraska. The sky ahead looked hazy with dark clouds, but he soon realized it was a column of black smoke.

Parker rode directly toward it and soon spotted the burning wagon.

CHAPTER 7

The landscape remained predominantly prairie, but there was a scattering of hackberry trees about a hundred yards from the burning wagon. Parker tied his horse to one and proceeded cautiously, his right hand resting on his Peacemaker.

It was—or had been—one of those Conestogas usually found in long wagon trains. It had almost finished burning, the remaining few flames licking the wagon bed, the wheels blackened, the bonnet pulled off and lying in a crumpled heap several yards away in the knee-high grass. He scanned the horizon. If there'd been other wagons, they were long gone.

As he moved closer, he saw a dead horse on its side. He tried to remember the wagon trains he'd seen, how many horses had pulled a single wagon. Two? Four? More than one certainly. Had the wagon been hit by bandits, the horse killed accidentally? He was far from an expert on the subject but figured bandits would rather a live horse to sell as opposed to killing the animals for no reason.

The thought made his mind wander. Dead horses were one thing. What about people?

He froze, his eyes raking every inch of the scene. Clothes, both men's and women's, were strewn across the ground, many of the garments ripped and ruined.

His gaze landed on a charred lump near the wagon, and as he got closer, he could see it was a body, a man most likely, judging from the size. Parker winced and turned away, feeling a sudden lack of curiosity. He saw the wagon's bonnet again lying nearby and thought the least he could do was cover the body. Any poor Christian soul deserved at least that much respect.

He grabbed two handfuls of the bonnet and began to pull—

Something darted from beneath the bonnet, springing at him like a wild animal, a blur of red and black, the glint of flashing metal catching sunlight, and Parker felt a sharp sting across his forearm.

He yelped, slapping one hand over the shallow, bleeding gash as he continued to backpedal, trying to put as much space between himself and the snarling creature.

But the girl didn't advance on him. She stood trembling, panting, eyes wild, blade held out in front of her, dripping red with Parker's blood. She was a skinny, squashed-looking thing, face and arms smeared with mud or maybe ash, or both, black hair a matted tangle, sweaty and greasy. She wore a man's flannel shirt with a red-and-black-checkered pattern, and it was far too big for her, cuffs coming past her wrists to swallow her slender hands. Men's trousers rolled at the bottom. Boots laced tight. Maybe fifteen years old.

Parker risked a look at the gash on his arm, and hissed at the mild but insistent pain. "What'd you do that for?"

"Stay away from me!" Her voice had a rough edge to it, like maybe she was about to scream or to start crying—like it could go either way.

"I ain't gonna hurt you, stupid girl," Parker said. "I didn't even know you were under there. I was going to cover up—"

He was about to say *cover up the body* when it occurred to him it was probably the girl's ma or pa. "I'm not going to do anything to you, okay? Just stay calm. Maybe put the knife away."

But she didn't put the knife away, just kept looking at him, scared and bewildered, as if he was speaking a foreign tongue. Her eyes frantically took in the whole scene, and Parker wondered how long she'd been hiding under the bonnet.

"Who did this?" Parker gestured at the wagon. "Bandit attack?"

Her eyes went to the burning wagon for a moment, her mouth falling open like she wanted to tell him something, but then nothing came out but a frightened little choking sound and she closed her mouth again. A quick shake of the head which Parker didn't know how to interpret. Was she saying she didn't know? Didn't remember? Couldn't talk or wouldn't?

Parker sighed and looked at the wagon again. It had mostly finished burning. He wondered how long ago it was set ablaze, how long it took one of those big Conestogas to burn. Whoever set it on fire might still be in the area, in which case, hanging around was probably a lousy idea.

"We should go."

No response.

"Let's look around, see what we can salvage," Parker suggested. "Long as we're quick about it."

Still nothing from the girl.

Parker bent down and snatched a white article of clothing from where it lay in the grass. A woman's cotton shift, half ripped. It was ruined anyway, so he ripped it into strips and bound his arm. A red splotch seeped through, but it did an okay job of stanching the blood. He picked up a few articles of clothing that still seemed usable, all men's. Other than the shift, there was barely anything else for a woman to wear.

He glanced back at the girl. She'd lowered the knife but made no move to help salvage anything from the burning wagon. She stood and watched, wide-eyed, face blank, which Parker reckoned was an improvement over looking panicked and terrified.

"What's your name?"

She stared at him a moment, then looked away.

Parker sighed. *Fine.*

He circled the wagon twice, but there was little worth saving. He reckoned that made sense, since bandits would have made off with anything useful. There wasn't even any food.

Parker trudged back to where his horse was tied, mounted, then rode back toward the girl. He reined in close to her and held out his hand. "Take hold. I'll pull you up. You can ride behind."

She took a slow step backward, eyes wide and un-blinking.

Parker bit off an unkind word. He was losing patience, but the girl had probably been through some horrors. "I can't just leave you. Get up here."

She didn't move.

He snapped his fingers. "Let's go!"

A blank stare was all he got in return.

"I'll go," he threatened. "I'll ride away and leave you here."

She didn't seem to care.

Parker clicked his tongue, and his horse eased forward at a walk. "I'm really going. I'll leave you."

The girl didn't budge.

"Suit yourself."

Parker rode away, keeping the horse to a walk. He looked back a few seconds later, and the girl hadn't moved, but when he looked again, she was following. Parker reckoned she had no other choice. How long had she expected to cower under the wagon bonnet in the middle of nowhere?

They went on like that for an hour. Progress was agonizingly slow, but he didn't want to speed up and leave her in the dust. A little while later, Parker tugged on the reins and eased the horse to a stop. He'd wait for the girl to catch up, and then maybe she'd see reason. Parker wasn't sure how far away the next town might be, but farther than anyone wanted to walk if they could

ride, he figured. A couple of sore feet, and she'd be ready
to climb onto the horse soon enough.

But soon after Parker stopped, she stopped, too.

He waited.

She waited.

"Well, come on," he shouted to her.

Nothing.

Parker cursed a blue streak as he nudged the horse
forward again. He was tempted to spur the animal on
and gallop away. That would serve her right, stubborn
thing.

He immediately chastised himself. She was scared.
She didn't know Parker from Adam. Could be she
wasn't right in the head. Parker had heard of such a
thing before, somebody going through a bad fright
and then not being right in the head. He needed to get
her to a town and a doctor. Then she'd be somebody
else's concern.

Parker glanced back. The girl was following again,
maintaining her distance. They went on like that the rest
of the day until they came to a sparse stand of trees.
Parker stopped about an hour earlier than usual when he
found an open grassy area among the trees, good, level
ground. He built a fire and began to prepare supper. He
watched her out there among the trees, not quite trying
to hide, but not coming forward, either.

Soon it would be dark. Parker guessed a cozy campfire
would be a heck of a lot more attractive than skulking out
there in the woods. If not, he had another trick up his
sleeve, and he began to make biscuits and cook up a pan
of bacon. The smell made his mouth water, and he

didn't doubt the girl could smell it, too. How long since she'd eaten, he wondered.

When the biscuits were ready, he set them aside on a tin plate. The girl was right at the edge of the camp now, the fire flickering and gleaming in her wide, hungry eyes.

He half turned around as if paying her no mind, but then asked, "Hungry?"

She entered the circle of firelight, tentative.

"There's biscuits here." As if she needed to be told. "Want one?"

She began to move toward the tin plate.

"Hold on now. If you expect me to feed you, then we need to come to an understanding. Like maybe you can answer some questions about who attacked you and such."

Her eyes went from him to the biscuits and back again, desperate. Her lower lip began to tremble, tears leaking from the corners of her eyes and rolling down her cheeks, leaving smudged lines in the dirt and ash on her face.

Parker felt like a first-class heel. He was about to tell her never mind. Go ahead and eat.

"Indians."

The word blurted out of her so suddenly, it made Parker flinch.

"Them that attacked us was Indians," she said.

He was about to ask her another question, her name maybe, but it was no use. She'd already wolfed down the first biscuit and had begun to attack a second like a wild animal.

CHAPTER 8

Her name was Annie Jolene Schaefer.

"What tribe?" Parker asked.

She tried to talk around a mouthful of biscuit but couldn't, so she finished chewing first. "I have no idea." She grabbed another biscuit and bit into it.

Parker had quickly grabbed a biscuit and a few strips of bacon before Annie devoured everything. She'd told Parker she'd lost track of how long she'd been hiding under the wagon bonnet, but it was long enough for her to be half starved.

"How could you not know what tribe?" Parker asked.

She rolled her eyes. "They didn't say."

"They didn't have no identifying marking or war paint or anything?"

"How in the world would I know anything about that?" *Crunch crunch*, and a strip of bacon vanished down her gullet. "Do *you* know one tribe's war paint from another?"

She had a point, he supposed, but didn't say it. "I haven't heard any of the tribes are at war in this area. Maybe some rogues."

"I don't know what that means."

"Just Indians running around making trouble but not at war, although I guess that's a distinction without much meaning if your wagon's being attacked. Were you part of a wagon train?"

Annie shook her head. "Just us. Me and— just us." She grabbed the last biscuit. "We were supposed to be in a wagon train for the Oregon Trail but we arrived late, and Pa didn't want to wait for the next one. If he'd listened to me— Well, Pa didn't want to wait. Better to get where we were going before winter, and well— It don't matter. Not now."

Parker didn't know what to say to that, so he kept shut.

Annie burped. "I'm so sorry."

"Never mind."

"Is there more?" Her eyes went to the empty tin plate.

"Not that's cooked. You might want to let what you've eaten digest. Could make you sick to overstuff, if you haven't eaten in a while."

"You're probably right."

"You okay?" Parker asked.

"I've eaten plenty, I guess."

"No, I mean are you . . . okay?"

A pause, her eyes on the fire, unblinking. "I think I am. I mean— I was sort of numb. Some part of my brain was making my legs walk and my eyes see, but the rest of me was sort of shut off. I think smelling the bacon snapped me out of it."

Parker grinned. "I always said bacon's good for what ails you."

Annie smiled at that, a new and different kind of light coming into her eyes, but both smile and light faded as fast as they'd come, her whole body slumping back into darkness, fatigue, and memory.

"We'll try to get you to a town or someplace tomorrow." Parker had said it like it was something helpful, but, of course, then what? He'd take her to a town, but she'd still be a penniless orphan, stranded halfway between home and Oregon. What next? Where would she go? Back home maybe.

"Where are you from?"

"Louisiana."

"Your folks didn't like it there no more?"

"My pa was a foreman on a big plantation," Annie said. "Things changed after the war, I guess. Leastways, that's what he said. He wanted something new. A fresh start. Ma had to leave some of her kinfolk, but that's just being married, she said."

"Maybe your ma and pa—"

"I don't want to talk about my folks."

Right.

Parker poked at the fire with a stick. "Probably best to get some shut-eye."

He gave her half the blankets and was thankful he'd grabbed extras at Eiger's. He lay with his head on his saddle as usual, and she curled up in her blankets on the other side of the fire. It crackled and burned low. She turned over, put her back to it. Parker shut his eyes but didn't sleep.

"Hey," she said in a small voice.

"Yeah?"

"You never told me your name."

"Parker Jones," he said, then added, "Deputy Sheriff out of Rory's Junction, Missouri."

She laughed softly.

Parker frowned and was about to ask her what was so funny, but the soft, even sound of her breathing suggested she'd drifted off.

He thought about his own dead parents. He tried to put himself into Annie's head, but he could only get halfway there. His parents had died, yes, but of sickness. Parker could only imagine the ugly, abrupt violence of an Indian raid. Had Annie watched as they'd slaughtered her parents? Had one of them been burned alive?

Parker turned to less gruesome thoughts. Annie would slow him down, especially if she kept refusing to ride double on his horse. He didn't know this part of the country at all and had no idea when they'd happen upon the next town. He felt bad for the girl but didn't want to be stuck with her any longer than he had to.

He didn't notice when he finally fell asleep, but he woke up with a start, something nearby making strange sounds. Parker sat up, hand going to his Peacemaker as he blinked the sleep from his eyes.

The sounds came from Annie, a sort of desperate, forlorn bleating. Parker circled the fire to her side, stood a few feet away, and called her name softly. "Annie."

She twitched beneath her blankets, and Parker could guess what she might be feeling. He'd had awful nightmares, too—not recently, but vivid enough to stay alive in his memory. He recalled his mouth unable to form words, eyes unable to open, a heavy weight on his chest.

Parker reached out carefully, shook the girl's shoulder. "Annie."

She flinched but didn't wake.

He leaned closer, shook her with more vigor. "Annie."

She sat up and gasped, the knife swiping in a fast arc right at his face.

Maybe she was sluggish with sleep, or perhaps Parker was ready this time, but he managed to back out of the way just in time, the tip of the knife missing his nose by an inch.

Parker threw up his hands in a placating gesture. "Whoa! Just me."

She looked at him, eyes glassy with bewilderment, chest heaving as she panted for air, hair matted with night sweat.

"It's okay," Parker assured her. "You're okay."

She looked at him another long moment as if lost, then broke down sobbing, shoulders shaking, tears and snot streaming down her face. She sucked haltingly for breath, the sobs redoubling.

Parker was at a loss. He reached a tentative hand toward her shoulder. "Hey— Hey, now. Come on."

Annie threw herself on him, arms going around. She sobbed against his chest, a wet spot seeping through. She cried and cried, and Parker had no idea what to do except return the hug, patting her back, and they stayed like that for a while.

* * *

"Daddy worked down at the waterfront after he left the plantation, but it didn't agree with him." Annie clung to Parker's back, riding double on the horse. "Daddy never did like water and boats. I don't think he ever learned how to swim, although he taught me when I was six by tossing me in a pond and telling me to swim fast before the gators got me."

"Uh-huh." Parker kept the horse pointed northwest, clomping along at a steady pace.

"Momma's friend from church Daisy Clayborn's cousin got his hand bit off by a gator," she said. "And now there's a hook where his hand used to be, and now he can spear fish with it if the water is shallow."

"Uh-huh."

"But then another time he went to scratch his face and forgot and almost took an eyeball out. Can you imagine that? Skewering your own eyeball? Can't say as I fancy that."

"Uh-huh."

Annie had not shut up since they started riding that morning. Parker had almost told her to pipe down, but then thought better of it. Maybe she needed to talk, maybe the constant yammering drowned out the bad thoughts. If so, then Parker reckoned he could put up with it. Better than her crying and crying, and going to pieces.

She talked straight through lunch when they stopped for a few bites of jerky and to rest the horse. She kept talking when they mounted up again.

About an hour before sundown, Annie went silent. Parker thought she must have finally taken a breath, but when a minute passed without a word, he glanced over his shoulder, as if wondering whether the girl had fallen off the horse.

"You okay?"

She looked confused. "Why wouldn't I be?"

"You stopped talking."

"Well, I mean, you could try to keep up your end of the conversation."

Parker frowned. "*My* end?"

"I been keeping you entertained for miles and miles," Annie said crossly. "And you ain't done nothing for me."

Parker held back on the first thing he was going to say and on the second one, too. He gave the third thing some serious thought but decided it bordered on impolite. So he settled for saying, "Not sure what you'd be interested in hearing. Maybe ask me questions."

"What do you do for work?"

"I told you last night. I'm a deputy sheriff from Rory's Junction, Missouri."

"You were *serious* about that?"

Parker fought down a wave of annoyance. "Why in the world would I make that up?"

"I thought you were trying to make me feel safe or something."

"You *are* safe," Parker insisted.

"You're not old enough to be no deputy," Annie insisted.

"Look who's talking. Some scrawny twig of a thing barely fifteen."

"I'm eighteen!"

Parker rolled his eyes. "You ain't been within ten miles of eighteen."

"I am too," she insisted with heat in her voice. "I am short and slight of build, so I don't look it."

"Well, it don't matter if you're eighteen or a hundred. I'm a deputy and you can take that to the bank." He took the tin star out of his shirt pocket and handed it back to her. "See?"

She took it in one hand, still holding on to him with the other. She looked at the star, eyes narrowing. "Huh."

"So there you go," Parker said. "Although I guess I'm a good ways from my official jurisdiction."

Annie gave him the star back, and he returned it to his shirt pocket.

"You ever shoot anyone?" she asked.

"No."

"Arrest anyone?"

Parker considered his ill-fated attempt to arrest Grady Jenks. "Not exactly."

"Sounds like you don't do much."

Parker couldn't deny it. He thought about all the things Sheriff Crabtree had told him about being a lawman. "If you're doing your job right, you don't have to shoot nobody. Nor arrest anyone, neither. If the town knows you're there, and what you're made of, then things'll go like they should. People will go about their business with no trouble."

"Well, you can talk the talk," Annie said. "I'll give you that."

They stopped again for the night, and Annie kept

talking, although it wasn't the previous relentless yammer. Parker let her go, nodding along and grunting now and then to show he was listening. The girl probably didn't want the silence closing in on her, and it was no effort to listen, so Parker listened. Bacon, biscuits, beans. Annie didn't wolf her food down like an animal this time, but she did eat her share. They slept through the night without incident.

They started out again the next morning after coffee and cold leftover biscuits.

It wasn't even midmorning yet when they spotted the little town in the distance, and Parker nudged the horse more westward and headed for it.

"What are we going to do there?" Annie asked.

"Got to take you somewhere."

A pause. "Oh."

It was as if she hadn't thought about it, Parker mused, hadn't considered that anything might exist beyond the minute she was living in right now.

Farmhouses at first and tilled land, the soil not so rich, in Parker's opinion, as to invite attempts at agriculture, but he was no farmer, so what could he really say about it. The town itself was just one main street with a dozen buildings along each side. Why somebody decided to get a town going on this exact spot in middle-of-nowhere Nebraska was none of Parker's business, either, and he wasn't curious enough to ask.

The street was mostly empty, and Parker reined in his horse in front of a man in a wooden chair, leaned back against the wall, an unlit cigar in his mouth and a tin star on his vest.

"You the law around here?" Parker asked.

"And the mayor. Welcome to Gurley."

Parker considered telling the man he was a deputy, but some instinct told him not to. The man was big, a bloated belly hanging over his belt, with a wild red beard and mustache that had yellow teeth in the middle. He didn't seem the sort that wanted a couple of port-siders to interrupt the nothing he was doing all day long.

Parker briefly related finding the burning wagon, the Indian attack, and so on. He jerked a thumb over his shoulder to indicate the girl. "She's the only survivor."

The sheriff shifted his cigar from one side of his mouth to the other. "Ain't heard of no Indian trouble hereabouts. Not lately." His eyes shifted to the girl. "What tribe?"

Annie shrugged. "Indians."

"I'll wire over to Fort Sidney and let them know," he said. "That's about all I can do. Unless they come storming down Main Street."

"What about her?" Parker asked, meaning Annie.

"Yeah, what about her?"

"Well, I couldn't just leave her there."

"Reckon not." He shifted the cigar back to the other side of his mouth. "Very Christian of you."

"So what do I do with her?"

The sheriff scratched at a spot behind his ear, thinking it over. "Can she work?"

"I can work," Annie said.

The sheriff leaned his chair forward and stood up with a grunt, hitching his pants up as he came to the porch rail and leaned there, giving Annie a closer look. "Elmer Pitts is always on the lookout for a new girl. He's at The Lucky Aces at the end of the street. This one looks fairly young, but there's some as likes 'em that way, I reckon."

"Sweeping up and washing dishes and such?" Annie asked.

The sheriff gave Parker a look, the expression plain. *Do you want to tell her, or shall I?*

"Obliged, sheriff. We'll get out of your hair now." Parker clicked his tongue and the horse headed down the street.

"Safe travels," the sheriff called after them.

"Are we going to see this Elmer Pitts fella?" Annie asked.

"Nope."

"Why not?"

Parker didn't know a delicate enough way to explain it, so he said nothing.

A minute later, they passed The Lucky Aces on the left as they headed back out of town. It was a two-story building, with swinging saloon doors marking the entrance below. Three ladies leaned on the rail of the balcony above, watching them pass. Their stockings were rolled down below their knees, corsets laced tight, the ladies overflowing the tops. Painted faces. Silky robes flapping in the dirty breeze.

A woman with an abundance of red hair piled on

top of itself waved at Parker with wiggling fingers and a sly grin.

Annie looked up at the women, face blank. "Oh."

"We'll think of something else," Parker said.

And they rode out of town.

CHAPTER 9

There had been a time not so very long ago when Red Pony considered himself a man of honor. He had been among the most fearsome braves to fight against the blue coats when the Cheyenne had risen up. Little Wolf himself had singled out Red Pony as one of his mightiest warriors.

But those glory days were behind him now. Dull Knife had surrendered. Little Wolf had fled to parts unknown—Montana some said. Now, Red Pony was reduced to leading a ragtag group of braves, preying on the weak and isolated, people who had little ability to defend themselves, often families with young children. They'd already eaten the food and drunk the single bottle of whiskey from the recent wagon they'd sacked. There had been a time when Red Pony and his war party would have attacked and looted an entire wagon train.

His so-called war party was nothing more than a bandit gang of cowards and outcasts, those no longer welcome in their tribes, Cheyenne mostly, but others, too. Not that it mattered. They were tribeless renegades now, more scavengers than warriors, eagle feathers traded for those of the vulture.

At least looting the wagon had produced a good rifle. Red Pony had taken a fine Winchester from the dead hands of the old man. In his band of eleven, only he and three others had repeating rifles. The others had the single-shot carbines made commonplace by the coming of the blue coats. Red Pony chuckled to himself at the thought of going into battle with bow and arrow. It had been so long.

Yellow Feather pulled his horse up next to Red Pony's. "We need food again."

"I know." Red Pony stopped himself from snapping at the other brave. Yellow Feather was a scrawny, twitchy little man who'd been run out of his camp for stealing. He'd feigned illness when the rest of the men in his tribe had gone on a raid, and while they were away, he'd moved from tent to tent, taking whatever he pleased. He'd thought himself clever, but one of the women had seen him.

But even cringing cowards and sneaky thieves had to eat. Had it really been so long since Yellow Feather or the others had stalked game or waited patiently by a stream for a deer to come and take water? All they wanted to do now was to take from the weak, to steal what others had and leave naught but destruction and death in their wake.

Red Pony could think of nothing, no aspect of his existence of which he was proud. He loathed the others, but was he any better? He had no ambition other than finding his next meal.

"Take another and scout north," he told Yellow Feather. "You know what we're looking for, a lone farmhouse. Someone isolated. I'll send others to scout to the south."

Yellow Feather went away to do as he was bid. He was replaced by a brawny Arapaho who'd nudged his horse within a few feet of Red Pony's. His name was Howling Bear, and he was the perfect square-jawed image of a warrior brave. Muscles in his arms. A keen glint in his eye. Howling Bear had been coy about why he was no longer with the rest of his tribe, but even though he was curious, Red Pony refused to press the other Indian on the matter, since Howling Bear seemed sensitive about the subject.

"Is this all we're ever going to do?" Howling Bear asked. "Little raids for a bottle of whiskey or a scrap of food?"

"If you have a suggestion, I am happy to listen," Red Pony said. "Shall we overthrow the Blue Coats in Fort Cottonwood and proclaim ourselves kings of the united tribes?"

Howling Bear snorted, half contempt, half resignation. "If I had a good idea, we would not be having this conversation. I would lead the braves to make it happen." He abruptly turned his painted horse and trotted away.

Lead the braves? By all means, have them—and curse the lot of you, Red Pony thought. Now that he gave it thought, he had no idea how he'd ended up as leader of this band of misfits. Still, Howling Bear would need to be watched. If he intended to take over, he'd likely start by killing Red Pony.

Two hours later, Yellow Feather returned.

"What did you find?" Red Pony asked him.

"A fishing camp along the river," Yellow Feather reported.

"Good for a raid?"

Yellow Feather hesitated. "We saw three of them at first, but we watched for an hour and there was a fourth."

"A family? Women and children?" Red Pony asked. "Or men with rifles?"

Yellow Feather blew out a sigh and looked away. "Men."

Red Pony grunted, thinking it over. Four men with rifles. Maybe more if they came from up- or downstream with their catch.

"There are eleven of us, and we'll have surprise." Howling Bear edged his horse in between them. "Are we so craven? Do we hesitate at the thought that we might have to earn it this time. Four men—so what?"

Red Pony frowned. "Don't rush me, Howling Bear."

Howling Bear rolled his eyes.

"Is the tree line close to the river?" Red Pony asked Yellow Feather. "Can we hide the horses and sneak in on foot?"

Yellow Feather brightened, a hint of enthusiasm creeping into his demeanor. "On our side, yes. And the babble of the river will cover our sounds. It is no more than knee-deep."

"*I* will make no sound," Howling Bear said with inflated pride. "Some of us still remember the ways of stealth."

"Then Walks as a Ghost, I will rename you," Red Pony

said. "The rest of us mortal men will be glad for the cover of the river. I will have any advantage the circumstance offers."

Howling Bear scowled but said nothing.

"Tell the others," Red Pony said. "We hit the fish camp tonight."

They followed Yellow Feather to the pocket forest along the river and dismounted, hobbling their horses out of sight. After nightfall, they crept to the edge of the tree line and watched the fish camp. The camp consisted of three buildings, and it wasn't difficult for Red Pony to guess the use for each. The main building was a rough log cabin with a turf roof and a chimney that looked little more than a pile of rocks. Windows small and shuttered. To Red Pony it looked like a hastily built structure, low and squat. A man would need to duck his head to go in and out the front door. He wondered if there was another door on the other side.

The farthest building was a barn with a corral attached. Red Pony couldn't see any animals from his spot at the tree line, but it would be good if there were horses to steal. Or pigs to slaughter. Red Pony had developed a taste for pork. He looked for but didn't see a chicken coop.

The third building was the smallest and most obvious since the place was a fish camp. The little wooden building was slightly larger than what the white man called an *outhouse*. Smoke came from a stovepipe chimney on the roof, and when the wind shifted just right, Red Pony imagined he could get a whiff of what was inside. Smoked fish was good eating and would travel well.

They watched and waited. The white men had built a fire halfway between the main cabin and the smokehouse. They did not appear to be cooking a meal, but rather sitting around, perhaps engaging in casual fellowship before settling down for the night. Their silhouettes passed back and forth in front of the fire, blurring into one another. Red Pony couldn't be sure, but there did seem only four men, as Yellow Feather had reported.

Eventually, the men around the fire went into the cabin. The Indians waited a little longer, until they felt certain the white men had gone to sleep. Then Red Pony gathered the braves around him.

He communicated in hand gestures. It was unlikely the men in the fish camp could hear whispers at this distance, but Red Pony took minor pride in maintaining even a small discipline. He pointed at one of the braves then at the barn, and the brave nodded. The men were probably all sleeping in the cabin, but it was prudent to check. Then Red Pony pointed at another brave, made a climbing gesture and then a stuffing something gesture. The brave nodded. Red Pony pointed at the rest of the braves and made a circling motion with one finger. *Surround the cabin.* They'd all done this before and understood.

Red Pony motioned for the others to follow him. They emerged from the tree line, moving fast and silently down the bank and into the river. The water was cold but not bitterly so, the current quick. As expected, the water never got much beyond knee-deep, and they crossed with minimal splashing.

The Indians took a knee on the other side, waiting to see if they'd been heard. Apparently, they hadn't. The brave tasked with securing the barn broke off at a quick trot, and another climbed to the cabin's roof, a thread-bare horse blanket thrown over his shoulder. Red Pony made the circular motion with his finger again, and three braves broke off to go around to the other side of the cabin.

The brave atop the cabin stuffed the horse blanket into the chimney and jammed it home with the butt of his rifle.

The Indians waited.

A few minutes passed and then a few more, and Red Pony began to wonder if blocking the chimney was going to have the desired effect or not.

Then he heard voices from within, muffled and faint, then stronger and edged with panic. Coughing.

Red Pony grinned. The inside was filling with smoke just as he knew it would. There was no reason for the white men to suspect anything more amiss than a blocked chimney, clogged with soot perhaps. Certainly not that they were under attack.

Shouts. Then the front door flew open, smoke billowing out followed by two of the occupants. They jammed in the doorway, both trying to get out at the same time, ragged coughs and watery eyes. They finally pushed their way out, gulping clean air, and Red Pony raised his rifle.

Not yet. Wait for the other two. They haven't seen us yet.

But Yellow Feather kneeling next to him whooped and fired. One of the white men clutched his guts and pitched forward. The other was turning to run, and Red Pony shot him in the back.

He glowered at Yellow Feather. *Fool.*

He opened his mouth to tell Yellow Feather he should have waited, but Yellow Feather was off and running, charging for the open cabin door with a shrill war cry as he levered another shell into the chamber of his Henry rifle.

The next white man to appear in the doorway stepped through the smoke with a six-shooter in each hand, thumbing the hammers back and firing wildly. His eyes were narrow slits, tears streaming from the smoke. He could not possibly see what he was shooting at but was game for trying, blasting lead in every direction.

He got lucky on his last shot, the slug punching through Yellow Feather's skull just above his right eye and exploding out the back of his head in a thick, greasy mess of blood, brain, and bone.

Howling Bear raised his rifle and shot the white man dead.

The last white man came out coughing, hands raised, eyes closed. "Wait! I give up! Don't shoot! Don't—"

All the Indians fired at once. The white man twitched and shook as lead ripped into him, splatches of blood erupting all over his torso until he finally fell dead in a heap in front of the open doorway.

"Take the blanket from the chimney," Red Pony

yelled to the brave on the roof. "Let the inside clear. Somebody check to make sure there aren't any left."

Howling Bear eased up to the door and peeked inside. "Empty."

That was it then. They'd taken the fish camp. It had only cost them Yellow Feather.

The other braves began to whoop and holler, realizing their victory. Such as it was. Red Pony told them to search for anything useful. That was the point after all. He walked toward the smokehouse hoping for a good haul, resting his Winchester on his shoulder. If they could take an ample supply of smoked fish with them, maybe they would not have to do one of these raids again for a while. Trout would be nice, but he wouldn't turn up his nose at anything.

He reached the little smokehouse, opened the door, and—

Another white man lunged out at him, waving a fillet knife, eyes blazing with a heady mix of fear and hatred. Screaming his face off. If the white man had known anything about fighting with a knife, Red Pony would have been dead.

But the man slashed sloppily at the Indian's face. On pure reflex, Red Pony swung the rifle barrel in front of him, deflecting the knife. He brought the Winchester's butt around and cracked the man in the jaw. The pale face's head snapped back, hat flying.

Red Pony stepped forward and hit him with the butt again, smashing his nose flat, blood shooting from each nostril. He stumbled and went down. Red Pony hit him again and again with the rifle butt, the man's skull cracking beneath flesh and hair.

When Red Pony saw the man was dead, he stepped back, panting, heart racing. Blood dripped from the butt of his Winchester. His hands shook.

So close. The man had surprised him, could have just as easily slid that fillet knife right into Red Pony's belly. He walked away on weak legs.

The other Indians danced and whooped around the fire. They'd found several jugs of homemade whiskey in the cabin and were celebrating their great victory. Yellow Feather still lay dead in the mud.

Four had been too many. And there had been five. They'd been fortunate to lose only Yellow Feather, although it was hard to think of the craven Indian as a loss.

Red Pony saw Howling Bear kneeling over one of the dead white men, the one with the pistols who'd killed Yellow Feather. Howling Bear held a knife in one hand, and a fistful of the white man's shaggy hair in the other. He brought the knife to the man's hairline and began to saw back and forth. A moment later, he had the scalp. Howling Bear held it high with a triumphant whoop.

What was the point? Who would be impressed? What woman would he win for a wife? What sons would tell of his deeds around the fire in the years to come?

Red Pony shook his head and sighed. "Tomorrow, we go west."

There was no reason to it. Any direction was as good as another, but it sounded decisive.

Howling Bear looking up at him, still clutching the scalp in a sticky, bloody fist. "What?"

"West," Red Pony said. "I have decided."

CHAPTER 10

"How long we gonna keep going west?" Annie shifted behind him in the saddle. It was clear she didn't like riding. Her backside hurt.

Parker felt the same, and he'd put in a lot more miles in the saddle than she had, although he wasn't about to let on to being in pain. A rear end could only take so much punishment. Even so, he was starting to get used to it, which he supposed was good, since he still had a long way to go.

"I keep going until I get where I'm going," he said dryly. "As for you, well, we're still trying to figure that out."

Although, truth be told, he had no idea what he was going to do with the girl. He couldn't leave her stranded in the middle of nowhere, and he wasn't about to just drop her off at some random brothel and wish her luck. Parker wouldn't be able to live with that.

"And we're not just going west," Parker added. "We're veering a bit north, too."

"Can we stop?" She shifted again like she had ants in her pants.

"We'll never get there if we keep stopping."

"Never get where?" she asked.

"Wyoming," he told her. It was the first time she'd been curious about where he was going.

"Why Wyoming?"

To find a bunch of stolen gold.

But he didn't say that. For one thing it was none of her business. But Parker knew the real reason he didn't say it—it sounded ridiculous. He already suspected Annie didn't really take him seriously, thought he was too young to be a deputy.

"It's a long story."

Annie spread her arms to indicate the endless nothing of Nebraska's sand hills. "Not a lot else going on right now."

"You want to talk, or do you want to give your backside a break?"

"Backside."

"Good choice." Parker reined in the horse and dismounted. "The horse needs more rest, anyway, with us riding double."

Annie slid down from the horse, walked in a little circle, rubbing her rear end and stretching. "I sure as heck prefer riding in a wagon."

Parker put his hands on his hips and looked ahead. The grass-covered dunes stretched on to the horizon, rolling and dipping, then rising up again. The trees had vanished completely, and the land, spreading on until it met the wide, blue, cloudless sky, had a sort of dizzying effect. Wyoming still seemed a long, long way away.

And what happens when you get there, fool? Nothing maybe. You got a map with a picture of a tree stump and no idea what you're doing.

Well, he'd come this far. No turning back now.

"What's that?" Annie pointed.

Parker looked where she was pointing, a little more westward than where he'd been looking as he pondered his choices. At first, he didn't see a thing, neither tree nor shrub, not even a bird flitting across the sky.

Then he saw it, perched atop a distant hill.

"A little shack," he said.

Annie squinted, then shook her head. "It's moving."

"What?" Parker looked again.

Just as Annie had said, what Parker had taken as a tiny shack was indeed moving. Very slowly. Some kind of wagon, then, but not an easily recognizable Conestoga. Parker watched it disappear down the other side of the hill slowly, slowly, slowly, until it was out of sight.

"We should follow it," Annie said.

"Why should we do that?"

"Maybe they know where they're going. A town or someplace."

Parker thought about that. It had been a while since they followed a road. Cutting cross-country might make it less likely for them to happen upon a town. Then again, there was no guarantee the people in the wagon ahead of them knew where they were going, either.

"And when we catch up to them?" Parker asked.

Annie shrugged. "Say howdy."

Parker shrugged, too. "I guess it don't matter either way."

They climbed back onto the horse and went after the wagon.

They kept a steady pace, up one hill and down another. The hill where they'd seen the wagon was farther away than it had first appeared, and it was late afternoon when they'd reached it. From the top they looked down and were surprised to see a small lake. The wagon sat on the edge of the lake, a cook fire already going nearby, an iron pot hanging from a tripod over the flames. The wagon's two horses were hobbled off to the side.

Parker watched for a moment but didn't see any people. Maybe they were inside the wagon.

They were close enough now to see that the wagon was basically a big wooden box, a bench out front, lanterns hanging from each corner. The whole thing was painted green with bright yellow writing on the side. As they got closer, Parker could make it out:

☞ Professor Xavier T. Meriweather. ☜
Elixirs for the Body and Spirit.
Purveyor of Scientific Miracles!

Parker dismounted fifty yards from the wagon and handed the reins to Annie. "Wait here!"

He called out as he approached on foot. "Hello!"

No reply.

He stopped within the circle of firelight, eyes slowly moving over the scene, wondering where the people were. Whatever was cooking in the pot smelled mighty good, and Parker's stomach rumbled. He'd had a bite of jerky for lunch and a swallow of water, but that seemed a long time ago.

"Anyone around?"

The familiar *clack-click* of a hammer being thumbed back on a revolver. Parker froze.

"Who's on the horse?" asked a voice.

"Annie," Parker said. "Just a friend. We don't mean nothing. Just saying hello. It looks like we're going in the same direction. Thought maybe we could share the fire. Okay if I turn your way?"

"By all means."

Parker slowly turned to see the man coming around from the other side of the wagon. He held a bucket in one hand. The other hand held an enormous Colt Walker pointed right at Parker's chest. He looked maybe mid- to late fifties, white hair curling from under a gray top hat. A bulbous nose, shining red, and an elaborate white mustache, drooping and curling at the ends. A powdering of stubble on his jaws and chin. He wore a white shirt with the sleeves rolled up, and a vest with such a busy purple, black, and silver paisley pattern that it almost made Parker's eyes cross.

"And may I ask your name, young man?"

"Parker Jones, sir."

"I see. And what does Parker Jones mean to the world?"

"Sir?"

"A rose by any other name can still shoot me in the back when I'm not looking," he said. "Who are you, and by what circumstance do we find ourselves in this exact spot on this vast spinning planet of ours?"

"Like I said, just happen to be going in the same direction. I'm bound for Wyoming." Parker slowly reached into his shirt pocket and pulled out the tin star. "I'm a deputy sheriff out of Rory's Junction, Missouri. I'm out of my jurisdiction and off duty, so I don't bother wearing it."

"Ah, man of the law, is it? Well, I don't suppose I can ask for a more trustworthy fellow than that."

Parker's eyes went to the Colt Walker. "Uh, if you don't mind."

The man looked at the revolver as if only just remembering it was there. "My pardon. A precaution only." He slowly lowered the hammer, then tucked the Walker into his belt. "A man alone in the wilderness cannot be too careful."

"I didn't catch your name, sir."

"No? Truly? Then allow me to introduce myself." He then set the Walker on the wagon bench where his coat was draped. He shrugged into it. It was such a deep purple as to nearly be black. He smoothed the lapels then doffed his hat, gesturing to the side of the wagon. "Professor Xavier T. Meriweather at your service, from the great state of Connecticut, by way of the finest medical institutions of Europe, where I learned the secrets of body and mind. My elixirs are no less than miracles of internal medicine. I cured the prince of Albania of his constant snoring. I made Countess Zalinski of Poland fertile again when she could not bear children. When the Sultan of Baghdad suddenly found himself as bald as a cueball, to whom did he come begging for a cure? Why, to the indomitable Meriweather, of course. He soon had a flowing mane that even Samson would envy. Come now, Deputy Jones, is there not an ailment that plagues you, which the great Meriweather could easily cure?"

"No," Parker said. "But that stew smells good."

"Ah. Yes, well, nourishment has a healing power all its own, I suppose." Meriweather raised his voice for Annie's benefit. "We are at peace, madam. Please join us."

The girl slipped down from the horse and led it in by the reins until she stood next to Parker. "Hello."

"And hello to you, young lady," Meriweather said affably. "We are all weary travelers who happen to find ourselves in the same place at the same time. Your gentleman friend has suggested you'd both like to share my campfire and perhaps even the stew currently simmering in the pot, and while your warm fellowship would undoubtably be reward enough, I'm forced to inquire how you might positively enhance our impending repast."

Annie's face went blank. "Huh?"

"What can you bring to the table, kids?"

"Biscuits would go good with that stew." Recent practice had improved Parker's biscuit-making skills, and he felt confident Meriweather wouldn't be disappointed.

Meriweather scratched behind the ear, considering. "Well, that's not bad, I suppose. Not a bad start."

"I've got whiskey, too," Parker said.

"Sold!" Meriweather gestured for them to come forward. "Make yourself at home. Hobble your horse next to the others, if you like. I've bowls and spoons in the wagon. I'll be but a moment."

Soon the three of them sat comfortably around the fire, spooning stew into their mouths and dipping biscuits into the broth. With great pride in his culinary skills, Meriweather explained that his stew contained a couple of fat coneys, potatoes, onions, carrots, salt, pepper, basil, and thyme. He told Parker and Annie to have as much as they liked, which seemed fair, since he apparently intended to take the same liberty with Parker's whiskey.

"An excellent meal!" Meriweather tipped the bottle back, drank deeply, and smacked his lips. "I don't suppose you happen to have a cigar on you, to go with this excellent libation hooch."

Parker shrugged. "Sorry."

"Never mind, young man. Never mind. We shall pass the time with scintillating conversation." Meriweather looked from Annie to Parker. "You two are . . . siblings?"

Annie shoved a biscuit into her mouth and shook her head. She chewed and swallowed. "My folks was killed. Parker found me." She filled her mouth with stew, signaling that was all she cared to say about the subject.

But Meriweather's curiosity had been piqued, and he clearly wanted to know more. "This is obviously a terrible tale of woe. Tell me, deputy, how did you happen upon Miss Annie in her time of need?"

Parker explained finding the burning wagon and Annie hidden under the bonnet. He didn't try to make the story exciting or make himself sound like a hero. He just related the facts. He then told the professor about finding a town where he thought Annie might get some work only to discover the work was in a brothel.

"I didn't really feel I could just leave her there," Parker said.

"I should say not," Meriweather agreed, then turned to Annie. "What in the world do you plan to do now, my dear?"

Annie shrugged. "Find work somewhere. Proper work. Then start my life."

"Pragmatic and levelheaded." Meriweather tipped the bottle back again. "You know, it occurs to me I might have an opportunity that would fit the bill perfectly. Are you by any chance acquainted with my particular line of work?"

Annie squinted at him. "Some kind of doctor?"

"In the most general sense of the word, yes, I suppose so," Meriweather said. "But there is so much more. I am equal parts medical professional and sensational showman. In this regard, I find an assistant very useful. I lost a most ungrateful young girl to a man in Topeka. She insisted she was in love and needed to get married. Imagine that! After all I'd done for her. Ungrateful child."

Annie narrowed her eyes, intrigued. "What does an assistant do?"

"Oh, this and that." Meriweather waved the notion away as if the details were inconsequential. "Often it's enough that a pretty young thing in a nice dress holds up the bottles of elixir while I explain the intricate science behind the medical miracle." He leaned forward and squinted at the girl. "I take it there is a pretty girl under those layers of grime."

Annie looked down, embarrassed.

Parker hadn't wanted to say anything, but he could smell the girl the whole time they'd been riding double. He supposed he could use a bath himself, but Annie was the filthiest creature he'd ever seen. Now that he thought about it, he doubted the brothel would have taken her.

"Wait here a moment."

Meriweather went to the wagon and returned a few minutes later with clothing and a towel in his arms. Also a cake of white soap and a small bottle.

"This is good, strong soap," Meriweather said. "The bottle contains a cleanser for your hair and smells of lilac. My former assistant left behind a few articles of clothing to which you are welcome, if you decide to enter my employment." He handed Annie the armload of items. "The lake water is clean. Cold but not *too* cold."

Annie looked down at the bundle in her hands, then stole a quick look at Parker.

"Fear not," Meriweather told her. "Deputy Jones and I shall remain on this side of the wagon. Your privacy is assured."

"Well, okay." She held the items close against her chest, then went around the wagon, out of sight.

"Thanks for that," Parker said. "She sure needs it, and that's the truth. Can't say a bath would hurt me none, neither."

"If you like, feel free to use the soap after she's finished," Meriweather said. "If there's any left."

Parker chuckled at that. *She might need every bit of it.*

"So what about you?" Meriweather asked.

"I reckon I'll bathe next," Parker said. "As long as we've got the lake handy."

"No, no, no." Meriweather took another slug of the whiskey. "I mean, what's your story? You said you happened upon our poor Miss Annie after her unfortunate incident, but you neglected to explain why you were crossing the wilds in the first place."

Parker spooned stew into his mouth to buy a few seconds. "It's kind of a long story."

"I see. Secret lawman business, is it?"

"Well, indirectly," Parker said. "I'm sort of looking into something. It's one of those things that if I'm right, everyone will think I'm a genius. If I'm wrong, I'll be a dang fool."

Meriweather laughed. "Say no more. I've had some experience with that sort of thing. Trust me. Can I at least know where you're headed?"

"Wyoming."

"Ah, yes, so you said. Well, you're certainly pointed in the right direction."

"It's a long way, and that's for sure," Parker admitted. "I just hope it's worth it when I finally—"

Parker's eyes went directly to the woman coming around the side of the wagon. She wore a green dress, her glossy black hair pulled back in a ponytail. He was wondering where in the world this strange woman had come from when it struck him like a bolt of lightning he was looking at Annie.

The oversize man's shirt she'd been wearing had hidden what was, indeed, a woman's figure—still slight, yes, but clearly feminine—and Parker guessed she might actually be eighteen years old, as she'd claimed. Face fresh, eyes glittering and refreshed. Annie sat back next to Parker, still clutching the bundle, which now contained her old, dirty clothes. She sat with her eyes on the ground, as if embarrassed. The subtle scent of lilac reached Parker.

She looked up briefly at Parker and the professor, then back down at the ground again. "Well, what's everyone staring at?"

Meriweather leaned forward, smiling warmly. "Quite an improvement. I knew there was something worth looking at under all that dirt." He turned to Parker. "Don't you agree, Deputy Jones?"

"You smell—" Parker cleared his throat. "You don't smell so bad anymore."

Annie's face went deadpan. "High praise."

Parker stood abruptly, snatching what was left of the soap from Annie. "Well, then. My turn, I reckon."

CHAPTER 11

"Let's face it. We're stuck." Farkas tossed back a shot of whiskey, grabbed the bottle, and refilled his glass. "We don't know where that gold is, and we'll never know."

Grady Jenks frowned. "You wanna just give up?"

Farkas scowled. "A fella should know when he's licked."

Grady Jenks, Bill Farkas, and Little Joe Tillis sat at a corner table in a dank Denver saloon called The Lumberman's, making their second bottle of whiskey slowly disappear, talking about how it had all gone wrong, and trying to figure out how to make it right again.

After chewing it over, nobody had really thought Tanner Best showing up at Eiger's had been a coincidence. A U.S. marshal was nothing to sneeze at, and the train robbery had been in all the papers. The outlaws had asked around about the lawman with the two-gun rig. What they'd heard hadn't been encouraging. Turns out Best was exactly the sort of lawman to go after men like Jenks and the boys. The marshal must like to see his name in the papers, because he seemed to hanker after jobs that everyone talked about like the train robbery. Best wanted the bragging rights for capturing outlaws like Jenks and the reward to go along with it.

They'd gone to see Filmore's mother, hoping to find out where Gerald was hiding himself. They didn't want to attract attention or accidentally intimidate the old woman, so Jenks had shaved and combed his hair and paid her a visit without Farkas and Tillis in tow. He'd told Mrs. Filmore that he was one of Gerald's old pals from the railroad. She'd confirmed Jenks's worst fear. Not only had the law been there ahead of him, but Gerald Filmore was now dead. He should have expected it. That dolt Lester had shot him, but Jenks had held out hope the wound wasn't so bad and they'd still find the man alive. Jenks wanted to make him talk—which was a tough row to hoe when the man was dead.

If Lester hadn't already been a corpse, Jenks would have shot the man himself.

There no longer being any point to lingering in Missouri, they turned around and headed west again. Kansas had recently proven inhospitable, so they crossed it as quickly as possible, avoiding towns and people in general. They felt safer in Colorado, and by the time they reached Denver, they were all more than ready for soft beds, thick steaks, and strong whiskey. Now their bellies were full, and the whiskey had sent that pleasantly warm, numb feeling into their extremities.

But they still had the same old problem.

Somewhere out there an enormous pile of gold

remained hidden, and Jenks had no earthly idea where it might be.

Except, well . . . that wasn't exactly true.

Jenks and the boys had talked it to death around the campfire during their breakneck trek across Kansas. Gerald Filmore had clearly not taken the gold with him. It wasn't like he could just put it in his pocket and walk off. That much gold was heavy and bulky, and Filmore would need some sort of wagon or cart, and they knew he hadn't left Wyoming with either.

In a way, Gerald Filmore had made it easy for Jenks. Filmore still had all the bad habits of an honest citizen, giving his real name when buying train tickets and checking into hotels. This kind of information was supposed to be confidential, but it was no surprise at all how often ticket sellers and hotel clerks were willing to part with a name when there was a six-shooter pointed at their nose.

Gerald Filmore had left Cheyenne by train and had gotten off in Omaha, where he'd purchased a horse, then headed due south. Jenks had found the hotels where he'd stayed. The man must have had no idea in the world he was being pursued, because he sure didn't seem in a hurry. They caught up with him in Kansas, and that's where it all went down the drain. They'd almost gotten their hands on Filmore when he pulled a pistol, shooting every which way as he made for his horse and not coming within a mile of hitting anything.

That's when that dang fool Lester had put a slug into the man. In fairness, when a man starts shooting at you, your natural inclination is to shoot back. Still, Lester should have shown restraint. Filmore hopped onto his horse with alacrity and rode away, giving Jenks the impression his wound hadn't been of the fatal variety. They'd pursued.

But it's funny how the law doesn't like folks just randomly shooting at each other and putting innocent folks in danger. So, yeah, they'd had a posse on their tails almost immediately.

And now they were in Denver, tired and drunk and no more gold in their pockets than when they'd started.

"He must have caught Frenchy by surprise," Tillis said, not for the first time. "No way that lily-livered railroad man outdraws Frenchy. Probably caught him by surprise or backshot him or some such."

"And why wouldn't he catch him by surprise?" Farkas said. "There was no reason to think he was pulling a double cross. No way the guy had the stones for that, leastways that's how he seemed."

"Well, I guess he did, after all," Jenks said. "But none of this is getting us anywhere. The question is, what do we do now?"

Nobody had an answer for that.

"It's a shame we can't find the gold as easy as Tanner Best found us." Farkas blew out a sigh, shook his head, and tossed back another gulp of whiskey. "I hate to say it, but it's probably me. There's a good number of folks know I frequent Eiger's. Probably, he asked around."

Jenks sat up straight, eyes slowly widening as an idea approached from a long way off. "Wait a minute. Say that again."

Farkas frowned. "That it's my fault?"

"Before that."

"Tanner Best found us easy enough," Farkas said.

Jenks grinned. "Fellas, we've been going about this all wrong. We should let Tanner Best do all the hard work for us."

"I don't follow," Tillis said.

"If the marshal is investigating anything to do with the train robbery, then that includes the gold, right?" Jenks explained. "All we got to do is let him do his job, and I'll bet he leads us right to it."

"You're maybe forgetting he's looking for *us*, too," Tillis said. "It's not like we can just follow him around until he happens to lead us to the gold. He's seen our faces."

"And there's no reason to believe he can find the gold any better than we can," put in Farkas.

"He's a lawman," Jenks said. "People are more apt to talk to a man flashing a badge—honest citizens, I mean. He probably thinks if he finds the gold, then he finds us. Or if he finds us, he finds the gold. Point is, he'll be looking all over, and he's probably better at it than we are."

"He still knows what we look like," Tillis reminded him.

"That's a concern," Jenks admitted. "But my brothers are in Fort Collins. They've never been arrested for nothing and don't have their faces on any wanted posters."

Tillis made a dissatisfied grunt. "Don't get me wrong, I'm sorry we lost Lester and Eugene and Frenchy, but I was sort of getting used to the idea of splitting the loot three ways instead of six."

"*What* loot?" Jenks asked. "What do you think we've been talking about? There ain't no gold unless we figure out a way to find it. And if Best does track us down again, he might have a posse with him, and that's no time to be shorthanded."

"I agree," Farkas said. "We're getting nowhere on our own. I say we try Grady's plan."

Tillis held up a hand. "Fine, then, I won't be the only naysayer. Can your brothers handle themselves?"

"They're dependable enough," Jenks said. "We'll head to Fort Collins first thing in the morning."

"What about tonight?" Tillis asked.

Jenks reached for the bottle. "Finish getting drunk, I guess."

And they did just that, woke up in the morning with headaches, and got a late start. The sun was just setting as their horses clopped through the mud into Fort Collins.

"They got a shack on the edge of town," Jenks told Tillis and Farkas. "Best if I go see them on my own. You boys go get yourselves a meal."

Tillis and Farkas dismounted in front of a grubby-looking hash house and went inside.

Jenks kept riding through town until he reached the other side.

He pondered what to tell his brothers. They weren't what anyone would call geniuses, but if he asked them to pick up and go to Wyoming—that's where Jenks figured Tanner Best would end up eventually—and then follow a U.S. marshal around, they'd darn well want to know why and what was in it for them. He thought hard on Tillis's notion to split the gold three ways and had to admit he liked the sound of it, too. But then he'd have to tell his brothers—what?

He shook his head, discarding the idea. The best thing would be just to level with them. Anyway, they'd give their best effort, knowing there was a heap of gold waiting.

It occurred to Jenks his brothers might not even be home. They did this and that for a paycheck, never sticking with one thing for too long. They might be off on a cattle drive or working a mining claim somewhere. There was nothing to do except knock on the shack's front door and see if anyone answered.

Jenks hadn't been to see his brothers in a while, so he paused on the edge of town, looking over the scattering of shabby shacks, trying to remember which was the right one. He spotted it after a minute, the one with the bent stovepipe chimney and the rusty horseshoe over the front door. It badly needed a coat of paint, and the roof was missing shingles. He tied up his horse and knocked on the front door.

At first, Jenks thought he'd struck out, but then he heard movement come from within, followed by grumbling. A moment later, the door creaked open, and Jenks's older brother stood there rubbing his eyes.

Jimmy Jenks was three years older and an inch taller, but lanky and frail-looking from drinking too much and not eating healthy. Streaks of gray in his hair, five days of stubble on his jaw. He resembled Grady Jenks around the eyes, but that was about it. He wore dirty underwear and had the look of a man roused from bad sleep.

Jimmy blinked. "Grady! You got here fast, didn't you? I guess word's gotten around."

Jenks wasn't sure what his brother meant. Probably he was talking about the train robbery being in all the newspapers. Had Jimmy been expecting him to show up all along. "Let's talk about it inside. I don't want the whole world looking at us."

Jimmy stepped aside and allowed him to enter, then shut the door. Jenks pulled a chair over to the window so that he could sit and keep watch on the outside. Something had occurred to Jenks as he stepped into his brother's shack. If it was known Jenks had brothers, might Tanner Best or some other lawman have the place watched? Jenks vowed to be more careful in the future.

"You act like you was expecting me," Jenks said.

"Not really expecting," Jimmy said. "Just not surprised. You want a drink?"

"Not just yet."

Jimmy sat at a rickety table in the shack's only other chair and reached for the half-empty bottle in the center. He pulled the cork with his teeth, spat it across the room, then took a big gulp and wiped his mouth with his sleeve.

"I see you're living high on the hog like usual." Jenks glanced around the interior of the shack. Dirty plates and cups in the sink. Flies buzzing. Two narrow beds, one on one side of the room, the other on the other side. One mattress was bare. The other had a threadbare blanket thrown over it. No pillow. The place smelled like old food, stale whiskey, and feet.

Jimmy shrugged and took another drink.

"Maybe I got a way you can make some money," Jenks said.

Jimmy's eyes focused. "I'm listening."

"Where's Charlie?" Jenks asked. "I don't want to say this more than once."

Jimmy frowned. "What do you mean?"

"What do you think somebody means when they ask where somebody is?"

Charlie Jenks was Grady Jenks's younger brother by seven years. If Jenks was going to explain what he had in mind, he'd rather tell both his brothers at one time, especially since both brothers would probably ask the same idiotic questions, and Jenks wasn't keen to needlessly repeat himself.

"He's in jail, Grady."

"Jail?" Jenks's eyes went wide. "Charlie's in jail?"

"Well, yeah," Jimmy said. "I thought that's why you was here."

"Just tell me what happened."

"He robbed a guy in an alley behind Tillman's Saloon," Jimmy told him. "He hit him in the back of the head. Charlie was just going to take his wallet and leave him to sleep it off, but the guy didn't go down and pulled a knife. So Charlie shot him."

Jenks rubbed his temples. "Good Lord."

"They're gonna hang him on Tuesday," Jimmy said.

Jenks sighed and stood, and grabbed the whiskey

bottle off the table, titling it back and draining what was left. "Tuesday, you say?"

"Yep."

"Well"—Jenks set the empty bottle back on the table—"I guess we'd better bust him out."

CHAPTER 12

Parker Jones rode tall in the saddle the next morning, a good bath and clean clothes making him feel like a new man.

He kept stealing glances at Annie, who sat next to Professor Meriweather on the wagon's bench. Parker admitted to himself that he missed the weight of her clinging behind him as he rode. *Just figures as soon as she's clean and pretty and smelling nice, and I would have actually* enjoyed *her proximity . . .*

Well, never mind. That was life, Parker figured. Missed opportunities. Just like Bonnie Morgan. Thinking of Bonnie made Parker laugh. She seemed a thousand years ago and a million miles away.

"What's gotten into you that's so funny," Annie called from her place on the wagon.

Parker shook his head and smiled. "Just in a good mood is all."

As they rode along, something caught Parker's eye that threatened to put a dent in his good mood. In the distance to the north, he saw a line of riders, maybe nine or ten of them, at this distance just silhouettes of men on horses. Parker watched for a while, but the riders didn't come closer, nor did they go on their own way.

He nudged his horse alongside the wagon.

"I think we're making good time, don't you?" the professor said.

"Nice weather for it, too," Parker said. "Uh, say, Professor, what do you make of those fellas over there?"

Meriweather leaned away from the wagon and squinted until he saw the figures on the distant ridge. "Oh, have they been there long?"

"A while," Parker said. "I've been keeping an eye on them. They're dogging us, I think."

Meriweather looked again, opened his mouth to say something, then abruptly shut it again, his eyes going to Annie.

"Go ahead and say it." Annie was looking, too. Now that Parker had pointed them out, they were hard to miss. "Indians."

"I'm afraid that's the conclusion I reached, as well," Meriweather said.

"I don't suppose they might be friendly," Parker mused.

"Prudence would suggest we assume they're not," the professor said.

"Trust me," Annie said in a quiet voice. "They're not."

"The question is what sort of action do we take next," Meriweather suggested. "I haven't been out west for so very long, so I have no firsthand experience with the tribes. I've only heard stories. Deputy?"

Before undertaking this journey, Parker had never been any farther west of the Mississippi than Rory's Junction himself. He had no more idea what to do about

Indians than he knew how to grow corn on the moon, but he didn't think saying that would comfort his traveling companions. His only chance was to try to apply some common sense.

He hoped he had some.

"I don't suppose there's a town close by," Parker said. "Or a homestead or—well, anything. More people would be better. Might make them think twice before attacking."

The three of them craned their necks and twisted in their seats, looking in every direction, but that only confirmed what they already knew. They were in the middle of nowhere, without another white man for miles and miles. There was no place to run and hide.

"Let's just keep going for a while and see what they do," Parker suggested. "Don't let on like we notice them."

Parker stole a look at Annie. Her face had gone pinched and pale, and she bunched the material of her dress in tight fists, clearly anxious.

"We'll figure something out." Parker had said it lightly in the hope to sound confident, but it was so obviously put on, he was afraid his words had the opposite effect.

They rode for another hour, and the Indians matched them, neither drawing closer nor moving away, and now Parker decided some sort of action needed to be taken.

"We need to be smart about picking our spot when we stop for the night," he told Meriweather.

"What if we didn't stop?" Meriweather asked. "What if we just rode on through the night?"

"If they attack, then our choices are fight or flee,"

Parker said. "How fast do you think you can make this wagon go?"

"Not very fast," Meriweather admitted. "And not for long."

"That's sort of what I figured," Parker said. "If we run, they'll ride us down pretty easy. If we pick our spot and fight, then we can at least take cover and . . ." A shrug. Parker didn't know what he was talking about, but they had to try something. "I don't know. Maybe we'll get lucky. Maybe we can put up just enough of a fight not to be worth the bother. But if our choices are keep going or stop and get ready, then I vote we get ready for them as best we can."

Meriweather scratched behind his ear, thinking it over. "Neither choice appeals, but I yield to your logic. The next question is, where?"

Parker scanned the landscape then pointed. "That low hill. It's a bit steeper than the others. If we camp at the top, they'll be forced to come at us uphill, no matter what direction they choose. It's not much of an advantage but better than nothing. Anything that makes it harder for them might just be enough to make them change their minds."

"The hill, then," Meriweather said. "We should still have a good bit of daylight by the time we reach it."

Howling Bear brought his horse alongside Red Pony's. "What are we waiting for?"

Red Pony let out a long sigh and fought down the urge to snap at the impatient brave. "We have plenty to eat, and they aren't going anywhere. There is no rush. We can watch them."

"We have watched them," Howling Bear said. "There's only three, and one's a girl."

"We thought there were four at the fish camp, but there were five. It's better to be sure."

"Four or five. What's the difference?"

"Yellow Feather is the difference," Red Pony said. "It costs us nothing to be cautious."

"Yellow Feather." Howling Bear said the words as if they left a sour taste in his mouth. "Is he such a great loss?"

"Yellow Feather yesterday," Red Pony said. "Who will it be today? Who tomorrow? Small mistakes add up until there are none of us left—or is it your plan to act recklessly until you alone remain? A band of one, all unto yourself?"

"At least I would no longer have to put up with your so-called caution," Howling Bear spat back. "Are we a band of old women and cripples?"

Red Pony could see that a few of the others had edged their horses closer, listening. They'd all been well fed. The raid on the fish camp—Yellow Feather's death aside—had been successful. Red Pony would have thought them satisfied for the moment, but then he realized what was happening. The triumph at the fish camp had fed their egos, had made them feel like mighty braves again, instead of a chickenhearted rabble. They wanted more scalps and another night of victory and whiskey.

"We will watch until they make camp tonight," Red Pony said. "If all is as it seems, then we shall attack."

The gathered braves murmured approval. Howling Bear grinned.

They rode another hour, keeping pace with the wagon. It veered a little south, but Red Pony saw nothing interesting in this until he noticed it seemed to be heading straight for a hill which humped up all by itself from the flat grassy plain. Soon the wagon had reached the top of the hill, and it was clear they'd stopped for the day, going about the business of making camp.

"They've stopped," Howling Bear said. "We should attack at night. Let them get comfortable, even asleep. It worked at the fish camp."

"It will not work here," Red Pony said.

Howling Bear's face hardened. "And why not?"

"Surely they have seen us," Red Pony said. "There is no forest in which to hide and bide our time as there was at the fish camp. They know they cannot run, so they have taken to high ground and will wait."

"The high ground? What of it?" Howling Bear said dismissively. "They don't seem to be doing anything out of the ordinary—tending to horses, preparing a fire to cook a meal."

"You're wrong."

Howling Bear looked so angry, Red Pony worried he would pull the tomahawk from his belt and attack him. "How am I wrong?"

"They're building a fire." Red Pony said. "But not to cook a meal. Look."

Howling Bear looked. A plume of twisting black

smoke rose into the air from the top of the hill, reaching high into the blue sky. It would be visible for many miles, and there was still plenty of daylight left.

Parker threw another coil of old rope onto the fire, and the black smoke billowed as it rose.

Professor Meriweather approached with the tripod and iron cooking pot.

"I thought maybe we should have a cold dinner tonight, Professor," Parker told him.

Meriweather paused to look at what Parker was doing with the fire. "A distress signal? That seems rather a slim chance."

"*Two* slim chances, actually," Parker said. "First, maybe we'll get lucky. Like you say, who's out here to see it?—but you never know."

"And the other chance?"

"Maybe the Indians will think we know something they don't," Parker said. "If they think help's on the way, they might not want to stick around."

Meriweather nodded. "That's worth a chance, I suppose. What else can we do to prepare?"

"How are we fixed for guns?"

"I believe you're acquainted with my Colt Walker," Meriweather said. "In addition, I have a Sharps carbine."

"One of them single-shot trapdoor jobs?"

"Yes, that's right."

"Use that first," Parker said. "Only switch to the Walker if they get close. It's an old cap and ball, and reloading will take forever, so make every shot count. When's the last time you checked the load?"

"Young man, I can't even recall the last time I fired it," Meriweather admitted.

"Then empty it and reload," Parker told him. "Old powder maybe. Or maybe it got damp. Who knows? In the middle of a fight is a bad time to find out."

"Smart. I'll change it out now." Meriweather turned and headed back to his wagon.

Parker took a deep breath. Strangely, he felt calm. Would reloading the Walker help? Maybe. Would sending up smoke bring help or dissuade the Indians from attacking? Probably not. Would he and Annie and the professor live through this?

Good question.

But even with his lack of experience, Parker felt right making decisions. Anything was better than sitting around crying that they were doomed. Might as well get ready for what was to come. Maybe it wouldn't make a difference. Maybe it would make all the difference.

He considered his own weapons and lamented he'd never shown much interest in getting proficient with a rifle. It had seemed glamorous to Parker to practice his quickdraw skills with the Peacemaker, and he'd often fancied himself a storybook gunfighter. But what had he accomplished with that? Had Bonnie Morgan been impressed with Parker's gunslinging skills? Nope. He'd gladly trade all those hours he'd spent outdrawing bottles and cans for a solid Henry rifle or a good Winchester and a couple of boxes of shells. A practical weapon for a dire situation.

If I get out of this alive, I'm going to spend some of my money on a good repeater. A grown-up gun for real-world danger.

Parker turned his thoughts toward the scattergun he'd taken from Eiger's. Another close-range weapon. He wished he could exchange it for a rifle, but it could still shoot, and it could still kill. He was determined to make do with the resources at hand.

"Annie!"

She came around from the other side of the wagon where she'd been looking after the horses. "Yeah?"

"Ever shoot a shotgun before?"

Annie shook her head, but her eyes narrowed with determination. "Show me."

Paker broke the shotgun, removed the shells, then handed her the weapon. "Feel the weight of it."

Annie took the gun, felt its weight in her hands, pointed it out across the prairie, and sighted along the barrels.

"Take your finger off the triggers," Parker said.

She moved the finger quickly, as if scalded.

"Never put your finger on the trigger until you're ready to shoot," Parker instructed. "Never point this gun at nothing you don't want dead. We don't want accidents. You point this at anyone, it means you're ready to kill them."

"I understand."

"Two triggers, one for each barrel," Parker said. "This ain't a rifle, so you wait until they're too close to miss. Get the butt up against your shoulder. Firm. Thing kicks like a mule. It'll knock you right over if you ain't braced for it."

She blew out a nervous breath. "Right."

"Let's load and unload it."

They spent ten minutes breaking the shotgun, taking out shells, putting them back in, going over every inch of the weapon. She started to feel more comfortable with it, or at least acted like she did. Annie feared what was to come but hid it well. She's going to do her part, Parker figured, and that was all anyone could ask.

Whether it was enough remained to be seen.

Parker tossed the last of the rope onto the fire, black smoke twisting high into the sky. He scanned the landscape but couldn't see the Indians. He would have liked to believe they'd gone, but he didn't. His gut told him they were just on the other side of one hill or another, likely waiting to strike at night.

Two more hours until the sun sets, more or less. Will they come right away or make us sweat first? Maybe they wait for us to fall asleep. Well, jokes on them. No way I'm falling asleep tonight.

How had he gotten into this? He let his mind wander and was surprised. He'd thought he'd regret all his choices. He thought he'd wish he was back in Rory's Junction with his sister. A boring, directionless life, yes, but safe from all the perils of the frontier. But he didn't wish to be home. Parker had found Annie near the smoking ruins of her wagon. Who would have found her if Parker hadn't left home? Would Professor Meriweather be all alone when the Indians came if not for Parker?

Parker's existence now mattered to others, affected their lives. As short as they might be.

They ate a bite of jerky and drank some water. None of them had much of an appetite, anyway. Darkness fell, and Parker put the last of the wood on the fire. He wanted the circle of light to be as wide as possible so that he could see the Indians when they attacked. They took positions under the wagon. Any cover was better than nothing.

"Professor, me and you'll take them head on," Parker said. "Annie, make sure nobody comes up behind us. Don't waste ammo. Wait until you can hit something. Don't be afraid. Be afraid after it's over. Deal with what comes."

He wasn't sure where the words had come from. Maybe something his father had told him as a child.

They waited.

Red Pony couldn't wait any longer.

Howling Bear was growing impatient and had riled the other braves against Red Pony. They wanted blood. They wanted to feel the pulse of battle in their veins and would not be held back.

Howling Bear brought his horse close to Red Pony, leaned toward him, pitched his voice low. "Lead us into battle. No more waiting. If you don't, I will."

Battle? That Howling Bear would consider attacking three people—one a girl, the other a gray-haired gentleman—a *battle*, was only proof of his self-delusion. But Howling Bear had picked his time just right. The rest of the braves were up for it, and it was no secret that Howling Bear thought he should be leader instead of Red Pony.

Red Pony would not be surprised at all if Howling Bear challenged him there and then for leadership if Red Pony balked at the attack. The braves would not intervene. Howling Bear was big and strong. Red Pony could not be certain he would prevail in a knife fight. He could not show weakness, not now.

He cast his gaze across the wide plain, the campfire atop the hill seeming small in the vast darkness. Perhaps he was being too cautious. Attacking the lone wagon didn't seem necessary, but neither did it seem so much a risk. Fine, then. They'd attack.

And at some later time, Red Pony would decide what to do about Howling Bear. Accidents happened, after all. Even the most sure-footed of braves could slip and fall off a cliff.

Red Pony turned to the others and lifted his rifle in the air. "We attack!"

CHAPTER 13

He supposed the sounds floating up the hill were meant to be animal sounds, or bird cries, or some such, but even to Parker's untrained ear, he could tell they were fake. Indian's calling to each other in the night, signals maybe, or it could be they were just riling each other up, getting ready for the attack. It all amounted to the same thing.

"Here they come!" Parker announced.

The whoops and hollers grew louder, and in the next moment, a half dozen mounted Indians broke into the firelight.

Professor Meriweather shot first, the carbine spitting fire, and a screeching Indian flew from his horse. Parker knew reloading the single-shot rifle would be slow and opened fire with his Peacemaker.

His first shot missed. Parker spat a curse and thumbed the hammer back again. He fired, and another Indian flew from his horse, landed hard in the grass, and didn't move. Rifle fire came at him fast, splintering chunks of wood out of the wagon and kicking up dirt an inch from Parker's elbow. He fired again and missed.

The professor had reloaded. He fired again but missed, too. The Indians weren't making it easy. They rode fast, their horses circling the wagon as they kept pouring it on with their rifles, lead flying every which way through the air.

Parker glanced back at Annie. "Doing okay back there?"

"I'm good!" But her voice was tight with fear. "Nobody coming at us from this direction."

The Indians circled and fired, and Parker shot back. They made a lot of noise but didn't hit much. Parker hurried to reload.

A scream. The thunder of the shotgun. More screaming.

"Annie!"

Parker crawled from beneath the wagon on Annie's side, hot lead whizzing past his ears. He saw a huge, muscled Indian dragging Annie away by her hair as she screamed and kicked. The shotgun lay on the ground by another dead Indian.

Parker raised his pistol to shoot at Annie's captor, hesitating, not wanting to hit the girl. The hesitation cost him. Another Indian came riding around the wagon, the horse barreling into Parker and knocked him to the ground.

He landed hard, grunted, and fired his Peacemaker, but from his prone angle hit nothing but sky. He stumbled awkwardly to his feet, fanning the six-shooter's hammer, spitting lead at the Indian, but the rider had already turned his horse and fled back around to the other side of the wagon.

Parker chased after the Indian who'd grabbed Annie,

following them into the knee-high grass. He caught up, just as the big Indian turned and saw him coming, Parker right on him now. The Indian's eyes went big as Parker aimed the Peacemaker, right at his face, and squeezed the trigger.

Click.

Panic seized Parker as he realized he'd run through his lead.

The Indian's startled look shifted to a contemptuous sneer, and he brought his rifle butt around fast and cracked Parker on the chin. Stars exploded in Parker's eyes, and he staggered back, legs weak, the ground going out from under him. He blinked the stars away, found he was on his back in the tall grass, looking up at the big Indian.

The Indian's sneer widened as he brought up his rifle and aimed it at Parker's chest.

Parker swallowed hard. *This is it. I'm going to die.*

A rifle shot split the night. Parker flinched, looked down at himself, surprised he hadn't been shot.

The Indian looming over him went rigid. His eyes rolled up. His mouth fell open, then blood poured out, dripping down his chin. He swayed a moment then fell over. Annie crawled away from him, eyes still wide with terror.

Another Indian stood ten feet away, smoke oozing from the barrel of his rifle. He swung the weapon toward Parker.

Parker was up on one knee now, pointing his six-shooter at the Indian. Maybe he'd know the gun was empty or maybe not. Parker replayed in his mind what had just happened. The other Indian had just shot his friend. He was too close for it to be an accident. They stood facing each other a long moment.

Then with his free hand, Parker made a slow gesture. *Go on your way.*

A slow nod from the Indian who then turned and stalked off into the night.

Annie threw herself into Parker's arms. "Parker!" She hugged him tight, trembling.

"Come on. The professor's still fighting them."

They rushed back to the wagon, the sound of Meriweather's Colt Walker booming across the landscape. They dove under the wagon to see the remainder of the Indians gathering for a final charge. Parker hadn't reloaded. He fumbled at his belt for fresh shells.

"I'm empty!" Meriweather tossed the Walker aside and hastily reloaded his carbine.

The Indians whooped and charged. Parker tried to thumb the fresh shells into his Peacemaker, fumbled them into the grass. He cursed. The Indians were upon them.

A spattering of rifle shots crackled across the hill. Indians screamed and fell bleeding in front of their horses. Landing dead in the dry grass. A horn sounded. The remaining Indians wheeled their horses in a panic, and the next volley of gunfire sent them to their deaths.

A dozen horses erupted into the circle of firelight, each ridden by a man in blue. One carried a standard and blew on a bugle.

"The cavalry!" Meriweather shouted.

More rifle shots.

An officer with lieutenant's bars on his shoulders dismounted, went to one knee, and peered under the wagon. "Are you folks okay?"

"We are now!" Meriweather said with relief. "Thanks to you!"

"You folks sit tight." The lieutenant turned and shouted, "Sergeant Bellamy, form a defensive perimeter, then send squads after any of those Indians that slipped away."

"Yes, sir!" a man shouted back at him.

Parker crawled out from under the wagon, put his hand against it, leaning, his heart racing. He felt suddenly exhausted. "Where did you come from?"

"We saw your smoke just before sunset," the cavalry officer said. "Weren't sure what it might be but thought we should investigate."

The smoke. Parker couldn't believe it.

"You're safe now," the officer assured him. "We've got the situation under control."

"Obliged," Parker said. "I'd better check on our horses."

Even as he went around the wagon to where the animals were hobbled, he could already feel his legs going watery. He stepped between two of the horses, took a deep breath, and started to shake. His legs went, and suddenly he was sitting on the ground, gasping for air, sweat drenching him.

It's okay. You made it.

It was only after it was all over that Parker realized that he'd fully expected to die.

* * *

The lieutenant's name was Jacobs. He explained he was out of Fort Sidney. They'd received a wire about Indian trouble from the sheriff in Gurley.

"My major sent out two forces to reconnoiter," Jacobs explained. "Captain Bostwick took his men farther south."

Parker hadn't thought much of Gurley's sheriff, but he made a point to thank the man if they ever crossed paths again. If Jacobs hadn't been patrolling with his men, they'd never have seen Parker's smoke. Parker decided he'd better play it safe from here on out, because he'd just used up his luck for the whole year.

"My men have set up a perimeter. We'll hunker down and get some sleep, then head out in the morning," Jacobs said. "If any of those Indians managed to escape, my guess is they'll still be running this time next year. Still, me and my boys can escort you as far as Kimball. You can make it to Cheyenne from there with no trouble."

Parker had told the cavalry officer he was heading to Wyoming. He must have assumed Annie and Meriweather were going with him. Now that he thought about it, he didn't know what their plans were, not really. They'd been taking things one night at a time, heading generally west. Maybe it would be safer for them all to stay together for a while.

"We appreciate it," Parker told the lieutenant.

They slept, and Parker had to be shaken awake the next morning. He was that exhausted. The cavalry boys broke camp with military precision, Parker helped the professor hitch his team to the wagon, and they were soon on their way from the site of the Indian attack.

It wasn't quite Custer's Last Stand, but Parker wondered if the incident would be remembered, if they'd name that hill or something.

Probably not.

They headed west.

Red Pony watched them go.

He did not feel bad about murdering Howling Bear, not in the least.

He did feel a passing regret that the rest of his braves had been killed by the blue coats. That had not been part of his plan.

Although calling it a *plan* was too generous. It had been more of a feeling that something had to change, and the most obvious place to start had been with Howling Bear. The world would be better off without him.

When the blue coats had attacked, Red Pony had gone low in the tall grass. He'd remained perfectly still in the darkness even as one of the searching blue coats had come within three feet of him. He stayed there all night, not moving until, finally, the blue coats and the other whites moved off west. He stood, watching until they were nothing more than dark dots on the horizon.

Red Pony looked back at the hill which he would always think of as Howling Bear's Bane. He doubted he would ever come this way again.

The Indian turned north and began the long hike toward a different life.

CHAPTER 14

"Are you sure your pal's gonna have dynamite?" Grady Jenks asked his brother Jimmy.

"Boris? Oh, sure," Jimmy said. "Whenever he leaves a job, he usually takes a few, uh, *souvenirs* with him. He was blowing holes through mountains to make railroad tunnels, and they had a few leftover sticks."

"And we can't just buy the dynamite from him?" Jenks asked.

Jimmy had explained that his pal Boris would be an asset to his brother's gang. Boris hadn't been interested in selling the dynamite for a few bucks. He wanted to be a full-fledged member of the gang, and Jimmy had vouched for him, saying that Boris was good in a tight spot, handy with a revolver, and a crack shot with a rifle. Grady Jenks hadn't relished explaining to Bill Farkas and Little Joe Tillis that they'd be splitting the gold six ways again, but all he'd had to do was remind them that Marshal Tanner Best might have a posse in tow next time he came after them, and suddenly having an extra gun on their side didn't seem like a bad idea.

Jenks had considered that there might be some better

way to break Charlie out of the clink that didn't involve dynamite. He'd still had a few sticks after robbing the train but had gotten rid of them because they made him nervous just being around. He just wasn't keen on explosions. Still, after scouting the jailhouse, Jenks had to admit that blowing the bars in the jail's back window was the best way. It would be loud and attract attention, sure, but they'd catch 'em by surprise and be out and away in a heartbeat. By the time the smoke cleared, they'd be on their way out of town.

So that's how Grady Jenks found himself riding with his brother Jimmy out to Boris Ivanov's remote cabin, to invite a short, mean Russian to be part of his gang.

"The only thing is, Boris can be a bit . . . intense," Jimmy said.

Grady's eyes narrowed. "Intense?"

"Yeah."

"Care to elaborate?"

"Well, the thing about Boris is, well"—Jimmy scratched his chin, thinking how best to put it—"Boris never does nothing halfway. You don't want to get him going on something and then try to call him off. Like trying to unshoot a pistol. Once the bullet has left the barrel . . ."

Grady Jenks supposed that could be a good thing under the right circumstances. (On the other hand . . .)

"Sounds like he's maybe not the best choice when a more subtle approach is called for," Grady said.

Jimmy nodded. "Right. Fortunately, there's nothing subtle about blowing a jailhouse window."

They took the narrow trail along the river until they

spotted the log cabin on a high bank overlooking the water. It was a tidy building, with a solid, peaked roof and a straight stone chimney. They dismounted, tied their horses to a post, and Jimmy knocked.

"Boris, it's me," Jimmy said. "I brought my brother Grady."

The door opened a second later, and Boris stood there grinning, the gaps between his big white teeth making him seem like a simpleton. His round melon head was bald, with dark stubble on a rocklike jaw. Short but wide with broad shoulders and muscles. He wore pants and suspenders but no shirt, his chest and shoulders covered with coarse black hair.

He stepped aside and gestured they should enter.

The interior of the cabin was clean and orderly, a bearskin rug stretched across the rough floorboards. The stone fireplace was cold. The three of them sat at a small round table. Boris produced a bottle and filled three glasses with clear liquid.

"What's this?" Grady Jenks asked.

"Vodka," Boris told him. "Very good."

They drank.

Grady didn't dislike the vodka, but he didn't quite like it, either. It was just, well, different. It burned going down, but not like whiskey. He could feel the vodka in his nose. It would probably be a bad idea to light a match near his breath.

"Your brother has talked to you, yes? He tells you I would be very good for your gang." Boris's accent was thick but not to the point he couldn't be understood.

"He told me," Grady said. "You can shoot?"

"Good with pistol, yes," Boris confirmed. "Also very good with rifle. I have killed men. I am tough customer, as you say. A hard man from a hard land."

"And you have dynamite."

"*Da*." He held up his hand. "A moment."

Boris crossed the room, went to one knee, and opened a large ceder chest. He moved some quilts and blankets aside and fished out a smaller wooden box, maybe pine. He brought it to the table and opened it.

Grady Jenks leaned in and took a look. He counted nine sticks of dynamite. "That should be more than enough."

"*Da*," Boris said, eyes glittering, face nearly giddy as he looked at the dynamite. "Such wonderful stuff. You can solve many problems with dynamite, my friend. Solve a problem so good and final, that it never comes back again."

Grady shot Jimmy a look. *Intense, huh?*

"So what is plan?" Boris asked.

"The sheriff knows my face," Jimmy said. "If I come within a hundred feet of the jail, that'll raise suspicions. He usually gets over to the saloon right around sundown every evening. I'll get there about the same time and make sure I'm seen. Then he'll know I'm not up to anything. I'll have my horse tied up in the alley behind the saloon, so I can slip out the back when things get loud. I'll meet you guys wherever you say."

"My boys will be standing by with horses, so we can get out of town fast," Grady said. "Boris, you and me will sneak around the back of the jail. You're good to handle the dynamite?"

"*Da.*" Boris held up both his hands and wiggled his fingers. "I am very good and careful. See? All fingers and thumbs. Nothing blown off by accident." He laughed as if he'd just made the world's greatest joke.

They drank more vodka. Discussed some of the plan's finer details. To Grady Jenks, the best part about the plan was its simplicity. The only real worry was that the local sheriff was likely to get a posse after them, so they were extra careful about choosing a rendezvous point and a good place to hunker down and stay out of sight until the heat was off.

"That's it then," Grady announced. "We've figured it as good as it's going to get figured, I reckon. Let's head back to town."

Boris packed up his dynamite, saddled his horse, and rode back with Grady and Jimmy Jenks.

Jimmy went to the saloon to wait. Grady took Boris to meet up with Tillis and Farkas, and they all got a bite to eat at a shabby place called Mama's, a few blocks down from the jailhouse. The café wasn't much to look at, mismatched chairs and tables, windows without curtains, but an old lady brought plates of food that smelled better than any grub Grady Jenks had eaten in a long time. Pot roast. Mashed potatoes and gravy. Corn on the cob. Carrots. Buttermilk biscuits.

They ate slowly, partly to enjoy the meal, but also because they knew they had to kill a certain amount of time before making their next move. Jimmy was in the saloon by now, making a point of being seen. As far as the local sheriff and his deputies knew, there was no reason to expect trouble.

Grady shoved a final biscuit into his mouth, chewed, swallowed, then said in a low voice, "Okay, time to get a move on. Little Joe, you and Bill position yourself out of sight with the horses, like we talked about. There'll be no mistake when it's time to bring them horses fast as you can, because it's gonna be good and loud. Boris, we'll give them a few minutes head start, then you come with me."

Grady Jenks watched Tillis and Farkas leave and sat a moment, sipping a cup of coffee. He waited five minutes, then paid for the meal.

"Let's go," he told Boris.

They left Mama's café and crossed the street, circling around behind the buildings the next street over, darker, narrower, and less trafficked than the town's main thoroughfare. Grady had scouted the place earlier, and the jail's back wall faced this quiet street. The barred window was a foot above his head.

"Give me a boost, Boris."

Boris knitted his fingers together and held his hands low. Grady stepped into the cradle they made, and he was hoisted level with the bars. He looked into the cell. It was dark. He thought he could make out a narrow cot on the other side, a lump under some blankets. He waited a moment, listening, but heard nothing. He glanced over his shoulder. The street was quiet.

Grady faced the cell again. "Charlie." His voice a barely audible whisper.

No reply.

"Charlie." A little louder, but not too much. The last thing they needed was for curious deputies to be investigating strange sounds from the holding cells.

Something stirred beneath the blanket, and the figure in the cot sat up, rubbing his eyes. Just enough light from the outside fell across his brother's face to confirm it was Charlie.

"Charlie, wake up, you dang fool."

Charlie sprang from the cot and rushed to the window. "Grady! Thank God!"

Charlie was young, with his shock of blond hair disheveled from sleep. He was a thin and wiry kid, all crazy jumping-bean energy when he wasn't just waking up. Clean-shaven.

"Keep your voice down, idiot," Grady said. "How many deputies in there?"

"Two in the front office, I think," Charlie whispered. "Playing cards. You here to bust me out?"

"Gonna blow this window with dynamite."

Charlie glanced over his shoulder. "Not a lot of places to take cover in here."

"You prefer we leave you?"

"Just tell me what to do."

"Get the mattress off that cot," Grady said. "Huddle in the farthest corner and cover yourself with the mattress."

"That'll work?"

"You'd better hope."

"Dang it, Grady!"

"There's no time to argue," Grady insisted. "Now get under the mattress."

Charlie did as he was told.

"Boris, let me down," Grady said.

The Russian lowered him to the ground, then took two sticks of dynamite from inside his vest. He seemed to hesitate.

"What's wrong?" Grady Jenks asked.

"I'm not sure if to use one or two," Boris said. "One is *maybe* enough, but if not, then noise will bring deputies, and we won't have time to try again."

"Fine, then use two."

"*Da*, of course, but—"

"But what?"

"But maybe, well, you know explosion will be big," Boris said. "Maybe blow your brother to bits."

"*You're* supposed to be the expert," Grady reminded him.

"Two." A crazy grin and a hint of madness in the Russian's eyes. "Bigger explosion."

"Okay, then."

Grady hoisted the Russian up, and Boris tied the two sticks to one of the bars with some twine. There was the sound of a match striking, then the hiss of a burning fuse. Jenks hated fuses. They were so unpredictable.

Boris jumped down. "Run!"

The Russian ran down the street, and Grady Jenks sprinted after him. They dove behind a stack of barrels at the rear of a mercantile and huddled on the ground with their arms over their heads. Grady had braced himself, but the blast still made him flinch.

The explosion rocked the entire street, a thunderous crack filling up the world.

Grady scrambled to his feet and jogged toward the back wall of the jail. The entire wall had been demolished, bricks and iron bars spilling out into the street. A cloud of dust hung in the air.

He waved the dust from in front of his face. "Charlie?" He could already hear Tillis and Farkas coming up behind him with the horses.

Charlie came stumbling out, almost tripping and falling on the loose bricks. He coughed. Charlie was covered in dust and little bits of rubble.

"You okay?"

"What?" Charlie stuck a pinky finger in one ear and shook his head. "I can't hear nothing. I got bells going off."

"Never mind." Grady Jenks pushed his little brother toward one of the horses. "Let's just get out of here."

They mounted up and headed down the street.

Right when two deputies rounded the corner, blocking their way. Both went for their six-shooters.

Grady Jenks's Schofield was in his hand in a heartbeat as he galloped toward the two deputies. He fired, and one of the deputies spun around, blood spraying from his shoulder. Jenks swung the revolver at the other deputy and fired, but the man had already jumped out of the way, throwing himself to the ground as Jenks and his gang galloped past in a racket of hooves and pistol shots.

Grady Jenks twisted in the saddle, squeezed off three more shots at the two deputies, not even trying to hit them, but making sure they stayed down. He started to make a right turn as planned, to lead the boys out of town, when a big freight wagon moved into the middle of the road, unexpectedly blocking his way.

His horse reared, and he jerked on the reins, wheeling the animal the other direction, not really thinking where he was going, just knowing he had to keep moving. The six of them rode like the devil himself was chasing them.

And unfortunately rode right past the saloon where Jimmy had been to show himself to the sheriff. The sheriff and a dozen men erupted from the saloon's swinging front doors. The explosion had grabbed everyone's attention, of course, and the shooting and galloping horses had brought them all spilling out into the street.

Grady Jenks fired twice and then the Schofield clicked empty. Farkas and Tillis took up the slack, blazing away with their six-shooters, spitting lead all over the place. The sheriff and the rest of them scattered, diving to the ground.

"Ride!" Grady shouted.

They kept going until they were well out of town, and Grady reined in his horse, the others halting also and gathering around him.

"It'll take them a bit to get a posse together, but probably not as long as we'd want. You know what to do," Jenks reminded them. "Teams of two. We'll meet at the rendezvous. Charlie, you're with me."

The others took off, and Charlie nudged his horse

alongside his brother's. "Don't think I ain't grateful for busting me out, but what exactly are we up to?"

Grady grinned. "Gold, little brother, gold. All you could ever want."

"Sounds like a story."

"That's for sure, but not here," Grady Jenks said. "Now let's ride!"

CHAPTER 15

They might have made it to Kimball by sundown that next day, but the professor's wagon was a cumbersome, slow-moving thing, so they were obliged to make camp short of their goal. Lieutenant Jacobs and the other troopers didn't seem to mind. They'd rescued Parker and the others and hadn't lost a man in the process and were still basking in the glow of a job well done.

They hit Kimball the next day, and Jacobs called a halt on the edge of town.

"We need to get back to our fort," Jacobs told Parker. "We've got good daylight left, so we should make a start. Kimball ain't much, but you can resupply before moving on. Some of the folks here still call it Antelopeville, so don't let that confuse you."

"Thanks again," Parker said. "We'd have been dead meat without you."

The two men shook hands, then the lieutenant led his men away.

"Let's get going and see what we have to work with." Meriweather flicked the reins, and the wagon lurched into Kimball.

They passed through an outer circle of low adobe buildings and then a shack and a short wooden platform that passed for a railroad station. Where the tracks went, Parker didn't have a guess. The main street wasn't much, as Jacobs had said, a half dozen buildings on each side. The few people out and about paused to gawk at Meriweather's wagon but offered little in the way of welcoming hospitality beyond an occasional polite nod.

Professor Meriweather brought the wagon to a halt in front of the livery stable. He climbed down from the bench and took a step out into the street, hands in his trouser pockets, as he made a slow turn, giving the town the once over.

Parker dismounted and looped his horse's reins over the nearest hitching post, then stood next to Meriweather. "Doesn't look like much, does it?"

Meriweather cleared his throat, made a *hmmmm* noise, then said, "I'm slowly reaching the same conclusion. I'm trying to judge if this is a likely town to set up for one of my demonstrations. On the one hand, I'm sure they don't get a lot of entertainment out this way, and I'm likely to be something of a novelty. On the other hand, I suspect these nice people might not have the required disposable income to purchase my admittedly exotic products."

Parker grinned. "I wouldn't mind seeing the show myself, but I'm definitely short on disposable income."

"Now, don't be silly, my boy," Meriweather said. "You would, of course, qualify for the friends-and-family discount."

They stood another moment, and then Parker asked, "So what's the verdict?"

The professor considered a moment, sucking his teeth, before finally shaking his head. "I think not. And anyway, I haven't trained our young Miss Annie yet how to properly assist me. Let us take advantage of our being in civilization—such as it is—and resupply as we think best, and then we can be on our way. I need more oats for the horses at the very least."

Meriweather entered the livery to ask about horse feed, and Parker took a slow stroll down the street, acutely aware the next moment that Annie was beside him.

"Going shopping?" Parker asked.

She shook her head. "No money."

Oh, yeah. "Don't worry. We'll feed you."

They entered a general store, and Parker bought more coffee, flour, and beans. There was a basket of fresh corn, and Parker grabbed three ears. Potatoes for boiling.

He spied bottles of whiskey on the shelf behind the clerk. "How much for the whiskey?"

"Two dollars," the Clerk said. "I got the good stuff locked in the cabinet."

"Never mind the good stuff. I'll take a bottle." The professor had put a significant dent in the supply Parker had taken from Eiger's.

He glanced at a glass jar of licorice sticks on the counter. "How much for those?"

"Two for a penny."

"Any meat?" Parker asked. "Pork or beef?"

"Nothing like that," the clerk said. "My brother's in the back butchering an antelope he shot this morning. I can give you two pounds off the haunch for a dollar."

Parker nodded, then asked, "Throw in two of them licorice sticks?"

"Sure."

"Wrap it up."

They left the general store a few minutes later with their supplies. Parker handed Annie one of the licorice sticks.

She beamed. "You're nice."

"Nice, huh? All it takes is a penny candy?"

"And saving me from Indians," she said dryly. "Twice."

Parker laughed and shook his head. "Only thing I did the first time was find you. And it was the U.S. Cavalry that saved all of us the second time."

"You thought of that smoke to bring them," Annie said. "Smart."

"Lucky," Parker corrected.

"I'm making a new rule starting right now," Annie said. "When I give you a compliment, you take it politely."

Parker raised an eyebrow. "I have more compliments coming my way anytime soon?"

"Let's see if you earn some." She bit off a chunk of licorice, grinning around it as she chewed.

They met the professor back at the wagon where he was loading oats into the back. "Never fear, my boy, I got enough for your horse, too."

"Obliged," Parker said. "And I think I can rustle us up a good dinner tonight."

"Then let us linger no longer," Meriweather told them. "I suggest we find a likely spot on the outskirts of this teeming city and set up a comfortable camp."

There was still plenty of daylight left after they'd finished setting up camp. They'd found a pleasant spot with a few trees along a shallow stream. Parker watered the horses as the professor built the cook fire. He glanced over and saw Annie a few yards downstream. She sat on the edge of the stream and hiked the bottom of her dress up to her knees, then she unlaced and pried off each shoe and set them aside. She edged forward, dangling her feet in the cool water.

Parker looked at her legs. They were a bit skinny, but long and smooth and white. He watched as she kicked in the stream, water splashing, feet slender, toes pink. He turned away before she caught him looking, feeling warmth flood his cheeks. He led the horses away and hobbled them in the shade beneath a tree, then joined Meriweather at the cook fire. Together, they went to work on dinner.

Corn. Biscuits. Potatoes boiling in the pot. Parker had cut the antelope haunch into chunks and cooked them on skewers over the fire. The smell hit them hard, making their mouths water. They served it all up on tin plates and went about the serious work of eating without conversation, chewing and smacking lips, with an occasional *mmmm* to indicate appreciation.

Finally, they all sat back, bellies tight. Parker broke out the whiskey bottle, much to the professor's delight.

"Pass that bottle this way," Annie said.

"You don't like it," Parker replied.

"I've nearly been killed by Indians twice," Annie said. "I'm not going through this life anymore without trying new things."

Parker passed her the bottle. She tilted it back, taking a sizable gulp, her face scrunching up as she swallowed, and for a moment, Parker feared she was about to give it back. Annie swallowed, winced, then coughed.

"Smooth, isn't it?" Meriweather laughed.

Annie passed the bottle back to Parker. "Okay. Now I can say I've had whiskey."

And maybe that's all she'd really wanted, Parker mused. To be part of things, to feel like she was joining in on the fun Parker and Meriweather were having. Her folks were dead, and maybe she just wanted to connect again with people, with a new family, and there weren't a lot of folks to choose from. Just a part-time deputy and an old medicine barker—but beggars can't be choosers.

Parker sucked down a double-size gulp, then passed the bottle to the professor.

Meriweather took a modest sip, and said, "You know, the three of us sort of fell in together as a matter of fate. Perhaps we should make it a more formal arrangement."

"How do you mean?" Parker asked.

"Well, we make a good team, don't you think?" Meriweather said. "Blooded together on the field of battle, so to speak. I propose we continue to travel together, and not only for the pleasant fellowship. There is also safety to consider. I shudder to think what might have happened if those red savages had happened upon me while I was still traveling the wilds all by my lonesome."

It struck Parker suddenly that he hadn't thought of doing anything else. He'd simply been rolling along with what each new day presented. But of course, Professor

Meriweather and his garish wagon might want to take off for anywhere—California, Oregon, Idaho!

"I need work," Annie said. "Sounds good to me. I mean, if you still want me to be your assistant."

"Indeed, I do," Meriweather assured her. "As a matter of fact, we should begin your training soon. Never fear, girl, it's nothing beyond your abilities."

That's when Parker realized that anywhere the professor went, Annie would go, too. In a short time, he'd become accustomed to her face, her laugh, her smile.

"I need to go to Wyoming," Parker told the professor. "If that suits you."

"I've heard good things about Cheyenne," Meriweather said. "I'm sure I could flog my wares there."

"Okay, then." Parker glanced briefly at Annie, then back at Meriweather. "I guess we can all keep on together. I mean, it sounds like the safe thing to do. Like you said."

"Then it's settled!" Meriweather said with enthusiasm. "Let's drink on it, shall we?"

They passed the bottle around again, Annie only taking a very tiny sip this time.

The three of them talked for another hour or so, Parker and Professor Meriweather slowly making the bottle disappear. Parker would have preferred a few cold beers, but he found, suddenly, he was in a good mood and wanted to drink.

"So why Wyoming?" Meriweather asked.

Parker almost muttered something about sheriff's business or some such other dodge. Maybe it was the warm feeling in his belly from the booze, or maybe the warmth of newfound friendship, but he found he didn't want to lie. He was far from home, and these people were all he was likely to get in the way of friends. He thought himself a coolheaded, stone-hearted loner when he'd set out to find the gold, but he'd been kidding himself. Normal human beings need other human beings in their lives.

And yet . . .

He'd feel a dang fool just to blurt out he was looking for stolen gold. He'd come to terms over the long miles that he was on a wild-goose chase. This wasn't really about gold at all, Parker was realizing. It was about forging his own path in this wild world around him. The whole fanciful notion of a treasure hunt was just the kick in the butt he'd needed to get him out the door.

"I, um, have this map," he heard himself say before he could stop the words from coming out of his mouth.

"Oh?" Meriweather's curiosity was piqued.

"I mean, it's probably nothing—"

"Nonsense!" Meriweather insisted. "Let's have a look at this map, eh?"

Parker felt he'd committed himself to a path there was no turning back from. He reached inside his vest and pulled out the map he'd found behind the old general's portrait in Dowager Filmore's house. As he unfolded it, Meriweather scooted in closer for a look.

Annie came from around the other side of the fire. "I want to see, too." She squeezed in close, and Parker was acutely aware that she pressed right up against him, her warmth seeming to flood Parker's cheeks and ears with a dizzying heat.

Forget it, idiot. Just show them the map.

Parker held it up, and the other two leaned in to look.

"If either of you two can make heads or tails of this, I'd be grateful," Parker said. "Lots of lines and places to go, and numbers, but it don't mean much without a starting point—which looks to me like a giant tree stump."

"An apt description," Meriweather said. "I have some experience with cartography, so—"

"Car what?" Parker asked.

"Maps."

"Oh."

"I see various lines . . . a river, and then a few roads or paths . . ." Meriweather sighed. "Yes, I'm forced to agree. Without knowing the starting point, it's all quite useless."

Parker's heart sank. It had been stupid to hope Meriweather might know something, but the professor was an educated man. Something on the map might have looked familiar.

"How do you even know it's in Wyoming?" Annie asked.

That was a pretty good question, actually. Parker had naturally assumed. The train robbery had happened in Wyoming, and that much gold would be heavy and difficult to move without attracting attention. But of course, there could have been a hundred other scenarios and factors Parker hadn't thought of.

Not that he planned to tell Annie any of this. It would only make him look like a dimwit. "Well, it's kind of a long story."

"What's that?" Annie leaned in to point to an *X* on the map. Doing so pressed her body even more against Parker's, and he began to feel lightheaded.

"That's the proverbial *X*, my dear," Meriweather said. "Haven't you heard that *X* traditionally marks the spot on treasure maps?"

"Treasure?" Annie sat up, excitement creeping into her voice.

"Now wait a minute," Parker said.

"That's it, isn't it?" Meriweather was sounding as enthusiastic as Annie. "Out with it, lad. Cortez's gold? The riches of the ancient pharaohs?"

"Nobody said nothing about no treasure. It's just deputy sheriff business." But it sounded feeble to Parker even as he said it. Why be so cagey if it was simply routine business?

Annie grabbed Parker's arm with both hands. "Tell us, Parker! You've just got to. It's too exciting to keep to yourself!"

Parker groaned.

"Now, are we comrades, or are we not?" Meriweather asked, with the authority gained by knowing the answer. "Did we not fend off a fierce Indian raid together? All three of us? Fate has bound us. Mystery and adventure calls. It has come to us in the form of this enigmatic map. We must pool our resources—*our brainpower*—and figure it out, surely."

"I suppose, and—I'm not sure, okay? But maybe"— Parker looked from Annie to the professor—"it's just possible that the map leads to a big pile of, well, gold."

Annie and Meriweather both whooped excitement at the same time.

Idiot, idiot, idiot, Parker chastised himself.

"Back in a moment," Meriweather said. "I think we have a cause for celebration."

He grunted as he rose and then hurried to the wagon.

"Is this really a map to gold?" Annie was no longer looking at the map but hadn't moved away from Parker, and her weight pressed against him was a distinct distraction.

"Uh, I don't know really," Parker said. "I didn't say anything before because I can't be sure. The whole thing might be a fairy story."

Meriweather returned with another bottle, long necked and fat at the base.

"This is quite a good brandy," the professor said. "I've saved it for, well, I wasn't sure *what* for, until now. Seems a fitting way to launch our new adventure."

The professor pulled the cork, took a swig, and sighed contentment, before passing the bottle to Parker.

Parker had never had brandy before. He tilted the bottle back. It went down warm and strong, but without the harsh bite of the cheap whiskey. He still would rather have had a beer, but the brandy was an improvement over the previous bottle by a mile.

Parker passed the bottle to Annie. "You'll like this better."

She hesitated, then took a sip. She still winced, but not so bad.

Meriweather took charge of the bottle again and drank. "Come now, my lad, tell us more of this gold. It would tickle an old man's fancy if it really *were* the gold of Cortez, but I'm sure it's something far more plausible, eh? Is it an abandoned gold mine? We're not going to have to dig this gold out of the ground ourselves, are we?" He chuckled.

Parker fought down a brief flash of annoyance. Who was this fella to horn in on his gold?

Then again, it wasn't really Parker's gold, either, was it? He was horning in as much as anyone. Maybe he was tired of carrying around the secret. Or maybe it was the booze, warm in his belly. Or maybe he just wanted to see the look on the professor's face. So why not? Why not spill the whole story.

"The gold is a stolen payroll from a train robbery," Parker said.

Meriweather froze, the bottle halfway to his mouth. "Oh."

"And there's a gang of murderous outlaws looking for the gold, too," Parker added. "And a U.S. marshal named Tanner Best is after the outlaws."

A long, quiet moment. The campfire crackled.

Meriweather looked at the bottle of brandy and sighed. "Well, it's already open. Might as well."

He took another drink. A big one.

CHAPTER 16

Parker sat slumped in his saddle, a dull headache behind his eyes. Too much to drink last night. Too much talk last night.

The news that the gold was from a train robbery and that finding it might involve running afoul of outlaws had put a damper on Meriweather's enthusiasm for the adventure. Annie understood right away that the gold, of course, would have to go back to the rightful owners. There was a part of Parker that knew she was right and another part that resented having it said out loud. He liked fantasizing about the gold, and how he'd spend it, and what his life of luxury would be like, riding back into Rory's Junction in a new suit—and then Bonnie Morgan could just eat her heart out.

But that was some kid's fantasy. Parker knew better. He should probably rip that stupid map to pieces and toss them to the wind.

But he didn't.

* * *

Cheyenne wasn't so terribly far away, but it was two and a half days going at the slow pace of the professor's wagon. They stopped on the outskirts of the town and made camp, built a fire, watered and fed the horses, all of it routine and habit by now.

Parker was restless. It was probably his imagination, but he had the feeling the other two—especially Meriweather—were disappointed in him, getting their hopes up about an exciting treasure hunt, only to have those same hopes dashed with a cold splash of reality. The stolen payroll, after all, was obviously something best left to the law.

"I'm going to ride into Cheyenne and have a look around," Parker announced.

Annie looked up, hopeful.

But before she could invite herself along, Meriweather said, "You go ahead, my boy. Annie and I will rehearse our presentation for tomorrow."

Annie tried to hide her disappointment, doing a poor job of it.

Parker climbed onto his horse and headed into town. A mug of beer in a proper saloon would do him a world of good.

Marshal Tanner Best tossed his cards on the table. "Fold." He hadn't had a good hand all afternoon.

Best had ridden into Cheyenne with only the vaguest of plans. He was out of ideas and only knew that he needed to start over. So he'd decided to go back to the beginning and see what he'd missed the first time around. The train robbery had been here. He could ask around. Maybe somebody had seen something or heard some loose talk.

He'd tried to pick up Grady Jenks's trail after the shootout at Eiger's, but the outlaw had gotten away with too much of a head start, and heavy rains had obscured the tracks enough to make picking up a trail impossible.

So here he was, still dusty from travel, nursing a warm beer and losing at cards in the Golden Buffalo Saloon. He hadn't really been paying much attention to the cards the last few hands, anyway. Instead, he kept a close eye on the man at the far end of the bar, trying not to be too obvious about it.

At first, he'd simply wanted the man to turn around so that he could get a better look at his face. The likenesses on the wanted posters could be notoriously unreliable. Eventually Best got the view he wanted and confirmed the man's identity.

Jasper Langhorne was wanted for cattle rustling, arson, highway robbery, and murder. An easy five hundred dollars. All Best had to do was stand, draw one of his Remingtons, and shoot the man in the head. It would cause quite a commotion in the Golden Buffalo, but then Best would flash his U.S. marshal's badge, and everyone would fall in line. Tanner Best hadn't come to Cheyenne looking for Jasper Langhorne, but he was loathe to pass up an opportunity. A payday was a payday, after all.

And if he was going to do it, then he might as well do it right and go all the way. Jasper was known to associate with a handful of other no-goods, who also had prices on their heads. If Best played his cards right, he could take them all, and that would be a hefty payday indeed.

Speaking of cards . . . Best threw in his hand and scooted his chair back from the table. "Gentlemen, it's been fun, but Lady Luck isn't with me today. I'll leave you to it."

The other men at the table mumbled various pleasantries, as Best stood and went to the bar. He ordered a beer and made sure to face away from Langhorne, keeping track of the man in a convenient mirror.

Langhorne leaned at the bar, hunched over his shot glass of whiskey, head down, keeping to himself. He had the look of a man who wanted a quiet drink, his posture indicating he was not in the market for friendly conversation. That suited Best. Maybe the man would finish his drink in a timely fashion and be on his way, and then Best could trail him—hopefully, to the rest of his gang.

It occurred to Best that Langhorne might want to take some time with one of the Golden Buffalo's sporting ladies. That would be inconvenient. Best didn't want to wait around that long, and he also didn't want to lose sight of Langhorne. Glancing about the interior of the saloon put that concern to rest. It was too early in the day for the ladies to be about selling their goods.

A few minutes passed. Langhorne looked at his pocket watch, tucked it back into his vest pocket, downed the remainder of his whiskey, and turned to the front door.

Best finished his beer and let Langhorne exit before following.

Best left the Golden Buffalo, and stood in front of the saloon a moment, letting his eyes adjust. It always struck him as odd coming out of a saloon into the harsh sunlight. He generally didn't frequent such places in daylight hours. He caught sight of Langhorne heading up the street and followed at a discreet distance.

Five minutes later, Langhorne turned in to the livery stable.

Best frowned. If Langhorne was fetching his horse, then possibly, he was heading out to meet up with the rest of his boys. That would put an end to Best's plan to take the whole gang. Best's horse was tied up back at the Golden Buffalo. The only thing to do was take Langhorn in the stable and leave the rest of the gang for another time.

He took the badge from his pocket and pinned it on the lapel of his coat. Then he swept the coat back, his twin six-shooters gleaming in the sun.

Okay, let's get this over with.

He entered the livery stable—and immediately saw he'd made a miscalculation.

Jasper Langhorne had indeed been on his way to meet the rest of his gang. In fact, he was meeting them right here in the livery stable.

Langhorn and three other men were in the middle of saddling horses and chatting back and forth. They didn't take much notice of Best, at first, but then the talk died away. All of them going stone still, and Best knew they'd seen the badge.

"Jasper Langhorne. I'm Marshal Tanner Best. Looks like you got Fox Thorndyke and Bob Gordon with you." Best squinted at the fourth man. "I don't know you, but I'm assuming you're in with the rest of these scoundrels, so I reckon you all should just throw down them guns and come quiet."

A bunch of eyeballs bounced back and forth, all four of them waiting for somebody else to do or say something.

"Four of us against one of you," Langhorne said finally. "Trust me, lawman, that tin star ain't bulletproof. Walk away, or you'll get yours—and that's a promise."

"Throw down the guns, boys," Best told them with mock patience. "You've been warned. I'm now at the end of any obligation I might have had to take you in alive."

They looked at each other for a long moment, and Best considered the situation, deciding who'd get it first. Langhorne was closest, his hands free, one hanging loose down by his six-shooter. Fox Thorndyke was a lanky man with a hawk beak for a nose. He stood behind his horse, so that would be a harder shot. Bob Gordon was beefy and short, and had his hands full of his saddle so would be slow on the draw. The fourth one was all the way in the back. If he was smart, he'd take off for the back door when the shooting started.

It always amazed Best how few of these fellas were smart.

Best opened his mouth to give them a last warning. Maybe they'd wise up, after all, and—

Langhorne went for his six-gun. It was only halfway out of his holster when Best's Remingtons appeared in his hands as if by magic. He squeezed off two shots, the racket startling the horses, who moved around, creating confusion. Langhorne clutched his bloody chest and dropped.

As predicted, Bob was slow on the draw, having to drop the saddle first. Best took the easy shot, plugging the man right between the eyes. Bob's head snapped back, and he staggered into one of the horses before going down. The horse spooked and kicked, its rear hooves slamming into the fourth man, sending him flying across the stable with a grunt.

Thorndyke wasn't a fast draw, but he didn't need to be from his place behind the horse. He squeezed off three quick shots with his Colt Thunderer, but Best was already moving to one side and going low, Thorndyke's shots chewing up wood in the stall behind the marshal.

Best went to his belly and saw Thorndyke's legs between the horses. He squeezed the trigger, and the Remington in his left hand spat fire.

Thorndyke's right knee exploded in a burst of blood and bone. He hit the ground hard, screaming his face off.

Best shot again, blasting a bloody hole in the top of Thorndyke's head.

Everything went suddenly quiet, smoke hanging in the air, the horses calming a bit. Best stood slowly, holstering one Remington, but keeping the other ready. A groan from back in the stable drew his attention.

Best maneuvered between the horses and found

the fourth man—the one he didn't know—lying flat on his back, holding his ribs, wincing and groaning and generally acting like a man just kicked by a horse.

"Busted ribs, I reckon," Best said.

The man held out a trembling hand. "Please . . . *please . . .*"

"Uh-huh." Best lifted the Remington and fired.

The man on the ground took the lead square in the chest. He kicked once and died.

"Sorry about that," Best said. "Looked like you were going for your gun."

Best holstered his six-gun and took out his pipe. He glanced around the stable, spotted a small stool, had a seat, and lit the pipe.

Now, to wait. He figured they'd be along in a minute.

And they didn't disappoint.

Four deputies burst into the stable, all pointing rifles at Best.

"Don't you move, mister!" one of the deputies ordered. "We've sent for the sheriff."

"Good, he can sign a voucher for me." Best thumbed the star on his lapel. "Tanner Best, U.S. marshal."

They traded words, and the deputies lowered their rifles. If anyone was allowed to go around shooting folks, they reckoned it was a U.S. marshal, although they still respectfully requested that Best come along with them to the jailhouse and get things sorted with the sheriff.

Best agreed. He knew the routine.

They arranged for some men to come pick up the

bodies while Best cooled his heels and waited for the sheriff. He smoked his pipe and waited.

The sheriff arrived, harried and shouting. Local law almost always had the same reaction to lead flying in their town, but the sheriff was polite enough when he learned it was a U.S. marshal doing the shooting. The sheriff was a reasonable man named Baker, and he offered Best a shot of whiskey while they went over the details.

"Langhorne, Thorndyke, and Gordon," Baker said. "We've confirmed their identities, and you're right. They all got paper on them. Even that other fella you didn't know. Name's Earl Price. A hundred dollars for cattle rustling."

"I'd appreciate a voucher, if you don't mind, sheriff," Best said.

"Of course. The bank's still open for another forty minutes. They can handle the transaction for you," Baker explained. "You know I've got a few salty deputies on the payroll here in Cheyenne. Next time you're hunting down villains, there's no need to go it alone. A heads-up would do us both some good."

Best smiled. "Well, it was just one of those things, sheriff. Sometimes the fish jump right in the boat."

Baker signed the voucher and handed it to Best, who went down a few blocks to the bank. Usually, Best would have to wait for the reward money to be wired, but sometimes you shoot the right man in the right town, and with the right bank, things just work out. Best walked out of the bank ten minutes later with eleven hundred dollars.

The marshal felt like celebrating his windfall. He got a nice room at a swanky hotel, and by the time he walked out of the lobby, the day had cooled into evening. Best walked back to the Golden Buffalo, wondering if the sporting ladies had come out of hibernation yet.

CHAPTER 17

Night had fallen, and the sound of laughter and a tinny piano drew Parker Jones toward the Golden Buffalo.

He pushed through the saloon's flapping doors, and smells hit him, tobacco and booze, and the sound, too, lively conversation, the man in the corner attacking the piano like it had insulted his sister. Men drank and played cards, and saloon gals made their rounds, looking wonderfully garish in skimpy outfits and too much makeup. There was a good crowd, but no doubt it would get more crowded still, as the evening wore on.

Parker claimed some real estate at the bar and waved down the burly man in the apron.

"Haven't seen you before, stranger," said the barkeep.

"Just rode in," Parker said.

"Ah, then you missed the excitement," he said. "They captured some outlaws earlier. Well, maybe *captured* ain't exactly the right word. Shot 'em all up pretty good, I heard tell."

Parker's ears perked up at the word outlaws. Was it possible Grady Jenks and his boys had made it back to Cheyenne? "Who was it, do you know?"

"Jasper Langhorne and his gang," the barkeep said. "Some bad men. Jasper drank right at this very bar."

"You don't say." Not Jenks, then. "How about a beer?"

"Coming right up."

The barkeep brought the beer, and Parker took a long swig. To say it hit the spot would have been the understatement of the decade. He drank the beer in record time and made himself take the next one slowly.

He leaned against the bar, feeling good, and took a nice long gander around the interior of the Golden Buffalo. It was bigger and grander than Clancy's back home, and big mirrors stretching up and down the walls made it look grander still. Light fixtures painted gold. An oil painting at least eight feet wide showed off a woman, naked as a jaybird, reclining on a chaise longue. She definitely caught the eye, although she was a bit chubby for Parker's taste.

Whatever lingering whiff of guilt Parker might have felt leaving Annie and the professor to run off and have a good time vanished with the next beer. He struck up a conversation with a cattleman, and then had a short talk with a haberdasher. Seemed all kinds came and went in the Golden Buffalo.

The crowd had doubled since Parker had entered the saloon. Watching all the different people fascinated him. So many different types of—

He did a double take, eyes landing on a familiar face across the saloon, near the piano player. Marshal Tanner Best. There could be no mistake. What could that man be doing here?

The answer was obvious. He was on the trail of

Grady Jenks. Maybe he was even looking for the gold. Surely, one led to the other. He screwed up the courage to cross the room and say hello to the man who'd saved his bacon back at Eiger's.

Then stopped himself.

Best had put his arm around one of the saloon gals who'd been working the room. She had a mess of impossibly yellow hair piled on her head, and her bodice threatened to burst. The two of them were obviously getting acquainted, and Parker was not about to interrupt. He'd trade pleasantries with the marshal another time.

Parker ordered another beer and continued watching the saloon patrons. A bevy of saloon gals had appeared and wove in and out of the crowd. When one walked within a few feet, Parker was hit by an overpowering perfume, too sweet. In a way, the ladies were off-putting, with so much makeup and their brazen demeanor.

But then again, those were the exact qualities that held his attention.

Parker tore his eyes from the ladies and gulped beer. *Behave yourself, fool.*

His eyes roamed the room again until they fell on the one man who seemed to be having a bad time, a hard-looking hombre sporting a scowl, eyes sharp with hate, a lean and angry fellow with his black hat tugged low over his eyes. Maybe ten years older than Parker. Five days of black stubble down each jaw.

The hombre's eyes never wavered, looking daggers at something. Parker followed his gaze and realized he was looking straight at Tanner Best. Parker watched as the hombre slowly started walking toward the marshal, hands held low.

Nobody but Parker saw when the blade dropped from the man's sleeve, six inches of gleaming razor-sharp steel. Parker's eyes went wide, not sure if he was seeing right. By chance, the crowd parted, giving the hombre a clear path to the marshal. Best turned his back, his attention completely on his female companion.

It was clear as day to Parker what was about to happen next.

He grabbed a bottle off the bar and chased after the hombre.

The man headed for Best drew the knife back to strike just as the marshal turned, eyes going wide as if he was trying to figure out what was happening.

Parker cracked the bottle across the back of the hombre's skull, shattered glass raining and whiskey splashing everywhere. The hombre's eyes rolled up, and he wilted into a pile at Best's feet.

"Hey, somebody just clobbered Hank!" a voice shouted.

Hands grabbed Parker from behind. From out of nowhere, a fist slammed into Parker's gut, doubling him over. His stomach churned, and he threatened to give back all the beer he'd been drinking.

In the next moment, Parker was curled on the floor, men shouting and cursing and kicking him.

Then the thunder of a pistol shot shook the room. Everyone fell quiet, backing away from Parker, who looked up to see Tanner Best pointing a smoking Remington at the ceiling.

"Everyone, just calm down," Best said. "I know this man."

The next few minutes were a bit of a blur for Parker. He was helped to his feet. The sheriff arrived, again looking perturbed, and there was a lot of talk and questions.

"That's Hank Langhorne," Sheriff Baker said. "It's obvious he wasn't too pleased about you gunning down his brother."

Best sighed. "Wouldn't be the first time."

"Okay, show's over, everyone," Baker told the crowd. "Go about your business."

Parker was helped onto a barstool, and a few of the men who'd been kicking him mumbled apologies and slapped him on the back. The barkeep poured him a free beer. Parker sat a few minutes, taking deep breaths. The gut punch had hurt like the dickens, but he was okay now. No permanent damage.

"You do turn up in the damnedest places, son."

Parker looked up to see Tanner Best moving to lean against the bar next to him. "What brings you to Cheyenne?"

Parker had a strong urge to tell the marshal everything, but something stopped him. Maybe he just didn't have the energy for it. "Just passing through. Trying to find my place."

"A young man off on an adventure, eh?" Best stuck his unlit pipe in his mouth.

"Something like that," Parker said.

"I appreciate your timely intervention," Best told him. "I was obliged to gun down Hank Langhorne's big brother today. It would appear he took it awry. Anyway, I owe you."

"I reckon we're pretty much even," Parker said. "I was in a tight spot in Eiger's. Hate to think what would've happened if you hadn't showed up."

Best shrugged as if to acknowledge maybe Parker had a point. "The point is that six inches of cold steel would have ruined my whole night, and I've got plans with a lady. When somebody does me a favor like that, I make it a point to show my appreciation."

"I appreciate that, marshal," Parker said. "I wouldn't want you to go to any trouble."

"No trouble at all, son." Best pointed at the ceiling. "Upstairs. Room Three."

Parker frowned. "I'm not sure I understand, marshal."

Best winked. "Room Three."

The marshal turned, waded back into the crowd, and caught up with his lady friend.

All the way on the left side of the saloon, a flight of stairs led upward, then a railing around the second floor so people could stand up there and look down. Parker was suddenly very tired, his enthusiasm for the evening draining away after getting kicked and punched. Would Best be insulted if he didn't accept his token of appreciation?

Slowly he rose from his barstool and crossed the room. He went up the stairs, a mixture of curiosity and nervousness mixing in his gut. At the top, he found himself at the end of a long walkway, doors on one side, the railing on the other. There was a thick haze up here, the smoke from all the cigars and pipes and cigarettes gathered and trapped.

He glanced at the first door on his left. Door of Room One. He kept going, two doors down, and lifted his fist to knock, hesitated.

Parker took a deep breath and knocked.

"Come in." A woman's voice.

Parker opened the door and walked in.

She was young, maybe even a year or two younger than Parker. Red hair piled high. Makeup too heavy. Lips as red as fresh strawberries.

"Come in and close the door." She sat on the edge of the bed. "I'm Louise."

Parker stepped into the room and pulled the door shut behind him.

"Marshal Best sent me. He said Room Three."

Louise smiled. "I know." She brought one foot up on the bed, rolled the stocking down over her knee then her ankle and off, pointed her toes, the nails painted a bright red. She repeated the process with the other leg.

Parker swallowed hard, felt his heart bang around inside his chest.

Louise leaned back on the bed, her grin showing straight white teeth. "He wanted to thank you with a nice gift. I suppose he didn't reckon buying you a drink was enough."

"I, uh . . ." Parker suddenly felt dizzy and hot, sweat behind his ears.

Louise stood and stepped close to him, putting a cool slender hand on his chest, her grin falling, expression going curious. "You want your gift, don't you?"

Yes, yes, yes, yes, yes—"No."

One of her eyebrows went up. "No?"

"I mean, it's not that I—not that I wouldn't—you *are* very pretty, but—" Parker felt like some bumbling fool had taken charge of his mouth.

The curiosity in her eyes deepened, her head tilting to one side as she considered. "This is your first—I mean, you've not done this before, have you?"

Parker sputtered and fumbled over a bunch of words that made no sense before finally saying, "Well, I mean— not exactly."

"You got another girl?" Louise asked.

"Yes."

Parker had no idea why he'd said that. Was he thinking of Annie, or was it just easier to say his heart belonged to another than to admit he was so nervous, it felt like all his insides were about to come up and shoot out his mouth?

Louise shrugged. "Well, I'm bought and paid for."

Parker didn't know what to say to that.

"Go down to the end of the hall," Louise said. "There's a little door. It's the only door without a number on it. Go in and there's a narrow flight of stairs. They're steep, so be careful. Go up to the roof and wait for me. I'll be along in ten minutes or so."

"The roof?"

"Go on."

Parker hesitated only a moment, then left the room. He went to the end of the hall as instructed and through the unmarked door. The stairs were as steep and as narrow as Louise had said, but Parker had no trouble climbing to the top and throwing open a trapdoor above his head. Cool air washed down through the opening. He climbed out onto the roof.

There were two rickety tables and a half-dozen old chairs. Maybe this was where the girls took breaks. Parker went to the edge of the roof and looked down into the street. People came and went, on horses or on foot. A glow came up from the town below, and from three stories in the air struck Parker as an odd but not unpleasant way to take things in. He sat on one of the chairs and waited, then waited some more. Louise had told him ten minutes, but Parker reckoned it had been more like twenty. Maybe she'd played a joke on him or wanted him out of the way so that she could get on with her next client.

But a moment later, she came up the steps carrying a big wicker basket.

"Sorry," she said. "It took a little longer than I thought to get everything together."

Parker noticed immediately Louise no longer wore her saloon gal outfit. She wore an ordinary dress, a pale mint-green color, with white buttons down the front. She'd wiped off all the excessive makeup, so now there was only a natural spray of freckles across the bridge of her nose, red hair loose down over her shoulders. She didn't look like any woman you'd see in the Golden Buffalo. She could have been tagging along after Bonnie Morgan and Mary Lou Shaw on the way to church.

Louise set the basket on one of the tables, and a good smell hit Parker, making his mouth water.

"Fried chicken and biscuits," Louise said. "The woman at the café down the street brings in meals for the girls in the evening. Slade says our time is too valuable to cook meals for ourselves."

"Slade?"

"Bernie Slade," Louise said. "He runs the Golden Buffalo. Anyway, there's always plenty extra."

Parker bit into a thigh. Flavor exploded in his mouth. It was the best thing he'd eaten in a long time.

"I got this, too." Louise took a bottle from the basket. "Wine."

"I never had wine before," Parker admitted. "What kind?"

"Red."

Parker took the bottle and squinted at the label. "Cab— Cabber—"

"Cabernet sauvignon," Louise said. "I didn't say it right the first time, either. Sure ain't how it's spelled. Dang, I forgot glasses."

"We can share out of the bottle," Parker said. "I don't mind, if you don't."

She laughed. Maybe that was actually kinda funny considering all they might have shared.

He pulled the cork and drank. It didn't burn like whiskey. It didn't foam and fizz like beer. He didn't hate it, but he wasn't quite sure what to think about it yet. He handed the bottle back to Louise.

She drank. "Most of the men drink whiskey, but sometimes a fella will want something fancier."

They ate chicken and drank wine.

A few minutes later, Louise blew out a sigh and sat back in her chair, one hand on her stomach. "I'm tight as a tick. You finish the rest if you like." She took another sip of wine.

He grabbed a drumstick from the basket. "Why are we eating up here?"

"I knew there'd be nobody around this time of night," she told him.

"Makes sense."

"And, well, I like it," she said. "It feels so closed in down there sometimes, all the loud talk and the smoke. I hate the smoke more than anything else. Smoking is a filthy habit. It makes a man's breath bad— Oh, no offense if you smoke. A lot of men do."

"I don't," Parker said.

Lousie nodded. "Good. Don't never take it up. The smoke gets all in your clothes and everywhere. But up on the roof, it's clean and quiet. There's air. I like it at night. It's like being in the wide open and hidden at the same time."

Parker understood what she meant. None of the people walking in the streets below had any notion he and Louise were even up there. It was an odd sort of privacy.

"And the stars," Louise said. "I like all the stars. Down on the street, all the light floods in from windows, but you're above that up here on the roof, and all the stars just twinkle and dazzle."

Parker looked up. The sky was beautiful and clear. "You're right. This is a nice spot."

"I'd come up here every night, if I could," she said. "And just sit in the peaceful quiet and watch the stars."

It struck Parker suddenly how relieved Louise must have been that he hadn't wanted to take advantage of Tanner Best's gift. Instead, she'd used the time to bring Parker up to her favorite spot. What had been meant as a gift for him turned out to be respite for her. He was glad. He couldn't change her life, but he could give her an hour of peace and fried chicken, stars and wine.

He took another hit of the cabernet. "This stuff grows on you." But he still liked beer better.

A breeze came out of the west and lifted Louise's hair. She tilted her head back and closed her eyes, letting it wash over her. She was pretty. Parker liked freckles.

Louise opened her eyes and turned to him. "You ever kissed a girl, Parker?"

He blinked, surprised. "Uh—"

She leaned toward him, pressed her lips to his. He froze, heart going like a jackrabbit. He felt his teeth mash against the inside of his lips. She pulled away and laughed.

Parker felt himself go red.

"Relax," she told him. "Part your lips a bit. Let it be soft."

She leaned in again, her lips brushing his, then pressing in a little more. Parker felt he might float away. She pulled away more slowly and didn't laugh this time.

"You're nice, Parker," she said. "If— Well, never mind. Anyway, you should get something from Marshal Best's money." Another long, lingering kiss.

If, she'd said. Parker wondered. *If* he wasn't passing through on his way to somewhere else. *If* she wasn't a saloon gal at the Golden Buffalo. *If* he'd been somebody else, or if she had been. *If* things had been different. Another time. Another place.

A man could choke on so many *ifs*.

"I've got to go." Louise gave him another kiss, a quick smack this time. She stood up from the table. "I need to get back to work. You can finish the wine, if you like." She went to the stairs, paused on the way down to wave, and was gone.

There were a couple swallows of wine left, so Parker emptied the bottle. He waited a bit then went downstairs. He didn't see Louise or Best, or anyone familiar. He got back on his horse and rode out to the camp. He took the saddle off his horse. The fire had burned low. He pulled off his boots and stretched out, head on his saddle. He didn't go right to sleep. But lay there looking up.

The stars went on and on. He wondered if he'd ever look at them the same way again—then laughed, thinking he was being too dramatic—but he could still feel her lips on his, and he knew it didn't matter, that he'd never see her again, and that was fine. But it was a different sort of night than he'd ever experienced before, and that was for sure.

Eventually, he drifted off, the stars keeping watch.

CHAPTER 18

People love spectacle.

At least that's what Professor Meriweather had told Parker, and so far, he was doing a good job of making one of himself.

The medicine show hadn't even begun, and already folks were gathering to gawk. The morning had started late and had proceeded slowly from there. Meriweather had found that late afternoon was the best time to put on one of his medicine shows: when people were closing up shop and on their way home or to dinner or for a well-earned drink at their favorite watering hole. A busy street with many pedestrians was what he wanted, and that's exactly what Meriweather got.

The professor had parked on a street corner, the colorful wagon drawing eyeballs. What happened next completely took Parker by surprise. Meriweather unhooked a couple of latches, and Parker watched as one entire side of the wagon swung down to create a makeshift stage, legs on the forward corners swinging down to provide support. Closed curtains concealed the wagon's interior on the now open side. Meriweather set up a small table on one side of the stage, with a large bowl and various glass vials and bottles full of liquids of all different colors. He lined up some wooden crates on top of which he set up small corked bottles. The label consisted of ornate yellow writing on a black background: *Professor Meriweather's Fortifying Elixir of Miracle Health.*

Annie emerged from between the curtains and strode out onto the stage.

And Parker's eyes almost popped out of his head.

Annie carried what looked like a large metallic dish, black with the outline of an oriental dragon on it in gold. The professor had called it a gong, and Annie had practiced with it earlier that day, smacking it with a drumstick, which produced an eerie ringing sound, deeper and more exotic than the bell Parker's teacher had used in grade school.

But that's not what had caught Parker's attention.

Annie wore a black dress of form-fitting silk. With its high collar buttoned under her chin, the body of the dress wrapped around to button down one side. A long, snarling dragon was stitched in gold down the other side. Even though the dress was long, it was slit up one side to reveal an alarming length of white leg as she walked. Her face had been powdered a stark white, pink blush on the cheeks. She'd put some kind of coloring in her hair to make it look glossy, wet, and midnight black. It had been slicked back, close to the skull, the length of it gathered at the nape of her neck and held together by two thin sticks crisscrossing through the bun. A grease pencil had been used at the corners of her eyes to complete her mysterious, Far-Eastern look.

Her appearance had a confusing effect on Parker. On the one hand, Parker couldn't help comparing how Annie looked to Louise's appearance when Parker had first seen her, all dolled up to catch a man's attention. On the other hand, Annie's getup didn't seem as wanton as Louise's. It was more like Annie was dressed up for playacting.

But the simple fact was, Parker couldn't take his eyes off her. It seemed laughable. He'd thought Annie barely an adolescent when he'd found her, caked in grime, wearing a man's shirt that was oversized on her.

Annie was a woman—young, yes, even younger than Parker—but a woman still.

And Parker felt a flush in his face and a flutter in his chest, and wondered what in the world he was going to do with that realization.

Professor Meriweather raised his hands, and in a loud booming voice said, "Ladies and gentlemen!"

Annie struck the gong three times. *Klong. Klong. Klong.*

The crowd around the wagon stage ceased their muttering to give the professor their attention. Pedestrians passing by paused, some moving toward the garish wagon, their curiosity getting the better of them.

"I am Professor Xavier T. Meriweather, and I've studied at the finest scientific institutes across Europe, where I learned to unlock the secrets of alchemy and the wonders of the natural world."

Annie struck the gong again, and Meriweather pulled

the cork on a tall, thin bottle filled with pink liquid. He poured a liberal amount into the bowl.

"But I did not stop there," Meriweather continued. "I traveled the world and found myself in the Far East, where I delved into ancient oriental secrets."

Annie hit the gong again. The crowd had grown larger. People wanted to see what was going on.

"And finally, after decades of exploration and study," Meriweather said, "I became a master of alchemical manipulation!"

He tossed a pinch of powder into the pink liquid.

A flash and an explosion and a *whumf* as a black cloud of smoke mushroomed into the air, the hint of something fiery orange within the black cloud. The crowd gasped, some taking a step back.

"My friends, I must confide in you." The professor's voice still carried but had simultaneously lowered to a conspiratorial tone. "I have unlocked some of the darkest secrets both modern and ancient science has to offer. Heads of state have approached me with dire propositions, that I should create powerful weapons to help them defeat their enemies." He lowered his voice still further. "It is without exaggeration that I tell you the world would be a different place, if I had accepted some of these offers. If I had taken the obscene amount of gold dangled in front of me, would we at this very moment be living in the Confederate States of America?" A shrug. "I'm not at liberty to say."

A murmur rippled through the crowd, some incredulous, others amazed or intrigued.

Meriweather held up his hand, shook his head. "No,

my friends, no. I am human, and I am ashamed to admit I was tempted. I could be sitting in my own castle in France, sipping fine wine, but that's simply not me. I am a man of science for one simple reason—to aid my fellow man. And that's why I am here with you today."

Annie had set the gong aside, and she now held a bottle of the elixir in each hand. She stood with her hip cocked at an angle, allowing the slit in her dress to fall open, revealing plenty of leg. Parker felt a stab of annoyance when a number of men in the crowd took notice.

"I have dedicated my life to relieving the everyday plagues and ailments of my fellow man," Meriweather said. "I am currently on my way to Denver, where a terrible outbreak of dysentery ravages the citizenry, but close confidants of mine have informed me that the people of Cheyenne are highly intelligent, so I've stopped here, for one day only, to give each and every one of you this rare opportunity to purchase—at an incredible discount, I might add—a highly effective tonic, which will change your life!"

The professor paused a moment to let that sink in.

"How many of your lives are interrupted by everyday ailments, your jobs and marriages, your lives held up by common but annoying—often debilitating—infirmities?" the professor asked. "Professor Meriweather's amazing elixirs have been known to cure or alleviate ninety-three common ailments that keep us from living our lives to the fullest every day." He picked up a bottle and looked at it with reverence. "I have taken the very best of modern medicine and combined it with the ancient secrets of the Far East to create this medical miracle. Sleeplessness, constipation, hangover, fatigue, headaches, sore joints, fuzzy thinking, cloying body odor, belly cramps, chronic tooth pain, stuffy nostril syndrome—and *more*! All cured or alleviated by my miracle elixir!

"*How* does it work? *Glad* you asked!" And then the professor launched into some ten-dollar words that were too long and encumbered with multiple syllables for Parker to follow, the point being that a lot of complicated science had gone into the making of the potion.

Parker had to hand it to Meriweather. The professor knew how to get a crowd riled up in just the right way, and pretty soon they were handing over hard cash for bottles of the miracle elixir. When the crowd thinned and customers began to drift away, Meriweather motioned to Parker.

"Help me reassemble the wagon, my boy." The professor raised his voice. "And we'll be on our way to Denver!"

Parker helped Meriweather put the stage back up and relatch it to the side of the wagon, as Annie took in the bottles and vials.

"Professor, I hate to break it to you, but I'm not really looking to go to Denver," Parker said.

Meriweather hastily made shushing gestures, looking both ways over his shoulders and lowering his voice. "That was a slight ruse, my boy, in case a dissatisfied customer should come looking for me. The infirm are notoriously impatient, and often they do not give the product a fair chance to work before complaining. Due to the rare and expensive nature of many of the elixir's ingredients, it's not possible to offer refunds, so I find vacating the vicinity directly after one of my shows to be best for all concerned."

Not for the first time, Parker wondered if the professor's elixir was completely on the up and up.

They finished packing and headed out of town. Parker hadn't really accomplished the things he'd wanted to do in Cheyenne. He'd meant to ask around about Grady Jenks and the train robbery and the gold, trying to find anything that might be a clue about what to do next, but Meriweather seemed anxious to get out of town in a hurry. He'd humor the man, then tonight, around the cook fire, explain that he had to return to Cheyenne to get a few things done.

With Cheyenne safely behind them, Annie stuck her head out the back of the wagon. She wore normal clothes again. "How'd you like that gong work, Parker Jones?"

Parker grinned and nudged his horse closer to the wagon. "I never knew you were so musical."

"And how about that dress?" Her smile almost knocked him right out of the saddle.

He recovered quickly and put an expression of mock innocence on his face. "What dress?"

Her smile twisted right quick into a scowl. "Dang it, Parker, you know very well I looked *good*."

Parker shrugged. "Oh, I don't know. I sort of cotton to a big, oversize man's shirt, and a woman covered in mud."

Annie threw an empty elixir bottle at him.

* * *

"You ever seen that sort of thing before?" Little Joe Tillis asked.

"One time in Dodge City," Grady Jenks said. "But he wasn't as good as this fella."

They watched from across the street, occupying two rocking chairs in front of the mercantile. They'd been waiting over two hours, and at least the medicine show had been a distraction.

Jenks squinted at one of the men helping the medicine show fella pack up his wagon. "He look familiar to you?"

"I never seen no medicine show before," Tillis said.

"Not the professor fella," Jenks said. "I mean that younger one helping him with the—"

Something caught Jenks's eye. Bill Farkas coming through the crowd. "Never mind. Here comes Bill. Maybe he's got some news."

Bill arrived and said, "He was holed up in his hotel room near all day, but your brothers saw him come out. I guess he was up there with some sporting lady. But he's out now and was seen headed toward the livery stable. Charlie figures he's going for his horse, maybe fixing to leave town."

Jenks chewed that over for a few seconds. "Okay, you and me and Little Joe has to stay out of sight. Best will recognize any of us straight off. Tell my dimwit brothers to take turns and stay back. Tanner Best ain't no fool. He'll spot a tail if they're clumsy about it. One can watch him and the other report to you, and then you tell us. We'll all keep tabs that way."

"Right." Bill Farkas went back the way he'd come.

"Think this'll work?" Tillis asked.

Jenks thought about it. "Best's job is investigating. Tracking. He'll stumble over something before we will. We'll give it a chance for a while."

Tillis grunted, which might have been agreement or not.

Jenks watch the green medicine show wagon rock and sway as it rolled away down the street. He sure liked it when that fella made the big cloud of smoke poof out of the bowl.

CHAPTER 19

There were still a few hours of daylight left when they made camp in a copse of trees near a wide stream. When Parker took the horses to get watered, he saw fish jumping from it. Trout, maybe? He'd been fishing plenty of times in the ponds and creeks around Rory's Junction but didn't have a clue what swam in the streams of Wyoming.

He took the horses back and tied them, in a line, to a tree limb. He went to his pack and dug through it until he found the fishing gear he'd taken from Dowager Filmore's house. He glanced around to see what the others were doing. Professor Meriweather had just carried in an armload of wood and was about to build a fire. Annie had strung a line between the wagon and a nearby tree, and was hanging up wet clothing.

He kept the fishing gear hidden as he turned his back on them and headed back to the stream. Parker liked the idea of surprising them with a fish dinner, but he didn't want to actually promise until he caught something.

The stream babbled in front of him, the water clear, the late afternoon sun glittering on the surface. He knelt at the bank, picked up a stick that would work for his purposes. Parker would have preferred a proper fishing pole, but he'd just have to make do.. He wrapped the fishing line around the stick. Then he perused the flies, picking the one that looked like it was meant to resemble a small insect, a little spoon curving into a barbed hook, green feathers fashioned to look like insect wings.

Parker tied the fly to the end of the line then tossed it in the water. The fly floated downstream ten or twelve feet then stayed there, buffeted by the current, bouncing on the surface. He watched, willing a fish to take interest.

"Try letting out a lot more line," somebody said off to his left.

Parker whipped around, the Peacemaker in his hand in a flash. He pointed it at an old man, sitting with his back against a tree trunk, in faded trousers, checkered shirt, and suspenders, a drooping, battered hat that had seen better days. He held a fishing rod and didn't seem alarmed to have a six-shooter pointed at him.

"Pretty fast with that thing," the old man said. "But there's no need. I'm unarmed."

"Sorry." Parker slipped the Peacemaker back into its holster. "You startled me."

"Beg pardon," the old man said. "A good spot for fishing. I don't mind sharing."

"Obliged. I'm Parker."

"Master Sergeant Jeremiah Scruggs," the old man said. "Retired."

"You said to let out some more line?"

"Your fly's bouncing on the surface. It should float more gentle-like," Scruggs told him. "Look down about fifty feet where the stream makes a slight turn. Deep spot in the bend. Let the current take your fly that far."

Parker let out enough line, and the current took the fly. He gave it a slight tug to encourage it to go where Scruggs had indicated. The current took it into the calm, deeper area, where it floated, making a gentle spin, but staying put and not taken by the swift current farther downstream.

Barely a minute passed before something struck.

Parker excitedly wound the line around the stick, pulling in the fish. He grabbed it, and took it carefully off the fly, tossed it into the grass behind him where it flopped.

"Yellow perch," Scruggs said. "Good eating."

Parker tossed the fly back into the water and let it float to the same spot. In the next ten minutes, he caught seven more fish.

Scruggs whistled. "Dang, boy, that must be some fly you're using. You caught more fish in ten minutes than I have the last two hours. Let me see it, if you don't mind."

Parker took him the fly and let him examine it.

Scruggs held it in the palm of his hand, squinting at it, then held it between his thumb and forefinger, turning it this way and that. "Well, no wonder. This is one of Gus Mendelson's flies."

"Gus Mendelson?"

"Best dang fisherman I ever met," Scruggs said. "And that's saying something, because all I've done since retirement is mostly travel around and fish. Got a nice little pension from the army—not much, but enough to eat—so I don't have to work. My two daughters are married off to good men, and my son works for the railroad. And it suits my old woman for me to get out of the house, so, yeah, I just take the pole and do a lot of fishing. Pretty good at it, if I do say so myself—but I can't hold a candle to Gus Mendelson. There's many a man that's traveled hundreds of miles to buy flies off him. Men serious about fishing anyway."

The beginnings of an idea began to stir in the dusty backrooms of Parker's brain. "This Mendelson fella live around here."

Scruggs shook his head. "Way up north. A stone's throw from Montana. A place called . . . well, I forget the Lakota word, but it basically translates into the Bear Lodge. Mendelson's fished all over, of course, but he mainly fishes the Belle Fourche these days. Lots of flatheads, and small-mouth bass and such. Walleye, now and then, but you practically need to be Mendelson himself to find them."

"Bear Lodge is the name of a town?"

"No," Scruggs said. "Towns are few and far between, up there. People, too, for that matter. But there's a trading post, and that's where you can find Mendelson, often as not. It's near Sundance, which is trying hard to be a town. They're new. But it's been a while since I've been up there myself. I was with Dodge, when he scouted the place. My last mission before retirement. They had another name for the place besides Bear Lodge, but— No, I can't think of it just now. But if it comes down to an Indian name or something a white man called it, you just know which one'll end up on the map sooner or later."

Parker nodded, thinking. "Bear Lodge. Sundance. Mendelson. Got it."

"If you get up that way, tell Gus old Sergeant Scruggs said hello."

"I will. And thanks for the fishing tips."

They talked another minute about towns in the area and other good fishing holes.

They shook hands, and Parker took the perch back to camp where Annie and Meriweather were delighted to learn of the change in menu. Bacon and beans were filling but had lost their glamor after so many meals in a row.

Parker cleaned the fish and fried them up in a skillet. The three of them ate until there were only tails and heads and bones left, nothing else.

"That was a most excellent repast, my boy." Meriweather belched, then hastily covered his mouth. "I had no idea you were such a skilled angler."

"I guess it's a popular spot," Parker said. "Fella there gave me some tips."

"Oh?" Meriweather raised an eyebrow. "Well, then I shall thank him as well should we ever cross paths."

"I was wondering if you'd given any thought to what direction we should travel." Parker had meant to announce he was going back to Cheyenne, but his chance meeting with Jeremiah Scruggs had set him on a different path.

"I suppose I hadn't thought about it, not completely," Meriwether admitted. "Somewhere I can peddle my merchandise. Cheyenne was a good town, much better than average." He turned toward Annie. "Much of that thanks to you, my dear. The first job of any good sale is to catch and hold the customer's attention. I daresay you accomplished exactly that with a number of the men in the crowd."

Annie shot Parker a look and stuck out her tongue as if to say, *see?*

Parker rolled his eyes.

"I thought we might turn west," Meriweather said. "I've heard good things about Rawlins."

Parker cleared his throat awkwardly. "I'd like to head north. A fisherman I ran into said there's a community north of here called Bordeaux Crossing. It's, well, not as big as Cheyenne."

"But it's a town, yes?" Meriweather looked hopeful.

"Maybe sort of a crossroads?" Parker said. "People, anyway."

"Let us be off early in the morning, then," Meriweather said. "We shall size up the situation and see if we can do business."

Annie stood and began to gather the cooking pots and tin plates. "I'll take these to the stream and get them washed. Then it's bed for me."

Meriweather waited until the girl was out of earshot, then leaned close to Parker, lowering his voice. "North, eh? So why this sudden premonition we should trek north?"

Parker didn't want to reopen gold as a topic for conversation again, and anyway, there was no reason to believe the information he got from Jeremiah Scruggs would actually lead anywhere. "Just a feeling, I guess. Might keep going to Montana. Who knows?"

Meriweather lowered his voice yet again, a cool edge creeping into his tone. "My boy, I am not a fool. This has something to do with that gold again, doesn't it?"

Parker froze, not sure what to say.

Meriweather's demeanor softened, and he chuckled. "Never mind, my boy. Never mind. A man must have some secrets after all. But sooner or later you'll need to take *someone* into your confidence, and I'd like to put myself forward as a candidate. Sometimes a man's got to do what he's got to do all by his lonesome, but other times he needs someone to lean on—or at least a friendly ear to fill with all his doubts and worries. I'm known in some circles to be wise and educated. You could do worse."

Parker considered the professor's words. "I appreciate what you're telling me, Professor Meriweather. I'll think hard on it."

"You do that, my boy. You do that," Meriweather said pleasantly. "In the meantime, let's hear more about this Bordeaux Crossing place. How far is it?"

Parker's face scrunched up as he calculated. "If we start early and ride all day tomorrow, then I think we can get there middle of the next day."

"Eureka!" Meriweather snapped his fingers. "That's the answer, then. It'll be Sunday, don't you know? We'll get them coming out of church."

Parker slept hard, rose in the dark, ate a cold biscuit for breakfast, and they were on their way by first light. They pushed hard, only stopping for the bare minimum time needed to rest the horses. They camped in the open, the landscape having gone to gently rolling prairie, the wind constantly tugging at their clothes. They went about their evening routine, back to bacon and beans for dinner. There was no talk of fishing or gold, or what the future might hold for the three of them, and that suited Parker just fine. He didn't have it in him to think about any of those things again, not quite yet anyway.

Another early start the next morning. Wyoming stretched on.

A little before lunchtime, they started spotting farmhouses in the distance, or maybe ranch houses, or both. Parker didn't see any crops. Maybe it was the wrong time of year.

Soon afterward, the crossroads came into view.

A dozen buildings clustered around the X made by two roads crossing one over the other, one north–south and the other east–west. They'd already passed the church, perched on a low hill a half mile back, and Meriweather had wondered out loud if the people would melt back into the countryside or come into town after church let out.

Parker could only shrug.

He helped the professor set up his wagon stage on a spot more or less in the middle of the crossroads, but off to the side just enough not to impede traffic too severely. They'd just finished setting up when some folks came from the direction of the church, women in their best bonnets and men wearing their once-a-week ties. Annie gonged, and Meriweather launched into his pitch. The crowd gathered, not as big as in Cheyenne, but respectable.

Parker had seen this show already. He wandered across the street to the mercantile and took a gander at what was for sale. Once they left Bordeaux Crossing, they might not see another town for a while, so best to stock up while he had the chance.

Sugar. Coffee. Some sausages he was assured were "more or less fresh." On a whim, he bought a box of ammo for his Peacemaker. It had been a while since he'd practiced, and he didn't like the thought of getting rusty.

He walked back out to the wooden sidewalk with his purchases and leaned against a post, watching as the professor and Annie sold bottles of elixir. They'd be wrapping up soon. Parker wondered if the saloon would open on a Sunday.

"I thought that medicine fella said he was going to Denver" came a voice from the other side of the post.

Parker froze, eyes slowly widening. He recognized the voice immediately.

"Maybe he changed his mind," said a second voice. "What's it matter?"

Very slowly, Parker took a quick look around the other side of the post. He caught sight of the man's face in profile, and it was enough to confirm his suspicions. He backed around to his side of the post, heart hammering in his chest. Not a foot away from him stood the outlaw Grady Jenks. Parker didn't doubt the man he was speaking to was one of the other hardened killers in his gang.

The idea of pulling his six-gun and trying to arrest Jenks was so laughable that Parker didn't even bother to entertain it for a second. He would certainly have been killed the last time he'd tried that if Tanner Best hadn't come along.

"How long we gonna wait?" asked the other voice.

"I told them to send word here. One of them will be along," Jenks replied. "Unless they lost him."

"Which would put us back at square one."

"There's no use looking for something to worry about," Jenks said. "We wait."

Parker's horse was across the street on the other side of the medicine show wagon. He turned slowly so as not to draw attention and walked down the sidewalk to the end, then crossed the street, keeping people or wagons or the corners of buildings between him and the outlaws. He loaded his purchase into his saddlebags, mounted, then pointed his horse north, making sure to catch Meriweather's eye briefly as he passed. The professor looked confused for a moment, but then quickly went back to selling bottles of his miracle potion.

Parker went up the road about three miles and stopped under a lone tree for the shade and waited.

Maybe an hour later the wagon came swaying and creaking up the road. Meriweather reined in his team with a "whoa" when he spotted Parker.

Parker had been sitting with his back to the tree trunk. Now he stood, brushed off his pants, took his horse by the reins, and walked toward the wagon. He'd been rehearsing what to say.

"Where did you run off to, my boy?" Meriweather asked. "I'd been hoping to enlist your assistance again in putting up the stage elsewhere and so on."

"Yeah, sorry about that," Parker said.

Annie fixed him with a curious look.

Parker opened his mouth to tell them the whole story, about running afoul of Grady Jenks and his ruffians at Eiger's Trading Post, how he'd almost been killed, and how he suspected these outlaws must surely be looking for the same gold he'd told them about a few nights ago. How he had been obliged to cut out before one of those bad men recognized him.

But then Parker closed his mouth again, second-guessing what he should say. Those men might have recognized him, but he'd left before they did. But what about tomorrow or the next day, or next week? If Jenks was following the same trail as Parker, then their paths might cross again. And if the outlaws found Parker, then that meant they'd find Annie and the professor, too, and there was no such thing as innocent bystanders.

Parker told them none of those things, but took a deep breath, and said, "I've been thinking it over, and I feel like—well, like I need to strike out on my own."

Annie's eyes shot wide with surprise. "What?"

Meriweather's face hardened. He suspected something was afoot but said nothing.

"It's nothing personal," Parker said. "That wagon just moves so slow, you know? And I need to be getting on with some things."

When he saw the look in Annie's eyes, he almost reconsidered. Maybe he should just tell them he was doing this for their own good, that they might fall prey to bad men simply because of their association with him. But, no, he couldn't chance it. They'd want to stick with him, insisting they could help him in some way. At least, he wanted to think that's what Annie would say.

The professor was something else. Friendly, yes, but Parker suspected a practical streak in the man. He doubted the professor would think the pleasure of Parker's company was worth getting murdered by outlaws.

"I'm sorry to hear it, my boy," Meriweather said. "But if a man sets out to do something, then I suppose it's best he gets on with it."

Parker climbed onto his horse, feeling sick in his gut.

"Parker!"

Annie hopped down from the wagon and ran to him. She grabbed him by the forearm with both hands. "But why? What's got you in a hurry?"

"Annie, you'll be safe with the professor."

"But—" Her eyes were suddenly huge, going glassy and moist.

"I've got to go."

Parker turned his horse and headed north at a gallop.

CHAPTER 20

He stopped a couple times, only briefly, to rest his horse. Parker knew Meriweather's slow-moving wagon wouldn't be able to catch up, but Parker wanted to be sure, wanted to know he wouldn't see them again, because he knew his resolve wouldn't hold. He was already feeling alone, second-guessing leaving the others. The days ahead would be long.

He made camp late, ate a cold dinner, and was up and going again early, without coffee.

Parker camped the next day near a stream and tried his hand at fishing again. It was slow going, but he sat on a rock near the water and forced himself to be patient. He let his mind wander. The breeze rustled the leaves in the trees overhead. The sound of the water flowing was pleasant and tranquil.

He sniffed, catching an odd smell, like something burning, but sweeter. He turned, looked behind him, and gasped.

"You're an easy man to sneak up on, Deputy Jones."

Tanner Best sat on a fallen log twenty feet from

Parker, the stem of his pipe between his teeth, the sweet smoke drifting on the breeze.

Parker nodded. "Marshal."

"After meeting you in Rory's Junction, I was surprised to see you again at Eiger's," Best said. "And then when I saw you again in Cheyenne, I thought, well, coincidences do happen." He took the pipe out of his mouth, eyes narrowing and going hard. "But when I run across you smack dab in the middle of nowhere, I start to wonder if maybe you just can't live without me."

Parker forced a laugh. "Funny thing is I was sort of wondering what you're doing out here, in the middle of nowhere, as you put it."

"I'm being followed," Best told him.

"Not by me," Parker assured the marshal.

"Couple of fellas I've never seen before. They're taking turns tailing me, and they aren't very good at it. I cut through this area to try to lose them. Imagine my surprise when I trip over Deputy Jones."

"I guess it does seem like a pretty far-fetched coincidence," Parker admitted.

"Maybe it's time you tell me what you're doing in Wyoming, son."

"It's, um, kind of a long story."

Best puffed his pipe. "How many fish you catch?"

"Two."

"That's one each, then." Best stood and dusted himself off. "Bring them. We'll talk and eat."

Marshal Best has set up his camp farther upstream. His fire had gone cold, and he worked to bring it back, blowing on the coals, then adding twigs, then larger sticks. Parker cleaned the fish in the meantime. When the fire was ready, he draped the perch over a stick that he set over the fire like a makeshift spit.

"That won't take long," Parker said.

Best took a bottle from his saddlebag and pulled the cork. He took a healthy swallow, then handed the bottle to Parker. "You being in Wyoming wouldn't have anything to do with some stolen gold, would it?"

Parker took a swig from the bottle. The marshal's question didn't rattle him. He's been expecting something like this and had been rehearsing what to say as he'd cleaned the fish. Tanner Best was a U.S. marshal, and lying to him was a bad idea, but Parker still wanted to tell his story in a way that didn't make him look bad. He'd tell Best the truth.—but maybe not all of it.

"I guess maybe it would have something to do with that," Parker admitted.

"I figured," Best said. "I guess it was foolish to think I'd be the only one after the reward."

Reward? Parker almost blurted out he had no idea what the marshal was talking about, but then wisely kept his mouth shut.

"I have a mind to pull authority on you and send you on your way," Best told him. "I generally work alone, and I don't need you crossing me up when I'm going after these bad men. It'll only be a distraction to have to pull your fat out of the fire, like I did at Eiger's."

Paker frowned. He didn't care to be characterized as a liability, but he couldn't deny what had happened at Eiger's. Best had saved him, and that was a fact. And when the shooting had started, Parker hadn't been much help.

"And I don't mind saying I'm not eager to share the reward," Best admitted. "A ten percent finder's fee on fifty thousand in gold is nothing to sneeze at. I got plans for that money. I like being a U.S. marshal—I'm good at it, maybe the best. I don't care if that sounds braggartly. Facts is facts. But the other fact is that I've been shot at more times than I can count and even hit three times in places that were thankfully not vital. I've been lucky, but luck can run out. I'd like to retire while I'm still young enough—and *alive* enough—to enjoy it. I've got plans to retire in comfort, but that takes money."

Parker had little interest in the marshal's retirement plans. He was distracted by the math. Ten percent of fifty thousand was five thousand big ones. It was a fortune. And it wasn't stealing. It was a legitimate reward for finding the stolen gold. It had always nagged at Parker when he'd begun this adventure that he intended to do something that wasn't strictly legal. He tried to tell himself that stealing from criminals wasn't quite the same as stealing from honest citizens, but when push came to shove, the gold still wasn't his. It was that simple.

But a reward! Well, that was legitimate. That was the kind of thing that Parker could—

No, it didn't matter. The marshal wanted that reward, and he didn't want Parker in the way. Parker wasn't about to cross a man like Tanner Best.

He realized the marshal was still talking.

"But then I got to thinking," Best said. "I've got people following me, and I don't know who they are.

That business at the Golden Buffalo demonstrated there's always a chance somebody can sneak up on my blind side. You managed to prove you weren't completely worthless."

Parker supposed that worked out to a compliment. Sort of.

"I'm thinking I might need somebody to watch my back," Best said. "And If I keep you where I can see you, then I won't be tripping over you later."

Parker blinked, not sure if he was hearing right. Was one of the toughest U.S. marshals in the West really asking him to partner up?

"Now, you need to understand I'm not talking about an equal fifty-fifty split," Best explained. "I'm the senior lawman here, the one with the skills and the experience, and frankly, I'm doing you a favor. I'm thinking twenty percent for you is generous. That's a dang sight more money than you've ever seen all at once, I'm guessing."

Ah. Yes, that made it more believable. Best didn't want a partner. He wanted a sidekick.

"I reckon that's a good offer, marshal," Parker said. "I'm for it."

Best nodded approval. "Then first we shake on it."

They shook hands.

"And then we drink on it." Best took a swallow from the bottle then handed it to Parker.

Parker took a bigger gulp than usual, wincing as it burned down his throat. He wanted to cough but refused to let it happen. He wasn't about to let on he couldn't handle his whiskey in front of Best. He wiped his mouth on his sleeve. "I reckon that seals the deal."

"Reckon so," Best agreed. "Now look after them fish. I'm so hungry I could eat the backside of a mule raw."

Parker served up the fish, and they ate, sitting on opposite sides of the fire.

Best finished eating, smacked his lips as he set his tin plate aside. "Now that we're teamed up, I think we should trade information. I'll start. I lost track of Jenks and his gang after Eiger's. Then I figured I'd come back to Cheyenne and question all the people that's already been questioned to see if I knock a memory loose. Maybe they'd seen something or heard something and hadn't realized it was important." The marshal shook his head. "No good. So there you have it. I'm at a dead end. Now you."

Parker raised an eyebrow. "Me?"

"You must have some notion," Best said. "Or are you telling me you're wandering the Wyoming wilderness hoping to stumble over the gold by accident? You're headed north. Why?"

"Well, it ain't much to go on."

"I'll be the judge of that," Best said. "Spill."

"I was fishing, pretty much how you found me today, but back south," Parker explained. "There was an old veteran there. He was fishing, too. He recognized the fly I was using."

Parker related the information he'd gotten from retired Master Sergeant Jeremiah Scruggs about Gerald Filmore's fly, expert fishermen Gus Mendelson, and a place near Sundance called the Bear Lodge.

Tanner Best sighed and shook his head. "It's thin, deputy, thinner than a pancake sat on by a circus fat lady."

Parker shrugged. "It's all I have."

"On that, we can agree," Best said. "At least it means Filmore's been there. It thin, but it's something. How in the world did you get ahold of one of his fishing flies?"

Parker had been expecting the question. He was ashamed he'd stolen it from old lady Filmore's house and didn't want to admit the minor transgression to the marshal. "It was in his pocket when he died back in Rory's Junction. I didn't think it was important at the time, so I kept it."

"I reckon it's a good thing you did," Best said. "Fortunate you happened to show it to the old man. Sometimes it's better to be lucky than good."

Parker couldn't disagree. He'd take all the luck he could get.

"Let's finish this bottle, then get some shut-eye. We'll get going at first daylight. At the very least, you can try your luck in the Belle Fourche. Maybe catch us another fish dinner."

They drank for another hour, Best getting drunk and pummeling Parker with story after story of his various close calls with wicked men and dangerous desperados across the West. Best eventually stumbled away to his bedroll to sleep. His snores rose above the crackling of the waning campfire.

Parker laid his head on his saddle and closed his eyes. At least half a dozen times, he'd almost taken out the map he'd found behind the portrait of the old general to show it to the marshal, but something always stopped him. Maybe it was because he didn't want to admit he had no idea what it was or even if it was important at all. A drawing of a tree stump and some lines. Why bother?

But there was something else, too—something Parker couldn't quite put his finger on.

Whatever it was faded, as slumber took him down into blissful darkness.

Best had a good sense of direction. They came out of the woods right at the road that would take them north. Parker supposed calling it a road was a stretch. Not more than a thinning of the grass, like a beaten down track with hoof marks in the mud. It was an indication, at least, that other travelers had come this way, so the road must lead somewhere worth going to.

After a couple miles, the road climbed to the top of a low hill, and Marshal Best reined in his horse and turned to look back the way they'd come. He twisted in the saddle, reaching back into one of his saddlebags and came out with a collapsible spyglass. He extended it, lifted it to his eye, and scanned the horizon to the south.

"Hmmm." He made a slow pan with the spyglass from east to west. "Hmmm."

Parker squinted south. "See anything, marshal?"

"No," Best said. "And that's good. I do believe cutting through the woods threw off my tail. For the moment anyway. Do me a favor, Deputy Jones, and glance over your shoulder every now and then."

They rode north, and for the next three nights, Parker cooked, cleaned up afterward, and tended to the horses. It soon became clear Best wasn't interested in a partner nor a sidekick, neither. He wanted a squire, like knights had in the old-time stories. For a thousand dollars, Parker was willing to do the work. Anyway, it kept him busy.

They stopped early the next day, so Parker elected to use the remaining daylight for target practice. He didn't want to get rusty. Professor Meriweather had let Parker have a dozen elixir bottles he'd deemed too scratched and chipped to sell. He walked a good quarter mile away from camp, across flat prairie, not wanting to shoot too close to the horses.

He lined up the bottles and shot, each time seeing if he could draw a little faster than the last. Fast as greased lighting would matter if he missed, so he kept trying to push his limit, drawing as fast as possible, but still hitting one of the bottles.

Parker paused to reload and smelled pipe smoke. "Everything okay, marshal?" he asked without turning around.

"Just come to watch the show," Best said. "You're fast."

"Lots of practice."

"You ever killed a man?" Best asked.

Parker turned to look at the marshal. He stood about

twenty feet away, pipe chugging like a locomotive. "Indians."

"Oh? All storming you at once?"

"Yeah."

Best nodded, coming closer until he stood right in front of Parker. "That's one sort of experience. All of them circling and screaming their war cries and lead flying every which way."

"More or less just like that," Parker said.

"Not quite the same as one man against another."

Parker wasn't sure what the marshal meant.

"A one-on-one gunfight is a personal, up-close thing," Best explained. "I've talked to men who've come back from the war, men who've survived some of the biggest battles—Bull Run, Gettysburg, and so on. Men colliding into one another a thousand at a time, pushing this way and that, firing into the chaos, never knowing the man you've killed or even if you've killed anyone at all. That ain't a gunfight. In a gunfight, the other fella looks you right in the eye, and you look straight back into his. You can see the sweat rolling down the side of his face. There's a tension, and the air between you is thick with it, and it connects you."

"But then the fastest wins, right?" Parker asked. "That's why you practice."

A half shrug from the marshal. "Let's say being slow won't help you win, that's for sure. But being fast ain't all there is to it."

"Being accurate?"

"Obviously, but there's something more than *that*.

Something that has to happen before your six-gun even clears the holster." Best puffed the pipe. "Heck, son, you're as fast as I am. And accurate, too. You hit them bottles, no problem."

Parker felt himself puff up with pride. "That's high praise, marshal."

"Not as high as you think," Best told him. "If both men are fast, then which one wins? I'll tell you. The one who don't mind dying. The one who knows he's dead already. That he's going to get a bullet right here." Best jabbed a finger into Parker's chest, making him flinch. "Or a bullet here." The marshal tapped Parker's forehead with the same finger. "You can't spare one ounce of desire on living. Some part of you will want to flinch or duck, and you're dead already. Accept that, and you can focus your full attention on killing the other man. Draw, shoot, hit your target, no thought for yourself. Then when the smoke clears, and he's flat on his back, then and only then can you think about living, thank any God you like, and pray it's a long time until the next gunfight."

Parker looked down at the Peacemaker in his hand, letting Best's words sink in.

"There is one more thing."

Parker looked up. "Yeah?"

Best grinned. "Even better if you can keep yourself from getting into a gunfight in the first place. A man survives one hundred percent of the gunfights he avoids."

Parker returned the grin. "I guess that's pretty good advice."

"Wish I would have followed it myself a few times."

Best sucked on the pipe, tilted his head back, and blew a long stream of gray smoke at the sky. "Come on, then. Rustle us up some beans."

Grady Jenks had just put his head back on his saddle and pulled his hat down over his eyes when he heard the all-too familiar sound of a hammer being cocked back on a six-gun.

He sat up and saw the Russian on the other side of the fire, gun in hand, a Smith & Wesson Model Three, the one they called—appropriately enough—the Russian model. He squinted into the darkness, bringing one finger to his lips in a *shush* gesture.

Tillis and Farkas snored gently, blissfully unaware anything was happening.

Then Jenks heard it, the sound of twigs snapping beyond the firelight, somebody creeping through the woods and doing a pretty lousy job of being quiet about it.

"Don't shoot." A familiar voice. "We're coming in."

Boris eased the hammer back down on his Smith & Wesson and returned it to his holster.

Charlie and Jimmy shuffled into the circle of firelight, shoulder slumped, faces long. That the two of them had come back together could only mean one thing.

"You lost him," Jenks said.

"He left the road, and we lost him in the woods," Jimmy said. "I think he spotted me."

Jenks rolled his eyes. "You think?"

Farkas and Tillis stirred, then sat up, rubbing their eyes.

"What's happening?" Farkas asked.

"The geniuses here lost the marshal," Grady said.

Charlie frowned. "Hey! You said not to get too close to him or he'd spot us."

"Well, he did anyway," Grady reminded his brother.

"Bickering like old hens ain't gonna solve the problem." Bill Farkas rubbed his face with both hands, still trying to wake up. "Point is, what do we do now?"

Grady twiddled his thumbs, thinking about it. "Which way was he going before he left the road?"

"Straight north," Jimmy said.

"And he was going north before he spotted you?"

"Yep," Charlie said.

"You're sure?"

Charlie looked put out, like he didn't want to be questioned. "Sure, I'm sure!"

"Okay, so then whatever he's doing, it's north," Grady said. "We have to assume that once he feels sure he's thrown you off, he'll want to return to his original course. So I say we head north, too, and try to pick him up again. What's north of here anyway?"

Charlie shook his head. "Not a lot. Plenty of open country."

"Some small villages." The Russian's accent made it sound like *zum zmall willages*. "Trading posts."

"No towns?"

"Sundance?" Boris looked at Jimmy and Charlie, eyebrow raised.

"Yeah, Sundance." Jimmy nodded. "That could pass for a town."

"So, there we go," Grady said. "We head for Sundance and keep our ears open along the way, in case anyone's talking about a U.S. marshal who's been through recently."

Little Joe Tillis blew out a tired sigh. "I dunno, Grady. That's a lot of wandering around, hoping to hear something, hoping to see something."

Grady fixed him with a hard look. "You want to kiss off fifty thousand in gold?"

Nobody wanted to do that.

"So we head north, then. And we pick up the marshal's trail again."

"Then what?" Charlie asked. "Start following him again?"

"Stuff that," Grady said. "My patience is about run its course. We find the marshal, get our hands on him, and make him talk."

CHAPTER 21

Bad weather drifted in from the west, dark, low-hanging clouds obscuring all but the base of the Bear Lodge Mountains. Cold rain fell steadily. It had started falling that morning and just kept on coming, neither growing heavier nor letting up.

By the time their horses clopped through the mud into Sundance, Parker was dripping wet, soaked through, and miserable.

"I wonder if there's a hotel," Best muttered.

Parker looked at the town ahead and didn't feel optimistic, a half dozen slouching buildings, only a couple with a second story, at the end of the street, but it was getting dark, and the rain obscured visibility. Maybe there was more to Sundance than first met the eye.

"That's a livery stable." Best pointed ahead of them. "We can get the animals out of the rain, at least."

The stable was empty, and the proprietor was glad for the business. The price of stabling the horses included feed and a rubdown.

"Okay if we bunk in here with the nags if we can't find better accommodations?" Best asked.

The stableman shrugged. "All the same to me, but Milly Blankenship rents a room over her slop house at the end of the street."

"Obliged, my good man." Best flipped the man a coin.

Parker and the marshal walked down the street, keeping close to the buildings, hoping the overhangs would keep the rain off, but they were still dripping by the time they reached the slop house and went inside.

The place smelled like grease and baking bread, and wet, sweaty men. The place was full, cowboys and farmhands and merchants hunched over plates at mismatched tables, mopping up gravy with biscuits, and spooning stew into their mouths. The place was poorly lit by a half dozen lanterns hanging from the ceiling at various spots. A woman came through a swinging door in the back, wiping her hands on an apron, maybe in her thirties, lines on her face from a life of hard work. Her brown hair was pulled back, but a few strands had broken loose to stream in her wake as she rushed about.

She stopped in front of Parker and Best. "Dinner?"

"Perhaps later, madam," Best said. "Would you be Miss Milly?"

"I would."

"The man down the street at the stable said you might have a room for rent," the marshal said.

"Around the back and upstairs," Milly said. "Two dollars a night."

"That strikes me as a bit steep."

Milly shrugged. "It's raining."

"A fair point," Best admitted. "I'll take the room."

Her eyes went from Best to Parker. "It's a single bed."

"Alas, I must claim seniority." Best turned to Parker with an apologetic smile. "It would seem the stable is for you, Deputy Jones."

"Right." Parker sighed. *Of course, the squire bunks with the horses.*

"I'll be back with the key in a minute." Milly left back through the swinging door.

"Never mind, boy," Best said. "I'll make it up to you. We'll go for a drink."

Milly returned and handed Marshal Best the key.

"Obliged." Best made the key disappear into a vest pocket. "Is there a place around here a man can get a sip of whiskey."

"The Broken Wheel," Milly told him. "You passed it on the way here."

Best touched the brim of his hat with two fingers. "Obliged again."

Parker and the marshal went back the way they'd come. The rain hadn't let up one jot, and now distant thunder rolled in, a low, strung-out rumble, promising the weather would get worse before it got better. The saloon didn't have a proper sign, just a wagon wheel with a few spokes missing hanging over the front door.

They went inside, glad to be out of the rain again, if nothing else.

To Parker, the interior of the Broken Wheel looked like someone had specifically set out to build a saloon the exact opposite of the Golden Buffalo. No gilded chandelier, no big mirrors. No fancy art. No piano player. Rough tables and a rougher bar, as if the furnishings had been made out of the leftover lumber from an old barn they'd torn down. The place was dim, even fewer lanterns than in the slop house, as if the proprietor thought the less folks saw of the place, the better.

Best crossed the room to the bar, and Parker followed.

The emaciated man behind the bar looked sickly and gray, but smiled his yellow teeth at the marshal in his best imitation of hospitality. "Get you something?"

"A bottle of whiskey," Best told him.

Parker would have preferred a beer, but Best was paying.

The barkeep brought the bottle and two glasses. Best filled the glasses and handed one to Parker, then raised the other. "To Sundance, the jewel of northeast Wyoming."

They drank.

The rain pelted them as they rode, single file, in the dark, thunder ahead of them. Flashes of lighting briefly illuminating black clouds from within.

Bill Farkas nudged his horse up alongside Grady Jenks. "How long we gonna keep riding in this? I'm wet all the way through. My underwear's sticking to my backside in a way I wouldn't call comfortable."

"We're all as wet as we're gonna get," Jenks said. "Might as well keep going. If I'm figuring right, Sundance ain't too far ahead. Maybe we can put a roof over our heads."

Farkas grunted, which might have meant anything,

not that Jenks gave a damn one way or another. He was just as wet and miserable as the others, and in no mood to listen to bellyaching.

"What if we don't find him?" Farkas asked.

"We'll find him."

"Then what?"

"I told you," Jenks said. "We make him talk."

"What if he don't know nothing? What then?"

"Then we think of something else!" Jenks snapped.

Jenks found that line of questioning galling for the simple reason that he'd been asking himself those very same questions and didn't have any answers. The simple truth was that somewhere out there, there was fifty thousand in gold, and Gerald Filmore might very well have taken the gold's hiding place to his grave. For Grady Jenks, it was a notion too bitter to contemplate.

No. I refuse to believe it. Somebody knows where that blasted gold is, and we're going to find it.

"Look, we'll get some whiskey, okay?" Jenks said to Farkas. "We'll get to Sundance, get someplace dry, and get a bottle. We're all tired and crabby."

"And hungry."

"And hungry," Jenks said. "We'll get a bottle and some grub."

Farkas blew out a sigh. "I guess that can't hurt."

"How much longer we going to ride in this dang rain?" Jimmy Jenks called from the back of the line.

Bill Farkas twisted in the saddle and shouted back, "Pipe down back there! No point complaining, is there? We're all wet. We'll dry out and get a sip of whiskey in Sundance."

Grady Jenks grinned. *Now, why didn't I think of that?*

They rode toward Sundance, the rain coming heavier.

They'd made half the bottle of whiskey disappear, Marshal Best doing most of the work, Parker sipping along just enough to be sociable. Men had drifted into the Broken Wheel, taking tables and occupying space at the bar. Best had his eye on a card game in the corner, but at the moment, all the seats were taken.

Parker sighed, sipped whiskey, and looked around, again comparing the Broken Wheel to the Golden Buffalo. The Broken Wheel didn't come out well in the comparison. The saloon back in Cheyenne had been a jovial place, filled with music and laughter, and pretty ladies. The Broken Wheel almost seemed like a saloon designed to go along with the dismal weather, a place where men sat quietly and stared into the bottom of their shot glasses.

"If someone leaves that card game, I might jump in," Best said.

"Uh-huh." It was the third time the marshal had said that, and Parker was barely listening. He had no interest in cards. He knew about as much about playing poker as he knew about the ingredients of Professor Meriweather's elixirs.

Parker's thoughts drifted back to Louise. Had he made a mistake, thrown away an opportunity? She'd been pretty, even prettier when she'd wiped off all that makeup.

No. That wasn't something he could do. He just—couldn't. What would his sister say?

He wondered what Sarah was doing, and his brother-in-law. Sarah probably missed him. He should have sent her a letter long before now to tell her he was doing okay. Caleb probably hadn't given him any thought at all, except occasionally, to be glad he had one less mouth to feed.

Parker sipped whiskey and wished he were somewhere else.

"There's a fella taking his leave," Best said. "I'm going to try my luck."

"I guess I'll head back to the stable," Parker said, "catch some shut-eye."

"I'll fetch you in the morning," Best said. "We'll get breakfast at that slop house. Give you a break from cooking, at least."

"Right."

Parker finished his whiskey, then headed outside, hoping the rain had let up.

It hadn't.

They'd been happy to have Best fill the empty chair, mostly because the marshal was from out of town, and talk of doings elsewhere was always welcome. The other four men at the table all seemed cut from the same cloth: tired middle-aged men, who'd stopped off for whiskey and cards before going home to tired middle-aged wives. Three of the men—a couple of shopkeepers and a rancher who'd come into town to buy feed—were polite enough, but unhappy in general. The fourth man was downright jovial—the local undertaker, oddly enough, who seemed determined to be in a good mood no matter how many hands he lost.

Best lost three small hands in a row before raking in a sizable pot on his fourth go. That's when the rancher bowed out, saying he needed to head home.

They played another hour, and Best won two more pots.

The marshal played cards and drank whiskey. He was having a very good time.

Which is probably why he failed to notice the man who walked into the Broken Wheel next.

Parker ate a strip of beef jerky and washed it down with a swallow of water from his canteen. He'd have preferred a hot meal at Milly's slop house, but that would have meant walking there in the rain, sitting there, wet, to eat, then walking back to the stable in the rain again, and Parker had had enough of the rain.

Back at the livery stable, Parker squirmed out of his wet clothes and hung them on hooks in the back of the stall. He changed into dry duds, then plopped down in the hay, pulling a horse blanket over him. He was dead tired, but he knew from experience that he'd need to let his mind settle before he could finally drift off to sleep.

He'd just entered that first part of sleep where thoughts melt into dreams. Louise brushed her lips against his, but when he pulled away, it was Annie in front of him, not the young saloon girl from the Golden

Buffalo. In the way of dreams, this didn't seem strange. He leaned in to kiss her again and—

Voices.

Parker's eyes flickered. Opened.

A group of men looking to board their horses, all grumbling about the rain, which was understandable. Parker closed his eyes again and tried to ignore them.

"Don't bother unsaddling them nags just yet. Wait and see if we find a place to stay," said a cranky voice. "Are we getting a bottle or not?"

Parker's eyes popped back open. He recognized that voice.

Grady Jenks had come to Sundance.

Grady Jenks pushed on the batwing door and entered the Broken Wheel. He felt the boys trying to crowd in behind him, but he stood a moment taking the place in. Not the grandest of saloons, but he'd seen plenty worse. Anyway, a place to drink was a place to drink.

He began to walk inside, eyes going here and there, and he saw—

Jenks turned abruptly to walk out again, bumping into Farkas right behind him.

Farkas frowned. "What in blazes are you do—"

"Shut your mouth," Jenks whispered. "Turn around. Get out."

Farkas looked cross but did as he was told, and bumped into Tillis right behind him, resulting in an angry grumble from the big man. Half of them were trying to get in and half of them trying to get out, looking like a bunch of idiot circus clowns. Grady muttered a string of curses under his breath but somehow managed to herd them all outside without drawing attention.

Charlie Jenks threw up his hands in a *what gives?* gesture. "I thought we was getting a drink of whiskey."

"Settle down!" Grady Jenks said. "Tanner Best himself is sitting in there, playing cards."

"That's good, ain't it?" Jimmy said. "We were looking for him, weren't we?"

Charlie started walking back toward the entrance of the saloon. "Well, okay then. What are we waiting for? Let's grab the son of a—"

Grady grabbed a fistful of his jacket and shoved him back. "Moron. There's a saloon full of people in there."

"What then?" Charlie asked.

"We pick some spots out here and keep watch," Jenks told them. "He's laying his head around here somewhere. We'll follow and then get our hands on him when nobody's looking."

"A shame about the bottle," Little Joe Tillis said. "I been looking forward to it."

Grady turned to the Russian. "Boris, you're the only one of us he hasn't seen. He only saw Jimmy and Charlie from a distance, but there's no sense taking that chance. Can you go in and get us a bottle?"

The Russian nodded. "*Da.*"

He headed for the saloon.

"Boris," Grady called after him.

The Russian paused and looked back.

"Get two."

* * *

Parker pulled on his boots, strapped on his gun belt, and donned his hat.

Somebody's got to warn Marshal Best. I reckon that somebody is me.

He made to leave, paused, went back to get his jacket and put it on. He reached into his pocket and fished out the tin star. He pinned it to his lapel. He had no jurisdiction here. Likely the star wouldn't mean a darn thing to anyone in Sundance.

It means something to me. That's enough.

He snugged his hat down low and huddled in the horse stall, listening to be sure Jenks and his gang had really gone, straining to hear over the rain battering the tin roof and the thunder moving ever closer.

Grady Jenks and his two brothers waited in the deep darkness of an alley across the street from the Broken Wheel. It was a good spot to keep an eye on the saloon's front door. They were partly sheltered from the rain, but not enough, and water dripped from their hats.

They couldn't get any more soaked than they already were. *I guess that's something, at least*, Jenks thought.

"How long we gonna stand out here, Grady?" Charlie asked. "I hate this."

Grady tried to keep his temper. Didn't these boys know what fifty thousand in gold was? Didn't they think it worth some hardship and discomfort? Charlie was the worst. Their mother—God rest her soul—had babied the boy, and he hadn't come out the better for it.

"Just have a drink and relax." Grady handed Charlie the bottle. "Good things come to those who wait."

"That ain't been my experience." Charlie tilted the bottle back and took a big gulp. "I been waitin' all my life, and nothin' good's come along yet."

"All your life." Grady snorted. "Takes God longer to blink than you been alive."

Jimmy laughed.

"Yeah, laugh it up," Charlie said. "Just keep laughing."

"Some gratitude for getting you out of jail," Jimmy said.

"You didn't get me out. It was Grady," Charlie shot back. "Him and Boris."

"Who do you think organized it?" Jimmy said. "Should have just let you sit there. More gold for the rest of us."

Grady snatched the bottle back. "Shut your mouths, the both of you."

Miraculously, they did shut them, and the three brothers drank in silence for a minute, but of course, the peace and quiet didn't last for long. It never did.

"What you gonna do with your share of the gold, Grady?" Charlie asked.

Grady froze, the whiskey bottle halfway to his mouth. He'd never asked himself that question before and had literally no idea what his future plans might be. Of course, there'd be a time of celebration, women and booze in a fancy hotel suite. Maybe a slick new set of duds.

But all of that was short term. Short term had been the way he had thought for years. He and the boys would rob a stagecoach or a bank, and then they'd spend it on a wild spree until the money ran low again. They'd either have to lay low until the heat was off or move on to a different territory, where they'd do it all over again.

But this gold—well, that was a different sort of proposition. His share could potentially be a life-changing amount of money. He could set himself up somewhere.

But where? Doing what?

"I don't rightly know, not exactly," Grady admitted. "What about you?"

"I'm going to buy a villa in Veracruz," Charlie said.

Jimmy rolled his eyes. "This again."

Grady blinked. "A what? Where?"

"A villa," Charlie said. "In Veracruz."

"Veracruz?"

"It's in Mexico," Charlie said.

"I *know* it's in Mexico," Grady snapped. "I want to know why you want to go there."

"He saw a painting," Jimmy said.

Grady rubbed his eyes. "Are you going to make me sorry I asked about this?"

"It was in a saloon in El Paso," Charlie said. "This long painting behind the bar. A villa in Veracruz. The colors were so bright, the ocean in the background so blue, like the painting had its own light glowing from within. And there was a lady on a— a—what do you call it? Like a porch, but open and wide?"

Grady drank whiskey. "A veranda."

"Right, a veranda," Charlie said. "With these wide archways, and you could look through the archways and see the ocean. And the lady was stretched out on one of those things that's like only half a sofa, open at one end."

"One of them chaise things," Grady said.

"That's it, and the woman is all stretched out on that, wearing nothing but what God gave her," Charlie said. "But it's not dirty. It's just beautiful, all that brown skin. And that's what I'll do, go down there and buy a villa just like that, maybe even that very villa where the painter did the picture, and it'll be like walking right into that painting. I'll walk right in and never come out again."

Grady had always thought Charlie a bit thick between the ears, but at that moment, it seemed like his little brother knew what he was saying, like he was on to something for the first time in his life. Grady Jenks hoped he'd do something as good and thoughtful when he got his share of the gold, and for just a brief moment, it made him sad, knowing he probably wouldn't.

The brothers stood in the alley, not talking, the *tap tap tappity* of the rain on their hats the only sound.

Jimmy jerked a thumb at Charlie and snorted. "Can you believe this dang fool? Wants to live in an oil painting."

Grady frowned, a flash of annoyance washing over him, and he wanted to punch Jimmy in his stupid face.

But what would that solve?

"Hush up now," Grady said softly. "Here he comes."

Tanner Best emerged from the Broken Wheel. Grady watched the man for signs he'd had too much whiskey. Did the marshal sway a bit? Maybe. Maybe not. He turned down the street and started walking.

Thunder rumbled in the distance. Lightning far off inside the low, black clouds.

Grady gave Best a few seconds head start, then motioned for his brothers to follow him out of the alley. He stopped at the street corner and looked back where the other three were hiding. Grady motioned after Best, then made a circular motion with his hand. *Go around the other way.*

Bill Farkas gave a wave to show he understood.

"Now what?" Jimmy asked. "We grab him?"

"We follow," Grady said. "Find out where he's bunking for the night. We need a place away from prying eyes to question him. And remember, he's dangerous. We can't just walk up and grab him. We need to be smart about this. Come on."

Jimmy drank the last of the whiskey and tossed the bottle into the mud.

They followed Best to the end of the street, past a slop house. He went around it, and Grady gave him a few seconds before following. The last thing he wanted was to follow too quickly and round the corner and find himself staring into the barrel of one of the marshal's Remingtons. When he finally circled around to the back of the building, the marshal was nowhere in sight.

"*Pssst.*" Farkas stepped out of the darkness.

Jenks could see dark shapes in the shadows behind him, Tillis and the Russian.

"He went up there," Farkas said.

Jenks hadn't noticed the steps up the side of the building in the rain and the dark. They went up the stairs to a door, a window beside it glowing with warm light.

Charlie leaned in and whispered into Grady's ear, "Let's just go up there and grab him."

"That's a good way to get a face full of lead," Grady replied. "Hold on. Let that light go out. We'll wait until he's deep asleep, and then we'll go up, nice and quiet."

CHAPTER 22

The tarp attached to the side of Professor Meriweather's wagon and stretched out about ten feet, tied at the corners of two thin poles stuck into the ground. Annie sat and listened to the patter of the rain against the canvas above, hugged her knees up under her chin, and watched the campfire dwindle.

Meriweather slept inside the wagon and snored, so Annie had taken her blanket outside.

Annie wondered where Parker had gone, wondered why he'd left so abruptly. Had she said or done something? She hadn't wanted him to go, and now she missed him even more than she'd expected to.

She pulled her blanket around her. The night had turned chilly.

Not that Meriwether was bad company, but he was more like a kindly old uncle than—

Than what?

Than a handsome young man who saved you from Indians, she told herself. *Face it, girl, you fell for him, and he left, and now you can't stand it.*

She supposed lack of options might have something

to do with it. It's not like the wilds of Wyoming teemed with eligible bachelors—not that she'd been looking for one. There'd been boys in the past who'd caught her eye, of course, but when she'd set out with her folks to head west, all she'd thought of was the path ahead. Her mother had often told her she'd meet a nice young man someday, but when that might happen—if ever—was simply not something that had occupied much of her thought.

Alone, parents dead, stranded in the wilderness, it was only natural she might cling to Parker. Her savior. And she'd let her imagination run away with the idea as she hung on to him from behind, riding his horse through the yellow wood and across the faded prairie, feeling how solid his back was, feeling the warmth of him.

And then she'd put on the dress the professor had given her, and that makeup around the eyes, looking like some doll from the Far East, hoping Parker would see her differently, like she was a woman and not some kid. But had it been working?

She thought she'd caught him looking at her once or twice, and maybe . . .

Well, maybe nothing. He was gone, and the thought he might never return ate at her something awful. She wondered where Parker was right at that moment. Probably at some saloon, sipping whiskey, with his feet up, a shady lady on each arm.

Annie scowled into the dying campfire, the rain coming harder. *Well, I hope you're just living it up, Parker Jones. While I'm here shivering under this thin horse blanket. You just go ahead and live it up.*

* * *

Parker Jones stepped in a fresh pile of horse dung and cursed.

Then he slapped his hand over his mouth. He hadn't meant to curse out loud. He'd still been huddling in the stall behind his horse, hesitant to show himself until he was sure Jenks and his gang had gone. It was when he'd tried to slip past his horse out of the stall that he'd stepped in the mess.

I reckon I better look where I'm going from now on.

He eased out of the stall, turning his head this way and that to see if the stable was empty or not, ready to duck back into the stall again at the first sign of Jenks or one of his men. He hadn't been able to work up the nerve to look, but from the sound of their grumbling there were at least four of them.

He listened now, trying to hear if any of them were still around, but it was nearly impossible over the rain, and Parker heard only the snorts and movements of horses in the adjacent stalls. He decided the coast was as clear as it was ever going to get, and he emerged from his hiding place with his hand resting on the grip of his Peacemaker.

Parker went to the stable's door, standing just inside as he glanced up and down the street. Nobody was about, hardly a surprise in this weather.

He had to find Marshal Best and warn him. His first thought was to head immediately back to the Broken Wheel, but then he thought better of it. If Best had gone back to the room over the slop house, then Jenks might catch him there all alone.

Parker left the stable and jogged through the rain toward Milly's, cursing again as he was slowly soaked. *Dang it, I just changed into dry clothes.*

Never mind. There were more important things at stake beside his personal comfort.

He ran, splashing in puddles, until he reached the slop house. It was dark, past closing time, Parker reckoned. He circled around to the back and rattled up the stairs without hesitation. The windows next to the door were dark.

Parker pounded on the door with a fist. "Marshal Best!"

He looked around, suddenly worried he was calling attention to himself, but nobody was in the alley behind the slop house. He pounded on the door again, calling the marshal's name.

No answer.

The only possiblility, that Best was still be at the saloon, playing cards. He was already flying back down the stairs and around to the front of Milly's slop house. He turned back the way he'd come but stopped himself. Jenks and his boys were out there somewhere, and Parker wasn't keen to be spotted.

He crossed the street and went up an alley toward the Broken Wheel. It was darker here, without candle or lantern light spilling from windows into the street. Rain lashed his face. Mud sucked at his boots as he jogged toward the saloon. He found a back door and tried it. Locked.

He muttered a string of curses as he circled around to the front. Parker didn't want to barge through the front door and run straight into Grady Jenks. He cupped his hand against the saloon's front window and peered inside. It seemed more or less the same crowd as had been there earlier, a few different faces maybe, but none of them were Jenks.

It didn't look like Best was in there, either.

Parker went inside.

He asked the barkeep if he'd seen the marshal—the man he was with earlier—but the barkeep said he wasn't really good with faces.

Parker went over to the men playing poker. "Sorry to disturb you fellas, but I'm looking for the U.S. marshal that was playing cards with you."

A tidy little man who looked like a shopkeeper glanced up at Parker. "Best? You missed him. Left a little bit ago."

"He was winning," said an older man in a long black coat. "Then he gave it all back in one big pot. His three jacks lost to my full house. Tens over sixes. He just laughed and said he'd better quit while he was still more or less even."

"Did he say where he was going?" Parker asked.

Everyone shrugged.

"He just bid us a good evening and left," the shopkeeper said.

But Parker was already heading for the door and was in the street standing in the rain again the next second. Could he have gone back to the stable for his horse?

Would he sneak away in the night and leave Parker? Maybe if he'd reconsidered having a partner?

Except Parker wasn't really a partner, not a full one, anyhow.

I'm the squire. And his lordship isn't going to give up the fella who cooks his meals and feeds his horse.

But mostly Parker had Tanner Best figured as a man who knew his own mind. He wouldn't have partnered up with Parker in the first place unless it was exactly what he wanted to do. Best wasn't the type to second-guess himself.

Parker turned back toward Milly's and walked fast through the rain.

The lights had gone out in Best's room, and Grady Jenks had stood across the alley, watching along with the rest of his gang. They gave it a few minutes and then a few more.

"Follow me," Jenks told them. "Boris, stay here in the shadows and keep watch. I don't want nothing coming up behind us. Clear?"

The Russian stuck a long, thin cigar in his mouth. "*Da.*"

Jenks blew out a sigh, clenched and unclenched his fists. "The rest of you, let's go. No talking."

Jenks crossed the alley to the stairs and started up, pausing immediately as the first step creaked under his weight. He looked back at the others and made a *go easy* gesture, then put his weight very gradually on the next step. Probably the marshal was up there, snoozing away without a care in the world, but the man was reputed to be a crafty one. It was easy to imagine him sitting in a chair, facing the door with a pistol in each hand and an evil grin on his puss, just waiting for somebody to barge in and catch lead.

Jenks put the notion out of his head. The man was asleep. All they had to do was bust in and grab him.

He took the next step and then the next, careful each time to step lightly, keeping the creaking of the old wood to a minimum. It likely couldn't be heard over the rain, anyway.

Thunder. Lightning crisscrossed the sky.

Jenks looked down at Boris across the alley. The Russian was barely visible in the shadows under the building's overhang.

Finally, Jenks reached the top, but there wasn't room for more than two of them to stand on the small landing in front of the door. He wondered if it was latched on the other side or locked, or what? They'd have to smash through, and they'd only get one chance. The racket would surely wake the marshal.

Jenks pointed at Little Joe Tillis and gestured *come up here*.

Tillis squeezed past the others on the stairway, trying to move as quietly as Jenks had. A moment later, he stood next to Jenks on the landing.

Jenks conveyed with hand gestures what he intended for them to do. He gestured back and forth between the two of them—*both of us*. Then he made a punching motion with his fist at the door—*gonna smash this door in*. He patted his shoulder to indicate how they should impact the door.

When Jenks held up three fingers, Tillis nodded.

Each man took a deep breath.

Jenks held up one finger. *One!*

Then he held up another. *Two!*

He held up the third finger, and he and Tillis leaned back and then rushed forward, slamming the door with all their weight. It cracked inward, splinters flying, the door swinging open much more easily than Jenks had anticipated. He went stumbling into the room, Tillis right behind him. Jenks hit the bed, and Tillis tangled with him from behind, and they both went down.

"What the Sam Hill—" Tanner Best, instantly awake.

"Get him!" Jenks shouted.

He and Tillis both jumped on the bed, and the marshal thrashed. The heel of a bare foot caught Jenks on the side of the head, and he blinked stars. He was aware of the others pounding up the stairs and crowding the room behind him.

There was a brief ecstasy of thrashing, the marshal trying to kick away everyone who was trying to get at him. Everybody yelling. Jenks grabbed an arm—or he assumed it was an arm, at least. Hard to tell in the dark.

A small flash of light. The acrid stink of a struck match.

Then the light grew stronger. Charlie had lit the room's oil lamp, and Grady Jenks could now see the situation with total clarity.

He did indeed have hold of one of Best's arms, the

marshal's hand reaching for the gun belt hanging from the back of the wooden chair next to the bed. Bill Farkas had hold of his other arm, and Joe Tillis sat on Best's chest, his vast bulk pinning the marshal down, one of Tillis's meaty hands around Best's throat. Jimmy stood in the doorway, six-shooter drawn but otherwise uninvolved.

"Close the dang door, will you," Grady said.

Jimmy closed the door.

"Get off me!" Best croaked. It wasn't easy to talk with a hand around his throat.

Grady grabbed the marshal's gun belt and handed it to Charlie. "Get him in the chair, Little Joe."

Tillis manhandled the marshal out of the bed. Best struggled at first, but then Farkas came over to help. They made him sit. Marshal Best had a reputation as a hard man, but he didn't look like much in his underwear.

But Best's hard eyes still flared with fiery indignation. "Well, aren't you outlaws just slick as snot on a doorknob? You've bit off more than you can chew with Tanner Best, you dumb sons of—"

Tillis punched him hard across the jaw, the smack of flesh on flesh so loud it made Grady flinch. Best's head snapped around, and he spit blood.

"There's plenty more where that came from," Grady warned. "Little Joe can punch all day and all night, if that's what you fancy."

"You're playing with fire, Grady Jenks," Best told the outlaw. "You're for the hangman's noose, every one of you. If you was smart—and obviously you ain't—

you'd be headed for the border instead of digging a deeper hole for yourself."

Tillis punched him again. Best didn't bother spitting this time, just letting the blood dribble down his chin.

"We're going to ask questions," Grady said. "I think you can imagine what's going to happen if we don't like the answers to them questions."

"You're all under arrest," Best said.

This time it was Grady Jenks who struck Best, a backhand across the marshal's face. Not one of Tillis's teeth-rattling punches, but a stinging slap, enough to get his attention without addling his wits completely. They needed the man conscious after all.

"Where's the gold?" Jenks asked.

The marshal laughed.

"Care to let me in on the joke?" Jenks asked.

"I've been looking for you lot to ask the same question," Best said.

"Except that's not how it works," Jenks reminded the lawman. "We ask. You answer."

"What's the matter?" Best asked. "You're the ones stole the gold. Forget where you left it?"

"Our friend Gerald Filmore pulled a fast one on us," Jenks said. "But I reckon you knew that already."

"Didn't know anything, not for sure," Best admitted. "But I had some pretty good guesses. Looks like I guessed right. I think we're all in the same boat."

Jenks frowned. "How do you figure?"

"I figured if I found you, then maybe you'd lead me to the gold. Looks like you were hoping *I'd* turn up something in my investigation and maybe lead *you* to the gold. We're all just chasing our tails in a circle, seems to me. How's that for a laugh?"

"I ain't laughing," Jenks said.

Best shrugged. "Well, we're both wasting our time, it seems. Laugh or cry. You choose."

"You're overlooking something," Jenks told him.

Best grinned, his teeth stained red with his own blood. "I just have a feeling you're going to tell me what that is."

"You've been heading due north ever since you left Cheyenne," Jenks said. "You weren't following us. We've been behind you. So what is it, marshal? What brings you to Sundance? There must be some reason."

Best shrugged again. "I reckon one direction's as good as another when I have no idea where I'm going."

"Or maybe you have a good idea. A very good idea," Jenks said. "How about it, marshal? That gold hidden around Sundance somewhere?"

"Turn the town upside down if you want to," Best told him. "If you find any gold, it'll be a surprise to me."

Jenks scowled. "Then why?"

"Why what?"

"Why Sundance? Why north?"

Best let out a long, disinterested sigh, as if the whole conversation was beginning to bore him. "Well, you know, I just heard the climate was nice."

Thunder picked that moment to crack overhead. Rain spattered against the window.

A slow smile spread across Jenks's face, but there was no mirth in the man's eyes. "I'm going to ask you some of these questions again, marshal. But not now, not just yet. First, I think we need to get you into the mood to talk." Jenks's eyes went to Tillis. "Little Joe."

"Right." Tillis took off his jacket and started rolling up his sleeves.

"I guess we're in for a long night, then," Best said, "because I don't know squat."

The rain came harder and stung Parker's eyes as he once again went around to the back of Milly's slop house. He looked up at Best's room, and this time there was a light in the window.

Good. He's up there. I need to warn him right away.

Parker started toward the staircase, then stopped abruptly, something catching his eye across the alley.

A red-orange light flared, and in the flickering matchlight, Parker saw a man in the shadows, leaning against the far building under just enough overhang to keep him out of the rain. He caught the briefest glimpse of his face in the matchlight, hard and lined. Bald head. He lit a thin cigar with the match—*puff, puff*—then shook the match out and tossed it away.

Parker froze, not exactly sure what to do next. The man didn't look familiar, certainly not one of Grady Jenks's gang he'd seen inside Eiger's. He supposed the man had simply come out for some fresh air and to smoke his cigar.

In a dark alley? In the rain?

Right.

Parker, slowly, with all the nonchalance he could muster, walked toward the staircase up to Best's room, right thumb hooked into his gun belt, about as close as he could get his hand to his Peacemaker without it looking obvious he was ready to draw.

He took a half dozen steps, keeping tabs on the stranger in his peripheral vision, and at first, Parker didn't think the man was interested in anything he was doing. He just stood there smoking, the cigar's cherry glowing red like a beacon. He supposed there was no reason to think the man was up to no good. It was none of Parker's business if the man wanted to come out in the driving rain to smoke his cigar, and as far as Parker was concerned—

Movement. The man reached inside his vest. Parker tensed, thinking he was about to pull a pistol, even though the man had a six-shooter on his hip. A second later, Parker relaxed, seeing it wasn't a gun. Something about seven or eight inches long, difficult to identify in the darkness, maybe another cigar. The stranger took the cigar out of his mouth and brought the glowing end to the thing in his other hand. It erupted suddenly in a showering of hissing sparks, and Parker turned and ran.

He chanced a glance over his shoulder and saw the stranger stepping closer, armed cocked to throw.

Parker ran faster, pumping his arms and legs and—

An explosion. A wave of heat slammed into Parker's back, lifting him, arms and legs churning uselessly as the world blurred and turned upside down.

CHAPTER 23

Jimmy Jenks blinked. "That weren't no thunder."

They all stood frozen, even Grady Jenks, all of them wide-eyed, mouths hanging open.

It was Tanner Best who recovered first. "Sounds like God's come a-knockin'."

"Shut up," Grady snapped. "We'll get back to beating on you in a minute."

"I'll be right here," Best said.

Grady pointed at his brothers. "Watch the marshal." Then he looked at Farkas and Tillis. "Come with me. I want to know what's going on out there."

"Bring back some coffee, will ya?" Best said.

"We'll see to you soon enough, funny man." Then Grady Jenks opened the door and stepped out onto the landing, Farkas and Tillis crowding in behind him. He looked down and saw Boris casually crossing the alley, angling toward the street. What was that ridiculous Russian doing now?

Jenks watched as Boris reached into his vest and pulled out—

"Dynamite," Jenks said. "That crazy Russian!"

For the tenth time, Jenks regretted bringing Boris in on this whole scheme. Brother Jimmy had vouched for him, but what was that worth? A letter of recommendation from a jackass.

"What the blazes are you doing, you dumb Russian?" Jenks shouted.

Boris paused, looked up, and grinned big, teeth like tombstones. "Solving a problem, *tovarisch*." The Russian kept walking.

Jenks looked where Boris was going and saw a man lying face down in the mud twenty yards ahead, not moving, probably dead.

But wait. No, the man lifted his head. Not dead after all.

Parker's ears rang.

For a brief moment, he wasn't sure where he was. Then he remembered the explosion, flying through the air, the splat landing in the mud. He was fairly certain nothing was broken. He pushed himself up and shook his head, trying to make the ringing go away.

It didn't.

He pushed himself up to his hands and knees, then staggered to his feet, stood there swaying a moment, trying to blink the world back into focus. He was dazed and knew it, but couldn't just stand there.

Got to . . . warn . . . the marshal.

Where was he going? Oh, yeah. The stairs. He turned toward them, the ground tilting this way and that, like he was on the deck of a ship in rough seas. He saw the stairs leading up to Best's room over the slop house and took a halting step toward them.

Parker saw men at the top of the stairs. They seemed to be saying something. Were they talking to him? They sounded like they were shouting from the bottom of a deep well, voices muted by the ceaseless ringing in his ears. He couldn't quite focus on their faces.

He shook his head. It didn't matter. This was all taking too long. He had to warn Marshal Best. He had to hurry.

Parker tried to run, heading for the stairs, but his legs wouldn't work, and the result was a stumbling, awkward lope. He almost went into the mud again but righted himself and kept going.

The men were coming down the stairs now, waving their arms and shouting, seeming to look at something. Parker tried to turn and look, his attention seized by the sparking thing arcing high over his head. The sight of it penetrated his addled brain.

Dynamite!

He turned and dove in the other direction.

Grady Jenks watched the man struggle to his feet and stand there, mouth hanging open and eyes blinking like he was lost. There was something familiar about him, but with the fella's face all covered in mud, Jenks couldn't be certain.

The man started walking toward Jenks, but his legs were so wobbly, it was a wonder he could stand at all. It was a wonder Boris hadn't blown his arms and legs off. He started down the stairs, Tillis and Farkas right behind him.

Jenks paused when he saw what Boris was doing. The Russian angled to intercept the mud covered fella coming toward the stairs. Boris grinned like a madman, and as Jenks watched what happened next, everything seemed to slow down, like when something horrible happened in a nightmare and Jenks could only watch dumbstruck, powerless to stop it.

Boris laughed liked a wild man, eyes wide and crazy. He took the cigar from his mouth.

And lit the dynamite.

Jenks waved him off and started shouting the word *no*, then stretching it out into a panicked animal sound. Boris lifted his arm to throw.

Farkas and Tillis had seen too, both of them trying to flee, one trying to come fast down the stairs, the other one trying to go back up into the room, the two men slamming into each other in a terrified tangle.

Boris tossed the stick of dynamite.

Jenks watched helplessly, mouth hanging open, as the stick of dynamite tumbled end over end through the air, trailing sparks through the rain, then coming down, down, down, to land at the foot of the stairs and—

A white flash and heat. Smoke and the crack of timber.

Jenks was briefly lifted—and then came tumbling down in a calamity of scorched wood and flailing bodies.

* * *

"What in the blue blazes was that?" shouted the one holding the gun on him.

He held Best's gun belt with the twin Remingtons in the other hand.

The second explosion sounded even closer than the first. Tanner Best sat in the chair, waiting for his opportunity. Everything had happened so fast, it hadn't occurred to the outlaws to bind his hands. Jenks, Farkas, and Tillis were known to him, but he didn't recognize the two in the room with him now, not that he really needed to. They were obviously in cahoots with Jenks. That was all the marshal needed to know for the moment.

The other one stood in the doorway, looking out. "Good Lord! The stairs are gone!"

That got the other one's attention. "What?" He turned to look out the window.

And that was all the opening Best needed.

The marshal stood, grabbed the chair, and flung it at the kid holding the six-shooter. It slammed into him just as he was turning back around, smashing the six-gun out of his hand and knocking him back against the wall.

Best leaped on him, yanking the gun belt free from his other hand. He went for one of the Remingtons.

But the one by the door jumped on both of them. The three rolled around, fell on the bed, then rolled off the bed and hit the floor, hard. Best threw an elbow and caught one of them in the jaw. A grunt and the rattle of teeth. Best twisted away, stood, headed for the door, and went down again, legs tangled, hands grabbing him and pulling him down.

The three wrestled and punched and rolled along the floor. Best looked up to see the combined mass of them heading for the open door. A shove from behind and out they went.

Best felt a bewildering moment of weightlessness, the three of them coming apart from each other, and then slamming—hard—into something. White-hot pain exploded in Best's side.

He discovered he was still holding his gun belt and drew one of the Remingtons, the nickel finish glinting in a sudden flash of lightning.

Parker had curled into a ball, braced for the explosion.

He looked back and saw the men and the ruined staircase all in a pile. The men groaned, slow to get up, and the man who'd been lobbing sticks of dynamite rushed to them, gibbering in a language Parker didn't know.

Parker pushed himself up to one knee, a vague ache all up and down his body.

The gibbering man was pulling wood off the other men. They were slowly coming back to their senses and—

Three more men tumbled from the room above to land on the men below, knocking the gibbering man to the ground. They all lay grinding and twisting among the lengths of cracked wood. The first man to recover and stand looked around him like he couldn't believe what had happened. Parker realized suddenly he recognized the man.

Grady Jenks!

Parker's hand fell to the grip of his Peacemaker.

Tanner Best rose from the pile of bodies, tilting to his left, one arm up against his side in obvious pain. He winced and grunted, going back down to his knees as he brought his six-shooter around.

Jenks kicked the six-shooter out of his hand, and it went flying back into the mud.

Lightning, jagged across the sky, blurred everything white for a brief moment.

Jenks went for his gun.

Parker drew and fired twice, rain in his eyes, palms slick on the Peacemaker's grip. He hit nothing.

But the gunshots got everyone's attention, all of them scrambling to their feet.

Best crawled toward his gun belt in the mud, reaching for the other Remington.

Thunder shook the world.

Everyone who hadn't already drawn a revolver did so.

They all fired at once, bullets whizzing past Parker's ear and churning up the mud at his feet.

Best drew his other Remington and fired wildly.

Grady Jenks was sore, disoriented, and was now being shot at from two different directions. He'd had stairs exploded out from under him by a crazy dynamite-tossing Russian, and the thunderstorm was getting fiercer by the moment.

In short, the outlaw had had enough.

"Let's get out of here!" he shouted above the storm.

They ran.

Tanner Best shot at them, but he was leaning over and holding his side, clearly injured, and his aim wasn't the best. The other one lifted his pistol.

And shot Charlie right in the gut.

Grady Jenks's little brother cried out, stumbled forward a few more yards, then went down.

Grady scooped him up, draping one of Charlie's arms around his neck, and supporting him with an arm around the waist, half-running, half-dragging him along. "I got you, little brother."

Charlie winced. "It hurts."

"I'm sorry," Grady told him. "You can rest soon. We'll get you fixed up, but right now you've got to grit through the pain and run."

He looked back over his shoulder. The man who'd shot Charlie was coming after them, although not very fast, sort of halfheartedly, as if not sure what to do. Grady Jenks briefly considered turning around and gunning the mangy polecat.

But as the people of Sundance spilled from the buildings, eyes wide at the commotion, Jenks abandoned the idea of fighting. Not with the whole town watching.

It was time to go.

The Russian lit another stick of dynamite from the glowing tip of his cigar and tossed it over his shoulder.

It shook the street with a deafening explosion. Women screamed, and half the people scattered, the others ducking behind whatever cover was available. Jenks looked back again and saw that the dynamite had discouraged Best's sidekick from following.

They reached the stable and got their horses. Jenks

draped his brother across the saddle in front of him. They rode hard out of town, thunder following them. There was still lightning in the sky.

They reined in their horses about a half mile out of town.

Jenks thought they'd probably gotten away clean, but he didn't want to assume anything. They'd roused the whole town, and for all he knew, Marshal Best was raising a posse at that very moment. They could be coming after them any minute.

"Split up!" Jenks shouted. "Meet at that place we talked about before."

Farkas, Tillis, and Jimmy turned their horses and headed south at a gallop.

Jenks spurred his horse west, the Russian right behind him.

Charlie's head lolled. Eyes closed. He'd passed out from the pain.

CHAPTER 24

The doctor had been awake, of course, because the whole town was up, and a-buzz with excitement and fear from the explosions. Marshal Best had done his best to calm everyone, told them the show was over and they should go back to bed, and that nobody was hurt.

The exception being Marshal Best himself.

"You'll need to rest," the doctor said as he finished wrapping Best's middle. "A cracked rib is no laughing matter."

The doctor had seen service during the war: he'd treated every manner of wound and injury from amputating a gangrenous leg to lancing a troublesome boil. He'd come west hoping for a quiet life and had settled in Sundance.

"Explosions woke me out of a sound sleep," he said. "Thought I was back at Vicksburg. Took forever to get the cannon fire out of my ears."

Parker stood off to the side, holding his hat and watching the doctor work on the marshal, who sat with his shoulders slumped on the examination table. Best winced as the doc wrapped his ribs tightly. Parker still had dried mud all over him.

"I'll rest if I can, doc," Best said, "but I'll need a ladder to get up to my room."

"Climbing ladders is probably not a good idea," the doc said. "I have a bed in the spare room. You can recover in there."

"Thanks."

"I have an analgesic which might ease the pain," the doctor told him. "I'll fetch it and be back in a moment."

He left the room.

Tanner Best shook his head and sighed. "I never seen so much shooting with nobody getting hit."

"I did hit one," Parker said. "In the belly."

"Oh?" Best looked hopeful. "Was it Grady?"

Parker shook his head.

"Little Joe Tillis? Great big fella. He worked me over good. I hope it was him."

"Sorry. Some younger guy. Maybe even a bit younger than me," Parker said. "Never seen him before."

"Well, at least you hit somebody," Best said. "All I did was fall out a doorway and roll in the mud like a clumsy idiot."

"Right." But Parker didn't feel particularly proud of himself. He didn't feel terrible about it, either. It had all been a blur of craziness: gunfire and explosion and mud and rain and thunder. He felt numb and tired.

"Do me a favor," Best said. "That ladder's actually a good idea. Ask around and borrow one and get up to that room and get my things, will you?"

"Okay." *The squire at work.*

"The room's paid until noon, so you might as well get some shut-eye while you can," Best suggested.

"That's a good idea."

The doc returned and gave Best some pills and a glass of water. "Time to get some rest."

Parker put on his hat and turned to leave. "I'll get your things for you, marshal."

"Obliged," Best said.

The stableman was up with the dawn and had a ladder Parker could use. He carried it back to the slop house and circled around back. He had to maneuver a bit to find a place to set the ladder, but soon enough he was climbing up and in the room. He didn't bother gathering Best's possessions. He could do that later. He was dog tired.

I guess there's something about being woke up in the middle of the night to go to a shoot-out in a thunder-storm and have dynamite tossed at you that just fatigues a man.

He pulled off his boots and flopped into bed, and was dead asleep in no time.

Parker opened his eyes. It seemed only minutes since he'd sprawled in the comfortable bed, but the sun slant-ing through the window told him a few hours had passed.

"Hey! Hey, up there!"

Parker sat up and rubbed his eyes.

"Hey!" A woman's voice.

Parker swung his legs over the side of the bed and stood, every muscle protesting. He could have used another ten hours in bed, but he didn't reckon that was an option. He went to the door, opened it, and saw the owner of the slop house.

"Miss Milly," Parker called, "I'm just gathering the marshal's belongings. I'll be out in a minute."

Milly gestured at the pile of debris which had once been a staircase. "Who's going to pay for this, that's what I want to know."

"Sorry, ma'am," Parker said. "I reckon a U.S. marshal is bound to make enemies. It's Grady Jenks and his band of outlaws who owe you for the staircase." *Good luck collecting, lady.*

Milly threw up her hands and then walked away, muttering discontent. Parker didn't blame her.

He gathered the marshal's things and went down the ladder. He carried them to the livery stable and stashed them in the stall with Best's horse. How long were they going to stay in Sundance? Would Best be well enough to travel?

Parker didn't have the answers.

They burst into the abandoned cottage, Grady Jenks carrying his little brother over his shoulder. There was no bed, just a couple of broken chairs and a table. No glass in the windows, thin shreds of old curtains wafting in the stiff breeze.

Grady laid Charlie on the table, his boots hanging over one end. His shirt was soaked with blood. Charlie had bounced on the horse as they'd fled Sundance until he'd eventually passed out. Grady took off his jacket, also covered in blood, folded it, and put it under Charlie's head for a pillow.

"Get the horses out of sight," he told Boris. "Put them in the barn."

"*Da.*" Boris rushed to do as he was told.

On their way to Sundance, as the last of the light was fading, they'd spotted the stone cottage, with its dilapidated barn, nestled in some trees next to a small stream—Cundy Creek, he thought it was called. Some had thought it a good place to spend the night, but Grady had wanted to press on to Sundance. Still, it had seemed a good place to meet if they got separated.

He just hadn't thought it would be so soon.

Boris returned. "The horses are out of sight."

"Good. Any reason you started throwing dynamite around back there?"

Boris grinned. "Solving problems."

Grady was about to tell the Russian where he could shove his next stick of dynamite when Charlie groaned.

Grady stood at the table, put a gentle hand on his brother's shoulder. "Easy, Charlie. We'll get you fixed up. We'll find you a doctor."

"The nearest doctor is back in Sundance," Boris said. "I am sorry, but he will die. This is obvious."

Grady frowned. "Shut up."

"He will only suffer. Better he be put out of his misery," Boris said. "I understand it is difficult. I can do it for you."

"I said shut up!"

Charlie groaned again. The kid was off somewhere in his mind. Veracruz, maybe.

"Easy," Grady said. "You're gonna be fine."

Charlie's eyes flickered open. "Muh— Mother . . . mother."

His eyes closed again. His face was covered in sweat. It soaked his collar.

"This place is not difficult to find. If the marshal has gathered a posse, they will find us easily," Boris said. "When the others come, we should go. I feel bad for Charlie, but he will slow us down."

"So what?"

"So better to do it sooner than later."

Charlie groaned again. He looked so pale.

"Some water," Grady said. "He could use some water. I'll be right back."

He went to the well out back, lowered the bucket, and brought up the water. He filled his canteen and went back inside.

Boris stood next to Charlie. He'd taken Grady Jenks's coat from under his head and was pressing it to Charlie's face to suffocate him.

"Get away from him!" Jenks dropped the canteen, rushed forward, and shoved Boris away from his brother with both hands. The Russian stumbled back and let loose a long bunch of foreign words that didn't sound friendly. He righted himself and came back fast, punching Jenks in the gut.

Jenks doubled over, the wind going out of him.

Boris pressed forward, threw another punch at Jenks's face. Jenks turned and took it on the ear, the whole side of his face going hot with buzzing needles. His hand fell to his six-shooter, but he never got a chance to draw.

Boris slammed into him, arms going around him as he carried Jenks to the floor. They rolled around, each trying to gain an advantage over the other. Jenks punched once, twice, three times into the Russian's ribs. It was like punching a brick wall. The Russian was a hard, compact little man.

They rolled around on the floor, and the Russian ended up on top.

Suddenly, Boris had a knife in his hand. He brought it down toward Jenks's face. Jenks grabbed Boris's wrist, halting the knife's descent. With his other hand, he pawed at the Russian's face. His thumb found its way into Boris's eye socket, and Jenks dug in hard. He forced his thumb in, felt the eye pop, blood flowing around his thumb and dripping onto his face.

Boris screamed but didn't let go, kept forcing the knife down.

The tip of the knife was just about to plunge into Grady Jenks's face. He rolled left, and the knife went into his shoulder instead. He screamed and bucked, trying to dislodge the Russian. He twisted, and both of them rolled over, and suddenly Jenks was on top.

He smashed his forehead down into the Russian's nose, cartilage snapping and blood shooting from his nostrils. Boris went limp beneath him, his grip on the knife going slack. Jenks knocked the blade away and punched Boris in the face, once . . . twice . . .

Three times.

Jenks rolled off him, chest heaving as he gasped for breath.

Boris lay dazed, bleeding from his nose and one eye

socket, mouth opening and closing like a fish gasping for breath.

Jenks tried to stand, legs going wobbly, and he collapsed back to the floor. He took a deep breath and then another, and another. He stood slowly, head swimming, blinking his eyes, trying to banish the dizzy feeling between his ears.

Boris muttered something in Russian, writhing on the floor. He pawed at his bloody face, whimpering and cursing, his one good eye bouncing back and forth as if seeing the world and all its ugliness for the first time.

His hand went for his gun.

Jenks drew and fired.

Blood erupted from a hole in the Russian's chest. He started screaming and wouldn't stop.

Jenks shot him again.

Everything went still, Boris not moving a muscle, mouth hanging open, one eye wide and staring up at nothing at all. A stink hung in the air, gunpowder and panic sweat and blood all mixed together, and maybe the stench of loosened bowels thrown into the bargain. It was all a horrible mess. Jenks hadn't meant it to go so far, had simply reacted from instinct when he'd seen the Russian trying to suffocate his little brother.

Jenks backed against the far wall and slid down into a sitting position. He took deep breaths, bringing his heart rate back under control.

Bill Farkas burst into the room, gun drawn, startling Jenks.

"We heard shots," Farkas said.

Jenks gestured to the Russian's corpse.

"What'd you do that for?" Tillis and Jimmy appeared right behind Farkas.

Jenks explained.

Tillis squatted next to the dead Russian and whistled. "Geez, he's a mess, ain't he?"

Jimmy went to the table where Charlie was sprawled.

"We need to find a doctor," Jenks said. "Charlie's gut-shot pretty bad. He's bleeding all over the place."

"Never mind, Grady," Jimmy said. "He's dead."

Parker took Best a few of his personal items, including a change of clothes. The doctor took charge of the items as the marshal was still resting.

Then Parker went to the general store and purchased a box of ammunition for his Peacemaker to replace what he'd already used up.

"There a post office in Sundance?" Parker asked the clerk.

"That'd be me," the clerk replied. "I keep outgoing letters in the lockbox until the mail wagon comes through. It's due in a few days, as a matter of fact."

Parker bought a sheet of blank paper and a pencil and an envelope. "I'm going to find a place to sit and write a letter. I'll be back for a postage stamp in a bit."

"Take your time," the clerk said. "I ain't going nowhere."

Parker left the store and sat on the bench out front. The sun was up, and the day was warm, baking the mud dry from last night's rain. He wished he'd had a few more hours in that bed.

He looked down at the blank sheet of paper, wondering how to begin. He'd told himself a dozen times to send his sister a letter but had never seemed able to get around to it. She was probably worried sick.

He wrote *Dear Sarah*.

Well, that was the easy part.

Parker supposed he could just tell her all he'd been up to since leaving home. Maybe she'd find it interesting. He thought about relating his encounter with the outlaw Grady Jenks at Eiger's Trading Post, but he'd frozen trying to arrest the man and probably would have gotten himself killed if Tanner Best hadn't come along. Parker decided he didn't come off that well in the story, so he skipped over it.

Instead, he told her about finding Annie and then falling in with Professor Meriweather. The professor was a colorful character, and Parker guessed Sarah would find that interesting reading. He wrote about fending off an Indian attack before the cavalry arrived and decided he came off a lot more heroic in that story. He tried to stick to the facts and not lay it on too thick.

Then he told Sarah he'd fallen in with a U.S. marshal named Tanner Best. He didn't say anything about gold, telling her only that he was helping the marshal with a matter of law enforcement.

He considered telling her about the shoot-out in Sundance, but it would probably only worry her, with bullets flying all around and a fella throwing dynamite and all.

And anyway, he'd almost filled up both sides of the paper, even after intentionally writing small to save space. He'd written slowly, too, since his penmanship wasn't the best, and he wanted the letter to be legible. He said he'd write again soon and signed it.

Parker folded the letter, stuck it in the envelope, and wrote the address on the front. He took it back into the store and bought a stamp.

"I'll make sure it gets on the next wagon," the clerk assured him.

"Thanks." Parker turned to go, then paused. "Say, you happen to know of a place called the Bear Lodge?"

"Sure, everyone around here knows that place."

"How would I get there?"

"Take the road west out of town," the clerk said. "Maybe thirty miles at most. Gonna have a look at it, huh?"

"There's some kind of trading post, right?" Parker asked. "I was, uh, looking to do some fishing maybe."

"Oh, you're looking for old Gus," the clerk said.

"I mean—maybe." Parker had hoped not to be too obvious. "He must be famous."

"Well, in some circles, I reckon," the clerk said. "I like to do a little fishing myself, when I can get away. And fishermen like to talk, compare stories, talk about the best bait for this fishing hole or that. Now, if you asked my wife, she wouldn't know Gus Mendelson from a jackrabbit."

Parker laughed. "Thirty miles, you say."

"Maybe not even that."

"Okay, then," Parker said. "I appreciate it."

The clerk waved. "Hope you catch a bunch."

Parker walked outside just in time to see Marshal Best coming from the other direction. He'd cleaned up and put on the fresh clothes Parker had brought him. Other than walking a little more slowly than normal, Best seemed none the worse for wear.

"Feeling okay, marshal?" Parker asked.

"Good enough, I reckon," Best replied. "The doc wrapped me up nice and tight."

Parker told Best what he'd learned from the store clerk.

"Then I guess we might as well get a move on," Best decided.

"Getting kind of a late start," Parker said.

Best looked up and down the street. "Well, I do believe we've gotten all we're going to get out of Sundance. Might as well get going to this Bear Lodge place and see if there's anything worth seeing. We won't get there in daylight, but we'll get there."

They went to the livery stable. Parker saddled his horse, and then he saddled Best's. *Squire Jones hard at work again. It sure didn't take the marshal long to get used to people doing his work for him.*

"Obliged for the help," Best said. "Hard to lift the saddle with cracked ribs."

Parker felt bad then for his earlier unkind thought. Of course, the marshal had been injured and would need help.

Best put his boot in the stirrup, tried to heave himself into the saddle, winced, and came back down again.

"Let me give you a boost," Parker offered.

"Obliged. But I need to be able to do this."

He heaved himself up again, grunting and flinching with the pain, face going red, but finally found himself in the saddle. He sat leaning over to one side, arm up against his ribs. He took a slow, deep breath, held it, then let it out slowly. He repeated the process a few times and then, gingerly, sat up straight.

"Okay, then," Best said. "Guess I'm good to go."

They headed west.

Chapter 25

The late afternoon sun beat down on the streets of Sundance without mercy as the blocky, garish wagon rattled into town, people on the sidewalk gawking at the sight. Professor Xavier T. Meriweather reined in his team of horses, and the wagon rolled to a stop in front of the general store.

Annie sat on the wagon bench next to Meriweather and cast a glance about, taking in her surroundings. "Not much of a town, is it?"

Meriweather shrugged. "We must play the hand we've been dealt. Even in such remote areas, people are often in need of my miracle elixirs. Are we to deny them the relief they so desperately crave just because we happen not to be impressed with their town?"

"I guess not," Annie said. "Should we set up? Want me to get dressed?"

Meriweather looked around, making his own appraisal of the town. "I think not. Tomorrow might be better. It's getting close to closing time for some of these folks, and they'd all be off home by the time we finish setting up."

Annie hadn't thought of that.

Meriweather climbed down from the wagon with a grunt, stood, and stretched his back. "I cannot sit on that wretched bench a moment longer."

Annie climbed down, too. It felt good to move.

"I'm going to have a look around and get a notion of what sort of place this is," Meriweather told her. "Then we shall make our camp for the night out of town and return tomorrow to put on our show. Meet me back here in an hour."

"Okay."

She watched the professor amble away and stood in the street next to the wagon, not really sure what to do with herself. There were a few shops, but she didn't have any money, even though she'd been working for Meriweather. The professor had never explained how often she was supposed to be paid, or even how much.

"Lordy, will you look at that," a voice said behind her.

Annie turned to see a middle-aged woman gawking at the wagon. She had a hardworking look about her, an open and pleasant face, if a bit tired.

"What kind of wagon is this?" she asked, squinting at the writing across the side. "What's an—*ee-licks-sir*?" she asked.

"Medicine," Annie said.

"Huh." The woman shrugged. "Maybe better just to say *medicine*, then."

Annie couldn't argue with that.

"This Meriweather fellow a doctor, then?"

Annie had noticed the professor had very specifically not claimed to be a doctor. "More like a professor."

"Huh."

"He's studied at some of the finest institutions in Europe," Annie said.

"Huh."

Annie couldn't quite tell if the woman was impressed or not.

"Well, it sure has been an interesting couple of days," she said. "First all that crazy ruckus last night, and now the craziest looking *elixir* wagon I ever did see."

"Ruckus?"

"You didn't hear? Woke up the whole town?"

"I been in Sundance all of five minutes," Annie said.

"Had a fella throwing dynamite around," she said. "Can you believe that? Like to blown the whole town to bits. Blasted my back steps all to kindling. And then they all started shooting. That Marshal Best and his young deputy and a bunch of outlaws who rode into town, God knows why."

Annie's ears perked up. "Would that be Tanner Best?"

"That's him."

"The young deputy with him. Would you happen to know his name?" Annie asked.

"Sorry, girl, I didn't catch it."

"Parker Jones."

Annie turned to see a little man who had approached from the other direction and was now inserting himself into the conversation. "He was in my store to mail a letter."

Annie's heart leaped with hope. "Please, sir, can you tell me if the young man is still in town?"

"I don't think so. He was asking for directions elsewhere." The man looked at the big, garish medicine show wagon, then back at the girl. "You must be Annie."

Annie blinked. "How did you know that?"

The woman frowned at him. "Henry Armstrong, have you been reading people's mail again?"

Armstrong lifted his chin, assuming a haughty manner. "That is a wild and baseless accusation, Miss Milly. I don't have to stand here and be insulted."

Milly offered him a quirky smirk. "Where do you usually stand?"

Armstong made an annoyed noise in his throat and turned to stalk away.

Annie chased after him. "Please, Mr. Armstrong, did Parker Jones happen to say where he was going?"

Armstrong paused. "He asked for directions to the Bear Lodge. It's a well-known oddity in this area."

"Mr. Armstrong, did he, uh, say anything very interesting about me in his letter?"

"I do *not* read other people's mail. Good day to you, madam." Armstrong turned abruptly and left, without looking back.

But Annie paid him no mind, already lost in her own thoughts.

Looks like I'll be talking Professor Meriweather into going to this Bear Lodge place.

* * *

They buried the Russian behind the barn, and they buried Charlie under a shady tree down by the water.

"He weren't a bad fella, really." Jimmy leaned on the shovel, looking down at the fresh mound of dirt. "Just a bit—intense."

Grady Jenks frowned. *Yeah, well, he almost intensed your little brother right into the grave.*

Not that it mattered. Charlie was in his grave, anyway. It had all been so stupid. The entire affair with the gold had been a debacle. They should never have trusted Filmore.

Little Joe Tillis hooked his thumbs into his gun belt. "Now what?"

"We shouldn't stay here anymore." Jenks said. "Maybe Best's got a posse after us, maybe not. But this is the sort of place they'd check. We need to get out of here."

"But get out of here to where?" Farkas asked.

Jenks sighed. "I can only figure two possibilities. Either we go back to Cheyenne and start asking around again, or we take another run at Tanner Best."

Farkas raised an eyebrow. "The marshal? That didn't work out so well last time."

"I know, and I feel a dang fool about it," Jenks said. "That was— That was six of us against one damn marshal."

"Two of 'em," Tillis corrected. "That other fella come along."

"Still, six against two," Jenks said.

"Who was he, anyway?" Jimmy Jenks asked.

"I don't know," Grady Jenks said. "For a second, I thought he looked familiar, but it was dark, and he was covered in mud, and all the thunder and lightning, and that stupid Russian throwing dynamite all over the place. That's what I'm talking about. We let ourselves get rattled and run out of town. There was only two of them. We need cool heads. We need to think before letting ourselves get flustered."

"So what do you want to do, Grady?" Farkas asked.

"Whatever we do, the first order of business is to make sure nobody's after us. I say we ride west for a day or so, and then double back, or maybe head south, depending on what we want to do next."

"Why west?" Jimmy asked.

"Because why the hell *not* west?" Grady Jenks was getting tired of so many questions. Maybe because he was sick of not having the answers.

"There's supposed to be a trading post, west," Farkas said. "Maybe a day's ride."

Jenks nodded. "Okay, then. That's something to shoot for. We could use some supplies and maybe ask around kind of subtle-like about the news of the day. Maybe hear about any posses running around."

"And then what?"

"I'm getting a little fed up with people asking *and then what?* all the time," Jenks said heatedly. "We're going west until we hit this trading post. I'm calling a ceasefire on all questions until then. We're going to ride in peace and quiet, and put some miles behind us. Now mount up!"

There was a bit of grumbling, but they all knew better than to pester Grady Jenks further.

He climbed onto his horse and turned west. A line of dark clouds loomed in the distance.

That just figures. More rain.

Blue skies turned gray, then black, and then the sky opened up and the rain fell hard.

Parker Jones hunched in the saddle, soaked through. He nudged his horse alongside the marshal's. "You want to keep going in this?"

"You see a hotel around here?" Best asked. "We're wet, anyway. Might as well keep going."

Night fell, and the rain eased. With the clouds obscuring the moon and stars, the night became implacable and unending. They paused while Best lit a lantern and held it up as they went. The small circle of light wasn't much, but at least they wouldn't run the horses into a hole.

The rain stopped altogether, and they spotted a copse of trees just off the road, with a clearing in the middle.

"As good a place as any to stop," Best said.

Thank God. All Parker wanted to do was go to sleep.

But Squire Jones had work to do. Lighting a fire with wet wood was tricky, but he at last got a blaze going— lots of smoke at first—and soon he had an acceptable campfire. He strung a line between two trees and hung up the wet clothes. Then he tended to the horses, feeding and hobbling them for the night.

Best sat with his back against a tree trunk, smoking his pipe.

By all means, relax, Parker thought sourly. *I'll fix dinner, too. Just leave it to your trusty squire.*

Dinner was bacon and beans. By the time they'd eaten, and Parker had cleaned up, he could barely keep his eyes open. He stretched out and put his head on his saddle. The fire burned low.

"Grady Jenks doesn't know where the gold is," Best said.

Parker sat up. "What?"

"All this time, I've been hunting Grady Jenks, hoping he'd lead me to the gold," Best said. "Turns out he was looking for me, hoping the same thing."

Parker let that digest, then said, "Are you telling me that nobody knows where the gold is?"

"Well, with Gerald Filmore dead . . ." Best let that hang there a moment as he puffed his pipe. "It might be gone, Deputy Jones. That gold could be lost forever."

Parker let that sink in. "Then what do we do?"

Best shrugged. "Go and find your fisherman, I reckon. Can't hurt. We'll see what tomorrow brings."

Parker lay back down and closed his eyes. His thoughts turned to Annie. He'd done the right thing, hadn't he, leaving her and the professor?

But of course he had. Last night was proof of that. The outlaws had come. Annie could have been right in the middle of it. What a waste it would have been saving her from Indians only to have her blown to smithereens by some madman flinging sticks of dynamite.

Sleep took hold and the rest of the night passed dark and dreamless.

* * *

Parker awoke to daylight and sat up, running his fingers through his hair as he yawned. He was usually up before now, getting coffee ready. He glanced over at the marshal. Best still slept. Bouncing in the saddle yesterday with those sore ribs had probably taken a lot out of him.

Parker stood, stretched, and fetched the coffee pot. He took a quick walk, hoping to find a stream to fill the pot and preserve the water in the canteens. He emerged from the copse of trees to an open area, blue sky stretching in every direction. Last night's dark clouds had cleared away and—

Parker dropped the coffee pot. He stood and stared, his eyes going wide. For a long moment, he thought he might have been imagining it—but he blinked, and it was still there.

He ran back to the camp, found his jacket, and took the map from the inner pocket, unfolding the map as he went. Then he just stood there for a minute looking at the huge monstrosity before him, then down at the map to compare, then back up again.

A mountain, looming large, but like no other mountain Parker had ever seen. It rose almost straight up from its base, walls deeply lined and grooved from bottom to top, as if scored by giant claws, and flat across the top.

In short, it looked like a gigantic tree stump.

He looked down at the map again.

Not a tree stump. A mountain.

Somewhere ahead, maybe in the shadow of the strange mountain itself, fifty thousand dollars in gold waited to be found.

CHAPTER 26

"Why didn't you show me this before?" Best asked.

An apologetic shrug from Parker. "I guess I felt fool-ish. Map didn't make no sense. Just looked like a tree stump to me."

But that was only partly true. For whatever reason, Parker had held the map back. Some instinct had told him to do it, but he couldn't exactly say why. Maybe for a moment just like this when all hope seemed to be lost. So he could whip out the map and be a hero.

Best looked at the odd flat-topped mountain, then down at the map. "I reckon it does look like a tree stump."

"How tall is it?" Parker asked.

"That's depends on how far away it is. Maybe a couple miles," Best estimated. "I'd say maybe five hundred feet from the base. We'll know more as we get closer."

Parker couldn't help but stare at it. Just a bunch of rock shooting straight up. "It sure is a sight."

"Is that our coffee pot there in the grass?" Best asked.

Parker looked down. "Yeah. Sorry."

"Bring it," Best told him. "We'll have coffee, at least."

No rest for Squire Jones.

They each had a strip of jerky for breakfast, washed down with black coffee, and soon they were back on the road, the strange stump-like mountain growing larger in their vision. By the time they reached the Belle Fourche River, the mountain was less than a mile away.

"Now that I see it up close, I'm thinking it's a bit taller than my earlier guess," Best admitted. "Maybe closer to a thousand feet. Let's cross the river. I want to get closer."

The Belle Fourche wasn't a particularly wide river, nor very deep. They found a spot to ford where the river was barely twenty-five feet to the other side, and the water just came up to the horses' bellies.

Best reined in his horse and motioned for Parker to stop next to him. "Let me see that map again. Maybe we can get ourselves oriented."

Parker handed the map to the marshal, who looked down at it, then off to his left, then down at the map again, then off to his right.

While Best tried to get his bearings, Parker took a deep breath and paused to appreciate the moment, his eyes drawn ever upward to the mountain of stone before him. Today, it seemed like Parker was living in an entirely different world than yesterday. Previously, the map he'd found—stolen, if he was being honest—was no more than a bunch of inscrutable nonsense.

Now it was a treasure map. With gold at the end.

Unfortunately, there was no *X* to mark the spot, like in some pirate story.

"I'm not sure where to start and where to end." Best squinted at the map.

"My guess was that the big stump was the starting point," Parker said.

"How do you figure?"

"It was something he'd recognize without having to write down what it was," Parker said. "Or he could give the map to a friend, to pick up the gold, if he was being watched. It was hid behind a painting at his house, and he could send somebody to get it, if he needed to. Maybe he did have a partner, but he never had a chance to pick up the map. Or— Well, I don't know, really. But it just seems to me with all them lines and directions, you'd need to start someplace obvious, but not too obvious, in case the map fell into the wrong hands."

Best looked at him, eyes narrowing. "You've given this a good deal of thought, haven't you, Deputy Jones?"

"That map's been weighing down my pocket since Missouri, marshal," Parker said. "Let's look at these numbers and lines."

Parker held one side of the map and Best held the other, as both men squinted at it.

"This wavy line I think is the Belle Fourche." Parker traced it on the map then pointed behind them. "See how it bends toward the east back where we crossed. I think it makes another bend back then heads north." He returned to the map. "Just like on here. See?"

"I see," Best said. "What's this on the northern part of the river? Some kind of triangle."

Parker traced the river with his finger up to the triangle. "See that line down the middle of the triangle?"

"Yeah."

"Sort of looks like a tent to me," Parker said.

Best nodded. "You're right. A camp."

"That's what I was thinking," Parker said. "Right on the river."

"A fish camp?"

"Maybe." Parker traced a line from the camp due west to the base of the big flat-topped mountain. Then he tapped another symbol on the map. "What's that look like to you?"

"An *X*."

"I thought that at first, too," Parker told him. "But one line's longer than the other."

"A cross? A peculiar place for a church."

"Or maybe it *is* an *X*, just written sloppy," Parker said. "But the rest of the map seems pretty neat and careful." He traced another dotted line going back northeast until it came to a symbol that looked like a *W*. What could *W* stand for? Water? Why not just write pond or lake? Parker had no idea.

"Why's that line broken up like that?" Best asked.

"I gave that a good bit of thought," Parker said. "Maybe the solid line is a trail and the dotted line isn't. Or it could be the other way around, for all I know. These are all guesses, marshal—but like I said, I been looking at this map a long time, and I tried to figure what sort of thinking would go into it if *I* was trying to hide something. If the gold was on a path or near a well-known landmark, then anyone might stumble over it, by accident. I guess you need landmarks to follow, so you don't outfox yourself. I wouldn't want to hide something so good that I couldn't find it myself, when the time come. But then at some point, I'd have to go off the beaten path, some out-of-the-way place nobody would find it by sheer dumb luck."

"I guess the only way to find out is to follow the map," Best said.

Parker sighed. "Unless I'm not figuring these symbols right—in which case we can run around the woods in a circle all week and never find a thing."

"Then let's start with the fish camp," Best suggested. "If the map is to be believed, then all we have to do is follow the river. That'll tell the tale soon enough."

"Sounds like a good plan to me."

They followed the river at an easy walk, Parker checking the map periodically, to see if it matched the bends and turns in the Belle Fourche River. It wasn't perfect, but it was very close, and Parker was confident Gerald Filmore had mostly got it right.

They'd gone maybe a mile and a half when Best was the first to spot the tent under some overhanging tree branches near the riverbank. As they got closer, they saw a circle of stones off to the side for a sitting area, and a fire pit. An unsaddled horse was tethered nearby.

"Somebody's here," Best said.

They eased their horses to a halt, eyes scanning the tree line, but didn't see anyone.

"Maybe inside the tent," Parker said.

Best raised his voice. "Hello, the camp!"

"Over here!"

Their heads turned toward the river. A man stood thigh-deep in the middle of the current, holding a fishing rod. Best and Parker urged the horses along the riverbank until they'd drawn even with the fisherman.

"Catch anything?"

The fisherman tapped the wicker basket hanging from his shoulder strap. "A whole mess of bullheads."

The fisherman was old, gray hair thinning, face wrinkled, skin clinging to the bone. But he stood his ground in the river's stiff current and seemed spry enough. He wore a flannel shirt and a straw hat.

"Thought we might try fishing a little ourselves," Best said, tone affable.

The old man's eyes went briefly to Parker and Best, before looking to where he was casting. "Where's your rods?"

"We're just scouting good spots right now," Best said. "I heard there's a trading post hereabouts. Figured we could equip ourselves there."

"How'd you hear about this spot?" the old man asked. He wasn't unfriendly, but neither did he overflow with warmth.

Best opened his mouth to answer, but Parker found himself jumping in.

"Gerald Filmore told us." Parker figured it was true, in a sense. It was Filmore's map after all.

The old man seemed pleased to hear Filmore's name, although it might simply have been a trick of the light, the sun's reflection off the water doing things to his expression. "He was always keen to find my best spots. I must admit, I thought he'd keep my secrets better."

"Sir, are you Gus Mendelson, by any chance?" Parker asked.

Now the old man did smile as he wrist-flicked the rod, his lure dropping into the water a dozen yards away. "Just call me Gus. Everyone does. How's Gerald? I haven't seen him since he came up with those pack mules."

Parker didn't like breaking bad news to people, but he needn't have worried. Tanner Best took back control of the conversation.

"He's doing well. The railroad keeps him busy," Best said. "He'd rather be fishing, of course."

Parker's eyes flicked briefly to Best. The marshal had come up with the lie so quickly that Parker felt it must have been something he'd thought up ahead of time.

Gus chuckled. "That sounds like Gerald."

"I'm Tanner Best, and this is my partner, Parker Jones," Best said. "The afternoon's getting late, and I'm of a mind to climb down from this saddle and give my backside a rest. Mr. Mendelson—Gus—would it put you out if we shared your campfire tonight?"

"I suppose I wouldn't mind the company," Gus said. "And I got more bullheads than I can eat all by my lonesome, that's for sure."

"And I have a bottle of whiskey in my saddlebag," Best offered. "Never let it be said Tanner Best comes to the party empty-handed."

Gus grinned. "Now you're talking my language."

Squire Jones went back to work unsaddling the horses, gathering wood, and building the cook fire. He reminded himself that the marshal was still tender from his injury, wincing with every step.

Gus Mendelson was not only an expert angler, but he turned out to be a sure hand at cleaning and frying the bullheads. He sprinkled them with salt and pepper and some wild sage, and stewed a pot of mustard greens to go with them.

Best borrowed Gus's rod and tried his hand at fishing while Gus prepared the meal. Parker watched the marshal from the corner of his eye. Best stood on the edge of the bank, flicking the lure into the water. To Parker, it seemed Best didn't have the patience for fishing. He'd toss the lure to one spot, then jerk it back if he didn't immediately get a bite, and then fling the lure elsewhere. Parker shook his head. The marshal would probably have preferred to draw his Remingtons and gun the fish out of the river.

By the time Best called it quits, the meal was ready. The men ate in silence, tucking into the fish and greens like it was the first meal they'd ever eaten. After so many nights of bacon and beans, Parker considered the bullheads a treat, and he ate until his belly was tight.

Parker sat back and let out a sigh, one hand on his stomach. "Mr. Mendelson, that was about the best fish I ever had."

"Gus."

"Sorry," Parker said. "Gus."

"Nothing beats fresh-caught," Gus said. "Now, I think I heard something about a bottle of whiskey, yes?"

Best fetched the whiskey, and they passed it around. The sun had just gone down, and Parker put more wood on the fire.

Gus Mendelson loved to talk fishing. He seemed to know the perfect lure or bait for any sort of fish, what time of year was best for fishing which body of water, and what fish were good to eat and which weren't worth the bother.

Parker listened attentively, asking an occasional question. He could picture himself off somewhere alone and peaceful, catching fish, and not worrying about gold or outlaws, or anything.

Best listened, too, but Parker suspected the marshal was only pretending to be interested.

"That's how I became acquainted with Gerald Filmore," Gus said. "He wasn't having no luck in the Belle Fourche until I tied a couple of ties for him and told him where to go."

"You said last time you saw him, he had a string of pack mules?" Best asked.

Gus drank from the bottle, then passed it to Parker. "I asked him what he was packing, and he just said supplies. I said he must be going to the fish camp for a month with all that, but he just shrugged. Maybe he was meeting some pals."

Best took the bottle from Parker and drank. "How far back would this be?"

Gus tilted his head back, face squinting as he gave it thought. "Well, now, my memory ain't what it used to be." He pondered a moment and then told them the date.

Best shot Parker a significant look, and Parker knew

why. The date more or less corresponded to the stretch of time directly after the train robbery, when Filmore would have had the opportunity to make off with the gold and hide it somewhere.

Gus Mendelson stood and stretched. "Well, I reckon it's time to take these tired old bones to bed. I'll be getting up early to head out. You gents headed to the trading post to buy your fishing gear? If you want to ride along with me, I'll show you the way."

"Obliged for that," Best said. "But we thought we'd stick around and do some hunting before getting our fishing gear. Gerald maybe mentioned, uh, some kind of trail that would take us into the woods."

Again, Parker noticed how easily the lies came to Best. Still, what else could the marshal do? It probably wouldn't be smart to blab they were looking for a fortune in gold, hidden somewhere by a dead man.

Gus jerked a thumb over his shoulder. "Maybe twenty yards that way, but it's just a narrow game trail. Blink and you'll miss it."

"Obliged."

"I'm not much of a hunter, but there's plenty of mule deer, and I occasionally see a whitetail," Gus said. "I haven't been all the way down the trail, but I'm told it goes all the way to Devils Tower."

Parker raised an eyebrow. "Devil's what?"

"Tower. Surely you saw it. Can't miss it," Gus said. "Or maybe you know it by the old name, the Bear Lodge."

It all made sense now. The big flat-topped mountain of stone. They'd been riding straight for the Bear Lodge without even realizing what it was. "Why did they change it to Devils Tower?"

"Don't rightly know," Gus admitted. "Some army expedition came through, mapping and such, and suddenly everyone's calling it Devils Tower. My guess is somebody translated it from Lakota wrong, but that's just the sort of mistake that don't ever seem to get fixed."

"It looks a sight, whatever it's called," Parker said.

"It does seem to fill up the view," Gus agreed. "Goodnight, gents. Maybe we'll share some coffee before we part ways in the morning."

The old man went to his tent. Parker and Marshal Best spread out their bedrolls on opposite sides of the fire pit.

Parker lay awake awhile, knowing in part what tomorrow would bring. They'd follow the map, of course, and maybe they'd find the gold, or maybe they'd find nothing at all. And if they did find the gold, then what? It hadn't brought happiness to Gerald Filmore, only death.

The Devils Tower loomed ahead. Was the devil himself out there waiting for them? It didn't matter.

When a man was halfway to hell, he had no choice but to keep going.

CHAPTER 27

"Are you sure our young Deputy Jones is traveling with Marshal Best?" Meriweather asked.

"That's what they told me." Annie sat on the wagon bench next to the professor.

It was the lunch hour before they were finally able to pull out of Sundance. Meriweather had wanted to put on a medicine show midmorning. They'd drawn a tepid crowd and sold exactly two bottles of the professor's miracle elixir. Meriweather faced the poor sales with cheerful aplomb, acknowledging that into every life a little rain must fall.

"Then he was telling the truth, eh?" Meriweather said. "He's obviously off on some task for the law."

Annie nodded, eyes straight ahead as the wagon rocked and jostled, eating up the miles at its dogged, glacial pace. When Parker had left them, she'd assumed the worst, that he'd grown tired of being slowed down by a weird old man and his cumbersome wagon, that he didn't want to be burdened with some silly girl.

But now, well, she wasn't sure what to think, not completely. She knew the professor was trying to make her feel better, implying Parker had gone off because he had a job to do with the marshal and not simply to shed himself of her company. She wanted to believe it.

It might even be true.

"I don't mind going to this Bear Lodge place," Meriweather said. "I mean, I have to go in some direction, eh? But there's no reason to believe Parker will be there waiting for us."

Annie nodded slowly, still looking straight ahead. "I know."

"And if it's meant to be, then he'll come back and find you," added the professor. "That's how it is in the storybooks, eh?"

"I know." Although Annie had never read those kinds of storybooks. Her folks used to have a Bible, and she'd read from that a lot. She didn't remember reading anything in there about being heartsick for somebody she might never see again.

"Did I ever tell you I almost got married once?" Meriweather asked. "I was very young, of course, as young as our good Parker Jones, at least. Did I ever mention it?"

"No." Annie wasn't particularly interested, but if she let him talk, then she wouldn't have to. He'd been full of stories all through Wyoming—nothing else to do really but swap stories—and he was older, so he had more of them.

But she hadn't heard this one.

"She was a beautiful girl, from a good family in Savannah," Meriweather said. "This was before the

war, you know. Things were so different then. I went to
sea on a whaling ship, but it wasn't for me. I returned
eventually to find she'd married another man, someone
her family approved of just a little bit more. Those old,
established Southern families were nearly aristocracy
back then. Making a good match was far more important than true love."

Annie wasn't sure if this story was supposed to make
her feel better or not.

"I cried and carried on, and was quite the mess for a
while," Meriweather confessed. "It was all rather em-
barrassing. I thought I'd lost the love of my life, but
really, I'd gained myself. I was allowed to go on with
my life and be completely who I was meant to be. If
I'd married that girl—if I'd somehow gotten past her
parents—I would never have been me. I would just
have been the family problem, the disappointment,
and she'd have grown to resent me for it, and we would
not have been happy people." A shrug. "At least that's
the story I've told myself over the years. When one
pulls weeds to allow a garden to flourish, one seldom
considers the weeds a loss."

Annie supposed she was meant to think of Parker as
a weed, and now that he was gone, she could flourish.
She didn't have the professor's experience of the world,
but even to her it seemed a child's assertion of *I never
wanted that anyway* when a favorite toy was taken away.

Or maybe that was the point. Maybe a child had to
get rid of toys and childish things in order to grow up.

Or maybe there wasn't a point at all, and the professor

simply liked to talk away the hours and the miles, all down through the long years, until Annie was sitting beside him to provide ears to fill with his talk.

Her thoughts were unkind, she supposed. Professor Meriweather had taken her in and given her work, but she couldn't stop herself, because she felt sorry for herself and, therefore, angry with herself. She'd survived two Indian attacks and seen her parents killed. She'd felt terrified, worried, numb, exhausted, and maybe a dozen other feelings, all mixed together like one of the professor's elixirs.

But this was the first time she'd felt sorry for herself. And she didn't like it.

She didn't like not knowing what was going to happen. Would she still be the professor's assistant a year from now? Five years from now? Just for lack of other options? Even wearing the exotic dress no longer amused her, not without Parker around to see her in it.

Annie Jolene Schaefer had no idea what her life would be. All she knew was that Parker Jones was headed somewhere called the Bear Lodge, at least according to the man she'd spoken with in Sundance.

So that's where Annie was going, too.

Parker Jones woke, stoked the coals of the previous night's fire, and began the coffee. When it was ready, he poured himself a cup, took a big sniff of it, always loving the aroma, right when it was freshly brewed.

The morning was cool and damp.

Tanner Best was up and around a few minutes later, and Squire Jones brought him a cup of coffee before turning his attention to biscuits and bacon. By the time the food was ready, Gus Mendelson emerged from his tent, fully dressed with his pack over his shoulder and his rod in one hand.

"Morning!" he called.

Parker gestured to the food. "Breakfast, Mr. Mendelson?"

"You're a polite young man, but it's Gus," Gus reminded him. "Yes, please. And if you offered me a cup of that coffee, I wouldn't say no."

"Happy to, but we only got the two cups."

Gus took his own cup from his pack and let Parker fill it.

"Thanks," Gus said. "I'm going to do a little more fishing and then leave for the trading post this afternoon."

"Sounds like a good way to spend a few hours," Parker said.

They ate breakfast, and Gus took his rod to the river.

Parker didn't have a rod, but he still had the line and flies he'd taken from the Filmore home and thought he might try his luck in the Belle Fourche. It looked like it would be a good day for it, with blue skies and mild weather.

They had a late lunch, fried fish again, and then Gus went to saddle his horse.

Gus returned, leading his horse by the reins. "Obliged for the fellowship. I reckon I'll be moving along now."

"We appreciate the hospitality," Best said.

"Nice to have some company," Gus replied. "Feel free to use the tent while I'm gone. I might see you again down at the trading post when you come for your gear."

"That's appreciated," the marshal told him.

Gus turned to go, then paused. "Oh, one more thing I should mention. I saw a track in the mud down by the riverbank a few days ago. Pretty darn big, so I'm figuring it has to be a grizzly. We don't really see them much in these parts, and he's probably passed on through to wherever he's supposed to be by now. Still, might be good to keep an eye out."

"Thanks for the warning, Mr. Mendelson," Parker said. "I mean, Gus."

"You fellas take care." Gus tossed them a final wave, then headed downstream, following the river south.

They watched the old man go, and when he was out of earshot, Parker said, "Marshal?"

"Yeah?"

"How come you didn't tell Mr. Mendelson that Gerald Filmore was dead?"

Best took a sip of coffee, musing a moment before answering. "Something you should learn about people, boy. Hearing about death can affect someone in an unpredictable way. I see death all the time, but that's not how it is for most folks. If I'd have told old Gus that Filmore was dead, he might've just shrugged and said, *too bad*. Or he might've taken it as a bad surprise and gotten all moody and quiet, just when we needed him to be talkative."

The way Best explained it, Parker could see why breaking bad news like that could have soured the whole conversation.

"There was no need for Gus to know what we're doing up here or that Filmore was dead or any of it. That would only have muddied the waters," Best said. "A nice friendly chat, then let him be on his way none the wiser. Simpler all around."

"I guess that makes sense." Parker still felt bad about lying to the old man, but at least the marshal had good reason.

"That old saying, *Ignorance is bliss*? Well, that's unfortunately too true for too many people," Best said. "Folks ain't always built for hard news."

"I think you might be right about that," Parker said. "I sure wasn't happy to hear there's a grizzly bear prowling around here someplace."

Best chuckled. "Well, it's the bear's woods, not ours. We just need to remember to step lightly, keep our ears and eyes open, and stay out of the critter's way."

"I'll go my way, if he goes his," Parker said.

"He was probably just passing through, like the old man said," Best assured him.

Parker hoped so.

Best stood and tossed the dregs of his coffee into the fire.

"We'll take our ease the rest of the day and then get started fresh in the morning," the marshal said. "I don't want to start following that map and then lose the daylight. Last thing we need is to trip in the dark and break our necks. In the meantime, maybe get these dishes cleaned up."

Parker turned away so Best wouldn't see him roll his eyes. *Yet another chore for Squire Jones.*

CHAPTER 28

"What the hell is that thing?"

Grady Jenks paused halfway up the steps to the front porch of the trading post and looked back at his brother Jimmy. "What thing?"

Jimmy pointed.

Grady gazed out across the open grassland. In the distance, an ugly, gray flat-topped butte, like some giant tooth, sprouted from the ground. He had traveled farther west and seen buttes, huge orange things rising from the rough surface of the rocky desert, but this one did look sort of odd out there all by itself.

"Forget it," Jenks said. "Nothing to do with us."

He headed up the steps into Carlile's Trading Post, Jimmy in tow.

The interior of the trading post was much like any other, various sundries for people and livestock both. The only difference was a collection of fishing rods in a rack on the far wall. Jenks supposed that was due to the river less than a hundred yards away. They had crossed over it via a narrow log bridge to the trading post.

They'd been told the area was called Carlile's Junction,

although there was nothing there but the trading post as far as Jenks could see—supposedly, a few homesteaders scattered around the region.

Bill Farkas and Little Joe Tillis were already in a conversation with the man running the trading post when Jenks and his brother approached.

"No, it's been real quiet around here," said the trading post man. "Slow yesterday. And you gents are the first customers today."

"How about a bottle of whiskey?" Farkas said.

The man put a bottle on the counter. No label, but it was full, and that was good enough for Farkas

Tillis gestured to some chairs under the front table. "Okay if we take a load off while we have a drink?"

"Don't make no never mind to me." The trading post man set four glasses on the counter next to the bottle.

The four outlaws took the booze to the table and sat. Farkas pulled the cork off the bottle and filled each glass. They shot the booze back, smacked lips, and set the glasses back on the table for more, and Farkas poured everyone a refill. They hunched over their drinks, leaning in so they could converse in hushed tones.

"The guy running the place says there's been no law come through here," Farkas said. "Nor any talk of trouble. And he ain't heard nothing about no trouble in Sundance neither. I don't think there's a posse after us."

"I hope you weren't too obvious about asking," Jenks said.

Farkas frowned. "What am I, some dang greenhorn? I was casual about it, don't you worry."

"Okay, good," Jenks said. "Then the first order of business is deciding what to do next? I figure it comes back to one of two options. Either we circle back and try to pick up Best's trail again, or we go all the way back to Cheyenne and start poking around, and try to get some clue where that conniving railroad man stashed the gold."

They set about discussing the pros and cons of each path, but as the hour wore on, most of them were simply pro-whiskey and con anything that seemed like another wild-goose chase.

Not for the first time, Jenks wondered why he'd joined up with such men. They were tough men, and they'd all worked well together in the past, and Jenks mostly trusted them. But the good Lord knew they sure weren't famous for their patience, nor for their ability to press on doggedly in the face of adversity. He supposed with the loss of Frenchy LaSalle and the Morris brothers, it was likely Farkas and Tillis didn't have the stomach for it anymore. They'd all been together a long time, but this was the first job that had presented such difficulties.

There was also more money on the line than in all their previous jobs. If they were upset and discouraged, so what? Hadn't Jenks himself just lost one of his own brothers? And was Jenks giving up? Hell, no.

As for the Russian, well, Jenks didn't feel any loss for Boris. He should have seen right away that the Russian was a mad dog—and you shoot mad dogs. You don't bring them into the family.

Grady Jenks glanced at Jimmy. The only actual blood

relation he had left. Jenks had thought it a good idea to bring him and Charlie into the gang. Brothers were supposed to look out for one another, weren't they?

Except Grady hadn't looked out for Charlie. Just the opposite. He'd rescued Charlie from a jail cell only to get him killed.

Now what would happen to Jimmy? If anyone needed looking after, it was him. Grady Jenks hated to say it, but Jimmy Jenks didn't have so much between the ears.

Farkas refilled the glasses again. "We've talked this to death, and we're no closer to forming any kind of plan than we were when we started. I don't know about you fellas, but by the time we get to the bottom of this bottle, I'm going to want some grub. Probably, we should start thinking about that."

Grady stopped himself from muttering a curse. They'd sat there an hour and hadn't accomplished a dang thing.

Still, he supposed they did have to eat.

"We'll get fresh supplies and make camp somewhere," he said. "Who's turn is it to cook?"

"Mine," Jimmy said.

The other three groaned. Jimmy wasn't what anybody would call a gourmet chef.

"I'll talk to the proprietor and see what he has in the way of meat," Grady said. "I wouldn't mind a roast chicken or maybe some kind of—"

The sound of a snorting horse and the racket of wheels over rough logs drew their attention. A wagon was coming across the bridge, a square, bulky, garish-looking thing pulled by two horses. It was almost too wide for the narrow bridge, the wooden railings barely missing the sides of the wagon.

"Well, how do you like that?" Tillis said. "The medicine show man?"

"Has to be," Grady said. "There can't be *two* wagons that ugly."

Jimmy went to the window, grabbing the sill with both hands and leaning out anxiously. "That's the pretty gal, riding up front next to the old-timer. She's not wearing that dress. Dang it, I like her better when she wears the dress and shows off some leg."

"What are they doing here?" Tillis asked.

"They need beans and horse feed, just like anyone else, I reckon," Grady said.

"Hey, you think they're going to put on the medicine show here?" Jimmy asked.

Grady rolled his eyes. "Yeah, just for the four of us."

"That'd be fine by me," Jimmy said. "Oh, man, I hope she puts that dress back on."

As they came over the bridge, Annie spotted the horses tied up in front of the trading post. She wondered excitedly if they could belong to Parker and the marshal, but of course, she had no idea what the marshal's horse looked like—or what the marshal looked like, either, come to think of it—and the closer she got, the more obvious it became that none of the horses were Parker's.

Her heart sank, and she felt foolish.

I didn't really think it would be that easy, did I? That he'd be standing there on the front porch, waiting for me to ride up?

She shook her head and *tsk*ed.

"Over there." Meriweather pointed to a spot, about forty yards left of the trading post, where there was a circle of stones, blackened ash within, from campfires past. "I daresay that's where travelers make camp when passing through. A good spot for the night." He tugged on the reins, angling his team of horses toward the camping spot.

"Let me off in front of the trading post," Annie said. "I want to ask if Parker and the marshal have been through here."

"Good idea." The professor tugged the reins, and the wagon rattled to a halt.

Annie jumped down from the bench and headed toward the clapboard building. She heard the professor click his tongue, and the wagon got moving again.

"Hey, girl!" called a voice. "You gonna put on that silky dress?"

Annie stopped, her eyes scanning the trading post until she saw a young man hanging out the front window, slapping an open palm against the side of the building.

"You got some nice legs," the man called. "Why not show 'em off?"

Annie cleared her throat and said, "The professor doesn't plan to put on one of his medicine shows today."

"That don't matter," the stranger called. "You can put on a private show just for me."

A hand grabbed the man's shoulder from behind and abruptly dragged him back inside.

Annie hesitated, then turned on her heel and headed back toward the wagon. She'd return to inquire about Parker and the marshal at a later time.

Grady Jenks yanked Jimmy back from the window.

"Hey!"—Jimmy frowned—"I was getting on with her."

"You were making a jackass out of yourself," Jenks said. "And this is no time for any of us to be drawing attention to ourselves."

Jimmy sulked into his chair and grabbed his glass of whiskey.

"Now listen up, all of you," Jenks said. "We're going to finish this whiskey, get some supplies, and get out of here. We'll figure out our plan around the campfire later."

There were grumbles of agreement. Fifteen minutes later, they pushed away from the table, leaving an empty bottle behind. The four of them circled the room, picking out various supplies.

The front door of the trading post creaked open, and an old man walked in. He had a fishing pole leaning on one shoulder.

"How's your day going, Pete?" called the old man.

The trading post man came forward, wiping his hands on his apron and grinning a greeting at the old man.

"Gus Mendelson, you old so and so. Did you bring me back a mess of bullheads for my frying pan?"

"Sorry, Pete, met a few new friends up at the fish camp, and treated them to a fish dinner."

Jenks's ears perked up. He pretended to be looking at some canned goods on a shelf as he eavesdropped.

"You run into some fellow fishermen?" Pete asked.

"Potential fisherman," Gus told him. "They didn't have no gear, so I told them this was the place to come get outfitted proper."

"Obliged for that," Pete said. "Looks like I'm in for a regular rush. First these gentlemen, then the wagon, now you. And then your new friends coming to get fishing gear. I don't suppose there's a dozen of them. I could use the business."

Gus laughed. "No, just two. A hard-looking middle aged man, and a younger fellow with him. Friends of Gerald Filmore. I guess Gerald told them all about my excellent lures and flies."

Pete laughed. "I told you not to give all your secrets away to that railroad man. He'll blab, and soon the world will know all your secret fishing holes."

Upon hearing Gerald Filmore's name, Jenks had to make a physical effort not to look too eager. He cleared his throat and donned his most affable demeanor. "Beg pardon, sir, but I couldn't help but overhear your conversation."

"That's okay." Gus smiled. "Not like I'm giving out government secrets."

"My boys and I are looking to meet up with some friends, and it sounds like you maybe ran into the very fellas we're looking for," Jenks said. "One of them wouldn't happen to be called Tanner Best, would he?"

The old man brightened. "Why, as a matter of fact, yes. The very same. My goodness. Small world, ain't it?"

Jenks laughed, friendly-like. "It sure is. It sure is a small world."

"The other fellas name is, uh, it's . . ." Gus scratched his head. "Oh, fiddlesticks. It's right on the tip of my tongue. My memory isn't what it used to be."

"Don't fret about that," Jenks said hastily. It occurred to him that if the two men really were his friends, then he should know the man's name. He rapidly went on to another subject. "Say, could you give us directions to this fish camp? We'd love to meet up with them."

"Happy to." Gus gave Jenks detailed directions. "It's right on the Belle Fourche, so you can't miss it if you follow the river."

"Thank you so much," Jenks said.

"It'll come to me," Gus said. "The name of that other fella will come if I think on it enough."

Jenks hurriedly made his purchases, and the outlaws went outside to their horses.

"Well, that decides it then," Jenks whispered from the side of his mouth to Bill Farkas. "This won't be like in Sundance. We'll have the dirty skunks out in the wilderness, all alone. We'll make Best talk—or we'll toss him into the Belle Fourche, one little piece at a time.

* * *

Annie helped the professor with the horses, then built a campfire in the circle of stones.

She was eager to go into the trading post and ask the man running the place if Parker had come through. She wondered if those men were still there or not. She didn't want to encounter the rude young man again, but she was too anxious to wait.

"Go on then," Meriweather said. "I'll get started on supper. Let me know if you find out anything."

Annie headed toward the trading post, rounded to the front, and stopped at the edge of the porch just as four men emerged and went to their horses. The rude one who'd wanted to see her in the silky dress was with them but hadn't noticed her.

She waited. They'd ride off in a minute, and then she could go inside.

They mounted up and were just about to ride away when an old man came out and waved them down. "Hold on there, young fellas. I thought of it."

"How's that?" one of the riders asked.

"The name of that other fella," the old man said. "Parker Jones."

Annie gasped and felt her chest tighten.

"Obliged for that," said the mounted man. "We'll tell them you said hello."

The four men turned their horses and trotted away north. The old man went back inside the trading post.

Annie followed.

"Sir! Excuse me, sir!" She chased after the old man.

He turned and smiled. "Well, where did you come from, young lady?"

"Did you say Parker Jones?" she asked. "I know him."

"Good Lord, is there a family reunion or something in Carlile Junction this week?" he asked. "Seems everybody knows everybody else."

"I reckon the world is funny that way sometimes," Annie said. "When did you see him? Is he well?"

The old man told her all about Tanner Best and Parker Jones happening upon him while he was fishing, how they'd enjoyed a nice meal together, and so on.

"Nice fellas," the old man said. "The younger one—Jones—has good manners, too. Knows how to talk to his elders."

"Please, sir," Annie said. "Can you tell me where to find them."

"I suppose I could, but you needn't bother," he said. "They'll be coming here soon enough."

A huge grin split her face. "Really?"

"Yes, I told them this was the best place to get supplied and outfitted," he said. "Anyway, the wilderness is no place for a young gal like you. There's dangerous stuff up there and—uh-oh. Oh my . . ."

Annie's face fell. "What's wrong?"

The old man *tsk*ed. "I probably should have told them other fellas about the bear."

The outlaws made camp, and Jenks opened another bottle of whiskey. He'd made sure to buy a couple before leaving Carlile's.

"We might could've made it if we'd pressed on," Tillis said.

"Maybe in daylight and maybe not," Jenks said. "We never been to this place before, and I don't want to chance arriving in the dark. We're going to get up bright and early, and scout this place in the light, and not get caught with our pants down."

"We don't even know if they're still there," Jimmy said. "They could be getting farther away every moment we dawdle."

"Or we can blunder into the fishing camp all in a hurry and get shot to pieces by one of the toughest U.S marshals this side of the Mississippi River," Jenks said. "No, thank you. We're going to do this methodical-like."

"Who was that kid with Best?" Farkas asked. "What did the old man say his name was? Parker Jones? We had Best dead to rights, and then he just showed up out of nowhere. And then that fool Russian started throwing dynamite around and—"

"I know what happened, I was there. It don't matter his name," Jenks said.

But that wasn't quite true. He felt sure he'd seen the man somewhere before, and if his face hadn't been covered with mud, maybe Jenks would have been able to figure where. So, yeah, curiosity had got ahold of him. *Just who in the blazes are you, Parker Jones?*

"Here's the long and the short of it," Jenks said. "We need Tanner Best alive. We need him to talk and tell us where the gold is. We're going to get to the end of this sorry quest once and for all. Now, you heard that old man. Gerald Filmore was up here, and now so is Tanner Best. I don't believe in coincidences any more than I believe in flying buffalo or honest roulette tables. That gold is around here somewhere, and we're going to make Best talk, and we're going to do it right this time."

"And what about Parker Jones?" Farkas asked.

"We need Best alive, so we can get answers," Jenks said. "As far as Parker Jones is concerned, I say shoot him as soon as you see him."

CHAPTER 29

The lawmen stood at the head of the narrow game trail, trying to decide if they should take the horses or not.

"It's overgrown," Tanner Best said. "And we'll be ducking the low branches of those ponderosa pines all the way, and I don't fancy hunching over in the saddle that long with my bad ribs. You think Filmore rode or walked?"

"I don't know," Parker said. "I don't even know it's the right trail."

"It's the right trail," Best insisted. "We're nearly at the end of this thing. I can feel it. Filmore hid the gold somewhere at the end of this map, and we're going to find it. The trail leads away from the fish camp." Best jerked a thumb over his shoulder to indicate the tent behind them. "*That's* the fish camp. This has to be the trail."

Parker scratched his chin, considering. "Okay, here's how I have it figured. It's too much gold for one man to carry, and Gus Mendelson said he saw Filmore with a string of mules. That makes sense because there's no way he'd get a wagon down this narrow trail. I think he leads the mules in on foot, stashing the gold whatever place he thought was good, then came back out. Probably sold the mules to somebody on the way home."

"That's how I have it figured, too," Best said. "I reckon he'd need to stash it until the heat was off. It was a lot to transport, and Filmore couldn't just run off to Mexico with a ton of gold, without attracting attention. The law is looking for the gold. The outlaws are looking for him. That much gold weighs a man down. Hard to outrun the world with so much wealth dragging your pockets along the ground."

"Then he goes back to Missouri one last time, to see his mother," Parker said. "But that's his mistake. He's on his way to a place where people can find him, and that's exactly what Jenks does. Doesn't matter if they catch him coming or going, they still caught up with him long enough to put a bullet in him. He lives just long enough to stagger into Rory's Junction, and that's as far as he ever gets."

"And now all that's left is to go get this gold."

Parker nodded. "I say we leave the horses for now. No sense dragging them around if we make a wrong turn."

Best nodded. "Okay, then. You take the lead."

Parker headed down the trail, pushing pine branches out of his way. According to Filmore's map, they'd be taking the trail all the way to the big gray monstrosity known as Devils Tower, where a cross—Parker still wasn't convinced it was an *X*—indicated some sort of landmark or turning point. Then the path took another direction to, well, something else. And then . . .

Well, Parker didn't know. He had a vague hope the solution would be self-evident when they reached the end of the map.

A few hundred yards in, and the path opened up a bit, but not by much. The closeness of the trees and thickness of the underbrush blocked any breeze that might have mitigated the rapidly warming day. After a mile, Parker had an annoying trickle of sweat down his back.

The Devils Tower loomed over them, immense and strange.

Another mile, and they were slap up against the tower's base.

Best sat on a small boulder, holding his side and panting. "Thought my ribs were healing better than this."

"The doc did say to rest," Parker reminded the marshal.

Best grinned. "Gold first. Then rest."

"The trail sort of ends here," Parker said "But I don't see a cross. Maybe we passed it."

Parker tried to imagine what Filmore had done. Had the man taken two fallen branches and made a cross out of them? Maybe stuck them in the ground, like something over a man's grave. No, that was a bad idea. A storm could blow through and knock something like that right over. No, the marker would have to be something more permanent, something that would still be there if Filmore came back a year later.

"It doesn't have to be a cross. It could be anything,"

Best said. "All Filmore had to do was put something on the map to jog his memory."

Parker didn't want to believe that, but he had no good reason to dispute it.

He looked around, making a slow circle of the area, searching for anything that resembled a cross. Marshal sat on the boulder and lit his pipe, puffing thoughtfully, as he let Parker search.

An hour later, he still hadn't found a thing. He was hot and thirsty, wishing he hadn't left the canteen back with his horse.

The sun continued to rise as the morning grew late, bathing the eastern side of Devils Tower in fresh light. Parker's eyes were drawn to it. It was difficult not to stare. Something so enormous and so odd just demanded to be looked at. Grooves shot up the side of the stone almost like something carved on purpose, even, and spaced just so . . .

Parker blinked and looked again. About a third of the way up, some of the stone had fallen away, weathered, chipped a bit here and there by the passage of time and the relentless elements. The even vertical lines, interrupted here and there, formed the shape of—

"Hey, marshal."

Best looked up, a bored expression on his face, pipe dangling from his mouth. "Hmmm?"

"Come look at this."

Best heaved himself to his feet and went to stand next to Parker.

Parker pointed. "What's that look like to you?"

Best turned to look, then took the pipe from his mouth and smiled. "That, Deputy Jones, is quite obviously a cross."

They'd dismounted and tied the horses to a tree as soon as they saw the tent ahead of them, perched right on the riverbank.

"Spread out," Jenks whispered. "Remember, we need Best alive. Kill the other one."

They approached the camp slowly, guns drawn, eyes searching, ears open. Jenks saw the horses a moment later, unsaddled and hobbled just beyond the tent.

They're definitely still in the area.

Jenks caught Little Joe Tillis's attention and motioned toward the tent. Tillis nodded. They approached so slowly, it almost tested his patience, stepping softly. When they were right in front of the tent, Jenks looked at Tillis, pointed at it, and Tillis nodded.

Tillis swept the tent flap aside, and Jenks brought up his six-gun, ready to blaze.

The tent was empty.

Jenks lowered his gun and looked around.

Jimmy and Farkas walked toward him. They'd been looking around the rest of the camp.

"I don't see nobody," Jimmy said.

"Cook fire's still warm," Farkas said. "I don't know where they went, but they had breakfast first."

"Okay, let's take a look around," Jenks told them. "Maybe we can figure out where they went."

A few minutes later, Bill Farkas called them over. He knelt at a spot just on the edge of the tree line, looking at the ground.

"Looks like a game trail." Farkas indicated a print in the dirt. "Boot heel. Made fresh. And there's broken limbs a few feet along the trail. They went this way, I'm sure of it."

"Or somebody did, if not them," Jimmy said.

"It's them. Who else?" Jenks squinted at the sky, then looked down the trail. "Plenty of daylight left. Let's get after them. But no talking, and step softly. We'll either find where they ended up or catch them coming back."

They headed down the trail, the enormity of the Devils Tower beckoning them on.

Parker and Best skirted the base of Devils Tower until Parker judged they were more or less even with the cross. It wasn't a perfect cross, but against the even vertical lines of the tower's face, it was plain enough. Parker turned, holding the map in front of him to try to match the angle where the dotted line branched away northeast. Parker had figured the dotted line indicated a direction but no path, but he and Best looked around just in case.

No luck.

No game trails nor even a marker to indicate where a trail might have been. The number scratched over the line was 325.

Parker discussed it with the marshal. Feet? Yards?

Parker questioned how that could be accurately measured over rough terrain.

"I think it's steps," Parker said. "I can't think of anything else that makes more sense. Then I guess at the end of the steps is whatever this *W* is supposed to be."

Best knocked the ashes out of his pipe against a tree trunk. "Lead on, then, Deputy Jones. I'm right behind you."

Parker made a start, counting his steps. He tried not to let his mind wander, but of course, he couldn't stop from second-guessing himself. What was a step anyway? One man's stride might be longer or shorter than the next. What if they were off even just a little bit to the north or east?

Pay attention, you fool. You want to lose count?

Three hundred and twenty-five steps later, they entered a wide clearing.

Best pointed to his left. "There it is."

Parker wasn't sure what Best meant at first. All he could see was a cluster of quaking aspens in the center of the clearing, but when he looked closer, he realized that the four pale trunks sprung from the ground at just the right angle to form a huge *W*.

Parker nodded, appreciating what Filmore had done. "Smart. If you're off just a little, it don't matter because the clearing's so big. You can still see the *W*."

They went to it. Stood in front of it. Looked at it.

"Now what?" Best asked.

"I don't exactly know," Parker admitted. "You think he buried the gold between the tree trunks?"

"We didn't bring shovels." Best kicked at some loose

leaves and twigs at the base of the *W*. "Not that it matters. Nobody's moved this earth an inch since the beginning of time."

"Maybe around back." Parker circled the aspens, eyes on the ground, but it was obvious nobody had dug any holes.

Best sat on the ground, stuck his pipe in his mouth, and began to thumb fresh tobacco into the bowl. "My ribs are throbbing. I need to sit a spell."

Parker saw no reason to object. He had no idea where to go next anyway. He circled the *W* more slowly, this time his eyes up instead of on the ground. Best puffed his pipe, in no hurry to budge another inch.

When Parker went behind the cluster of aspens, he saw it. Filmore wasn't a bad artist. The image carved in the thick trunk of the largest aspen looked exactly like a human skull with its mouth gaping wide. Underneath the skull was an arrow pointing due north. No other instructions. No number to indicate how many steps.

Just the skull and the arrow.

"Marshal, come look at this."

Best groaned. "If I get up, it better be good. I just got comfortable."

"I reckon it depends on how you define good," Parker said. "But it's, well, something."

Best muttered a string of complaints, but he stood, then came around behind the aspens to stand next to Parker. He looked up at the skull and the arrow.

"Huh." Best puffed the pipe hard. "Gerald Filmore's trying to tell us something, Deputy Jones. But what?"

"I guess we follow the arrow," Parker said.

"The skull might be a warning," Best said. "Maybe he's telling us there's danger that way."

"Not like there's a bunch of other options," Parker said. "If you see a picture of gold and an arrow pointing in some other direction, please tell me."

Best laughed. "You make a good point. A bit smart-alecky, but a good point, nonetheless."

"So I take it we're going to—?"

"Follow the arrow, Deputy Jones."

They began to hike again, Parker glancing back often at the *W* formed by the aspens to make sure he stayed lined up in the direction the arrow pointed, but soon the *W* was out of sight, swallowed by the forest of ponderosa pines behind them. Parker did his best to stay on course. The ground was uneven and rocky.

"How do we know when we get there?" Best asked.

Parker had no idea. "We've got to hope it'll be obvious."

The terrain became even rockier, and they were forced to maneuver around boulders of varying size. Then the ground fell away before them, and they stood on the edge of a gorge.

Best looked one way and then another. "Going around will take a minute."

The boulder that humped up from the edge of the ridge was like a smooth stone dome. Parker stepped out onto it, so he could look over the side at the floor of the gorge immediately below them.

Parker pointed off to the right. "It's not so steep there."

"Steep enough, with these ribs throbbing," Best said. "I'd hate to climb down there for nothing."

"Let me go first," Parker told him. "I'll see if it's worth the trouble."

Parker picked his way down, sliding on loose rocks and dirt a few times, but managing to maintain his footing. He reached the bottom with a sigh of relief.

"Anything?" Best called down.

Parker looked ahead, then side to side. The bottom of the gorge looked exactly like the bottom of a gorge. So what now? Were they supposed to keep going?

He turned around to shout back up at the marshal. "I don't know what I'm supposed to be looking at. Maybe if we—"

"What's wrong?" Best asked.

"I think I found it."

The rock formation Parker was looking at was very much like a human skull. The smooth domed rock on the edge of the gorge was the top. Two gaping holes halfway down made the uneven eyes, a jagged gash in the face of the stone for a nose. A hole five feet high arched up from the ground to form its yawning mouth, clearly the entrance to a cave.

Parker described what he saw to the marshal.

"A cave, you say?" Best called down to him. "Sounds like the perfect place to hide some stolen gold."

Parker grinned up at him. "My exact thought."

"Then proceed, Deputy Jones," Best said. "Go forth and explore."

Parker took three eager steps toward the mouth of the

cave, then abruptly stopped. He looked down. There in the mud was a claw print as big as a dinner plate. Slowly, Parker lifted his head and squinted into the darkness of Skull-Mouth Cave.

He thought it his imagination at first, the subtle movement in the depths of the cave, but then slowly it took shape, something bulky and shaggy coming into the light, with a snort and a growl, the scrape of claws on stone. Parker knew already what was coming even before the enormous beast stepped into the light.

When it finally emerged from the cave, Parker felt cold fear chase down his spine. The big grizzly bear was even larger than he'd imagined. The animal tossed its head, a low growl emanating from deep in its belly.

Parker desperately wanted to run, but he found somehow his legs couldn't move. Hadn't he heard somewhere that you were supposed to play dead when confronted with a bear? To Parker, it seemed terrible advice.

The bear came toward him.

Parker swallowed hard. *I'm going to die.*

The grizzly suddenly reared up on its hind legs. It was at least eight feet tall. Its mouth gaped open, teeth long and sharp, and bellowed a deafening roar. Parker found his legs and backpedaled as fast as he could, eyes wide with terror. He tripped over his own feet and went down into the mud.

The bear roared again, and Parker felt parts of his body twitch and pucker, certain the bear was about to pounce.

The bear dropped down on all fours and ambled past.

He gave Parker a final backward look, as if slightly bored, before loping down the length of the gorge and finally vanishing into the underbrush.

Parker let his head fall back as he lay on the ground, panting, heart thumping so hard he thought it might burst out of his chest.

CHAPTER 30

"You okay?" Best had both his Remingtons drawn and looked down from the edge of the gorge.

Parker propped himself up on one elbow. Miraculously, he was okay. He hadn't even soiled himself. "Why didn't you shoot it?"

"It was a bad angle," Best said. "I didn't want to hit you by mistake."

Parker didn't see how the marshal could miss anything the size of that grizzly, but it had all worked out, so Parker didn't quibble. Parker stood, saw his hands were muddy, and wiped them on his pants.

"What about the cave?" Best called.

Parker hesitated.

"Bear's gone," Best said. "You'll never have a better chance."

"Well, if he comes back, yell or shoot or something."

"Don't worry, I'll keep watch," Best assured him.

Parker looked back the way the grizzly had gone. He wished he hadn't left his shotgun with Annie and the professor. He'd let her keep it in the wagon with her after the Indian attack, thinking it would make her feel safer. Right now, *he* wanted to feel safer.

No more stalling. He ducked his head and entered the skull's mouth.

The cave wasn't so very deep after all, and after pausing to let his eyes adjust, he could see all the way to the back wall where there was a lump of something piled up. He edged closer, careful not to bump his head.

Burlap bags stacked neatly against the wall, maybe twenty-five or thirty of them, cinch-tied at the top. He grabbed one and tried to lift it. It didn't come at first. It was heavy. He grunted, lifted it, carried it to the mouth of the cave, and dropped it on the ground, where it landed with a metallic *chink*. Parker knelt next to the bag and began to open it with shaking hands, loosening the drawstring. He spilled the contents on the ground in front of him.

The gold coins glittered in the sunlight.

Parker's face felt strange, and he realized he was grinning so widely it threatened to break his face.

"You find anything or not?" Best called.

Parker took one of the coins and slipped it in his pocket. Then he cinched the bag closed again and shoved it back into the cave.

"I'm coming up!" he called.

By the time he climbed to the top, he was so sweaty his shirt stuck to him.

"Well?" Best was clearly anxious.

Parker took the coin from his pocket and handed it to him.

"Oh my." Best held up the coin, letting it catch a ray

of sunlight, his eyes slowly widening. "Oh my, will you look at that. There's more?"

"Bags of it," Parker told him.

"Fifty thousand in gold." Best whistled. "What a man could do with that."

"I'll settle for a thousand," Parker said. "My cut of the reward money."

Best's face grew serious. "Of course. We'll be returning the gold like law-abiding citizens. But it sure is nice to dream about. Next question is, how do we get it up here?"

"Filmore didn't get mules down there, that's for sure," Parker said. "Not unless he went around the long way."

Bust grunted. "I don't care for the sound of that."

"I guess we could bring the horses and rope," Parker suggested. "I'll climb back down, and you can pull the bags up one at a time."

"Okay, then," Best said. "Let's get to it."

They headed back, the route no longer seeming so mysterious now that they knew what to expect. They reached the cluster of quaking aspens that formed the *W* then angled back toward the cross. They were skirting the rocky area of the tower's base, when Best called a halt.

"My ribs are screaming." The marshal sat on a boulder, took off his hat, and wiped sweat from his forehead. "Just give me five minutes."

Parker leaned against the trunk of a pine, wishing for the tenth time he'd brought his canteen along. "It's hot enough. I've a mind to jump in the Belle Fourche."

"Let's secure the gold first," Best said. "Then you can swim all the way back to Cheyenne if you want."

Parker laughed. "Just enough to cool off will suit me. I wouldn't mind a bite, either. After all this hiking around, I'm hungry enough to—"

A pistol shot split the air, and bark chips flew up two inches from Parker's face. He dove to the ground.

More shots passed overhead as Best rolled off the back of the boulder, using it for cover. He came up with a six-shooter in each hand, peering over the top of the boulder into the trees and underbrush below. "You see 'em?"

Parker was flat on his face and not eager to get up. "I don't see a thing."

"Get up and find some cover," Best said impatiently. "Get that Peacemaker out. We got trouble."

Parker elbow-crawled behind another boulder, rose to one knee, and drew his six-gun. He scanned the forest in front of him and thought he saw some movement. "Off to the left, but I can't be sure."

"I got two more over in the other direction," Best said. "There's at least three or four, and they're spread out."

"Now what?" Parker asked.

"I'll keep them distracted," Best said. "You keep low and circle around behind the one you seen on your side."

"And then what do I do?"

"Shoot the dirty skunk, of course," Best said.

Parker blanched.

"They've already fired on us, Deputy Jones," Best said. "Now listen, and listen good. These men want the gold. They're outlaws. No matter what they say, they're not letting us down from here alive. This is a kill or be killed situation. We clear on that?"

Parker nodded. "Clear."

"I'll give you a couple minutes to make a start, then I'll draw their attention," the marshal told him.

Parker nodded.

He skulked off to the left, scooting from boulder to tree trunk to bush, whatever would keep him concealed. He took an occasional peek, trying to keep whoever it was in sight with intermittent success. The other guy was trying to stay hidden, too.

"I'm guessing that's you down there, Grady Jenks?" Best called from his spot behind the boulder. "You and your mouth-breathers looking to take another run at Marshal Best, are ya?"

A pause. Then: "There's more of us than there are of you, Best."

Parker recognized Jenks's voice.

"The only chance you got to get out of this alive is if you throw down them guns and show us where the gold is," Jenks shouted. "And don't try to tell us you're up here on a fishing trip. We know Filmore hid the gold around hereabouts, so don't waste your breath with bad lies."

Parker had been listening to the exchange with rapt attention, barely remembering he was supposed to be trying to outflank the fella on his side. He started moving again, downhill this time, after he estimated he'd gone far enough to come up behind the man.

"Gold or no gold don't make no difference," Best

called back. "I got the high ground. If you want to come try and dig me out, I'm happy to shoot down on you all day long."

Parker eased through the underbrush and saw his target not more than six feet away, a huge bruiser of a fella. Just as the marshal had predicted, the bruiser's attention was fixed on the exchange between his boss and Best.

"How you fixed for water?" Jenks shouted. "Or food. I can wait you out. I can wait longer than you can."

The marshal and Jenks kept shouting back and forth, alternating between trying to goad each other and trying to talk sense into each other.

Parker eased closer to the bruiser and lifted his Peacemaker. It would be easy. Parker could squeeze the trigger and blow the bruiser away right now.

But he just couldn't. Yes, these men were actively trying to kill Parker and Best, but Parker just couldn't bring himself to shoot a defenseless man in the back. The right thing to do would be to bring him in alive.

Parker steadied himself, and in a low, calm voice said, "Freeze, mister."

The bruiser started to turn, looking back over his shoulder.

"I said freeze," Parker barked.

The man froze.

In the background, he could hear Jenks and the marshal still gabbing at each other.

The bruiser had a hard look in his eyes, no sign that Parker worried him in any way.

Parker licked his lips nervously. "Toss that gun aside."

The bruiser turned slowly toward Parker, face blank and as cold as stone. He held his six-gun out to his side, letting it dangle.

"Go on," Parker said. "Toss it."

The bruiser let the pistol swing back and forth a moment as it dangled, but his eyes never left Parker's. Finally, the bruiser tossed his six-gun.

Parker followed the arc of the pistol's flight with his eyes.

A mistake.

It was all the distraction the bruiser needed. The big man leaped at Parker, knocking the gun out of his hands. A fist the size of a baked ham came up and cracked Parker on the jaw. The world upended, down and up rapidly trading places in a bewildering blur, and suddenly Parker was on the ground, blinking stars from his eyes.

He looked up to see the bruiser looming over him.

"You stupid little runt," the bruiser growled. "I'm going to break every bone in your—"

A blur of fur and enormous dripping fangs.

The grizzly roared and pounced, huge jaws locking on the side of the bruiser's neck. The bear dragged the man away, the bruiser screaming and screaming, trying to wriggle free, to no avail.

Parker watched wide-eyed as the man vanished into the underbrush, his screams still echoing throughout the forest.

* * *

"You're playing with fire, Grady!" Marshal Best shouted to Jenks. "At the moment, I'm willing to let bygones be bygones. You and your boys should turn around and walk away. But if you fellas are keen to end up in a prison cell, or worse, a shallow grave, then by all means—"

Screams interrupted the marshal's conversation with the outlaw. Screams and more screams that wouldn't stop.

"What the hell's that?" Jenks shouted. "Is that Little Joe?"

Best realized Jenks was shouting to his fellow outlaws. Now was the time to move while they were distracted.

Best darted to his right, hiding behind another boulder. The screams kept coming, the outlaws confused about what was happening. Was that something Parker Jones had done? Best hadn't heard a gunshot. He scooted to another boulder, then another, and began to make his way downslope. If he'd figured properly, he'd come upon the outlaws from the side, catching them by surprise.

But when he pushed through the underbrush, the three of them surprised each other. Best recognized Bill Farkas immediately. The skinny one with him, the marshal didn't know, but both looked surprised to see Best where he shouldn't have been, turning to bring their guns up fast.

But not fast enough.

Tanner Best blasted Bill Farkas with one of his Remingtons and shot the other man with the other, both clutching their chests, bloody as they went down.

He thumbed back the hammers as he turned, looking for his next target.

But he looked the wrong way.

"Hold it." A voice behind him. Grady Jenks.

Best muttered a curse. Jenks had him dead to rights.

"Go ahead and flinch," Jenks said. "Just move one muscle. Give me an excuse. That's my good pal Bill Farkas lying dead there and my last brother next to him, so go on and give me a reason to shoot."

"What's stopping you?" Best asked.

"I didn't come all this way to leave without that gold," Jenks said. "You're going to show me where it is."

Best chuckled grimly. "Let's not kid each other, Grady. You're going to shoot me anyway."

"Maybe," Jenks said. "But you want to get shot now or shot later?"

I suppose that's something to ponder, Best thought.

Best considered turning and shooting, and taking his chances, but Jenks wouldn't hesitate to fire in those circumstances. Sure, the outlaw wanted the gold, but Best figured Grady Jenks probably wanted to live even more. He tensed, readying himself.

Then both heard the cock of a pistol behind them. "Don't move, Mr. Jenks."

Parker pointed his Peacemaker right at Grady Jenks, and the three of them stood like that for a long moment, Parker taking aim at the outlaw, and Jenks with his pistol on the marshal.

Jenks didn't move, but his eyes slid to Parker. "I remember you now. Eiger's."

Parker nodded. "That's right."

"So what are we going to do now?" Jenks asked. "Gonna try to arrest me again?"

"I guess that would be easiest for everybody," Parker said. "Now drop that gun and we can—"

Jenks spun and brought his six-gun around on Parker.

Parker fired.

He caught Jenks high in the shoulder and sent the outlaw stumbling back. Jenks lifted his pistol to try again.

Parker fanned the hammer of his Peacemaker once, twice, three times.

Blood exploded from Jenks's chest three times. The outlaw fell over, landing flat on his back, and stayed there.

Parker stood, looking at the dead body he'd just made.

Best holstered his Remingtons, then came over and slapped Parker on the shoulder. "Good shooting, Deputy Jones."

Parker let out a breath he hadn't realized he'd been holding.

It was over.

CHAPTER 31

They trudged back to the fish camp, neither man speaking. They were both exhausted, Parker numb from the gunfight, Best's sore ribs screaming bloody murder.

"There's still daylight left, but my ribs need a break," Best said. "I say we rest, then go get the bodies and the gold in the morning."

Parker raised an eyebrow. "The bodies?"

"There's rewards for Grady Jenks. Might as well take Farkas, too, just in case. I don't know about that other fella," Best explained. "There's money for Little Joe Tillis, too—but I don't think I'll be fighting a grizzly for his corpse."

Best went into the tent and dropped onto the cot, groaning relief.

Parker fetched his canteen from his horse and drank until it was empty.

He retrieved the dead outlaws' horses, removed their saddles, and tethered them along with his own and the marshal's horse to a picket line. He made sure they were fed and watered. They'd need all the horses to bring back the gold and the corpses of the outlaws.

Parker stripped off his sweaty clothes and jumped into the Belle Fourche. The water was cold enough to bite but the perfect balm for his aching body. He dressed in fresh clothes and felt like a new man.

He used Filmore's fishing line and fly to catch three bullheads, and by the time he'd finished frying them up, Best had emerged from the tent, rested and hungry.

They ate.

"We'll get the gold, and then fetch the bodies on the way back," Best said. "You go down to the cave, and I'll haul up a bag at a time with rope."

"Can you do that with your ribs?" Parker asked.

"Easier than if I can climb down to the bottom of that gorge," Best said.

"What about the grizzly?"

Best shrugged. "We'll cross that bridge when we come to it. He's probably off somewhere sleeping off a bellyful of Joe Tillis."

They went to bed early, rose with the dawn, and made an early start, right after coffee. They made their way back to Skull-Mouth Cave, taking the same route as the previous day, and Parker climbed down to the bottom of the gorge. He drew his Peacemaker and approached the cave with caution.

The bear wasn't there.

Best tossed down the rope, and they began the sweaty task of hauling up the gold, one bag at a time. They packed it onto the horses and headed back, stopping to get the dead bodies of the outlaws and draping them limply over the horses.

Parker noticed that Best had gone pensive, maybe

lost in his own thoughts, answering Parker's questions with a terse *yes* or *no*.

They returned to the fish camp.

"What in tarnation is that?" Best asked.

Parker looked to see a garish green wagon parked along the banks of the Belle Fourche.

"That's Professor Meriweather's wagon," Parker said excitedly.

"Who?" Best didn't seem pleased.

But Parker didn't care. He jogged forward, eyes darting around for his friends.

"Parker!"

Parker turned his head and saw Annie running toward him. "Annie!"

She threw herself into his arms and planted a huge kiss his on his lips, her arms going around his neck and holding him close as the kiss went on and on.

Parker finally pulled back, catching his breath. "Oh."

"Don't you *oh* me, Parker Jones," Annie said. "Do you think you can save a girl's life and then just run off and leave her? I'm not letting you out of my sight again."

Parker's head swam. "Well, uh, I . . ."

She kissed him again.

Meriweather came up behind him, taking Parker's hand when he broke from the embrace, and shook it enthusiastically. "Good to find you well, my boy."

Tanner Best came up behind Parker, leading the horses.

Parker made introductions all around. Again, Parker thought Best seemed cross for some reason, but the marshal exchanged polite greetings with Annie and the professor.

Then Annie saw the corpses draped across the horses and gasped.

"It's okay," Parker said quickly. "They're outlaws. Me and the marshal took care of them."

"Outlaws?" Meriweather looked astonished. "Oh, my! Does that mean you found the gold?"

"We sure did!" Parker beamed.

But Best looked more furious than ever, and turned away grumbling.

"Is he okay?" Annie asked.

Parker wasn't sure.

"He cracked his ribs," Parker said. "He's feeling pain."

That explanation seemed to satisfy Annie and the professor.

They built a cook fire and had bacon, beans, and biscuits for dinner—all too familiar fare, but filling. Meriweather produced a couple bottles of whiskey, recently purchased at Carlile's Trading Post. Even Best's unexplained sourness seemed to ease after a couple swigs.

Best and Parker regaled Annie and the professor with harrowing tales of grizzly bears and outlaws.

As the evening went on, Parker and Annie glanced across the fire at each other, exchanging looks and smiles, and Parker understood what they meant to each other, something that had happened while he hadn't been paying attention but was now undeniable.

They all went to sleep, but not before agreeing to all travel together south in the morning. Best had explained that Cheyenne was the nearest place to find a marshal to unload the corpses of the outlaws and also to put in a claim for the reward money on the railroad gold.

In the dwindling firelight, Annie came to Parker and kissed him softly. "Good night," she whispered before melting into the night.

Parker went to sleep feeling about as happy as a man could feel.

When he awoke, it was already daylight. He sat up. The fish camp was silent, nobody in sight. The rush of the Belle Fourche was the only sound. He stood, yawned, stretched, and put on his hat and boots. He strapped on his gun belt and looked around again but still didn't see anyone.

He checked the tent. Marshal Best wasn't there.

Parker left the tent and looked upriver, where he saw Best standing with his hands on his hips, looking across the river. As Parker went to him, he noticed Best wasn't wearing his hat.

"Deputy Jones, you're up," Best noted.

"Where is everybody?" Parker asked.

"There's juniper berries back along the path aways," Best said. "Your pal Professor Meriweather said they were an important part of his elixir, which I suspect is mostly gin. I told him where he and your young Miss Annie could pick some."

"Juniper berries? I don't remember seeing any." Although truth be told, Parker wasn't sure what they might look like.

"I need you to do me a favor," Best said.

"Oh?"

"My hat blew off," Best told him. "It's out there in the river."

Parker looked. The marshal's hat was hung up on some rocks in the middle of the river.

"Fetch it for me, would you?" Best asked. "I don't want to slip and fall in the current with my ribs."

Parker blew out a sigh. "Sure." *No rest for Squire Jones*.

"Take off your gun belt," Best said.

Paker paused. "What?"

"Don't want to soak your gun, do you?"

"I'll be okay," Parker said. "Ain't but knee-deep."

"I said, take off that gun."

Parker looked back at the marshal. Best stood square to him, his coat swept back to allow easy access to his Remingtons. Best narrowed his eyes.

Parker slowly turned to face him, keeping his hand away from his Peacemaker.

Best stared at him hard a moment, before a smile quirked to his lips. "I was going to give you a fair chance. Figured you deserved that much at least. Jenks had me for sure, yesterday, would've killed me, if you hadn't come along and gunned him. But then I thought to hell with a fair chance, you know? I come a long way, been through a lot for this gold, and I've seen you shoot, seen you drilling those bottles. You're fast, plenty fast, and I'm not at my best with these ribs—so, well, I'll admit it. I chickened out at the last minute.

Thought I'd get you to take off your gun, so I could do it the easy way. Sorry, Deputy Jones."

"You didn't shoot the bear yesterday" Parker said. "You were going to let him have me."

Best nodded. "Guilty as charged. It would have saved me an unpleasant task, but then you told me how heavy them sacks of gold was. I knew I'd need you to help me bring them back. I was going to have it out with you yesterday, but then your friends happened along."

"So now what?"

The smile leaked away from Best's face, his features going hard again. "Now I guess we do it proper."

"What about Annie and the professor?"

Best sighed. "Can't have no witnesses, son."

Something went cold and hard inside Parker. He remembered Best's words of gunfighter wisdom. A man had to figure he was dead already. Parker had wondered how a man could think that, but now he knew. Parker's living or dying wasn't the point. But Annie. That was different. If a bullet streaked right for Parker's nose, he wouldn't flinch a muscle. He'd take whatever lead was coming. He was dead already. And that was fine.

As long as he took Best with him.

The world was suddenly quiet and still, like he was living inside some old oil painting. No breeze. No chirping birds. Everything seemed to slow, time itself grinding to a halt.

Best's hands fell to his guns.

Parker drew.

Two gunshots shook the world.

Parker felt something tug at his sleeve.

Tanner Best was knocked back, a neat red hole in the center of his chest. He took a halting step backward, wobbled, then collapsed into a heap.

Dead.

And then there was a scream.

Parker looked up and saw Annie running toward him, the professor right behind. She flung herself into his arms, panic in her eyes.

"What happened?" she demanded.

Parker explained, the words falling out of his numb mouth. The marshal had wanted the gold. He hadn't wanted witnesses. Parker fingered the hole in his left sleeve where the bullet had passed through. His legs felt funny, and suddenly he was sitting on the ground.

Annie knelt next to him. "Parker!"

"He's had a shock," Meriweather said. "Annie, run to the wagon and fetch that bottle of brandy."

She ran away to do as she was told.

"He . . . wanted the gold." Parker was alive. Somehow. He'd outdrawn the marshal and was somehow still alive. He felt sick. He looked down at the Peacemaker still in his hand. He threw it away.

Meriweather went to the marshal, then came back to Parker. "He's dead, and that's for sure. That's quite a favor for me, I can tell you. The marshal was the one I was most worried about."

Parker had no idea what the professor was saying. He felt warm and dizzy. All he wanted to do was lie down. He looked up and—

Professor Meriweather came at him, a huge river rock lifted over his head with both hands, a mad look on his face.

Parker turned just as the professor struck and took the blow on the shoulder. Pain flared, and Parker screamed. The professor lifted the rock for another blow. Parker rolled away, taking the blow to the back. White-hot agony.

A scream. Was that Annie?

Parker tried to crawl and then roll into a ball, arms over his head. Meriweather was trying to stave his skull in, and all Parker could do was try to fend him off. Another blow and the rock smashed into his hand, and Parker heard more than felt the snap of bone.

He was on his back now, trying to squirm away. He looked up.

Meriweather stood above him, face a mask of insanity, stone held high. He'd bring it down and crush Parker's skull, and that would be the end.

Thunder shook the earth.

Half of Meriweather's face was torn away in an explosion of blood and bone and flesh. The old man fell backward, landing with a thud.

Parker turned his head to see Annie holding the shotgun, her eyes wide with the horror of what she'd done. She dropped the weapon and sank to her knees, sobbing.

Parker stood, legs weak, but he made himself put one foot in front of the other and went to her, sinking down next to her, gathering her in his arms, and they stayed that way awhile, as she cried it out. He wiped the tears, leaving dirty smudges across her face, and kissed her.

"It's okay," he said. "We're okay."

They stood and stumbled toward the wagon, clinging to each other.

EPILOGUE

The marshal in Cheyenne hadn't much liked Parker's story, and that was putting it mildly.

A U.S. marshal had turned bad and attempted to steal the railroad gold? Well, greed could get its claws into anyone, the marshal reckoned. It was, after all, a hell of a lot of money. But some greenhorn kid from Rory's Junction had beat Tanner Best in a straight-up gunfight? Fat chance. There had to be more to it.

But the more they dug into the story, the more it seemed it had all happened just exactly as Parker had said.

Maybe it was the fact that Annie Schaefer had corroborated the whole tale—although she was obviously not an impartial party.

Or maybe it was the fact that sending a telegram to Rory's Junction had resulted in a return telegram from Sheriff Crabtree, assuring the Cheyenne authorities that Parker Jones was an upstanding citizen.

Or maybe it was the simple fact that there was no evidence to contradict Parker's story, and what fool would ride into Cheyenne with five corpses and a ton of gold, as pretty as you please, unless his story was true?

The railroad had been much easier to please. They were so happy to see their gold again, they paid the five-thousand-dollar reward to Parker, no questions asked.

And so it was that six weeks later, Parker Jones rode back into Rory's Junction on his brand-new buckboard, in a new suit, with Annie by his side, in a dress that would have made the grand ladies of Paris look like beggars.

It just happened to be a Sunday, and who should they happen to pass on their way into town but Mary Lou Shaw and Bonnie Morgan, going to church. They walked with chins up and backs straight but couldn't help but glance at the unfamiliar young couple in their finery.

Bonnie did a double take. "Parker Jones?"

Annie took Parker's arm, leaned in close, and kissed him on the cheek.

Parker touched the brim of his hat with two fingers and winked at Mary Lou and Bonnie. "Ladies."

He left them wide-eyed, as the buckboard passed and continued into town.

"Was that her?"

Parker nodded. "That was her."

"Well, I did my best," Annie said. "I don't know if she was jealous or not."

Parker grinned. "I reckon she knows what she's missing."

Annie laughed. "Think you're slick, don't you? That's what everyone will call you. Slick Parker."

Parker shook his head. "I doubt that'll catch on."

She held on to him. "Well, that girl missed her chance."

Parker took her hand and squeezed. "Strange, but I don't seem to care about that anymore."

She squeezed back.

They reached town, and Parker tugged the reins and brought the buckboard to a halt in front of the sheriff's office. He hopped down and then helped Annie down. They went inside.

Sheriff Crabtree stood behind his desk, all smiles. "Well, if it isn't Parker Jones. I was wondering if you'd be drifting back our way."

The two men shook hands, and Parker winced.

Crabtree frowned. "You okay?"

"Busted a couple of fingers. Long story," Parker said. "They're still a bit tender."

Parker introduced Annie.

Crabtree took off his hat and bowed. "Miss."

"Annie, go down the block to Lana Ross's place, like we talked about, and see if she has any rooms to let," Parker said. "If she's gone to church already, we'll catch her after. I'll be along directly."

Annie offered the sheriff a smile. "Nice to meet you, sheriff," and then she left.

"Sheriff, I'm hoping to ask you two favors," Parker said.

"If I can, I will," Crabtree told him.

"I want you to stand up for me," Parker said.

Crabtree's eyes widened. "You mean you and that young thing?"

"Yep."

"Well, look who's all grown up." The sheriff took

Parker's hand again and pumped it, much more gently this time. "Congratulations, son. Of course I'll be your best man. What's that other favor?"

"I want your job."

The sheriff's face went blank. "Do I have some terminal illness nobody's told me about?"

Parker laughed. "I don't mean today. I was hoping I could get my old deputy job back. You could teach me to do it proper. Then in your own good time, when you're ready to put your feet up and enjoy the golden years, maybe I could take over."

Crabtree looked Parker up and down with an appraising eye. "You came back different."

"Better, I hope."

"Still got your tin star?" Crabtree asked.

"Yes, sir!"

"Then you can start tomorrow."

Parker rubbed the back of his neck, shifted awkwardly. "Well, actually—that is to say . . . I was hoping the justice of the peace could— And then maybe some kind of honeymoon or, uh . . ." His cheeks flooded pink.

Crabtree laughed and slapped him on the back. "Take a few days, son. Whenever you're ready, we'll get started."

"Thanks, sheriff."

Parker left the sheriff's office and caught up with Annie as she was coming out of Lana Ross's boardinghouse.

"She had one room left, so I took it," Annie told him. "Where will you be?"

"My sister's," Parker said. "Unless they rented out

that room in the mill while I was gone. It'll just be for a few nights. Have you decided where you want to live yet?"

"I don't know." Annie's forehead creased as she thought about it. "In town would be convenient, but a little land on a pond or a river would be nice, too. What do you think?"

"Anywhere you are is perfect."

"Someday, I'm going to think it corny when you say stuff like that," Annie told him, "but not today."

"Crabtree said I didn't have to start right away," Parker said, "so we can have a few days for ourselves. You still got that medicine-show dress that shows off your legs?"

Annie giggled, her hand slipping into his as they strolled the main street of Rory's Junction.

**TURN THE PAGE FOR
A NO-HOLDS-BARRED PREVIEW!**

**JOHNSTONE COUNTRY.
NEVER RUN A BLUFF WITH A SIX-GUN.**

A legend, his name is mentioned
alongside Buffalo Bill Cody and Wild Bill Hickok.
He casts a storm cloud–size shadow across the
untamed Western frontier.
Men on both sides of the law fear his wrath.
For Nathan Stark is the army's avenging angel,
waging war against the hostile Indian tribes
that threaten the nation—
and murdered his family in cold blood.

In the Arizona Territory,
the Apache have been raiding both sides of the border,
slaughtering anyone who gets in their way.
This is the same Indian band that kidnapped
the children of the Navajo chief whose scouts
serve the U.S. Army—and the Navajo will not
engage the Apache as long as the chief's children
are in harm's way.

Now, Stark and Crow scout Moses Red Buffalo
have been tasked with rescuing the Navajo.
But they aren't the only ones on the trail
of the kill-crazy Apache. A group of unhinged
scalp hunters are looking to collect
the Mexican government's bounty on the Apache.
Now the territory is about to explode
in an avalanche of violence and death . . .

National Bestselling Authors
William W. Johnstone
and J.A. Johnstone

PURGATORY CROSSING
A Nathan Stark Western

On sale now, wherever Pinnacle Books are sold.

Live Free. Read Hard.
www.williamjohnstone.net
Visit us at www.kensingtonbooks.com

CHAPTER 1

A lone buzzard circled high above the mesa, too far up to cast a shadow. Like all desert creatures, he survived by adapting to the harsh climate. He moved sparingly in the heat. Took care to drink whenever he could. And patiently observed the stillness below for the movements of creatures that would one day die and upon whose carcasses he would feast. For everything dies eventually, and opportunists thrive in harsh climates.

The buzzard had known many fat seasons. For a time, the creatures in the wilderness below had been frantic in their activities. The buzzard recognized Man and knew him to be different from other creatures, had learned to track and follow his armies for the refuse and bodies left in their wake. For a time, the sands below had exploded in a blood-soaked fury of battles. Those had been the best times for the buzzard. But those days had passed.

The desert had returned to stillness as Man migrated away, back to the softer lands in the East from which he had come. The sands blew, erasing traces of his passage and returning the desert to stillness. For the buzzard, the lean seasons returned.

Now a plume of dust rose from a man on a horse on the mesa below. The buzzard circled, assessing the creatures' relative fitness and the likelihood of survival. Instinct had taught the bird to read the signs of health and vigor, even from this lofty altitude. He could tell the rider and the mount far below were fit enough, yet it remained to be seen if they would survive the other perils of this wilderness.

He would return later and find out.

Nathan Stark, Army scout, lifted his gaze and tilted back the brim of his hat. High above the mesa, a lone buzzard had been circling. Now it peeled away to points west in search of sustenance. Stark knew that buzzards did not hunt but, rather, waited for others to die so that they could feed. And there was plenty of death out here in this desert.

He brought his gaze back down, repositioned the brim of his Stetson, and leaned forward to stroke the neck of his mount. Feeling the sweat beading in the hairs of Buck's coat, Stark reined to a halt, dismounted, pulled one of the large canteens from the assemblage dangling from his saddle horn, and unscrewed the cap. Buck stamped immediately upon smelling water.

"Thirsty?" Stark chuckled, untied the kerchief from around his neck, and removed the Stetson. "We'll take care of you, buddy."

He reversed the Stetson, poured a quantity of water

inside, and set it on the ground before Buck, then squatted as the horse leaned down to take a drink. Stark moistened the kerchief in the hat and wrung it out before retying it around his neck. Then he examined his surroundings.

Bleakness.

Nathan Stark was a well-proportioned man with broad shoulders and a steely gaze. A thick shock of black hair framed his lean, firm-jawed face. He moved with the practiced ease of an experienced trail hand and navigated even unfamiliar territory with a scout's professional eye. When his term of service with the Confederacy ended at Appomattox, he continued his chosen profession as an army scout, going to work for the Union forces. He had served under numerous generals as a civilian subcontractor, including the infamous George Armstrong Custer. Hard, blood-soaked trails were familiar to him.

He had journeyed through Arizona Territory before. There had been much cavalry activity here before the War Between the States. Arizona had voted to join the Confederacy . . . a dream that had ended after the Battle of Picacho Peak. Cavalry had played its decisive role in that engagement, as it had throughout the Territory's history. For here was an unwelcoming and unforgiving land whose inhabitants, both human and animal, resisted newcomers.

Stark knew the people native to these sands: the Navajo, the Yuma, the Apache, the Papago. Some farmed, like the Navajo and Papago. Others hunted and gathered, like the Yuma. And some raided.

Like the Apache, he thought. *The harsher the climate, the greater the likelihood of conflict over scarce resources.*

Cavalry out this way had their work cut out for them. The Apache were canny, aggressive opponents. They had set to raiding and killing the earliest settlers with brutal efficiency and then engaged the mounted military sent to oppose them. Amazing horsemen, the Apache inflicted coordinated guerilla attacks upon the sophisticated, drilled soldiers they fought against. Dealing with them became something of an art form, a sub-specialization of the grueling and terrible years known collectively as the Indian Wars.

A succession of generals had made their bones fighting those Wars. Sherman had served on the frontier, calling for the utter extermination of the Sioux. Sheridan had worked to deplete game on traditional hunting grounds and force hostiles onto allotted reservation land. And men like General Crook had been given the thankless task of fighting the Apache—an enemy well aware of how things had gone for other tribes and determined to resist a similar fate at all costs.

The heat of the day was coming on. The air shimmered as the ground temperature rose. The animals were still and a thick coating of dust lay upon everything. As Stark watched, a lizard crawled to the top of a nearby boulder and paused, its tongue flicking in and out of its mouth seeking moisture in the heat.

The Apache somehow survive in this horrible climate, he thought. *No wonder they're so tough.*

Buck drank his fill, raising his head and shaking his

mane. Still squatting, Stark tilted the opening of the canteen to his lips and took a long, deep, grateful pull of water. And as much as he liked a drink of beer or whiskey now and again, the water trickling down his throat in that dry furnace heat was the most delicious thing he had ever tasted, prompting feelings of gratitude within him that were downright religious.

All them fellas in the Bible were always hanging around in the desert, Stark thought. And considered that he might, squatting there in the sand, understand something about how they must have felt. Folks said, *Hard times make hard men*, he remembered.

He stood, dumped the remaining water from his hat, and replaced it atop his head, recapped the canteen, and remounted. Then he and Buck resumed their journey.

Hard men had been the topic of discussion with the man who'd sent Stark on this assignment. He had made the acquaintance of Mr. Alexander Obediah Greerson, Indian Agent, at Fort Billings, Montana. The man had been about as blunt as could be.

"We created the worst possible outcome in the Arizona Territory. Did it to ourselves," Greerson admitted, gazing around the sparsely furnished office the fort commander had placed at his disposal. "The first waves of settlement from down south in Mexico encountered brutal Apache resistance. So when Americans began heading out that way, we were prepared. We sent scouts ahead of the earliest wagon trains. Began building forts and settlements. There was a military presence there before the War Between the States. An effective one.

Good men served on the frontier, learned the craft of cavalry warfare, and implemented what they knew skillfully. For a time, we had the frontier under relative control.

"Then the war broke out. We had to bring those units home. Some went with the Confederacy. But those were federal troops out there, so for the most part, they rejoined the ranks of the Union Army. But the ensuing few years caused a great deal of attrition. We lost a lot of good riders during the war with Johnny Reb. When we turned our attention back to the Arizona Territory, it was with depleted ranks. And the game had changed."

The war had given the tribes the time to regroup and become better organized. The resulting war on the settlers approached levels of brutality rarely seen before. A new generation of leaders was emerging . . . men toughened by the experience of first contact with the Bluecoats. Men determined to take revenge. One of them was named Geronimo.

Of course, Stark knew the name. Anyone familiar with the war on the frontier did. It was a name to strike naked fear into the hearts of any man living in the Arizona Territory. For here in this sunbaked, coyote-haunted, scorpion-strewn land, it was a name synonymous with Death itself.

Geronimo.

The man was a force of nature. It was one thing for someone to command a room when he entered. But it was another thing for mere mention of that man's name to silence a room in his absence. The Apache war chief had risen from prominence within his own band to a broader prominence within the Apache nation itself. He cast a long shadow over the Arizona Territory—a bloody trail of vengeance and death that threatened even the very military itself.

He was the master of the desert these days, a great tactician who fought the war-hardened cavalry divisions to a standstill with a mixture of brilliance and brutality. General Crook had been given command of the region precisely because of his long familiarity with Geronimo and his demonstrated talent for rescuing victory from the jaws of defeat. For the Union Army was facing defeat at the hands of a force half its size, commanded by a man who still lived as a primitive savage.

"Your orders are to board a train for Arizona Territory, disembark in Tucson, and journey south on horseback." Greerson had produced a map from the inside pocket of his tweed coat, unfolded it, and pointed at one section with a stubby finger. "When you come down through the hills near Tubac, there is a telegraph station . . . here on the plains beyond this mountain pass." He tapped it twice. "It will take time for you to get there, and the situation is fluid. They will take stock upon your arrival and issue your orders by telegraph. Army is coordinating closely with Indian agents on this. And we're much obliged for your help."

Now Stark was approaching the last leg of his journey through these hills. His sense of this was confirmed when he and Buck came around the side of a low rise to find a road cutting across the stony plain. Not a track but an honest-to-goodness road someone had taken the trouble to cut through this section of the wilderness to accommodate the increasing numbers of settlers and supply wagons flooding the Territory.

"Well, look here, Buck." Stark patted the horse's neck. "Signs of civilization. We'll be settled somewhere nice and cozy—a hotel room for me and a nice cool stable for yourself—sooner than you think!"

The road was indeed a sign of civilization. And they didn't have to travel it overly long to learn about the state of things in the Territory. Some enterprising soul had attempted to set up a trading post along the road. Keen to be the first to greet those coming into the area, he had built a large, comfortable storefront of hewn logs.

Even at a distance, their charred forms attested to the carnage that had befallen the place. Black smoke drifted lazily skyward from the ruins. Sections of the building had been knocked over, with logs piled in a haphazard heap where they had fallen instead of burning.

This looks fairly recent, Stark thought. He reined Buck to a stop a quarter mile off and looked around. Had the Apaches stormed down from their hidden base in the hills to do this? It seemed unlikely but not impossible. He set his tracker's eye on the road. There were signs of a group coming through here fairly recently. He dismounted and knelt to study the tracks.

A small group, he reckoned. *And shod*. Which meant

the riders had been white or Mexican, but definitely not Indian.

That was as far as he got before he heard a gunshot and a woman's scream. Then he was back on Buck and riding full gallop toward trouble.

CHAPTER 2

Buck streaked along the road toward the smoking log structure. Stark leaned forward in the saddle, knees tensed against the mount's sides as his right hand swept toward his holster. The building loomed before them now, with Stark urging Buck around the corner with a sharp pull of the reins. They rounded the edge on a greased streak and pulled up short, the scene before them ghastly.

To his way of thinking, it appeared as if the store owner and family had been making ready to light a shuck. For whatever reason, the cost of doing business in the region had become too high, so the father had drawn a covered wagon up to the side door of the building. Stark guessed the family kept their quarters in the rear of the log structure—the man had probably been preparing to load his wife and kids inside the wagon along with some supplies when the marauders struck. And now he lay dead, his body a heap where it had fallen from the driver's box to land in a gory tangle on the grass.

Stark registered the group of men a split second before they saw him and Buck. And that second made all the difference.

The raiding party was eight strong—six ragged and filthy men who stood in a crescent, ranged around two more of their number, who held the dead man's wife by her arms as she twisted and struggled to get loose. A nearby boy and girl looked on, their shoulders grasped by members of the "audience." Stark saw all this in the instant before the nearest men turned. Then their eyes widened in alarm.

Stark palmed his Colt into his hand, swung one leg over Buck, and dropped to the ground. Then all hell broke loose.

Two of the raiders advanced on Stark, fists and voices raised . . . until they saw the gun in his hand, at which point they backed off. Not everyone came armed to the party, but a few did. One man turned, raising a sawed-off shotgun.

Stark's response was instinctive. He turned sideways to minimize his profile, raised his arm, and fired, the Colt like an extension of his hand. A neat round hole appeared in the shotgunner's forehead, and he keeled over backward, collapsing to the grass.

Then three men's guns were parting leather, including one of the two holding the dead shopkeeper's wife. He let go of her arm and she immediately spun, kicking the other man holding her in the shin so sharply that he went down.

Stark's gun spoke: loud booms that scattered the group. Two gunmen ran, but a third stood his ground, his piece unpouched and coming up, sight centering on Stark a moment before the scout snapped off a shot that tore the man's throat wide open. He died choking on his own blood.

The children chose that moment to act, both struggling against the grip of their captors. The little girl managed to break free, but the boy's efforts earned him a brisk cuffing upside his ear. He yelped, head snapping sideways just as his mother broke free of her assailant. With a low growl that chilled even Stark's blood, she launched herself at the man who had struck her son, teeth bared, fingers clawed wide. She hit the man with surprising speed and force, knocking him off balance. Then her nails were raking his face, seeking his eyes.

The man screamed, thrashing against the woman's grip. The little boy tore free and grabbed his sister's hand.

One of the other gunmen fired, drawing Stark's attention from the melee. The gunman had retreated behind the wagon, firing from behind the rear edge. Stark dropped to his knees, scanned behind the wheels, and spotted legs. He aimed and let fly, firing twice. One bullet tore a leg in half at the knee and the man groaned, slumping to the ground alongside the amputation. Stark put him away with one in his wide screaming mouth before spinning and launching himself toward the mother and her children.

The man who had cuffed her son was now well and truly beaten. She had wreaked such havoc upon his face that he held his hands up to it now, moaning and sobbing as he sank to his knees. The mother had gathered her kids to her and was spinning around, seeking a place to run.

"Inside!" snapped Stark. He waved at the door.

He only had to tell her once. Grabbing both her children by the wrists, she made for the doorway as the remaining men came at Stark.

His ammunition was almost exhausted. Coolly as he could, he dropped the cylinder and began reloading, staring down the group of marauders descending upon him. Two noted his action and traded a glance. With a grin, they turned toward the doorway through which the family had disappeared.

One man found his courage—and his weapon. He snapped off a shot that narrowly missed Stark. A moment later, the scout had his Colt loaded and was spinning the cylinder back into place before triggering a shot of his own.

The gunman stiffened and collapsed. And the other men scattered. Two took to their heels while the other leaped into the rear of the wagon, possibly hoping to find a weapon. But somehow Stark doubted that he would. The father seemed to have been preparing his family to go hide in the wilderness for a spell . . . get away from whatever had been bedeviling his business. Most likely, it had been this gang of marauders Stark was set on finishing off. With that in mind, he stepped around the rear of the wagon.

A steel skillet flew out of the wagon, narrowly

missing his head. It was followed by a china plate, then a porcelain bedpan. Stark frowned and ducked, biding his time until the man within showed himself. And very shortly, he did, springing to his feet from behind a crate with another skillet cocked back in one hand and ready to fly. Stark fired, catching him in the chest and pushing him back to collapse with a crash among the family's effects.

He turned. The girl was in the doorway.

"Please! Mister!" she cried, plainly distraught. "My mother!"

That was all Stark needed. He turned and swept across the threshold, pulling the girl after him. "What about your ma?" he asked, looking around the blackened interior. "Where is she?"

"They went out the back door," she moaned, wiping tears from her cheeks. "They took Danny, too! Just grabbed him and dragged them off!"

"It's okay. It's okay." Stark squeezed her shoulder. "Come on."

He steered her into a side room and shut the door behind her with a promise to return. And he would. But meanwhile, she would not present a target for the remaining marauders.

Out of sight, out of mind, he thought.

He saw the back door. He sidled toward it, gun up, flattening himself on the wall beside the opening. Silence. He counted to ten and took a quick peek around.

The two men had their backs to the store, having dragged the mother and son outside a short distance

from the structure. They had forced them both to their
knees. At first, Stark could not fathom the reason.
Until it suddenly dawned on him that they intended to
kill both.

It was illogical. Insane. And yet . . .

They're going to slaughter them! He shook his head
at the realization.

Then he was moving, booted feet crossing the threshold and emerging outdoors. The mother had decided to
resist and was trying to struggle to her feet. As one of
the men turned to cuff her, Stark shot the other one
on the run with studied calm. The bullet tore the man's
life from his body. He was slumping to the ground
when his partner turned.

There!

Stark swung the barrel of the Colt toward the second
man. But he suddenly grabbed the woman by the hair
and yanked her upright, dragging her in front of him as
a shield. Stark cursed his bad luck.

"Steady on, friend," said the man. He flashed a smile,
twisting his fingers in the woman's hair clutched in
his fist. He flashed a smile that was as dull as it was
malicious. "Surely we can come to some arrangement
regarding this little dainty! I'll share if you will."

"You'll let her go," Stark replied woodenly. "You'll
do it now and we'll finish this, or else I'll just end you
here. Trust me. You don't stand a chance."

"Well! I'd say that's downright unneighborly!" The
man yanked the woman's hair brutally, causing her to
shriek. "Here I am offering to share, all gentleman-like,

and there *you* are, being a rude, condescending so-and-so!"

"It's a hell of a thing to call a man rude when you're dragging a woman around by her hair like that!" Stark thundered. "Let her go!"

The woman chose that moment to rear up like a snake and bite down hard on the gunman's hand. He screamed and released her, stepping back and raising his bleeding hand to examine it. The woman scuttled away and the man turned, leveling his pistol on her.

Stark squeezed the trigger. And nothing happened.

He cursed, tossing the Colt aside. It wasn't the first time in his life a gun had jammed on him, but the event was a rarity. He quickly drew his knife, grasped it by the point, and threw it at the man.

The blade sank into the gunman's shoulder, causing him to drop his iron. By then Stark had launched himself forward in a cannonball tackle, grasping the varmint around the elbows and waist, and pitching the two of them to the ground. Stark's teeth clinked painfully together as they landed. Then the man beneath him managed to land a punch on Stark's head before the struggle began in earnest.

Both rose to their knees. The knife fell from the man's shoulder and they both grabbed for it, fingers slipping across the blood-moistened handle. The blade evaded both of them, tumbling into a crevice in the ground. They returned to pummeling each other.

Stark blocked an awkward punch, then reared back and brought his forehead down sharply on the bridge of the other man's nose. The man howled and drew away, panting moistly through blood and snot. Stark's hand shot to his neck, finding tendons and squeezing, glorying in the rage and the kill.

The man gagged, hand rising to break the chokehold. Stark gritted his teeth and doubled down, squeezing as hard as he could, his face widening in a terrifying rictus. The man's face reddened to a mottled purple until Stark felt something snap between his fingertips and the man sank like a sack full of potatoes.

He was done.

Stark staggered upright and looked around.

The log structure still smoldered moodily. The bodies of dead men lay all about within and to either side. And huddled together nearby were the woman and her two children. Beyond the wagon lay the body of the dead father and husband, and for that Stark felt terrible sorrow.

"I'm sorry about what happened here," he told the woman. "I'm sorry about what happened to your store. I'm sorry I couldn't get here sooner."

Gratitude welled up in the woman's eyes. She was a plain woman, her face weather-hardened and unadorned with makeup of any kind, yet she was handsome in her way. Strong and kind, Stark suspected. She radiated that kind of light, even amid profound grief.

"We are grateful to you, Mr. . . . ?"

"Nathan Stark, ma'am."

"Well, Mr. Stark. My name is Annabelle Reed. And you saved my life and the lives of my children, Steven and Sarah. I can't thank you enough. I know my dear husband would thank you, if he could."

"I'm sorry for your loss, ma'am."

"He was a good man." She fought back tears. "The least I can do is give him a decent burial."